BEATRIX POTTER'S
LETTERS

For Dick

BEATRIX POTTER'S LETTERS

*Selected and introduced
by Judy Taylor*

FREDERICK WARNE

FREDERICK WARNE

Published by the Penguin Group
27 Wrights Lane, London W8 5TZ, England
Viking Penguin Inc., 40 West 23rd Street, New York, New York 10010, USA
Penguin Books Australia Ltd, Ringwood, Victoria, Australia
Penguin Books Canada Ltd, 2801 John Street, Markham, Ontario, Canada L3R 1B4
Penguin Books (NZ) Ltd, 182–190 Wairau Road, Auckland 10, New Zealand

Penguin Books Ltd, Registered Offices: Harmondsworth, Middlesex, England

First published 1989
1 3 5 7 9 10 8 6 4 2

Designed by Ron Callow

British Library Cataloguing in Publication Data available

ISBN 0 7232 3437 X

Typeset, printed and bound in Great Britain by William Clowes Limited, Beccles and
London

INTRODUCTION

The life story of Beatrix Potter has been frequently and variously told. Books have been written about her, television documentaries made and plays performed, all of them becoming in their turn good secondary sources of research for anyone wanting to tell her story afresh. For now, nearly fifty years after Beatrix's death, the primary sources of information are disappearing. Those who knew her, as a friend, an artist, a storyteller or a countrywoman, are a sadly dwindling band. The remembered details of her life are increasingly embroidered at every telling. The truest source of information about anyone is usually their own account and for Beatrix we have the 'secret' journal that she kept from the age of fifteen until she was thirty-one, we have her published books – some of which have an autobiographical strand that can be teased out – and we have her letters.

When I started writing my own biography of Beatrix in 1984, I was surprised to find how many of her letters had survived and that they were available for me to read. Her publishers, Frederick Warne, had in their archive nearly all her letters to them from 1901 to 1927, the vital years covering the publication of the little books; the National Trust had a small collection of her letters in their offices in Ambleside, most of them concerning the management of property; there were the letters that Leslie Linder had acquired for his Potter Collection and which he had bequeathed to the Victoria and Albert Museum; The Toronto Public Library had published in 1977 a private edition of Beatrix's letters to *Dear Ivy, Dear June*, a mother and daughter living in Canada; and Jane Crowell Morse's invaluable *Beatrix Potter's Americans: Selected Letters* had been published in Boston (The Horn Book, 1982).

What I was then to discover was just how many more of Beatrix's letters had been treasured by their recipients over the years, stored in safe deposit boxes and in attics, in cardboard boxes and bottom drawers. A batch of them came to light in the files of the National Trust in London; the family of one of Beatrix's shepherds deposited his letters from her in the Cumbria Record Office; the *Beatrix Potter 1866–1943* Exhibition at the Tate Gallery in London and The Pierpont Morgan Library in New York brought in visitors bearing their own memorabilia. Once my quest for Potter letters became known I began to flush them out all over the world, in Australia, New Zealand, Canada and the United States. I now have copies of more than 1,400, from which I have chosen 400 or so to publish here. My choice has been governed by my aim to allow Beatrix Potter to tell her own story in her own words, with as few interruptions as possible.

The letters are printed just as they were written, with Beatrix's somewhat eccentric spelling and punctuation. In the course of checking and rechecking it was discovered that the dates of two letters used widely by Potter biographers (including myself) had been wrongly transcribed, the letters to Harold Warne of 10 October 1905 and to Winifred Warne of 29 December 1908. The corrected date for the first letter changes the hitherto accepted story and we now know that Beatrix bought her field in Sawrey after she had acquired Hill Top and not before – a much more logical, if less romantic, thing to do.

There are still mysteries in the letters to be solved and worrying away at them should keep members of The Beatrix Potter Society busy for many long winter evenings. What, for instance, were Millie Warne's 'good works' (23 August 1910)? Was the rabbit shop mentioned in the letter to Millie of 13 December 1911 one of the moveable toys that Beatrix made for children or was it that year's Christmas card? Who was Tom Harding, for whom Beatrix described her farm in such detail on 21 December 1917? And who was 'Dulcie', with whom Beatrix had a regular correspondence (see 29 July 1924, 18 April 1925 and 18 November 1922)?

The collecting of letters is a fascinating but never-ending task, and even now 'new' letters arrive almost every week so I shall continue to build up the collection. I am most grateful to everyone who has been kind enough to send copies of their letters to me over the years, paticularly to those who have given me permission to reproduce the ones in this selection. Their names can be found on page 7.

In addition I offer my sincere thanks for their help in a variety of ways in the preparation of this book to John Clegg, Susan Denyer, Joan Duke, Jackie Gumpert, Karen Ferns, Anne Hobbs, Philip Hough, Libby Joy, Janice MacFarlane, Antonia McLean, Susan Manson, David Miles, Jane Morse, Norah Moore, Rosalind Moscrop, Mary Noble, Nancy Robertson, Justin Schiller, Anne Sinna, Christopher Hanson Smith, Willow Taylor, Sandra Thorogood, Peter Tuckey, Jennie Walters, Vivien West, John Wilson, and Juliet Wrightson.

The letters in this book are owned by the following (for full details see page 466): John E. Benson; Winifred Boultbee; Colby College Library, Maine; Henry P. Coolidge; Country Life; Cumbria Record Office; the Free Library of Philadelphia; The Field; Doris Frohnsdorff; Betty S. Hart; John Heelis; Jean Holland; The Horn Book, Boston; Richard Hough; The Houghton Library, Harvard University; Mrs Hilary Hutchinson; Urling Sibley Iselin Collection, New York; Miss E. M. MacIntosh; the relatives of Joseph Moscrop; Trustees of the National Library of Scotland; The National Trust, London; The New York Public Library; The Pierpont Morgan Library, New York; Rosalind Rawnsley; Robin Rogerson; the Board of Trustees, Royal Botanic Gardens, Kew; the Simmons College Archives, Boston; Janet Adam Smith; Toronto Public Library; The Times; Alexander Turnbull Library, National Library of New Zealand, Wellington; Board of Trustees, Victoria and Albert Museum; the Frederick Warne Archive; and various Private Collectors.

Publisher's Note: Beatrix Potter's spelling and punctuation have been followed throughout, and [sic] has only been added where we felt it was really necessary.

Where page numbers are given for Beatrix Potter's books they refer first to the original editions and then [in square brackets] to the current editions.

All the drawings and watercolours are by Beatrix Potter.

A complete list of Beatrix Potter's books is given on page 469, together with a list of Some Further Reading.

LIST OF COLOUR PLATES

Helen Beatrix Potter was born on 28 July 1866, the first child of Helen and Rupert Potter. Her father was a wealthy barrister and the family lived in London in Bolton Gardens, Kensington. There are only three letters that survive from Beatrix's childhood and they are all to her father. The first two are not dated, the third was written when Beatrix was sixteen and on holiday in Ilfracombe with her mother and her brother, Walter Bertram.

To Rupert Potter [?]

I am not to go out in the garden as I have got a cold. From your aff
H B Potter

To Rupert Potter
Monday
2, Bolton Gardens,
South Kensington. S.W.

If you see anything pretty will you please send me a picture of it and then I will send you a letter back, and send word how the dogs are and if it is fine and nice at Dalguise [the house near Dunkeld in Perthshire that the Potters rented every summer from 1871 to 1881]. A kiss from your affectionate daughter

H B Potter

Beatrix and Bertram with their mother on the beach at Ilfracombe in 1883

To Rupert Potter
10 Larkstone Road
Ilfracombe
April 3rd 1883

My dear Papa,

Mamma has just got your letter. Things are not nearly so far on here as I expected. I don't think the bushes are so green as those in the Park in London. The water meadows at Salisbury were still quite brown and the valley of the Exe was not so pretty as last year. We have not such a good view from this house as from Mr Hussell's. The harbour is quite out of sight because we are a good way along, almost in the middle of the row of houses. We see most of Hillsborough which is very uninteresting as it is being covered with manure which seems to be a mixture of cinders and of something which smells very bad and makes the fields black.

Mamma and Miss Hammond went went [sic] shopping in the morning and Bertram and I went with Kate past Hele as far as Watermouth. We hardly found any primroses as they are only just coming up. They were unloading coal in Watermouth Harbour. The tide was coming in very fast. One old lady who seemed very anxious to get her coal drove her horse and cart at full speed into the water making such a splashing. This afternoon we went on the pier as it was too rainy to go for a walk. I looked for the tame cormorant but he was gone. There are some beautiful sea-gulls flying about. I saw some very plainly through my opera glass sitting on the rocks at the Bathing Cove. We can't manage the telescope yet, it makes things very big but all out of focus. Perhaps it

12

is because it is misty. Several large steamers have past [sic] and four two-masted ships have come out of the harbour. There are still some people playing lawn tennis. Mamma has been to see the Hussells. The birds are singing so beautifully particularly the blackbirds. I think there must be a starlings' nest in the garden across the road, the birds keep coming down into the field and flying back over the house. I saw some little birds near Hele which I don't think I ever saw before. I think they were stonechats, they had black throats and a good deal of white and red chesnut [sic] about them.

Mr Poole was at the station yesterday with 'Prince' and another horse and carriage and Mrs Poole was looking anxiously out at her window. The towncrier has been going about shouting "Lost a young donkey strayed from his stable at ——. He was heard braying in Portland Street. —— will be much obliged if anyone will restore this young jack-ass to his mother." It looks finer tonight and it is almost unpleasantly warm though the sun has not been out.

I am your affectionate daughter
Beatrix Potter

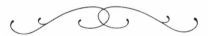

For two or three weeks each April, while the spring cleaning was in hand in Bolton Gardens, the Potters went to the seaside and in the summer they closed the house altogether for a three-month holiday. While she was away Beatrix sent picture letters to the young children she knew.

Beatrix's earliest known picture letter was written when she was twenty-five and was sent to Noel Moore, the eldest son of her last governess, Annie Moore, who as Anne Carter had been appointed in 1883. With only three years between their ages the two young women became close friends. In 1885 Annie left to marry a civil engineer, Edwin Moore, the following year. The first of their eight children, Noel, was born on Christmas Eve 1887. By the time the letter overleaf was written Noel was four-and-a-half and had a brother, Eric (three-and-a-half), and two sisters, Marjorie (two) and Winifrede (Freda, fifteen months).

To Noel Moore

Felmouth Hotel
Falmouth
March 11th 92

My dear Noel,

Thank you for your very interesting let , which you sent me a long time ago. I have come a very long way in a puf-puff to a place in Cornwall, where it is ver hot, and there are palm trees in the gardens & camellias & rhododrons in flower which are very pretty.

We are living in a big house close
to the sea, we go on the harbour
in a steam boat
+ and see ever so many big ships.
Yesterday we went across the water
to a pretty little village where the
fishermen live. I saw them
catching crabs
in a basket cage
which they let down into the sea
with some meat in it + then the
crabs go in to eat the meat + cannot get out.

I shall be quite sorry to come away from this nice place but, we have been here 10 days. Before we go home we are going for two days to Plymouth to see some bigger ships still, I shall come to see you and tell your Mamma all about it when I get home. I have got a lot of shells for you Erie, [I suppose they would not swallow them)

This is a pussy
I saw looking for
fish —
These are two little
dogs that live in
the hotel, + two tame
Sea gulls
+ a great many
cocks + hens in
the garden .

I am going today to a place called the Lizard
so I have no time to draw any more pictures,
+ I remain yours affectionately
Beatrix Potter.

17

The Potters went to Scotland for their three-month summer holiday throughout Beatrix's childhood, until they changed to the Lake District in 1882. Ten years later the family returned to Scotland taking Heath Park in Birnam from late July to early November. It was there that Beatrix met Charles McIntosh, 'The Perthshire Naturalist', now retired from walking fifteen miles a day as a postman. Charlie was an expert on the mosses and fungi of the district, a subject that had become a fascination for Beatrix and about which she was acquiring considerable knowledge. She was anxious to have Charlie's opinion of some of her fungus paintings (see Plate 1) and was delighted when he praised their accuracy and colour. He also agreed to post specimens to London for her to paint. Beatrix's letters to Charlie McIntosh are at first formal and unsigned.

To Charles McIntosh   Dec 10th 92.
                                                       2, Bolton Gardens,
                                                       S.W.

Miss Potter has sent off the drawings by parcel post, & hopes Mr McIntosh will think them sufficiently accurate to be worth his acceptance.

The last plants were particularly beautiful, *Agaricus variabilis* is almost like a pansy, and *A. velutipes* also very handsome. A curious thing has happened to the piece of broom on which the latter was growing, it was put away in a tin canister & forgotten, and now another species of fungus has sprung up. It is a pale straw colour, grown entirely in the dark, and there are nearly 100 'fingers', the longest measure $1\frac{1}{4}$ inch.

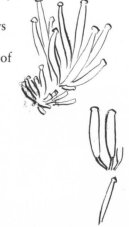

Miss Potter wonders whether it grows out of doors at this season or whether it is brought out by the heat of the room? It was about this size when first observed but being moved into a hot cupboard near the kitchen chimny [sic], it puffed out in a very odd shape. The last shoots that have grown are the same size all the way up. Miss Potter supposes the plants are over for this season, judging by the weather reported in the Perthshire paper, but when Mr McIntosh can get any more she will be glad to draw them, it is a real pleasure to copy them, they are such lovely colours. The moss is more trouble on account of being magnified, and Miss Potter thinks she will keep any drawings of moss, to add to her set. She has drawn most of the fungi twice. It might be well to mark the rarest plant in each parcel, (or that could not be replaced,) so that it might be painted first. *Stereum purpureum* went mouldy during fogs. *Agaricus fragrans* is curiously strong & *pleasant*. Miss Potter trusts Mr McIntosh will never send a horrid plant like a white stick with a loose cap, which smells exactly like a dead sheep! She went to look at a fine specimen but could not find courage to draw it.

To Charles McIntosh   2, Bolton Gardens,
                                                       S.W.
                                                       [?1893]
[The beginning of the letter is missing] . . . and ask if he would tell me, or you, the name of a book that would contain the other funguses, puffballs, *Helvella* etc. if there is one on the same plan as Dr Stevenson's I would prefer it. I have been looking carefully through part of the drawings at the museum, there are a number of portfolios with drawings & printed plates, which one may see at any time, but no one to give any information apparently. They have about 30 per cent of the funguses, rather more of the smaller divisions. There are the originals of the illustrations in Dr S's book, by Mr Worthington Smith. The drawing of *Strobilomyces* is dated Ludlow 1868. I did not hear whether it came up again. They are extremely anxious to have a specimen to put in methylated spirit, if Mr McIntosh finds it again he had better present it; it is a great curiosity, but they take no interest whatever in funguses at large.

All the plants we were doubtful about are marked? especially between *B. chrysenteron* and *subtomentosus*, *B. scaber* & *versipellis*; & varieties of *luridus*. *B. cyanescens* (mine) is like their *B. pachypus*, but I think there must be come confusion, as *pachypus* does not turn dark blue. *Hygrophorus coccineus* & *puniceus* also?? They seem to vary much in colour but it depends on the white foot of the stem. I have not looked at the *cortinariuses* yet. I think I will ask at Kew Gardens some day, whether there is anyone who knows more about the names.

Whether in London or on holiday Beatrix sent picture letters to all the Moore children but it was to Noel that she wrote most frequently. Not only was he the oldest but he was often ill and an attack of polio when he was seven was to leave him lame for the rest of his life. Noel was five when Beatrix, on holiday with her family in Dunkeld, Scotland, sent him what has become one of the most famous letters ever written.

To Noel Moore

Eastwood Dunkeld
Sep 4ᵗ 93

My dear Noel,
        I don't know what to
write to you, so I shall tell you a story
        about four little rabbits
                whose names were-

Flopsy, Mopsy Cottontail

and Peter

They lived with their mother in a
sand bank under the root of a
big fir tree.

'Now, my dears', said old Mrs Bunny 'you may go into the field or down the lane, but don't go into Mr McGregor's garden.'

Flopsy, Mopsy & Cottontail, who were good little rabbits went down the lane to gather blackberries. but Peter, who was very naughty

'an straight away to Mr McGregor's garden and squeezed underneath the gate.

First he ate some lettuce, and some broad beans, then some radishes, and then, feeling rather sick, he went to look for some parsley; but round the end of a cucumber frame whom should he meet but Mr McGregor!

Mr McGregor was planting out young cabbages but he jumped up & ran after Peter waving a rake & calling out 'Stop thief'!

Peter was most dreadfully frightened & rushed all over the garden for he had forgotten the way back to the gate.
He lost one of his shoes among the cabbages

and the other shoe amongst the potatoes.
After losing them he ran on four legs &
went faster, so that I think he would

have got away altogether, if he had not
unfortunately run into a gooseberry net
and got caught fast by the large buttons
on his jacket. It was a blue jacket with
brass buttons, quite new.

Mr McGregor came up with a basket which he intended to pop on the top of Peter, but Peter wriggled out just in time, leaving his jacket behind,

and this time he found the gate, slipped underneath and ran home safely.

Mr McGregor hung up the little jacket &
shoes for a scarecrow, to frighten the
black birds.

Peter was ill during the evening, in consequence
of over eating himself. His mother put him to
bed and gave him a dose of camomile tea,

but Flopsy, Mopsy, and Cottontail
had bread and milk and blackberries
for supper.   I am coming
back to London next Thursday, so
I hope I shall see you soon, and
the new baby   I remain, dear Noel,
yours affectionately
                                        Beatrix Potter

In 1890 Beatrix had been encouraged by her uncle, Sir Henry Roscoe, to offer some of her drawings for sale. They were bought by Hildesheimer & Faulkner and used as Christmas and New Year cards and as illustrations for a book of rhymes, A HAPPY PAIR. *Encouraged by her success, Beatrix submitted her work to a number of publishers of children's books, among them Frederick Warne. Although they could find no use for her drawings alone, they encouraged her to submit any ideas she might have in book form.*

Meanwhile Ernest Nister, a German firm of fine art printers, had also bought some of her work and they were now interested in a booklet she had sent them called A FROG HE WOULD A-FISHING GO. *They wanted to use the drawings in* COMICAL CUSTOMERS, *one of their Nister's Children's Annuals, and they offered Beatrix a guinea for the nine drawings.*

Draft letter to Mr E. Nister   June 2nd 94
                                                        2, Bolton Gardens,
                                                        S.W.

Sir,

I have received your letter of 2nd inst with reference to the pen & ink drawings, but regret to inform you that I am not satisfied with your terms. I offered to ac 25/- for 10 or 20/- for 8. A com between the two prices would be 22/6 and for 9 & unless you care to pay that price I am afraid I must trouble you to return the remaining 9 drawings which you still have, the 10th having been ret already. I am not willing to ac 21/- for 9 & I am of opinion that you had better return them without further discussion.

I remain Sir, yours sincerely
Beatrix Potter

Two days later Nister sent Beatrix 22/6 for the nine drawings.

From A Frog he would a-fishing go

To Noel Moore

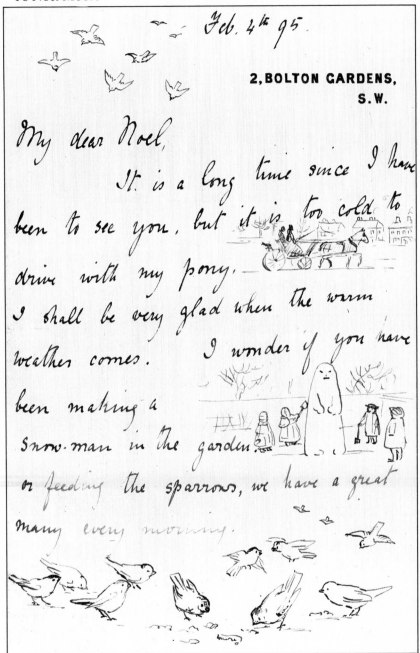

Feb. 4th 95.

2, BOLTON GARDENS,
S.W.

My dear Noel,

It is a long time since I have been to see you, but it is too cold to drive with my pony. I shall be very glad when the warm weather comes. I wonder if you have been making a Snow-man in the garden. or feeding the sparrows, we have a great many every morning.

My rabbit Peter is so lazy, he lies before
the fire in a box, with a little rug.
His claws grew too long,
quite uncomfortable,
so I tried to cut them with scissors
. but they were so hard that I
had to use the big gardens scissors
He sat quite still and
allowed me to do his
little front paws but
when I cut the other hind foot claws

he was tickled, +
kicked, very naughty.
If he were a wild rabbit digging holes
they would be worn
down + would not need
cutting.

Here are some rabbits throwing snow balls.

I wonder if your pussy cat
has learned to catch mice
yet. I think it would rather
lap milk, it is too fine
to work like a
common cat.

These mice are getting away down a hole.
I wonder if those dolls have any
hair still ?
whether they have
eaten all those nice
sausages.
I remain with love yrs aff.
Beatrix Potter.

In 1896 the Potters spent their first summer holiday at Lakefield, a large house on the edge of the Lake District village of Sawrey. Beatrix recorded in her journal at the time that Sawrey, 'Is as nearly perfect a little place as I ever lived in.'

To Noel Moore

Aug 7th 96

LAKEFIELD,
SAWREY,
AMBLESIDE.

My dear Noel,

I hope that you are all very well. We are having a very good time here. It is such a pretty place, and we have a boat

on Esthwaite Lake. There are
tall rushes at the edge of the
lake and beds of water lilies.

I sometimes sit quite still in
the boat & watch the water hens.
They are black with red bills and
make a noise just like kissing,
when they are hiding in the reeds.
They walk on the lily leaves, nodding
their heads
and peeping

underneath for water snails.
There are wild ducks too, but they are
not so tame. One evening I went
in the boat when it was nearly dark
and saw a flock of lapwings
asleep, standing on one leg in
the water. What a funny way
to go to bed! Perhaps they
are afraid of foxes. The hens
are.
There are
Some cocks & hens on the hill, who

sleep right at the top of a haw-
-thorn bush, the
branches are quite
covered with chickens. Those at
the farm go up a
stone wall into a
loft. The farmer

has a beautiful fat pig. He is a
funny old man,
he feeds the calves
every morning, he
rattles the spoon on the tin pail, to
tell them breakfast is ready, but
they won't always come. Then there is a
noise like a German band. I remain
yrs. aff. Beatrix Potter.

While staying at Lakefield Beatrix continued to collect fungi. As well as painting her detailed watercolours of them, she had been studying spore germination and had succeeded in sprouting spores of over forty species and making accurate drawings at × 600 magnification. In May, her uncle, Sir Henry Roscoe (himself a distinguished scientist) had taken her to The Royal Botanic Gardens at Kew, where he had introduced her to 'five different gentlemen' including George Massee, the Assistant Director, and the Director, William Thiselton-Dyer. After looking at her drawings, with which he seemed pleased, the Director had arranged for Beatrix to have an admission ticket to Kew – and then ignored her while he had an animated conversation with her uncle about politics and university problems.

To Charles McIntosh
Lakefield,
Sawrey,
Ambleside.

Do you think this is *B. versipellis*. I got it in the same place last year, always bright chesnut [sic] colour & rather velvety when first gathered. *B. scaber* does not grow at all freely here, and I think rather different to Dunkeld, generally hard shiny & wrinkled. I should be very glad of any *pezizas*, Mr Massee at Kew Gardens can name them from dried specimens. He says they have been drawn less than agarics & advised me to keep to one division of fungi. I find plenty of microscopic *pezizas* but no large ones yet and I should be very much obliged if you could send me any, especially any larger ones, which grow on the ground. The young specs of *B. versipellis* (?) have remains of a veil, it is always badly eaten by slugs, grows in gravel at the edge of lake.

Aug 20th 96

Working entirely on her own, Beatrix had made a number of remarkable discoveries, some of them at odds with the work being done by George Massee at Kew. She decided to share her knowledge with the Director there, and in December she submitted her findings and her drawings to him.

To William Thiselton-Dyer   2, Bolton Gardens,
                                             S.W.
                                             [3 December 1896]
Dear Sir,

Sir H. Roscoe sent me to ask whether you would be kind enough to look at some of my fungus drawings which he is interested in.

I do not quite like to give the paper to Mr Massee because I am afraid I have rather contradicted him. Uncle Harry is satisfied with my way of working but we wish very much that someone would take it up at Kew to try it, if they do not believe my drawings. Mr Massee took objection to my slides, but the things exist, and will be all done by the Germans. It is rather a long paper to ask you to be kind enough to read.

I remain, Sir, yours sincerely

Beatrix Potter

Beatrix's work was not well received by the Director and Beatrix recorded in her journal that she 'had it up and down with him'. However, George Massee had come round and was prepared to believe her findings, even accepting samples from her for his own experiments.

With her uncle's help and encouragement, Beatrix continued her research and began to revise her paper.

To Charles McIntosh　　　　　　　　　2, Bolton Gardens,
　　　　　　　　　　　　　　　　　　London, S.W.
　　　　　　　　　　　　　　　　　　Jan 12th 97

Do you think you could get me a fungus called *Corticium amorphum*? It grows on fir bark and looks at first like *Lachnea calycina*, but afterwards sticky like *Dacrymyces*.

Also I should be very much obliged if you could give me any information about *Merulius corium*. You told me some time since that you had not found it at Dunkeld with properly developed spore. Do you mean every season, or only in unfavourable seasons? Have you noticed the same thing with any other fungus? for instance *Chlorosplenium aeruginosum*?

I am doing some curious work with fungus spore, trying to draw up a paper with the assistance of my uncle Sir H. Roscoe.

Have you ever suspected that there are *intermediate* species amongst *Agarics* and *Boleti*? We are strongly of opinion for certain good reasons that there are mixed fungi – that is to say – either growing actually upon a mixed network of *mycelium*, or else hybrid species which have originated in that way. I do not express any opinion which way, only that they *are* intermediate.

Of course such an idea is contrary to the books, except for lichens but I should be curious to hear *whether you have had difficulty in naming any* of the *sorts* which I suspect. Have you noticed whether fungi described as "varieties", are constant in type? For instance does *A. aureus var. vahlii*, come up the same every season? and *all* the season? I mean to say are there poor specimens towards the end of the season more like the ordinary *A. aureus*? I do not mean to suggest the idea if you have not noticed it yourself. It may be a different species not a var. at all.

I have found a fungus very like *A. velutipes* which Sir Henry thinks is either a mixture or a new sort. There is no harm in giving an opinion, so long as it is made clear whether it is only an opinion, or the result of observation; we find some people make theories out of dried specimens without the least experience of the way things grow. If you find *Corticium* would you please wrap it up as soon as found, to keep the spore separate. If you take any interest in physiology I should be amused to send a copy later on, we have got into contradictions at Kew & Br. Museum already, but I think my uncle is a good judge.

Do you know anything about lichens?

　　　　　　　　　　　　　　　　　　　　　Beatrix Potter

To Charles McIntosh   Jan 22nd 97
                                       2, Bolton Gardens,
                                       London, S.W.

Thank you very much for your interesting letter, especially about the larch disease. I have taken note of it in the Lake district but never saw any aphis, but of course it is a disadvantage not to be able to examine the trees at different seasons.

I should think if a tree is weakened by one parasite it is less able to withstand the attack of another; or possibly the *peziza* spore may get into the larch through the blister & bleeding caused by the aphis. The *peziza mycelium* is very vigorous & spreads in the red lower layer of bark, I have seen it come out in that layer on a broken dead branch at several inches from the fungus. I quite came to the same conclusion about the bleeding of resin, = that it is the peculiar constitution of the larch which does the mischief; I think the fungus does not penetrate at all deeply but that the scar, being open, eats into the trunk. It is so bad in Westmoreland [sic] that one does not find a straight stem in 500. The woodmen think it is caused by replanting without cleaning up, & if the fungus *is* the cause they are right to some extent, because it breeds to an extraordinary extent on heaps of sticks. There is something odd about that particular fungus, supposing it is the cause of the disease for others very like it seem harmless. I have seen one very like it in Gloucestershire & Surrey but the live trees were scarcely diseased at all.

I think I have found the new fungus again, I can hardly describe the difference, it is drier than *velutipes*, both pileus & gills, rather broader & shorter & a peculiar smell, gills a deep yellow when old also inclined to become discoloured in patches.

My difficulty about lichens is to find ripe spore for experiments, I scarcely know what to look for. I have succeeded in growing spore of *Cladonia*, but *larger* spores would be more convenient. You see we do not believe in Schwendener's theory, and the older books say that the lichens pass gradually into *hepaticas*, through the foliaceous species. I should like very much to grow the spore of one of those *large flat lichens*, & also the spore of a real *hepatica* in order to compare the 2 ways of sprouting. The names do not matter as I can dry them. If you could get me any spore of the lichen & *hepatica* when the weather changes I should be very much obliged.

With regard to the drawings I have no objection at all, but wish that they were better worth lending. I think you have one of *S. strobilaceous* which is a curiosity. The fungologist at Kew said he had only seen it once

– in the summer of 95 – when he found any quantity in a wood nr Watford, Hertfordshire.

I remain yrs sincerely
Beatrix Potter

To Charles McIntosh

Feb 22nd 97
2, Bolton Gardens,
S.W.

I am very much obliged to you for the 2 parcels, the *hepatica* is particularly curious. I hope very much I shall succeed in getting the spore to sprout.

I have had a good deal of trouble about the paper, I am afraid the best part of my work will have to stand over till next season. The thing which causes so much contradiction is that I succeeded in sprouting the mushroom spore, which I supposed is what it is meant for; but it seems that no one else is admitted to have done it, and therefore no one except my uncle & one gentleman at Kew will believe that any of my slides are right.

I have grown between 40 & 50 sorts of spore, but I think we shall probably only send in *A. velutipes*, which I have grown twice and Mr Massee has also grown according to my direction at Kew. He did not previously believe in the things at all. I am just as much sure of the mushroom but unless I can get a good slide actually sprouting it seems useless to send it to the Linnaean [sic]. I should be obliged if you would *not* mention it to any one [sic] concerned with botany, until the paper is really sent, because without meaning to be uncivil they are more inclined to grow the things themselves than to admit that mine are right. What I have been doing is to sort out the "Hyphomycetes" which in great part are not real "species" at all, which has been suspected for a long time, but it was not previously known that they belonged to *Agarics* as well as to *pezizas*. Please do not send anything more just now because my slides are full of mushrooms, which refuse to grow when required.

Beatrix Potter

Beatrix's paper 'On the Germination of the Spores of AGARICINEAE' *was presented, possibly 'by title' only, on 1 April 1897 at The Linnean Society of London by George Massee. Beatrix was unable even to be present, as ladies were not allowed to attend the society's meetings, but she later reported to Charlie McIntosh that her paper was '"well received" according to Mr Massee, but they say it requires more work in it before it is printed'. Sadly the paper is lost.*

Lingholm (Lingholme), a large mansion on the wooded western shore of Derwentwater, was now the favourite summer home in the Lake District for the Potter family. This was their fifth visit since 1885. The Moores, who lived in Wandsworth, went to relations in Suffolk.

To Freda Moore

LOBBIN
June 14th '87
BE[ss] DARLING
JOAN APRIL

My dear Freda,

I think I must write you a letter too. What a nice time you are having, going to so many tea parties!

I wonder if there are going to be
any decorations at Wandsworth on
Jubilee Day. I shall not go to
see the procession; it is too hot.

I shall stop at home and have
a large flag out of
the window - 
At the last
Jubilee there was a
wind, and our flag
kept rolling up.

We had to reach out of the window with a broom to unroll it. We are going to have night lights on the window sills, red, blue, and white.

My rabbit is so hot he does not know what to do with himself. He has such thick

fur, I think he would be
more comfortable if he had

a little coat which would take

off. I shall send this to
Wandsworth; I daresay it will be sent
on to Ipswich, if you have not
come home. I remain
yours affectionately

Beatrix Potter

The little foal belongs to my uncle, it is so
tame.

To Freda Moore

LINGHOLM,
KESWICK,
CUMBERLAND.

July 30ᵗʰ 98

My dear Frida,

I am writing to you instead of Eric because I think you saw my tame snail, and he did not see it. I will write to him and Marjory next time. I had to dig up my snails' nest when I left home. I found there were 79 large eggs!

It was   such a queer
nest in   the ground
and the snail had covered it up
with soil. The eggs were white
just like the
eggs you
had for breakfast,
they would be just
the right size for little mice!
I brought them here in a little
box; the old snail did not take
any more trouble about them after

She had covered up the hole.
Yesterday morning, after 4 weeks,
the eggs began to hatch,
9 came out, and 4 more today.
They are such pretty little snails
with quite hard shells, but almost
like glass, I expect they will
soon go darker, they are
beginning to eat.
My brother has got
a jack daw, a
very sly bird.

Directly we let him loose he gets
into the fire place and brings
out rubbish which has been
thrown in the fender
I think he must
have lived in a
chimney, it will be very awkward
when the fire is lighted. We are
all quite well and there has not
been quite so much rain. as there
usually is here, but I shall be glad
to get home again, I don't like
going away for such a long time
remain yrs affectionately
Beatrix Potter.

Marjorie, Winifrede (Freda), Norah and Joan Moore in 1900

There were now six children in the still-growing Moore family – two more girls, Norah and Joan. Beatrix kept up a flow of picture letters to them all, letters that were highly prized and carefully preserved by the children, Marjorie tying hers in a bundle with yellow ribbon. It was their mother, Annie Moore, who one day suggested to Beatrix that the stories in some of the letters might well make into books. After borrowing them back to copy and to make one or two changes, Beatrix concentrated first on turning her rabbit letter to Noel into a book. There was a black-and-white drawing for each page and she prepared a coloured illustration for the frontispiece.

For help in approaching a publisher, Beatrix turned to Canon Hardwicke Rawnsley, a friend she had made on her first visit to the Lake District in 1892. As well as being the vicar of Crosthwaite, near Keswick, Canon Rawnsley was the author of a number of books, including the highly-successful MORAL RHYMES FOR THE YOUNG. *He agreed to use his influence to place* THE TALE OF PETER RABBIT AND MR MCGREGOR'S GARDEN *by H. B. Potter with a publisher. It was a frustrating time, with the book being repeatedly turned away, each publisher wanting something larger and with illustrations in colour.*

To Marjorie Moore

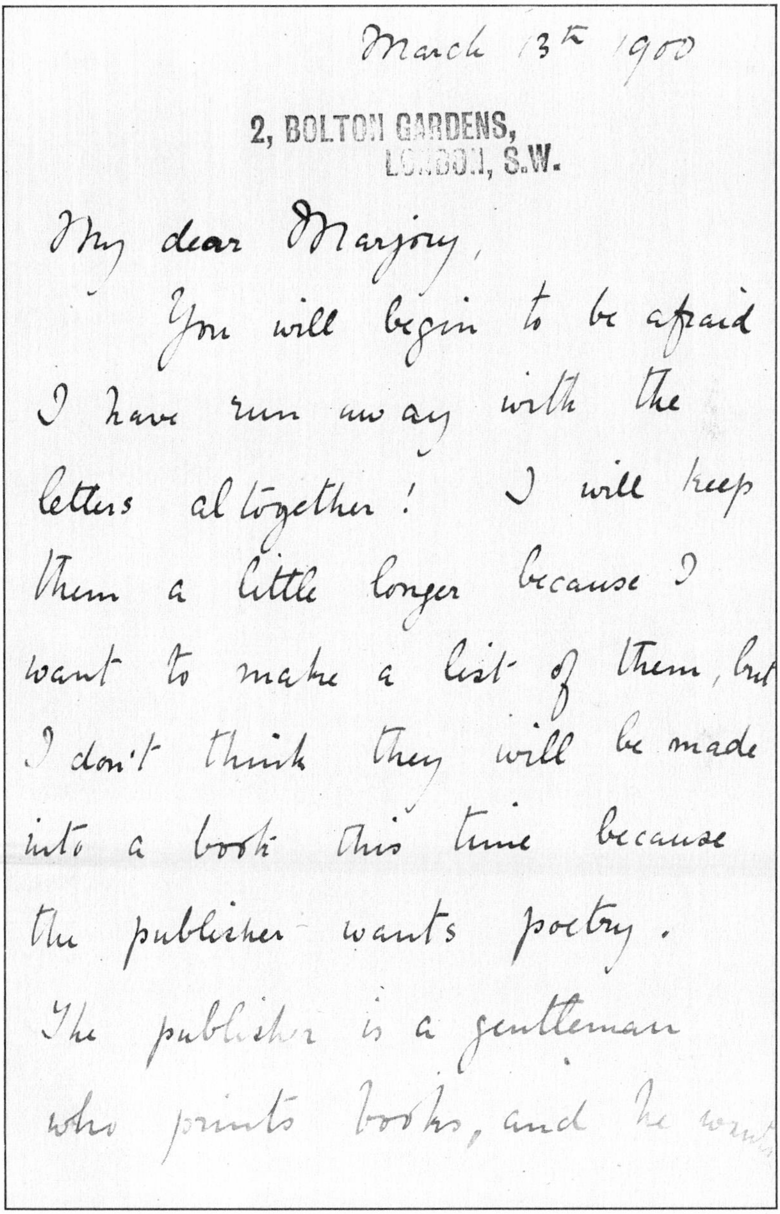

March 13th 1900

2, BOLTON GARDENS,
LONDON, S.W.

My dear Marjory,

You will begin to be afraid
I have run away with the
letters altogether! I will keep
them a little longer because I
want to make a list of them, but
I don't think they will be made
into a book this time because
the publisher wants poetry.
The publisher is a gentleman
who prints books, and he wants

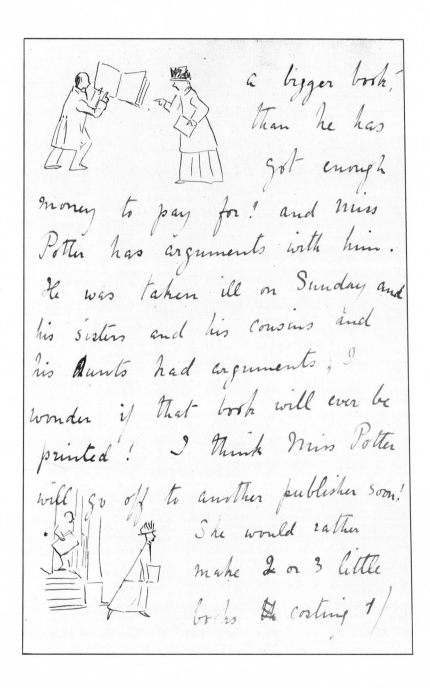

a bigger book, than he has got enough money to pay for! and Miss Potter has arguments with him. He was taken ill on Sunday and his sisters and his cousins and his Aunts had arguments; I wonder if that book will ever be printed! I think Miss Potter will go off to another publisher soon! She would rather make 2 or 3 little books costing 1/

each, than one big book costing
6/. because
she thinks
little rabbits
cannot afford to spend 6 shilling
on one book. and would never
buy it   I went to the
Reading Room at the British
Museum this morning to see a
                          old
delight-ful — book full of rhymes
I shall draw pictures of some
of them whether they are printed
or not.   The Reading room so

enormous big room, quite round. with galleries round the sides the walls covered with books, and hundreds of chairs and desks on the floor.. There were not many people but some of them were very funny to look at! And there are some people who live there always but Miss Potter didn't see them, although they are said to be the largest people of their sort in London! Next time Miss Potter goes to The British Museum she will take some Keating's powder! It is very odd there should be fleas in books!

MA 2009/125

54

By 1901 Beatrix's patience had run out and she made the decision to publish her rabbit story herself. She ordered 250 copies, with the colour frontispiece printed in the recently introduced half-tone process. There was a double quantity of frontispieces in case the book should be such a success that she might need a quick reprint.

Meanwhile Hardwicke Rawnsley was still trying to find a commercial publisher for Beatrix, even going to the length of rewriting her text in his own verse style. He sent the early part of the manuscript and all Beatrix's drawings to Frederick Warne, the firm that ten years earlier had expressed an interest in her work in book form. He told them about her plans for private publication and about the already-printed extra frontispieces. Warne were interested enough to ask for the rest of the manuscript and for information about the availability of the printing plant. They also asked if Canon Rawnsley would enquire of the author her reasons for the illustrations being in black-and-white rather than in colour. He handed the correspondence over to Beatrix.

To Messrs Warne & Co

Lingholme, Keswick
Cumberland
Sept 11th 01

Gentlemen,

Canon Rawnsley has shown me your letter and his reply, posted today, & he desired me to send back this part of the book after re copying the title page, which was blotted. I much regret I cannot call personally to explain about the blocks.

The 3 colour block [*see Plate 2*], by Hentschel, 182 Fleet St, has had 500 impressions pulled, but I do not think it would be at all spoiled for further use; and I could of course hand over the 500 if you & Canon Rawnsley come to terms.

I have only had proofs of the 42 zinc blocks (Art Reproduction Company, Fetter Lane). I have not got any block for the cover yet.

I obtained the blocks originally intending to print a small edition only for private circulation, & had thought of having a booklet 5 × 3¾ inches, on rather rough stout paper.

I did not colour the whole book for two reasons – the great expense of good colour printing – and also the rather uninteresting colour of a good many of the subjects which are most of them rabbit-brown and green.

I remain gentlemen, yrs sincerely
Beatrix Potter

On the receipt of Beatrix's letter Warne wrote again to Canon Rawnsley regretting that they would only be able to consider taking the book if the illustrations were in colour and the number of them reduced from forty-two to thirty-two. The text, they advised, would be better in simple narration rather than in verse. Hardwicke Rawnsley once again passed their letter to Beatrix who agreed to Warne's proposals. Warne then made an offer to pay her 1d a copy 'which would amount to about £20 on this first edition [of 5,000 copies]. On subsequent editions we should be able to pay about 3d per copy royalty. Of course we cannot tell whether the work is likely to run to a second edition or not, and therefore we fear it might not provide a reasonable remuneration for you.'

Beatrix meanwhile had received her first copies of the privately printed edition of what had now become THE TALE OF PETER RABBIT *by Beatrix Potter (see Plate 4).*

To F. Warne & Co.

2, Bolton Gardens,
London, S.W.
Dec 18th 01

Dear Sir,

I was on the point of posting the book, when I received your letter, of Dec 16th. I think Strangeways have printed it rather nicely. It is going off very well amongst my friends & relations, 5 at a time; I will spread it about as much as I can, especially in Manchester [where her father and mother were born]. Had you decided *not* to go on with it, I would certainly have done so myself, it has given me so much amusement.

I showed it this morning to some ladies who have a bookshop in Kensington who wanted to put it in the window, on the spot; but I did not venture to do so – though I would have been much interested.

I do not know if it is necessary to consult Canon Rawnsley; I should think *not*. Speaking for myself I consider your terms very liberal as regards royalty; but I do not quite understand about the copyright. Do you propose that the copyright remains mine; you agreeing to print an edition of 5,000, and having – as part of the agreement – the option of printing more editions if required? I must apologise for not understanding, but I would like to be clear about it. For instance who would the copyright belong to in the event of *your* not wishing to print a second edition? I am sure no one is likely to offer me better terms than 3d apiece, and I am aware that these little books don't last long, even if they are a success; but I should like to know what I am agreeing to.

I think it should certainly be kept down to 1/6; even if it took off my 1d royalty on the first edition.

I should be glad to call sometime at the office to hear what you decide about the coloured drawings. I still think the 3 colour photograph very nice; but I confess I had not thought of the plan of *brown* ink, when I expressed such a strong dislike to black outlines – I have put a X on some of the cuts which don't really seem to need alteration, but I am perfectly willing to redraw the whole if desired.

I remain, Sir yrs sincerely

Beatrix Potter

I have not spoken to Mr Potter, but I think Sir, it would be well to explain the agreement clearly, because he is a little formal having been a barrister –

From the privately printed The Tale of Peter Rabbit

To F. Warne & Co.

Jan 7th 02
2, Bolton Gardens,
S.W.

Dear Sir,

I send you another copy of Peter Rabbit. I did not remember to tell you when we were discussing Hentschel's blocks, that the set I have got here in my possession seems to be particularly well finished.

I know a little about copper as my brother etches in it, & have had some experience of printing. I work on stone myself but have never done coloured lithographs; but it is such an old fashioned expensive method it would not have been of much use, even if I had been competent to work out my own drawings.

I think Hentschel would make the best job of it; if the money part of the business can be arranged, which I do not doubt it can be somehow.

I remain, Sir, yrs sincerely

Beatrix Potter

On 4 January 1902 the 'Notes and Queries on Natural History' section of THE FIELD, THE COUNTRY GENTLEMAN'S NEWSPAPER *carried a letter from J. Whitaker (Rainworth, Notts) entitled 'White Hare at Rainworth'. Mr Whitaker was bringing readers up to date with news of a white hare he had found the previous October and had brought into the house to raise as a pet.*

To *The Field*   [published 11 January 1902]

TAME HARES.—I read your correspondent, Mr Whitaker's account of a tame white hare with great pleasure. The habit of tucking the forepaws backwards under the fur, and lying upon them when cold, is common to rabbits as well as to hares. For many years in a London House, I kept a Belgian rabbit (two bucks in succession), and they often went to sleep in that attitude. Both were fond of the fire, and one used to lie inside the fender; I have even seen him asleep under the grate on the hot ashes when the fire had gone out. Your correspondent does not mention whether his hare has the ludicrous habit of rubbing his chin upon objects in order to show contempt. For instance, upon his own reflection in a looking-glass, or upon a stranger's boots. I have noticed when carrying shot rabbits, that they generally have smeared chins. No doubt a hare would be more intelligent, but even the usually idiotic hutch rabbit is capable of developing strong character, if taken in hand when quite young. My first rabbit, Bounce, was exceedingly affectionate with myself; but suspicious, like a dog, of new servants or strange workmen in the house, at whom it would growl, the ordinary conversational noise being a low grunt. They can be taught tricks, playing tambourine and ringing a bell. I think their drawback as pets is, that although easily trained to cleanliness, they cannot be broken of the habit of nibbling; moreover, there is the risk of being injured or killed by strange dogs. I would warn your correspondent against giving his hare lump-sugar or hard comfits; I do not think the molar teeth grow again if broken, and as they cannot be reached owing to the smallness of the animal's mouth, it may suffer agonies from tooth-ache. My rabbit Bounce came to a premature end through persistent devotion to peppermints, which he begged from an old Scotch gamekeeper. I could feel the broken tooth with my finger, but could not get it out; he was not a healthy animal, and the toothache ended in a tumour, so he had to be destroyed. His successor, Peter, was in my possession for nine years; I then had him chloroformed, as he was getting very feeble but I have known two instances of rabbits living fourteen years. – H.B.P.

Warne were still wrestling with the costs for PETER RABBIT *and wondering how they could afford to use the three-colour half-tone process on which Beatrix was insisting. She had added colour to some of her original black-and-white pictures but she was not happy with the result and decided that, once she had cut the book to the required length so that it could be printed on one sheet of paper, she would redraw all the pictures in colour.*

On her visits to the Warne office in Bedford Street, Beatrix discussed her work with Norman Warne, the youngest of the three Warne brothers who had run the firm since their father's retirement in 1895. Harold was the senior partner and managing director, William Fruing was mainly concerned with the sales side of the business and Norman specialized in production, but also went on regular selling trips to booksellers round the country.

To F. Warne & Co.

2, Bolton Gardens,
London, S.W.
Jan 19th 02

Dear Sir,

I return the marked copy of Peter Rabbit. The present blocks are all within $2\frac{1}{2} \times 3$, (some being reckoned sideways). I find that 15 were reduced by $\frac{1}{3}$ and 17 by $\frac{1}{4}$.

I don't think this would signify, provided that the right sizes were mounted together in the way you suggest.

I suppose that you will not be doing anything just at present, with those already coloured. I think there was some paint used in some of them which would be better taken out before they are photographed.

The shapes of the zinc blocks, & also of the coloured drawings which you already have, were rather irregular.

Perhaps you will consider whether you prefer a variety of shape (within a certain size) – or whether you would like the backgrounds worked up to a more uniform shape.

I shall be very glad to prepare the drawings in any way to suit your convenience; I will set to work to colour the others & will bring them to the office.

I cannot call this next week as I am going into the country, but I can get on with the work now that it is definitely decided which process is to be used.

I remain, Sir, yrs sincerely
Beatrix Potter

I do not know if it is worth while mentioning – but Dr Conan Doyle had a copy for his children & he has a good opinion of the story & words.

To F. Warne & Co.   April 25th 02
                                                            2, Bolton Gardens,
                                                            S.W.

Dear Sir,

I think this is the drawing that Mr Warne was looking for yesterday; the gardener seemed to be better in the drawing I brought yesterday, but I hope you will use which ever you like.

I have been wondering whether the rabbit on the cover ought not to face the other way, towards the binding; it would not take long to copy again.

I should like to take the opportunity of saying that *I* shall not be surprised or disappointed to hear that the figures work out badly for the first edition of Peter Rabbit.

I remain Sir, yrs sincerely
Beatrix Potter

To Norman Warne   April 30th 02
                                                            2, Bolton Gardens,
                                                            S.W.

Dear Sir,

I am very sorry that I cannot call as I am going to Scotland tomorrow morning, my brother has made his arrangements & I don't want to miss travelling with him.

It is most provoking that I could not see the drawings before going, as I think I could very likely do them better there, as there is a garden. Would you be so kind as to post me the two that are the worst? I should be very glad to try them again; any that you are not satisfied with.

The address will be Kalemouth, Roxburgh, I expect to be at home again in a fortnight, & shall hope to call then at the office to hear what can be settled.

The book seems to go on of itself, I had requests for 9 copies yesterday from 3 people I do not know.

I remain yrs sincerely
Beatrix Potter

To Norman Warne

Kalemouth
Roxburgh
May 2nd 02

Dear Sir,

I have received the drawings and will do my best to make the alterations. I think they are all very reasonable criticisms.

My brother is sarcastic about the figures; what you & he take for Mr McGregor's nose, was intended for his ear, not his nose at all.

I have written for some 'Albinine', & will set to work at once.

The people are very suitable here, if one was not afraid of them; especially the cook. If I cannot manage any other way, I will photograph her in the right position & copy the photograph. I never learnt to draw figures, but it is much more satisfactory to have another try at them, & I am very glad that you have sent them back.

Believe me yrs sincerely
Beatrix Potter

The rabbits will be no difficulty, I had exactly the same opinion about the one under the gate, & those with the kettle.

To F. Warne & Co.

Kalemouth
Roxburgh
Scotland
May 8th 02

Dear Sir,

I enclose the drawings. I fear it is not of much use posting on Friday, but if any further alteration is required, you might have time to post them back here this week. If there had been time, I should like to have copied a photograph for "Mrs McGregor"; I have taken a very suitable person but cannot develop it here.

I think if you would kindly – as you suggest – draw out a rough draft of the agreement, & allow me to call at Bedford St in order to hear it explained, it would be the best plan.

The royalty upon the 1st edition of 6000 which you offer in your letter of May 7th is quite as much as I expected.

I should wish, before signing an agreement, to understand clearly what arrangement it would imply about the copyright; and what stipulations would be made about subsequent editions, if required.

I am very glad to hear that the book can be sold as cheap as 1/- nett; I should think at that price a large number will sell.

I wish that the drawings had been better, I daresay they may look better when reduced; but I am becoming so tired of them I begin to think that they are positively bad. I am sorry to have made such a muddle of them, 'Peter' died, at 9 years old, just before I began the drawings, & now when they are finished I have got another young rabbit, & the drawings look wrong.

I remain Sir, yrs sincerely
Beatrix Potter

To Norman Warne

May 22nd 02
2, Bolton Gardens,
S.W.

Dear Sir,

I am glad the drawings were received from Roxburgh, I had concluded it was on account of Whitsuntide.

I should have called but could not well leave Mrs Potter.

She is getting better now, but I am sadly afraid will be deaf; the drum of one ear being broken & the other very bad. It was influenza.

Perhaps you will kindly send a line when the proofs come, & I will call. I shall be very much interested to see them.

Believe me yrs sincerely
Beatrix Potter

If my father happens to insist on going with me to see the agreement, would you please not mind him very much, if he is very fidgetty [sic] about things. I am afraid it is not a very respectful way of talking & I don't wish to refer to it again, but I think it is better to mention beforehand he is sometimes a little difficult; I can of course do what I like about the book being 36.

I suppose it is a habit of old gentlemen; but sometimes rather trying.

Helen and Rupert Potter in 1907

Although copies of the Warne edition of PETER RABBIT *were due shortly, Beatrix decided to go ahead with the private publication of a second book. The previous winter it had been Freda Moore's turn to be ill and Beatrix had sent her for Christmas an illustrated story about a tailor in Gloucester, a story she had heard while staying with her cousin Caroline Hutton in nearby Stroud. Beatrix borrowed Freda's book back to make a copy of it.*

To Freda Moore

Laund House
Bolton Abbey
July 6th 02

My dear Freda,

I have kept your picture book a long time and I have not done with it yet. I had to copy out the pictures rather larger and it took me a long time, but you will get it back some day.

I hope soon I shall have the new edition of the little rabbit book with coloured pictures – I have had the pictures to look at and they were very pretty, but not made up into a proper book yet.

I have been such a fine long walk this morning right up onto the top of a hill, where there was heather and lots of grouse. We could see a very long way, hills & hills one behind another & white roads going up & down from one valley to the next. There is a beautiful old church called Bolton Abbey about a mile off, most of it is in ruins, but there is a little piece in the middle where they have service.

The river winds round about it and at the end of the lawn below the abbey there are stepping stones, like this,   such a width, I did not try to cross. I thought I should fall in. What a mess I have made with the ink! there is too much in the pot, and everyone is talking at once. I wonder how I am going to get to the station with my box, it is such a way!

I hope your Mamma is quite well, give her my love.

Your aff. friend,
Beatrix Potter

Lakefield in Sawrey had been renamed Eeswyke ('house on the shore') since the Potters' first visit in 1896 and now they were preparing to spend the summer there again.

Beatrix was anxious to interest Warne in an idea she had for a new book. Since the 1890s she had been collecting and illustrating nursery rhymes and she suggested that perhaps some of them might make a book in the style of two artists whose books for children she so much admired, Randolph Caldecott and Walter Crane. Crane's THE BABY'S OPERA *(1877) and* THE BABY'S BOUQUET *(1878) and the sixteen 'Caldecott Toy Books', published between 1878 and 1885, were extremely popular. Beatrix's father owned a fine collection of Caldecott originals. Beatrix's* APPLEY DAPPLY'S NURSERY RHYMES *was eventually published in 1917.*

To Norman Warne

2, Bolton Gardens,
London, S.W.
July 15th 02

Dear Mr Warne,

If you send my rabbit book would you be so kind as to mark it to be forwarded, or else direct it to Eeswyke, Sawrey, Lancashire? We go to the Lakes for 3 months, tomorrow, & it would be a long time to wait.

I will try to bring one of the frames of Caldecotts to Bedford St in the autumn. I have been looking at them a good deal.

They seem to have been drawn with brown ink & a very fine pen.

I wonder if it is the habit of Evans's [Edmund Evans, the printer used by Frederick Warne] line blocks to come out *thicker*? The one from Hentschell [sic] was rather the other way, inclined to be wiry & thin. It makes a good deal of difference; & I have been doing my larger drawings with a quill pen.

It may sound odd to talk about mine & Caldecott's at the same time; but I think I could at least try to do better than Peter Rabbit, and if you did not care to risk another book I could pay for it.

I have sometimes thought of trying some of the other nursery rhymes about animals, which he did not do.

Do you think everything has to be coloured now, or can one still have part in pen and ink?

I should not fancy 3 colour process for larger blocks, & I don't know anything about the other printing, which is my excuse for troubling you about it, & I very much enjoyed doing the rabbit book.

I would go on with it in any event because I want some thing to do, but I thought you might know about the printers. I did not mean to ask you to say you would take another book.

All our Caldecotts – about 30 – are the *same size* as in the books, & quite curiously fine. I wonder that they could be photographed at all.

It seems stupid to do a number of drawings all wrong, for I never can *re* copy them so well as the first time.

I remain, Sir, yrs sincerely
Beatrix Potter

To Norman Warne

Eeswyke,
Sawrey,
Lancashire.
July 21st 02

Dear Mr Warne,

The address is correct, (though difficult to write); Sawrey, Ambleside, also gets here.

I am very glad the book-sellers are going to give the little book a good start. It ought to sell in Manchester; I wonder if you happened to send it to Sherratt & Hughes, St Anne's St.

I am very much obliged to you for being willing to consider some more drawings. I am rather sorry that I did not bring them before leaving London.

The old drawings which I have done at different times are coloured, & various sizes – I mean to say they would have to be drawn again & it would take some time – but I am rather inclined to send them for you to look at as they are, to see what you suggest about the size of the plates & how much illustrations [sic] to each rhyme.

I would understand clearly that if I made them up into shape for a book – the book would still be only on approval.

I could make a rough plan of some of the pages & send them next week, or any other time.

This is a convenient place for subjects to draw, & it seems a pity to miss the chance of going on with them.

Thanking you very much for your letter,

believe me, yrs sincerely
Beatrix Potter

To Norman Warne   July 28th 02
                                                   Eeswyke,
                                                   Sawrey,
                                                   Lancashire.

Dear Mr Warne,

If 18 were a reasonable number of full page plates, I am inclined to think 7 rhymes would be enough; I should like to spin out the illustrations a little more.

I don't know whether it would be better to do the small ones in pen & ink, or in colour? The coloured sample page looks rather nice, & I think would make a prettier book. I don't understand whether colour can be printed on both sides, or to what extent one ought to consider the pages, if it cannot.

There is one pen & ink which I had processed two years ago, as an experiment. I think it is bad; but I might do better now.

I never met with Cecily [Parsley] in print; it is an old rhyme, there is another version in Halliwell's Nursery Rhymes.

The drawings seem to be in the direction of being too black *if* the outlines photographed any blacker; perhaps it might be mended by the use of brown ink in printing?

Most of them were sent to a small drawing society, I notice that those with a bit of landscape are the favourites. Nobody cares for the cocks & hens; & it comes rather near Caldecott's cat & fiddle, & comparisons are un desirable [sic].

I had thought the book might be in a style between Caldecott's & the Baby's Opera; I cannot design pattern borders, but I like drawing flowers.

I will go on with it on approval if you are undecided, or for myself if you decline it; I should not intend sending it to another publisher; but I hope very much you may like the drawings.

                                        I remain, yrs sincerely
                                        Beatrix Potter

To Norman Warne

Eeswyke,
Sawrey,
Lancashire.
Aug 17th 02

Dear Sir,

I return the proofs of Peter Rabbit, the only alterations I would like to suggest – there is a full stop on page 27, where there ought to be a coma [sic].

On page 75 it might read better if another line were crossed out, I have marked it in pencil; or if that is inconvenient you might print it "straight across the *cabbages*".

The word 'garden' has come twice close together owing to some lines having been cut out.

The blocks do not seem to have registered quite exactly but the only 2 that seem really unpleasant are page 65 & 74.

As long as it does not become worse, I rather like the effect in some of them; it makes them softer. I think your printer has succeeded much better with the greens than Hentchell [sic] did; I hope the little book will be a success there seems to be a great deal of trouble being taken with it.

It is a disappointing summer for work out of doors, I cannot get on at all so far.

I remain yrs sincerely
Beatrix Potter

Three suggestions for the title-page of The Tale of Peter Rabbit

To Freda Moore

Oct 6th 02
Eeswyke,
Sawrey,
Lancashire.

My dear Freda,

I had such nice letters from you and Marjory [sic] just after I came here, and I have been intending to answer them all summer, but I have left it till the last day! We are coming home on Wednesday. We have all got colds in our noses at present to end up with. I hope I shall be able to drive over to see your Mamma with the new pony; but I shall not keep him long if he does not improve his manners when he gets to London. One of his little games – when he is lazy and does not want to go – is to sail away round a corner & up a wrong road. Then I pull & scold, & then the groom takes the reins & pulls, & at last we stop, & then the groom gets out & turns him round and punches him very hard in the ribs! Other times he stands still at the bottom of a hill & won't go at all. When he does occasionally go, he is a very good pony indeed & nice looking.

Your mouse-book is not printed yet; but the coloured edition of Peter Rabbit is ready, & I think it is to be in the shops this week; if there are any book shops about Wandsworth you must look whether it is in the windows. The publisher has sold more copies than he printed (6000) so he is going to print another edition at once.

We have had a very cold summer, the last few weeks have been the pleasantest we have had; although it is sharp & frosty there is less wind & more sunshine than in August. My brother has been shooting pheasants & rabbits, lots of rabbits; the gardener puts a ferret into the hole & then the rabbit rushes out; he got 11 today. I have a little rabbit which I tamed, it jumps over my hands for bits of biscuit, but it is so frightened of everyone else I cannot show off its tricks to people. My brother was bitten with a snake a fortnight ago, he had a bad arm but it is all right again now. We have caught a good many pike in the lake, we fish with a thing they call a "wagtail"! It is a very ugly imitation fish made of bits of leather. I must do some more packing, so good night, & love to all of you.

from yrs aff—
Beatrix Potter

Warne printed 8,000 copies of THE TALE OF PETER RABBIT *in October, 6,000 of which were bound in paper boards for sale at 1/- and 2,000 in cloth at 1/6. There was a further printing of 12,000 in November and a third printing of 8,220 in December.*

Beatrix had printed 500 copies of her private edition of THE TAILOR OF GLOUCESTER, *slightly shortening the text of Freda's original and including all the pictures but two, the illustrations in colour throughout. Beatrix hoped very much that Warne would publish an edition, too. The nursery rhyme book had been set aside in favour of a story about a squirrel which was based on a picture letter Beatrix sent to Norah Moore in September 1901. To help her with the pictures Beatrix bought a squirrel from a pet shop to use as a model.*

To Norman Warne   2 Bolton Gdns
                                             Dec 17th 02

Dear Mr Warne,

I send the little book. I hope that at all events you will not think the story very silly. Two of the plates towards the end were intended for near to the beginning.

The colours for some reason seem better by gas-light; but if it ever were reprinted I would be strongly inclined to leave out several of the illustrations & put in some new ones, of the cat.

Also the words might be more compact.

I remain yrs sincerely
Beatrix Potter

I don't think they have processed as well as Peter, but it is my own fault. I used Indian ink rubbed off a stick instead of the ink in bottles, for the outlines.

I undertook the book with very cheerful courage, but I have not the least judgment whether it is satisfactory now that it is done, I'm afraid it is going to fall rather flat here.

Cover drawing for the privately printed The Tailor of Gloucester

To Norman Warne

Dec 19th 02
2 Bolton Gdns

Dear Mr Warne,

Thank you for your letter about the mouse book; you have paid it the compliment of taking the plot very seriously; and I perceive that your criticisms are just; because I was quite sure in advance that you would cut out the tailor and all my favourite rhymes! Which was one of the reasons why I printed it myself.

I don't mind at all what is done with it in the future; we will see how it goes off this Christmas, and if it is a success it might be improved & re-printed someday. At present it is most in request amongst old ladies.

I will work a bit longer on the squirrel drawings before showing them again, the squirrel is getting tame & I think they will turn out well, it is a great improvement to draw some of them length wise.

I think my sympathies are still with the poor old tailor but I can well believe the other would be more likely to appeal to people who are accustomed to a more cheerful Christmas than I am.

With best wishes believe me yrs sincerely
Beatrix Potter

To Norman Warne

2, Bolton Gardens,
South Kensington, S.W.
Feb 5th 03

Dear Mr Warne,

I have done this in rather a hurry [see opposite], if you think it requires more finish please send it to me at Denbigh.

I thought it had better be strong & distinct for the cover.

I will get the other squirrels done by the time you come back, & the tailor drawings planned out in pencil; I am very glad I came again to Bedford St; it seemed a pity to have different opinions about it, after having agreed so pleasantly about the rabbit book. I think it will work out all right.

I remain yrs sincerely
Beatrix Potter

Early in 1903 *Warne agreed to publish both* THE TALE OF SQUIRREL NUTKIN *and* THE TAILOR OF GLOUCESTER, *the latter only after a great deal of discussion about how much it should be shortened. As before, both books were to be issued in two editions, a cheaper one bound in paper and a de luxe edition bound in cloth, or possibly in a more elaborate fabric.*

To Norman Warne

March 12th 03
2, Bolton Gardens,
South Kensington. S.W.

Dear Mr Warne,

I have been thinking about your mentioning brocade.

I thought last year there was not sufficient difference between the 2 styles of bindings – that if the cloth binding had been more distinctly different, and pretty, there might have been more inducement to buy it.

The difficulty would be to get the lettering to show on a fancy cloth.

I don't mean to suggest that any of enclosed are suitable; I have a great quantity of samples but they are possibly out of stock, not having been to Manchester lately, but I should be amused to get another new bundle from the warehouse, if any chance of suiting.

If they had any *pattern* suitable there would of course be no difficulty in getting E. Potter & Co [her grandfather's calico printing factory in Manchester] to print in any desired shade of colour, or cloth.

I have nearly finished another drawing which looks promising.

Perhaps you would keep the samples till I call again.

I remain yrs sincerely
Beatrix Potter

Beatrix was asked to provide a full-colour design to be used for her books' endpapers. PETER RABBIT *had up to now had grey-blue, leaf-patterned endpapers. The new design would be printed on the same single sheet of paper with each book and that meant 'losing' four of the* PETER RABBIT *illustrations.*

To Norman Warne
March 20th 03
2, Bolton Gardens,
South Kensington. S.W.

Dear Mr Warne,

I have got into a perplexity about the end paper, those we looked at were all *line* blocks, but if Mr Warne wants it to go through the press with the others – does he mean 3 colour blocks?

Perhaps a line block could be printed once with one colour only, along with the others?

I will do whatever sort you wish but one ought to know, because it is useless to do anything in fine pen & ink for half-tone process; it cuts up the line, & there would be the tone all over the paper. I think you must have meant a line block.

I am vexed that the samples of print have not come yet, I hope they will by Monday.

I am looking over the other book [*The Tailor of Gloucester*] to see where I can shorten the words, before we decide where the pictures are to come in.

I ought to get it started before Easter because I have to go away for a fortnight always with my parents & I ought to be getting on with the work then.

I remain yrs sincerely
Beatrix Potter

To Norman Warne
March 21st 03
2, Bolton Gardens,
South Kensington. S.W.

Dear Mr Warne,

I think if the design [*see Plate 3*] were for a cover or title-page, occurring once, it is very good.

I am only afraid that when fully coloured & repeated 4 times, it may look rather heavy for so small book.

I always think that an end paper ought to be something to rest the eye between the cover and the contents of the book; like a plain mount for a framed drawing.

The one used for Peter Rabbit was in very good taste.

At same time – (having let off my objections) – I daresay it will come out all right; it is too late to object now, for we certainly cannot sacrifice the 4 extra drawings.

I don't think there is anything so elaborate as that in Mr Crane's; at least if there were there would be some white pages as well, to tone it down.

I am afraid I generally say what I think, but I assure you I will draw it any way you like!

I remain yrs sincerely
Beatrix Potter

I think if it were kept rather small, or rather light coloured, it would look very nice.

I will bring them on Monday afternoon.

To Norman Warne

March 27th 03
2, Bolton Gardens,
South Kensington. S.W.

Dear Mr Warne,

I should be very much obliged if you would look over this [*The Tailor of Gloucester* text] before I think out the drawings, in case any part of the story is too much spread out compared to the rest.

I ought to make something good of the coat; I have been delighted to find I may draw some most beautiful 18th century clothes at S. Kensington museum, I have been looking at them for a long time in an inconvenient dark corner of the goldsmith's court, but had no idea they could be taken out of the case.

The clerk says I could have any article put on a table in one of the offices; which will be most convenient.

I will call on Monday afternoon and bring the end paper – I thought my owls very bad when I went again to the [Zoological] Gardens.

I remain yrs sincerely
Beatrix Potter

At present there are 24 pages only, but I doubt whether they are not rather long towards the end; *you* would judge better about the rhymes. I am sorry it is so untidy.

To Norman Warne   April 13th 03
                                                   Melford Hall,
                                                   Long Melford,
                                                   Suffolk.

Dear Mr Warne,

I am posting back the patterns to Bedford St.

I had overlooked those in the small packet, they are rather quaint, especially one like pansies [*see Plate 5*].

I have been able to draw an oldfashioned fireplace here [the home of her cousin, Ethel, Lady Hyde-Parker], very suitable for the tailor's kitchen; I will get on with the book as fast as I can.

I stupidly left the end paper at home or I would have sent it before now.

                                   I remain yrs sincerely
                                        Beatrix Potter

Frederick Warne's New York office had failed to register the copyright in PETER RABBIT *there. Now news came of a pirated edition on which Beatrix would receive no royalty. Warne could not prevent it.*

To Norman Warne   6 West Terrace
                                                   Folkestone
                                                   April 30th 03

Dear Mr Warne,

I was very sorry to hear about the American edition, I trust they have not got hold of a copy of the mouse book also; but perhaps the private edition is not worth stealing.

I only wish I could finish the drawings faster, I can do a good deal here, but shall be travelling again after the end of the week, which is a very vexatious interruption of work.

I hope to bring some of them to Bedford St the end of next week; I have done 3 quite different of mice, I think I can make the story more clear, I hope you will approve of those I have done. I have got some live mice.

                                   I remain yrs sincerely
                                        Beatrix Potter

To Norman Warne   May 3rd 03
                                                   2, Bolton Gardens,
                                                   South Kensington. S.W.

Dear Mr Warne,

I think I ought to return these proofs [*The Tale of Squirrel Nutkin* text], though I should have been glad to look over them with you.

Do you really wish to put in all those 'Mr's?

Perhaps they strike me as being out of place because we had an aversion to the original (who was *not* an owl) & we always called him 'Old Brown'. The squirrels should address him as 'Old Mr Brown' to show extra politeness & it makes a change occasionally. I am afraid the page describing the tragedy will have to be altered because I altered the drawing.

Except that very awkward looking division of Twinkleberry, I think the pages look well – very much better than I expected; I do hope the blocks will come out all right, I think it might make a nice little book.

Enclosed slip was with the proofs, & all were in an envelope (of Evans) open at one end.

I have only written in pencil, not being very certain how to do it, and also you may not approve of them.

I remain yrs sincerely
Beatrix Potter

I think that division of Twinkleberry is rather unfortunate, the first time the name occurs in the book.

To Norman Warne

2 Bolton Gdns
May 10th 03

Dear Mr Warne,

If the drawings are returned from Hentschel's & you wish to have the 'fish' made more narrow will you post it to me at the 'Post Office,' Portinscale, Keswick Cumberland.

I am going to meet my brother at the Lakes tomorrow; I think *he* could very likely improve that owl, it is not worth a new block in its present form.

I notice one page of proofs is *all* too green, another *all* too red etc, so I think it is clearly the printer's fault.

The blocks seem very fine in themselves & register all right.

I did not expect to go away again, but I think I may come back Friday. But I will take the mice with me in case he wants to stay longer, so I can get on with them.

Perhaps you would care to have the enclosed drawings.

I remain yrs sincerely
Beatrix Potter

To Norman Warne   May 21st 03
                                                   2 Bolton Gdns
Dear Mr Warne,

I like the blocks very much on looking them over carefully. I cannot help thinking that some of your criticism is directed against their disagreeable heavy blue. I don't think the backgrounds will be too dark with Mr Evans' printing.

I have been a little sorry about one thing in the squirrel book; you said you thought there might be room to put in the child's name, but I intirely [sic] forgot when I looked over the proofs, perhaps there may be another edition some day. I remember there was a page with nothing but the title – I would have put The tale of S. N – a story for Norah, but it is my fault altogether I quite forgot about it. ['A Story for Norah' is the dedication in the first edition.]

I hope I have not made too many alterations, the eyes will be a great improvement; if they can make such small points.

                                        I remain yrs sincerely
                                            Beatrix Potter

I found some difficulty in making the white paint stick, but it shows sideways.

I have kept them rather long, I was hoping for an opportunity of bringing them.

I see the new edition of Peter is out, I bought a good copy.

[To Norman Warne]   June 2nd 03
                                                   2, Bolton Gardens,
                                                   South Kensington. S.W.
Dear Mr Warne,

I have 9 drawings almost finished [for *The Tailor of Gloucester*] & I shall be glad to bring them on Thurs. afternoon. I think they may want touching after you have seen them, but they can be ready by Monday.

I wonder if you have a board with 4 mounted on it, including the tailor & the dresser?

Also whether you found the rest of the calico samples?

I have had an amusing visit to Gloucester last week. I got a good deal of material in the way of sketches; but I flatly declined to interview the tailor after hearing my cousin's account of him. He has found out who did the sewing since he had the book!

                                        I remain yrs sincerely
                                            Beatrix Potter

Beatrix suggested she might add 'a line-work frame in pink or blue to the plates' of THE TAILOR OF GLOUCESTER, *so that they matched in size the facing page of type.*

To Norman Warne

June 23rd 03
2, Bolton Gardens,
South Kensington. S.W.

Dear Mr Warne

I was not thinking of a plain straight line; the enclosed may look rather heavy on the present bits of paper, but if you put them down on a page of the right size beside the sample page of type, it seems to me that they prevent the plates looking too dumpy. The plate that is cross-wise looks very squat beside a tall page of type.

If you thought it worth considering, it would be very little trouble to me because there are some m. s. illuminated books at the museum quite convenient to copy.

I could do a page-full to be processed all at once. They are very old books. If these are too much trouble, of course a *plain* line would help it; but it should not be at the sides; they are too wide for their height already, I think.

I remain yrs sincerely
Beatrix Potter

To Norman Warne

July 8th 03
2, Bolton Gardens,
South Kensington. S.W.

Dear Mr Warne,

I returned the proofs yesterday, I was pleasantly surprised to find the quantity so nearly right. I shortened p26 by taking something out of p24 and 25.

There seems to have been some confusion about the address, we are not leaving till July 16th. I understood that you were going away, and I thought I might not have another opportunity of calling at the office so I wrote it down then.

I had been a little hoping too that something might be said about another book, but I did not know that I was the right person to make the suggestion!

I could send you a list to consider, there are plenty in a vague state of existence, & one written out in a small copybook which I will get back from the children and send to you to read.

I had better try to sketch this summer, as the stock of ideas for backgrounds is rather used up.

I would very much like to do another next winter.

I sometimes feel afraid that the Tailor & Nutkin are rather too ingenious & complicated compared with Peter Rabbit; don't you think the next one ought to be more simple?

I never heard anymore about the mouse on reel (the cover) which you said might be wanted for registration in America; I will take it with me, so I can post it if wanted, I have cut up the board.

> I remain yrs sincerely
> Beatrix Potter

To Harold Warne   This date should be 14th [handwritten annotation]

> July 13th, 03
> 2 Bolton Gardens,
> South Kensington. SW

Dear Sir,

I notice that the date 1901 has been taken out after the dedication [in *The Tailor of Gloucester*].

I remember discussing it at the office, & I should very much like to leave it in. It is not very conspicuous. [It was restored.]

I think the new plates promise to be strong.

I have to apologize for not having answered your letter, & I regret that I cannot call again at the office before leaving town.

If I had not supposed that the matter would be dealt with through the post, I should not have mentioned the subject of another book at present. I have had such painful unpleasantness at home this winter about the work that I should like a rest, while I am away.

I should be obliged if you will kindly say no more about a new book at present.

> I remain Sir yrs sincerely
> Beatrix Potter

To Harold Warne

> July 15th 03
> 2, Bolton Gardens,
> South Kensington. S.W.

Dear Mr Warne,

I am delighted with the copies of the Squirrels which you have sent me. Mr Evan's printing is very much better than Hentschell's [sic], I hope the plates in the mouse book may be an equal success.

I should be very glad if you will let me have 12 copies at trade price *when published*; I think it is a little rash to send copies beforehand if they are *not* to get about – they will certainly be stolen!

I will make out a rough outline of the stories I know, & post it to you from Fawe Park, Keswick [that summer's holiday house]. I should not propose to work on any story while away, but if I knew what was likely to be chosen it would be a guide for sketching.

If you do not forward Mr Norman Warne's letters, will you please tell him sometime I was much obliged for his of July 4th, as he might think I did not acknowledge it.

I like the grey binding, but they are both very pretty papers.

I remain Sir, yrs sincerely

Beatrix Potter

To F. Warne & Co.

July 31st 03

Fawe Park

Keswick

Dear Sir,

I think these are very good blocks [for *The Tailor of Gloucester*]; but I am much afraid they have cut away my black line round the plates?

I am very much vexed if it is so; I think that one of the gateway is intirely [sic] spoilt by it, I relied on the line, to make the snow in the foreground look white. It is quite certain to look dirty against a white margin.

It is different when a thing is vignetted, but if there is an edge there ought to be a line, otherwise they look rotten; I asked particularly last winter if the line would be left.

I don't see how it can be remedied, but if there were time to get another of that one of the gateway I would gladly set the cost against one of the old blocks [from the privately printed edition] which you are taking over. That one is the most spoilt by it, I am really sorry.

It is very unlucky because I think they are good blocks.

I did not notice if they had done it with the last batch but I am afraid it is not unlikely, as I was very much puzzled why the street looked so different from the old illustration.

The black frame pulls them together & sends back the distance.

I have blacked my own outline a bit more in case you think it worth doing again; but it was quite sufficiently black to show originally.

The old one of the tailor's shop would be quite ruined if the line were taken away.

yrs sincerely

Beatrix Potter

To F. Warne & Co.

Fawe Park,
Keswick.
Aug 9th 03

Dear Sir,

I am much obliged for yours of Aug 7th enclosing Messrs Hentschell's [sic].

I was thinking afterwards I might rule the lines into my own copies, I hope I have not made too much bother about it.

I think it is not unfair to let them make a new plate of the gateway, I only hope it will be as good as the first one.

When I took the first mouse drawings to Fleet St myself I asked particularly about having that black line. I did not see the same gentleman that was at your office, an older one, he said nothing whatever about any difficulty.

I think it is rather a lame excuse to apply it to part only of a set of plates; and it is not a bad check upon the register of the printing.

I suppose Mr Evans won't take it off?

I shall be much interested to see the cloth covers. I hope the little books will repay you for all this trouble.

Thanking you very much. I remain yrs sincerely
Beatrix Potter

To Norman Warne

Aug 20th 03
(5th day of rain!)
Fawe Park,
Keswick.

Dear Mr Warne,

I enclose the reversed end paper, if it is not quite satisfactory in every particular please send it back again, I am afraid my hand is rather shaky, or else the sketching makes one careless.

I am *delighted* to hear such a good account of Nutkin, I never thought when I was drawing it that it would be such a success – though I think you always had a good opinion of it. I should be glad to have a few more copies when convenient; it must be a troublesome business to distribute 10,000.

I shall be very curious to see the Tailor. I expect the separate plates will be more pretty in themselves but rather too various, the squirrel illustrations go well together.

I remain yrs sincerely
Beatrix Potter

THE TALE OF SQUIRREL NUTKIN *was published in August 1903*, THE TAILOR OF GLOUCESTER *was scheduled for October, and already Beatrix was anxious to start on something new. She liked the variety of working on two books at once and had agreed with Norman that one of the new stories should be* THE TALE OF BENJAMIN BUNNY. *It would be published in the same format as the earlier volumes, which had become known as 'the little books'. The second book would be larger in size, possibly in the format of* JOHNNY CROW'S GARDEN *by L. Leslie Brooke recently published by Frederick Warne.*

Warne were meticulous in keeping Beatrix informed of everything in connection with her books, even sending draft copy of advertisements and advertising leaflets for her approval.

To Norman Warne

Fawe Park
Keswick
[? September 1903]

Dear Mr Warne,

Thank you for another advt. forwarded.

We are going home the end of next week; it has been so fine I am half sorry; three months is always more than enough, but autumn is far away the best time at the Lakes.

One of your travellers was in Keswick a fortnight ago & gave the bookseller a good account of Nutkin.

I think I have done every imaginable rabbit background, & miscellaneous sketches as well – about 70! I hope you will like them, though rather scribbled.

I had a funny instance of rabbit ferocity last night; I had been playing with the ferret, & then with the rabbit without washing my hands. She the rabbit is generally a most affectionate little animal but she simply flew at me, biting my wrist all over before I could fasten the hutch. Our friendship is at present restored with scented soap!

I shall be much interested to see the mouse book; little Lucie in Newlands [daughter of the vicar of Newlands and later to be the heroine of *Mrs. Tiggy-Winkle*] is delighted with Nutkin.

I remain yrs sincerely
Beatrix Potter

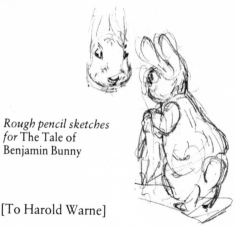

Rough pencil sketches for The Tale of Benjamin Bunny

[To Harold Warne]

Nov 6th 03
2, Bolton Gardens,
South Kensington. S.W.

Dear Mr Warne

I should be very grateful if anyone could find time to write me a line how the "Tailor" is going on?

I am afraid I am not making a good start yet with the rabbit book, I have been rather bothered but I hope it will come right; when will Mr Norman Warne be coming back? and able to look over it.

I have had a bad cold for two weeks, but I hope I may be out again next week.

I almost wish I could do the larger book first, I think I am getting a little cramped with those small drawings, I want to put too much in them.

I wish I could get the new books settled & go into the country for a week's sketching if it is going to be fine at last.

With apologies for troubling you

believe me yrs sincerely
Beatrix Potter

To Norman Warne

Nov 9th 03
2, Bolton Gardens,
South Kensington. S.W.

Dear Mr Warne,

I think I should be able to call on Wednesday afternoon unless it is very wet. If I don't come then I shall have to wait till Friday as my mother is busy on Thursday.

I have not seen that book but from the description in your catalogue I think it sounds a nice size, and I should very much fancy trying to do some outline drawings sometime.

The public must be fond of rabbits! what an appalling quantity of Peter.

Thanking you very much for your kind letter, believe me yrs sincerely
Beatrix Potter

There was still no decision about the larger book to pair with BENJAMIN BUNNY. *Beatrix had recently sent Norman a copy book containing three stories, one about a cat (an early version of* THE PIE AND THE PATTY-PAN)*, another about a long-haired guinea pig (later to be the first chapter of* THE FAIRY CARAVAN) *and the third about some mice and a doll's house called* THE TALE OF HUNCA MUNCA *or* THE TALE OF TWO BAD MICE. *While awaiting Warne's decision Beatrix turned her attention to the merchandising possibilities of her characters – and started making dolls.*

To Norman Warne

Dec 10th 03
2, Bolton Gardens,
South Kensington. S.W.

Dear Mr Warne,

I forgot to ask you whether you have got the original drawings of Nutkin & the Tailor, or whether they are still at the printer's? I don't want them in any hurry if you have got them all right, I could call for them sometime.

I am cutting out calico patterns of Peter, I have not got it right yet, but the expression is going to be lovely; especially the whiskers – (pulled out of a brush!)

I think I will make one first of white velveteen painted, like those policemen dolls are made of; fur is very difficult to sew.

I cannot tell what to do about those stories, it would certainly be more amusing to do the one with toys and I would have liked to do which ever you prefer; the first one seemed easier to manage in some ways. At present I intend to make dolls; I think I could make him stand on his legs if he had some lead bullets in his feet!

I also forgot about the French translation, I am glad you stopped it.

I remain yrs sincerely
Beatrix Potter

Beatrix's Peter Rabbit doll, registered at the Patent Office on 28 December 1903

Norman, who had acquired the nickname 'Johnny Crow' from Beatrix, was a keen carpenter and had recently made a doll's house for his brother Fruing's daughter, Winifred.

To Norman Warne   Dec 15th 03
                                                   2, Bolton Gardens,
                                                   South Kensington. S.W.

Dear Mr Warne,

My Father has just bought a squirrel in the Burlington Arcade, it was sold as 'Nutkin'; it is prettier than the rabbits, but evidently the same make. I wonder how soon we may expect to see the mice!

I hope the little girl will like the doll. There is some shot in the body & coat tail, I don't think it will come out until the legs give way, children sometimes expect comfits out of animals, so I give fair warning!

I wish 'Johnny Crow' would make my mouse 'a little house'; do you think he would if I made a paper plan? I want one with the glass at the side before I draw Hunca Munca again.

Mine are apt to be ricketty [sic]!

With best wishes for Christmas believe me yrs sincerely

                                                   Beatrix Potter

If you want to know anything about the doll my address for a week is c/o Rev. Sir W. Hyde-Parker, Bart, Melford Hall Long Melford Suffolk.

I shall try the new stories on the children there.

I wish you could do something at once about the doll; Harrod's [sic] said they were bringing out a doll like the advt. of "Sunny Jim", there is a run on toys copied from pictures.

Shall I make a mouse threading a rug needle?

To Norman Warne   Jan 1st [?1904]
                                                   2, Bolton Gardens,
                                                   South Kensington. S.W.

Dear Mr Warne,

I forgot to say that I received the squirrel drawings safely – they look very bad, as usual, after many days. I prefer the prints!

I am still puzzling about the larger book; I am inclined to the mice but it is difficult to spread them over so large a page as 'Johnny Crow'. They are more suited to the "Peter Rabbit" size as a matter of fact.

I think you said that you should be out of town after Christmas, if you were likely to be away from London for long I should have liked to get the book settled before. I thought I might get them roughly planned towards the end of next week, if that would be time enough.

If neither the cat nor the mice would do, one *might* fall back on the rhymes – "Applely [sic] Dapply".

I think you will see the difficulty with the mice from what I have sketched already, but I could make a nice *little* book of them.

I made another doll, I am sure they would sell, people are so amused with it.

With best wishes for the New Year,

believe me yrs sincerely
Beatrix Potter

It was agreed that the second book for 1904 should indeed be THE TALE OF TWO BAD MICE *and that it should match* BENJAMIN BUNNY *in the small format after all. Norman suggested that Beatrix might like to use Winifred's doll's house in his brother's house in Surbiton as a model.*

To Norman Warne

Feb 12th 04
2, Bolton Gardens,
South Kensington. S.W.

Dear Mr Warne,

When you have come back and can fix a time, I should like to show you the mouse book; I have planned it out, & begun some drawings of 'Hunca Munca'. I think you will like them.

I was very much perplexed about the doll's-house, I would have gone gladly to draw it, and I should be so *very* sorry if Mrs Warne or you thought me uncivil. I did not think I could manage to go to Surbiton without staying [to] lunch; I hardly ever go out, and my mother is so 'exacting' I had not enough spirit to say anything about it. I have felt vexed with myself since, but I did not know what to do. It does wear a person out.

I will manage to make a nice book somehow. Hunca Munca is very ready to play the game; I stopped her in the act of carrying a doll as large as herself up to the nest, she cannot resist anything with lace or ribbon; (she despises the dishes).

I have had so very much pleasure with that box, I am never tired of watching them run up & down.

As far as the book is concerned I think I can do it from the photograph & my box; but it is very hard to have seemed uncivil.

I have nearly finished B. Bunny except the cat. Please do not fix a Monday or Thursday afternoon, any other time would suit.

Believe me yrs sincerely
Beatrix Potter

From the manuscript of The Tale of Two Bad Mice

To Norman Warne

Feb 18th 04
2, Bolton Gardens,
South Kensington. S.W.

Dear Mr Warne

Thank you so very much for the queer little dollies, they are just exactly what I wanted, and a curiosity – coming from Seven Dials.

Allow me to congratulate you on your *unexampled success* in obtaining a cook & 2 kitchen maids so expediously [sic]! It makes me think of another publisher's establishment where they had 15 cooks in 6 years; & afterwards Mr M. did the house-keeping himself with 2 char-women!

I will provide a print dress & a smile for Jane; her little stumpy feet are so funny.

I think I shall make a dear little book of it, I shall be glad to get done with the rabbits.

I don't think that my mother would be very likely to want to go to Surbiton, you did not understand what I meant by 'exacting'. People who only see her casually do not know how disagreeable she can be when she takes dislikes. I should have been glad enough to go.

I did not know what to do.

I shall be very glad of the little stove & the ham, the work is always a very great pleasure anyhow.

I find the rabbits will be easy to alter with white paint.

Thanking you very much believe me,

yrs sincerely
Beatrix Potter

Meanwhile Warne asked Beatrix if she would take on some other illustration for them.

To F. Warne & Co.

Feb 21st 04
2, Bolton Gardens,
South Kensington. S.W.

Dear Mr Warne,

I do not think I can undertake the illustrations, but I have enjoyed reading the writing, it seems very pleasant and *fresh*.

What a pretty book Miss [Kate] Greenaway could have made of it.

It needs more capacity for drawing children & birds, than I possess.

With regard to illustrating other peoples books, I have a strong feeling that every outside book which I did, would prevent me from finishing one of my own.

I enjoy inventing stories – any number – but I draw so slowly & laboriously, that there are sure to be favourites of my own left undone at the end of my working life-time, whether short or long.

Illustrations soon begin to go down hill; I will stick to doing as many as I can of my own books – but I hope that Miss Fowler will find someone else to illustrate hers, for I think it is worth it.

I have written a letter for her which I enclose – if you think it would do.

I remain yrs sincerely
Beatrix Potter

Early pencil sketch for The Tale of Two Bad Mice

To Norman Warne

Feb 24th 04
2, Bolton Gardens,
South Kensington.
S.W.

Dear Mr Warne,

I received the parcel from Hamley's this morning; the things will all do beautifully; the ham's appearance is enough to cause indigestion. I am getting almost more treasures than I can squeeze into one small book.

I have had a nice letter from Miss Fowler; it is a pity one cannot turn them all over to one another. Yesterday I was bothered with a young lady who has drawn & published a book that won't sell. Also the Rawnsley's boy is about to set up a printing press (for type & bl. & white & calmly invites me to draw him a book. I should not wonder if he were to do good work in a small way; but I doubt the business part of it. I can only give him good advice of a depressing character!

I have borrowed a little *brown* velvet jacket, I think it will look better than the yellow [for *Benjamin Bunny*].

Thanking you very much for getting the things,

believe me yrs sincerely
Beatrix Potter

To Norman Warne

March 1st 04
2, Bolton Gardens,
South Kensington. S.W.

Dear Mr Warne,

Do you think this new drawing of Mrs Rabbit [for the *Benjamin Bunny* cover] would be sufficiently different from the frontispiece. The rabbits are not good, but I thought I would ask before working it up.

The little dishes are so pretty I am wondering if I have made enough of them [in *The Tale of Two Bad Mice*]?

Shall I squeeze in another dish? I regret the roast duck being left out!

I wish I could have brought the drawings but have got a cold which is provoking in this weather.

I have bought a gilt bookcase for 8½d, I wonder what is the colour of the Enc. Britannica, the advertisements don't say; it might be one of the things that would not go into the mousehole.

I don't much like the mouse drawings at present, but they are more like the originals of Peter; I am afraid I am getting into the way of making my work too soft & fine, forgetting that the process blocks will soften it. These are rather hard, but stronger.

I remain yrs sincerely
Beatrix Potter

[To Norman Warne]

March 3rd 04
2, Bolton Gardens,
South Kensington. S.W.

Dear Mr Warne,

If you could photograph the door side of the [doll's] house rather from the right it would be a great assistance.

I think I am glad that it is going to be the old size after all, we could not hope to do better.

I was very much amused about the money; I do happen to have been making myself an expensive present, but I think there is still plenty in the bank!

I had been wanting another bookcase and my uncle [Fred Burton] knew of a real good one in Denbigh, a Sheraton bureau it is such a beauty; 'Johnny Crow' would appreciate the joiner's work inside it.

Mr Burton has a fine collection of old furniture so I thought I could not do better than buy it under his careful advice – I also having a frugal mind! We tried vainly to get it down £5!

I am going to send one of the little [Moore] girls to college some day, either "Norah" of the squirrel book or "Frida" [sic], but there is time enough yet. Their mother was my governess.

I hope to send you the remaining rabbit drawings next week.

I remain yrs sincerely
Beatrix Potter

The Caldecott proofs are in the Art Reading room at S.K. museum, I am afraid the room isn't open on Sundays, I thought it was rather interesting to see how they were printed.

[To Norman Warne]   Gwaynynog
                                                     Denbigh.
                                                     March 15th 04

Dear Mr Warne,

I have not called about the book because I am here [the home of her uncle, Fred Burton] for 10 days till the beginning of next week; I think there will be plenty of time as the mouse drawings don't seem to take long.

This is such a pretty place and the air is so mild, I have been sketching out of doors all morning, and felt almost too hot in the sun in spite of snow on the hills.

I have been drawing the stump of a hollow tree for another hedgehog drawing; there is not much sign of spring yet but the moss is very pretty in the woods.

That letter you forwarded was from a lady in Pittsburgh who is of opinion that Peter Rabbit is 'exquisite literature'; also her gr. grandmother's name was Polly Potter, & she wants to know if I am a relation; I never heard of any in the States.

                    With kind regards believe me yrs sincerely
                                                     Beatrix Potter

Hunca Munca is very discontented in the small old box; I am also accompanied by Mrs Tiggy [a hedgehog] – carefully concealed – my aunt cannot endure animals!

To Norman Warne   2 Bolton Gdns
                                                     April 6th 04

Dear Mr Warne,

There are 8 more drawings [for *Benjamin Bunny*], so there were 20 last time.

One of these is not finished after all – the old rabbit jumping, unless I can do it before breakfast tomorrow.

I thought I would post them all in case any others want altering. My address for a fortnight from tomorrow is

Burley

Lyme Regis

Dorset.

I am sorry to have not quite finished them, but could let you have them by Monday morning if you post them back to Lyme at once I don't know whether you will like the little rabbit for the cover? Is it good enough?

I have not thought of any better name for the *Tale* of the two bad mice!

I was asked to pass a message to the publisher about the *tail* of the cat [sitting on the basket in *Benjamin Bunny*], its owner wants you to be assured that the real tail is even larger.

But if you think it looks exaggerated I will take it down; it belongs to old Sir J. Vaughan, late police magistrate & he is so very feeble I am afraid he will never see the book. He is very funny about the Tailor; he says I ought to have punished Simpkin.

I hope this weather will last, I hope that you had a pleasant holiday.

Believe me yours sincerely

Beatrix Potter

To Norman Warne

April 10th 04
Burley
Lyme Regis

Dear Mr Warne,

I agree with all your comments – including the '*troublesome*'! But I am only joking, it is much better to try to get them right. I think the snap dragon is much better for toning down & I have made those rabbits larger [p. 43 of the current edition of *Benjamin Bunny*].

The worst of copying drawings a second time is that I get so confused I dont [sic] know whether they are worse or better. Please don't hesitate to send them back if they are still wrong; and please direct them here, as our servant at home does not seem to be forwarding letters.

I went along the Pinney footpath yesterday, the birds were singing most beautifully & the banks were quite covered with primroses. I don't know whether I shall get as far as the big land slip by myself, I have not anyone to walk with.

There is a splendid view from this little house, it is at the top of the steep street & has a nice sunny garden. I have been able to sit on the verandah, so those 'troublesome' rabbits have not kept me indoors.

The weather has been delightful quite hot in the sun.

With kind regards believe me yrs sincerely

Beatrix Potter

No 6 is the one I am most doubtful about, the little rabbits have not much expression. I could do some pretty sketches along that path there is a broad space of grass beyond the farm just right for a picnic – or for rabbits to dance on.

To Norman Warne

Burley
Lyme Regis
April 19th 04

Dear Mr Warne,

Thank you very much for your letter of Saturday – if you have not already posted the photographs will you please send them to Bolton Gdns as we are going home tomorrow afternoon.

I think this is a delightful little place & the weather has been perfect, but I shall [be] rather glad to get home.

I am rather surprised to hear about 'Nutkin'; it seems a great deal of money for such little books, I cannot help thinking it is a good deal owing to your spreading them about so well. I see there are a lot of them in Dunster's shop here. The American letter was from a parent who wants a book about monkies [sic]!

I have been doing some pen & ink sketches in the town; but I will work hard at those mice when I get back. I shall be very much interested to have the photographs.

With kind regards believe me yours sincerely

Beatrix Potter

It is pleasant to feel I could earn my own living.

The country is getting quite green & there are such quantities of wild flowers.

Pencil and pen-and-ink drawing inscribed 'Lyme Regis'

To Norman Warne
April 20th 04
2, Bolton Gardens,
South Kensington. S.W.

Dear Mr Warne,

Thank you for the very satisfactory account received this morning, and also for the photographs of the little girl and doll's house. They are very good; & I have got an idea from the staircase & top floor.

The inside view is amusing, – the kind of house where one cannot sit down without upsetting something, I know the sort! I prefer a more severe style; but I do not see why you should be so depressed about the front door!

I was going to make mine white & I will alter the top a little.

I did not know whether I should have time to call tomorrow so I write to thank you for the account.

I shall be ashamed to show you how little I have done of the mice; but I did several rough sketches for backgrounds of the larger book, (Ap. Dap.) in case we should be doing it next winter. The spring colours are so pretty.

yrs sincerely
Beatrix Potter

To Norman Warne
April 29. 04
2, Bolton Gardens,
South Kensington. S.W.

Dear Mr Warne,

I find that Harrod's [sic] rabbits are *very ugly* after all; these cost 1/4 and 1/11, they are by the same maker as the policeman, & your samples. I had intended to colour the white *woolly* rabbit, but it will not take watercolour at all; I think that explains why the Peter dolls were coloured so coarsely.

I think on reflection that it was the colour which made them so frightful, in combination with the shoes & coat. I don't think the blue & red would have been too bright if the rabbit colour had been quieter.

I afterwards bought a fur rabbit at a shop near here, Porter, Sussex Place. They had a larger rabbit in nice brown fur. I really think that the fur ones are more tolerable, unless the velvet is well modelled, I am afraid the velvet needs a knowledge of bird stuffing. The fur covers up the defects in the anatomy.

I couldn't get them to tell me the fur maker's name, but they are made in England, I fancy in London – and Mrs Porter was very willing to get one made to order, if I would lend a model. Do you think it would be worth while to let them make a sample one? Telling them carefully that the doll is copyright. It is a shop I have known for many years, I think I could get at the maker's name by perseverance, they are civil people.

I have only enough velvet to make this head, & it is not very good, I will make a proper one when I come home, perhaps the little girl would like 'Flopsy' in a red cloak as 'Peter' is lost. I think it would be better to make them seated; it is hopeless to have the shop rabbits on their hind legs. Porters get 4 or 5 shillings for a large animal; I am sure the dolls would sell well, if they could be done properly, say at 2/6 or 3/-.

There were 2 large figures at Harrods, like people with rabbits [sic] heads, one was a lady in evening dress, I thought them very ugly.

I enjoyed going about the rabbits. I did not say who I was, Mrs Porter 'knew Peter Rabbit' & I thought seemed rather keen on the dolls idea.

My address is c/o Crompton Hutton Esq, Harescombe Grange, Stroud [her cousin Caroline's house], but I don't want the rabbits back!

With kind regards believe me yours sincerely
Beatrix Potter

Did you say that you were going away abroad in May?

I will try & think about things while I am away, I mean about the doll's house.

I have posted the rabbits.

To Norman Warne
2 Bolton Gardens
May 31st 04

Dear Mr Warne,

I have done 18 of the mouse drawings, I was wondering whether you are wanting them if you have come back?

I have begun the remainder, if I could go over them with you I should be rather glad as they may need altering.

If I could call, might we come as late as 4 o'clock because my friend cannot leave her work very early? I could come Thurs or Friday afternoon, or any day next week as far as I know.

I think some of the new mouse drawings are rather good, the dolls are still difficult.

When this book is finished I should like to get a rough idea of the 'Appley [sic] Dapply' book before we go away in July, I am very much inclined for working.

I remain yrs sincerely
Beatrix Potter

I got the drawings mounted to save time, but can gladly make any alterations, I hope you will like them I have been using the photographs.

To Norman Warne   2 Bolton Gdns
                                                          June 8th 04
Dear Mr Warne,

   As I cannot bring these today I think I had better post them to save time, but I will call on Friday aft. if I possibly can, about the endpapers, so if more highlights are still wanted I could put them in then. I could bring some white paint.

   I was rather disappointed at first with the proofs [of *The Tale of Two Bad Mice*] – but I happened to look at them by *gas* light & they look intirely [sic] different & better, which makes one hope that it is mostly Hentschel's heavy French blue which is to blame. It is the dark streaks & spots in the backgrounds that I dislike, but I think they will not show with the other printing.

   I should be delighted to try to make a design on approval for the book-list [Warne's seasonal catalogue]. I don't know if I should succeed but I can try. I think the usual price for that sort of thing is about £2 if you think that reasonable. The new end paper is coming out rather well, I have not quite finished it.

   I wish I could have brought the proofs for I am afraid now they are posted I have hardly put in so much white as you would wish. They are very confusing.

   I am very glad the little girl likes the rabbit & the story [?*Benjamin Bunny*]. I think it will be the next best to 'Peter' for little children.

                                              I remain yrs sincerely
                                                      Beatrix Potter

                                                              [?]
[To Norman Warne]   June 16th 04
Dear Mr Warne,

   I like most of the alterations – except the last pages in both books. A little doubtful '*Tale* of Two Bad Mice' – 'Story' was too long a word, I thought 'book' sounded well if you *had* wanted a change.

dedication – would not you put her initials to show more clearly that it belonged to a real child? [W.M.L.W. – Winifred Mary Langrish Warne]

p 15 [current edition p. 13]   transfer as you suggest

p 16 [14]   'drive'

p 21 [17]   I wish the printer could set Hunca Munca on one line – at all events on this page where first mentioned. If line is too long – "later" would be shorter than afterwards.

p 64 [46]   'Leant against' instead of 'stood'?

p 69 [49]   I think '*has*' not had. She '*has*' got them yet in permanent use – for anything we know!

p 80 [56] I have put your sentence the other way round; I am rather inclined to leave '*because*' Tom Thumb etc. there is another '*for*' in the same line.

85 [59] ⅔/ the *first* H.M. I think it did not balance properly the first way suggested.

9 *Benjamin Bunny* – p. 9. the type writers mistake,

15 [13] "That wood was full of rabbit holes; and in etc.

16 [14] Aunt Cousin

22 [18] 'conversed' children like a fine word occasionally. ⅔/ second Mr MGregor

33 [25] I think *spoils* is a good alteration

39 [29] yes, all 'for him'.

51 [37] 'winked' instead of looked?

58 [42] seems confused – I think we had better add the first paragraph from 63 [45]?

64 [46] 'under*neath*' you crossed out 'neath. I think that would a little alter the sense? by under*neath* I mean an inside view.

last page – 'they lived happily etc' in the first place it is inexact, also rather a trite ending.

"When Peter got home (to the rabbit hole,) his mother forgave him because she was so glad to see that he had found his shoes & coat. (Cottontail & Peter folded up the pocket handkerchief,) & old Mrs Rabbit strung up the onions and hung them from the kitchen ceiling, with the bunches of herbs and the rabbit tobacco."

If the above is too long – leave out C. tail & Peter etc & say "and she strung up etc"

I would like the book to end with the word 'rabbit tobacco' it is rather a fine word.

To Norman Warne   Melford Hall
                                             June 25th 04
Dear Mr Warne,

I have made a few alterations [to *Benjamin Bunny*]. I am perplexed about p. 52 [38] "Let go *of*". Someone put it into my head that it is bad grammar, but I am inclined to think a child would say "Let go of that!" If it does not strike you as wrong I think I would rather it stood as it is.

Had not you put the wrong front?

I have pasted in the one we chose first, it is the better block of the two.

                                             yrs sincerely
                                             Beatrix Potter

Rough pencil sketch for The Tale of Benjamin Bunny *cover*

To Norman Warne

June 28th 04
Melford Hall,
Suffolk

Dear Mr Warne,

I think that – 'Let etc. slip again' – is a very good way out of the difficulty. [This sentence finally reads 'Presently Peter let the pocket-handkerchief go again.'] I have thought of some covers; I am going home tomorrow, & thought I would call Thursday afternoon, unless I hear some other day would be more convenient to you. I am afraid they are only scribbled, for I have been rather miserable again with indigestion or something; but I have done a great deal of sketching, which is easy.

I should think your editor will be distracted when he has to correct 'Applely [sic] Dapply', I wonder if he knows how to spell the Suffolk way of calling ducks! It is very comical to hear the children – "KaDiddle C'Diddle K'Diddle!"

I think I shall manage the cover all right with perseverance, it is better to do several rough ones.

We shall be going to Keswick about July 20th.

I remain yrs sincerely
Beatrix Potter

Beatrix was working on her nursery rhyme collection, APPLEY DAPPLY, *whenever she could. The verse about calling the ducks was never used.*

To Norman Warne

Lingholme,
Keswick.
Aug 6th 04

Dear Mr Warne

Thank you very much for your letter & the proofs received this morning. I think the little medallions [for the covers of *The Tale of Two Bad Mice* and *Benjamin Bunny*] are very pretty.

The revised proof of the mouse & cradle is much better; it is a pity that my favourite little dishes were over-bitten, but they do not seem bad enough to ask Hentschel to make new blocks. I think we must trust that they will look better with the other ink, I should think there is no doubt they will.

Do you still wish for the catalogue cover? I did not hear any more about it? I could do it quickly if I knew the colour of the little people's clothes, & if you think this rough drawing a suitable design – I made it more like yr pencil sketch.

I have begun another more careful copy & I have taken a photograph of the little girl. I think I can get her right by making several copies & pasting on the best one. If you could *write* the colours on my drawing it would be less trouble than posting books.

I have made some more rhymes for the new book but I have not done much drawing yet, it would be a great pleasure to get settled to work again.

I shall be very interested to see little 'Benjamin'. I tried to look over into the Fawe Park garden [the setting for *Benjamin Bunny*] the other evening & got all over tar. He might well have had that adventure in addition to his other scrapes!

I think the new [catalogue] cover might look rather well, but I would have another try if it won't do [*see Plate 7*]. The pigs are rediculously [sic] little compared to the mice, but perhaps it does not signify.

I always forget to suggest would it be better to have the old date (on nut bag) scraped off the endpaper block?

I remain yrs sincerely
Beatrix Potter

Annie Moore had had her eighth (and last) child in November 1903.
The girl was christened Beatrix after her godmother, Beatrix Potter.
There were now two Moore boys and six girls, Hilda having been born
in May 1902.

To Hilda Moore

I gave away all the 4 little mice and got a brown mouse called 'Pippin', who lives with Thingummy-jig. Generally they are very good friends,

but sometimes there is a dreadful fight; They squeak very loud, and the piebald mouse raps her live

on the table, making quite a loud
tapping when she is very angry.

I do not think Pippin will be
able to wag her tail about — she has
had an inch bitten off the end!
I found the piece.

I was very much shocked; but
Pippin does not seem to care,
she walks about with her short
tail straight up in the air.

I do not think
that it was the piebald mouse
who bit off Pippin's tail; I think

it was a brown mouse called
Appley Dapply.

I hope that you are all quite well;
I wonder if you have any apples in
your garden -

yrs aff.
Beatrix. Potter

THE TALE OF BENJAMIN BUNNY *and* THE TALE OF TWO BAD MICE *were to be published in September, Warne printing 20,000 copies of each. The copies of* BENJAMIN BUNNY *lasted only a month before a reprint was needed.*

As well as her continuing work on APPLEY DAPPLY, *Beatrix was revising a story which she had first thought of in 1896 but had not written down until she was on holiday in the Lake District in 1901. It was about a hedgehog.*

To Norman Warne   Lingholme,
                                                         Keswick
                                                         Cumberland
                                                         Sept 12th 04

Dear Mr Warne

The original of 'Peter' is somewhere at Bolton Gardens – can it wait till I get home at the end of this month, or will this be sufficiently like?

It has been good weather & I have done a great deal of sketching for the new books.

I should be glad if you would let me know if you are likely to be out of town in Oct, like last season? It threw the new books late in getting begun, & I think I was back before you left if I had known in time.

Are you printing a large edition of Benjamin, does it seem to be liked?

I notice Muffettees is spelt wrong with an *a*; I know I do spell badly, but I cannot think how I overlooked it in the proofs. [This correction was not made until the third printing in March 1905.]

Longmans wanted a reader for elementary schools; I would have liked doing it for the children, but I thought it best to decline.

                                            I remain yrs sincerely
                                                 Beatrix Potter

I am hoping to get some more sketching for 10 days in Oct, so I thought you would excuse me asking, it always seems such a long time to be away & not to be able to attend to things.

I rather think the new rabbit is the better one.

To Norman Warne   Lingholme
                                                         Keswick
                                                         Cumberland
                                                         Sept 14th 04

Dear Mr Warne,

Thank you very much for your letter and for making out a plan of the larger book [*Appley Dapply*]; the plan of it which you suggest is just *exactly* what I should like. If my rhymes are good enough, I don't think I should have much difficulty in filling that number of pages! & I would rather try to make it a real pretty book than try to have more royalty.

I shall have to learn to do pen & ink better, but I daresay I shall get into it.

I think 'Mrs Tiggy' would be all right; it is a *girl*'s book; so is the Hunca Munca, but there must be a large audience of little girls. I think they would like the different clothes.

I am very much obliged to you for making out the dummy book, it gives one a better idea – even if subject to alterations.

I remain yours sincerely
Beatrix Potter

To Norman Warne

Oct 20th 1904
Lingholme

Dear Mr Warne,

Thank you very much for your letter, I will see what I can do about the cover drawings.

Muff etc is a regular puzzle; I wonder if little Miss Muffit (?) was the same person; it would have been best to follow Nuttall [Nuttall's *Standard Dictionary*, published by Warne in 1867].

I expect I will be able to call about the new books before you leave; but in any event I can go on with work all right; I was thinking when I wrote on 14th that you were going to leave them till I returned to London, your letter with the dummy crossed mine.

I am glad the new rabbit book is so satisfactory.

It is such perfect weather & I have done a great deal of sketching & thoroughly enjoyed the work.

We return to Bolton Gardens on Wednesday 28th & I am hoping very much to go away myself again the next week; our summer 'holiday' is always a weary business & Keswick pulls me down in August; though quite delightful in autumn when there is a bit of frost. The colours are most beautiful now the fern has turned.

I have thought of ever so many more rhymes, – most extremely odd ones some of them! but of course if they strike you as too fanciful they can easily go. I think it ought to make a nice book. I have been scribbling a great deal of pen & ink, not exactly useful subjects – but to get my hand into the way, I find it very interesting to do, & I think pretty good results.

I remain yrs sincerely
Beatrix Potter

To F. Warne & Co.   2 Bolton Gardens
                                                    Oct 23rd 04

Dear Mr Warne,

I have had a letter from a Mrs Garnett, whom I know slightly; she has made a frieze for her nursery out of Peter Rabbit, & it is so popular she would like to show it to a paper manufacturer, & she wants to know whether you would object to its being printed?

I am so much perplexed by this artless appeal that I have basely advised her to write to *you*; and I am now writing myself to apologize, but I rather hope you may hear no more about it. I am sorry if it gives trouble.

I told her that you would certainly exact a royalty from the wall-paper-mnftrr – so perhaps she will drop the idea.

I should think it would make a very popular nursery paper; but I do not know in the least whether Mrs Garnett can draw!

Of course if it were done at all it *ought* to be done by me – but *I* find it rather awkward to say so.

I think I could do it rather well – if it were not too much trouble. The idea of rooms covered with badly drawn rabbits is appalling; the American edition would be nothing to it.

                                                    I remain yrs sincerely
                                                    Beatrix Potter

To Harold Warne   Oct 25th 04
                                                    2 Bolton Gardens

Dear Mr Warne

I am very much obliged to you for your kind letter, and I am very willing to leave the matter intirely [sic] in your hands; I agree with all you say.

I said to Mrs Garnett that I thought it would make a popular wall paper, but that I could only refer her to you, as you were the registered owner of the copyright.

If I had known how to say it without rudeness, I should have said I thought her proposal rather cool; it is very odd how simple people seem to be about the profitable nature of the copyrights.

I think *you* could easily say that you think the wall paper ought to be undertaken by me – if at all.

I am glad to hear the books are doing well, they seem to be in all the shops.

I am going out of town for a week, & will call when I come back, I am sure that whatever you have chosen in the matter of cloth covers will be all right.

I should rather like a copy of the catalogue when it is out.

Thanking you very much believe me, yrs sincerely

Beatrix Potter

To Norman Warne   2 Bolton Gardens
                                                    Nov 2nd 04

Dear Mr Warne,

I am much obliged for the dummy book [for *Appley Dapply*] it is a very nice size – I only hope I shall do it justice.

I think you were right about pen & ink; I have done some with more decided shading & they do look much better. I should like to show them to you, but cannot call this week as I am going away tomorrow till Saturday.

I have not begun on the hedgehog-book yet I am ashamed to say; but I think it is not a bad thing to take a holiday; I have been working very industriously drawing fossils at the museum, upon the theory that a change of work is the best sort of rest! but I shall be quite keen to get to work on the books again.

If we get back Saturday I might perhaps call on Tuesday morning? It does not signify, as I have done so little, but I should very much like to show you the pen & inks.

Did you see that most amusing review in last Friday's Literary Sup. of the Times? There was a good one in the Scotsman. But I think it is a mistake to attend to them at all.

I remain yrs sincerely

Beatrix Potter

THE TALE OF BENJAMIN BUNNY *was reviewed in* THE TIMES LITERARY SUPPLEMENT *of 28 October 1904. 'Among the little books which have become as much a manifestation of autumn as falling leaves, one looks first for whatever Miss Beatrix Potter gives ... In her new book ... although there is no diminution in the charm and drollery of the drawings, Miss Potter's fancy is not what it was. The story is inconclusive. Next year we think she must call in a literary assistant. We have no hesitation in calling her pencil perfect.'*

From the manuscript of The Tale of Mrs. Tiggy-Winkle

To Norman Warne   Nov 12th 04
                                   2 Bolton Gardens,
                                   South Kensington. S.W.

Dear Mr Warne,

Thank you for forwarding a letter – a nice one from an appreciator of Benjamin, who signs herself "An Elderly Aunt"!

I am afraid I have not got on much, I was very disappointed that I could not call at the office; it sometimes gives me a fresh start to have the drawings looked at.

I will try to call on Thursday afternoon, unless I hear it would be inconvenient to you.

Mrs Tiggy as a model is comical; so long as she can go to sleep on my knee she is delighted, but if she is propped up on end for half an hour, she first begins to yawn pathetically, and then she *does* bite! Never the less she is a dear person; just like a very fat, rather stupid little dog.

I think the book will go all right once started.

I have been rather upset & very distressed about one of my aunts who is dying, but I hope she will be soon released.

I don't suppose there is any hurry about the books but I would have been glad to get settled to work.

I remain yrs sincerely
Beatrix Potter

To Norman Warne   2 Bolton Gardens
                                                Nov 17th 04

Dear Mr Warne,

I am very vexed I cannot come today. *I* don't mind fogs, but it was so thick this morning that I was afraid of confusion in meeting Miss Turner, & I sent back-word.

It seems useless to suggest coming tomorrow, while the weather is thick – Also there are muddles here with servants which make me rather tied.

I wonder whether you are likely to be reprinting Benjamin Bunny & could alter 2 words.

There are so many things I wanted to ask about, it is very disappointing.
                                    I remain yrs sincerely
                                        Beatrix Potter

I will try & get on with my work.

To Norman Warne   Nov 21st 04
                                            2 Bolton Gardens
                                      South Kensington. S.W.

Dear Mr Warne,

The 2 words are both on page 15 [13] – "Muff*a*tees" to be altered to Nuttall's spelling; and "what *we* call lavender" – I think '*we*' might be printed in italics? It means that the rabbits call the plant rabbit tobacco – but *we* call it lavender. [Both alterations were made.]

I had no idea that the little book would be reprinting already.

I wish that I had fixed to call today as it is so fine: I will call tomorrow afternoon on the chance of finding you at liberty to look over the sketches.

At all events I want some more copies of the little books which I can call for.

                                    I remain yrs sincerely
                                        Beatrix Potter

I cannot spell at all when I begin to consider the subject! I do not understand *why my* letter took 2 days; would you forgive my mentioning again this is *S* W, yours have several times gone to Chiswick where there is another B. Gdns

To Norman Warne

Nov 22nd [?1904]
2 Bolton Gardens,
South Kensington. S.W.

Dear Mr Warne,

I will make another attempt to call on Thurs. or Friday afternoon, it does seem almost hopeless to make *double* appointments at this time of year.

Before I come, would you ask Mr Harold Warne whether he heard any more of that tiresome Mrs Garnett & the wall paper?

I have discovered another lady – Mrs Spicer – who has had experience in the work; and if Mrs Garnett is disposed of, I think it might be a good idea if Mrs Spicer & I made a design and took possession of the field?

The rabbit dollies are in great force at Whitely's.

Did you ever happen to see a review of the 'Tailor' in the "Tailor & Cutter", the paper which the mouse on the bobbin is reading?

I have just been calling on my funny old tailor in Chelsea, & he said he had showed his copy to a traveller from the 'Tailor & Cutter', & told him about my drawing his shop, and they had "put in a *beautifull* review!" I suppose it would be last spring. I was very much amused with him, he is a very fat jolly old man on crutches.

I remain yrs sincerely
Beatrix Potter

The review in THE TAILOR AND CUTTER *had been in their Christmas issue of 24 December 1903.* 'A XMAS FAIRY TALE – *We have just reviewed with as much interest as any child ever read a fairy tale, a delightful little story entitled* THE TAILOR OF GLOUCESTER *by Beatrix Potter, and we think it is by far the prettiest story connected with tailoring we have ever read, and as it is full of that spirit of Peace on Earth, Goodwill to Men, we are not ashamed to confess that it brought the moisture to our eyes, as well as the smile to our face. It is got up in choicest style and illustrated by twenty-seven of the prettiest pictures it is possible to imagine as illustrations of the story . . . Perhaps some of our readers will have got past such fairy tales; but we like them, and if there are any others like us we strongly advise them to get this book . . .'*

To Norman Warne   Dec 5th 04
                                                   2 Bolton Gardens,
                                                   South Kensington. S.W.
Dear Mr Warne,

I am pleasantly surprised with the line blocks, I did not think they would have looked so well.

At the same time I can see their defects, and I shall learn a great deal from them.

I am afraid I *do* use process ink, and that the fault lies in my own work.

I think the catalogue design would have looked better if the ribbon had been pink, the lettering being red. It seems rather a jumble of colour. I like the simple fleur-de-lis pattern very much.

The hedgehog drawings are turning out very comical. I have dressed up a cotton wool dummy figure for convenience of drawing the clothes. It is such a little figure of fun, it terrifies my rabbit; but Hunca Munca is always at pulling out the stuffing.

I think it should make a good book, when I have learnt to draw the child.

With many thanks for the sample catalogues, believe me

                                                   yrs sincerely
                                                   Beatrix Potter

With this next letter Beatrix enclosed a sketch of a game board laid out as Mr McGregor's Garden and a set of detailed rules. THE GAME OF PETER RABBIT *was a square-to-square chase, 'If Mr McGregor succeeds in getting upon the same square with Peter – then Peter is caught.' Norman did as he was asked and duly registered copyright in the game at Stationers' Hall.*

To Norman Warne   2 Bolton Gardens S.W.
                                                   Dec 7th 04
Dear Mr Warne,

I think this is rather a good game. I have written the rules at some length, (to prevent arguments!) but it is very simple, & the chances are strongly in favour of Peter.

I was wondering whether you would cut out two little wooden pawns, to represent Peter and Mr McGregor, and try the game with some child at Christmas? If they like it, and it is worth bringing out, I should think the map might be printed a third larger, & mounted on a hinged paste-board. I remember when I was a child we played a game called 'Go-bang' on a board like that.

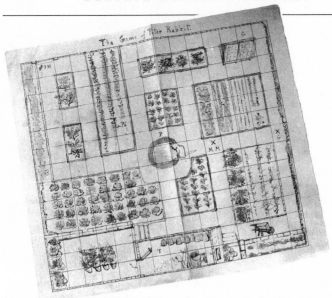

I have another copy of the map, in case you wanted to register this. It might be well to register it, & then put it aside till some less busy time; it is too late to do anything with it this season; but I think it is a game that children might find exciting, if they were fond of the book.

I remain yrs sincerely
Beatrix Potter

I made it yesterday in the fog, as I couldn't see to draw. I have tried it with the corks; it wants coloured wooden solid persons, like the old fashioned 'Noah'.

[To Norman Warne]
Dec 11th 04
2, Bolton Gardens,
South Kensington. S.W.

Dear Mr Warne,

I think it will be better to alter the map rather than the moves, I can very easily make it critical at corners. I think if a child were playing the game with a 'grown-up', the child would be sure to play the rabbit, so it ought not to be too difficult.

I will look it over & alter it a bit.

I am writing, with this, for books to be sent to the little people at Sawrey; I am much vexed to hear that half of them are down with scarlet fever & the school shut, I hope it is not a bad sort. I must stipulate that there are to be no letters of thanks!

I remain yrs sincerely
Beatrix Potter

THE TALE OF MRS. TIGGY-WINKLE *was to be Beatrix's next book, in the larger format proposed for* APPLEY DAPPLY. *The rhyme book was not ready so Beatrix agreed to cast around for ideas for a companion volume for* MRS. TIGGY-WINKLE. *She was also redrawing the Peter Rabbit wallpaper and devising a second version featuring Benjamin Bunny.*

To Norman Warne

Jan 30th 05
2, Bolton Gardens,
South Kensington. S.W.

Dear Mr Warne,

When you are in town & have time to look over my drawings I should be rather glad to bring them. I have partly done a number since you saw them last.

If you have already come back – would Thursday afternoon be convenient?

The wallpapers prove a heavy job; but I am hopeful about them, as my friend had done some before; so I trust she has understood the piecing together.

We have done them flat, like stencil colours; they are less frightful than might have been expected, and Mr McGregor is magnificent on the frieze.

I remain yrs sincerely
Beatrix Potter

To Norman Warne

2, Bolton Gardens
Feb 3rd 05

Dear Mr Warne,

I had concluded you were still away & I will come next Thursday afternoon; I shall get the wall papers done by that time. I am making a copy in a different colour of one of them.

I wonder if you will care for either of these [the draft texts of *Jeremy Fisher* and *The Pie and the Patty-Pan*], don't bother to read them before hand if you are busy. There is plenty of work to go on with; though I don't intend to finish the hedgehog book straight off, as I think I may have a chance of drawing a child conveniently later in the spring.

I shall be very glad to get my drawings looked over.

With kind regards believe me yrs sincerely
Beatrix Potter

I'm afraid you don't like *frogs* but it would make pretty pictures with water-forget-me-nots, lilies etc.

I should like to do both & I think I could, if the longer one were part black & white which takes very little time to process.

I don't know what to think about the second; it seems rather funny, but *very greedy*!

There is one thing in its favour, children like conversations.

From A Frog he would a-fishing go

To Norman Warne

Feb 14th 05
2, Bolton Gardens,
South Kensington. S.W.

Dear Mr Warne,

It is very kind of you to have taken the trouble to go personally to Sanderson's [with the wallpaper designs].

I should not haggle about the £10, (though worth more); but I am not very keen about selling it to a firm who don't fancy it much, as they might not push the sale like you have with the books.

I think Sanderson's are right in calling the design old-fashioned; but the books – which are certainly not new art or high art – have sold pretty well!

We had better wait & see what they say when the other Mr Sanderson comes home. If they were taking Benjamin Bunny only, & if that would preclude my offering Peter else where, I think that would be a pity. Peter would be the one that would catch the public.

The original Peter went all round the town before he found a publisher – but I should not like you to take all that trouble for the wall-papers.

I have asked an upholdsterer [sic] I know to look through his books & see which firm has most nursery patterns; I rather fancy Sanderson's are high art people.

I am working away at the large drawings of Mrs Tig.

I remain yrs sincerely
Beatrix Potter

Unfinished watercolour sketch of Mrs. Tiggy-Winkle and Lucie

To Norman Warne

Feb 27th 05
2, Bolton Gardens,
South Kensington. S.W.

Dear Mr Warne,

Would Thursday afternoon be convenient to you to look over the hedgehog drawings, if I arrange to bring them then?

I have finished a good many and should like to have them processed because I have used a different white. I expect it will photograph well, but I should be glad to be sure of it.

I have redrawn the birds & mice, it looks much better.

I wonder whether Liberty would care for that paper; they advertize wall-papers, and they would know how the book sells. I should doubt if they are manufacturing wall-paper makers; but probably they choose their own patterns

I remain yrs sincerely
Beatrix Potter

THE PIE AND THE PATTY-PAN *was chosen to be the companion to* MRS. TIGGY-WINKLE *and it, too, would be in the larger format. There would be ten illustrations in full colour, the rest being pen-and-ink drawings to be printed in brown (although when the book was finally published in October the latter were in black).*

To Norman Warne   2, Bolton Gardens
                                                   March 26th 05

Dear Mr Warne,

I will call tomorrow Monday – probably in the morning – to see if you have come back and whether the letter press has come to hand. I can ask for it anyway. I hope I may happen to see you, I am going away for a fortnight on Tuesday. The address will be Pullycrockan Hotel, Colwyn Bay until Friday, & then c/o Dr Bowen Davies St Asaph – or if you send anything here would you please mark it "to be forwarded", as our old servant is very stupid.

I think it is scarcely worth while sending the coloured proofs & drawings, as I shall be back before Easter.

But I should be glad to have the pie-book, because I generally find I can invent drawings when I am away.

I hope I shall be able to draw the child for the other book [Lucie for *Mrs. Tiggy-Winkle*]; my cousin at St Asaph has a little girl of the right age.

I hope I may find you have come back. I have been drawing the little dog.

I shall be very glad of a change, & it is nice weather now.

                                              I remain yrs sincerely
                                                   Beatrix Potter

Pencil sketch of Ribby and Duchess for The Pie and the Patty-Pan

To Norman Warne   March 28th 05
                                         2, Bolton Gardens,
                                         South Kensington. S.W.

Dear Mr Warne,

I was surprised last night to receive another letter from Mrs Garnett. She has taken the trouble to make a reduced copy of her frieze & I suppose that you will receive another specimen.

She is very pertinaceous [sic]. Her poor little drawing is so ludicrously bad that one cannot regard it very seriously.

I don't think it need be told to her that *my* first design has been refused with scorn! *hers* is still more unworkable; it would require such an enormous cylinder to print the whole story all round the room without repeats.

I am glad to see fine weather again.

                                         I remain yrs sincerely
                                         Beatrix Potter

I hope my letter – of which I enclose copy – is not rude; but you see yrs was not strong enough. She has no possible right to take possession of my book, & I should have much disliked her going to a paper firm because it might have put the idea into their head to work it out by one of their own designers, if unscrupulous.

To Norman Warne   2, Bolton Gardens.
                                         April 13th 05

Dear Mr Warne,

Thank you for your letter and the proofs [of the first *Mrs Tiggy-Winkle* illustrations]. Most of them are very good indeed – but one or two (as usual) are sadly over bitten.

I think the light coloured & yellow ones only want better printing. I will bring them on Monday afternoon as you suggest, I was looking forward to coming tomorrow but it would give me time to work some more at the other book [*The Pie and the Patty-Pan*].

Perhaps I can get tomorrow to draw a magpie at the Zoological Gdns while it is this pleasant warm weather. I am having the little dog again this afternoon.

                                         I remain yrs sincerely
                                         Beatrix Potter

To F. Warne & Co.   May 21st 05
                                               2, Bolton Gardens,
                                               South Kensington. S.W.

Dear Mr Warne,

I am much obliged to you for the statement, which is a very gratifying one. I am glad that the old books continue to sell, especially my favourite the Tailor.

I should like to do one or two other favourites before the numbers come down or I am worn out – whichever happens first.

I rather expected to hear that the price of Peter Rabbit *had* been cut in U.S.A. because a friend told me that both editions – yours & the pirated – were selling at an identical price (not named).

I have got on with the Pie book, I think I had better bring the drawings on Wednesday afternoon on the chance that Mr Norman Warne could look over them, I think it promises to make a pretty book.

I expect to be from home 26th to 29.

Thanking you very much for all the trouble you must have taken
                              believe me yrs sincerely
                                        Beatrix Potter

After Norman had seen the illustrations he asked Beatrix to change two pictures of the dog, Duchess. 'There seems to me to be too much bend about her nose and the division between the legs should be made clearer. My brothers find the same fault . . .'

To Norman Warne   June 1st 05
                                               2, Bolton Gardens,
                                               South Kensington. S.W.

Dear Mr Warne,

I have not yet worked out the two originals, but I will finish two new figures, like enclosed, to gum over them. I think they would be an improvement.

I enclose a photograph of the original Duchess (on a chair) in very bad coat, she was never much to look at herself, though a most valuable little dog.

The two I have been borrowing are more like the photographs in Country Life. I think I can get the things done by Monday afternoon, & I will try another scribble at the pen & inks which have come to hand from Euston. I received the originals of the last books quite safely.

There seem always to be some of the plates less satisfactory than the rest, but I hope that the good ones of the cat may pull the book through. I will go over the letterpress again.

I remain yrs sincerely
Beatrix Potter

To Norman Warne

June 5th 05
2, Bolton Gardens,
South Kensington. S.W.

Dear Mr Warne,

I am sure that your designer will draw a neater pie than I can!

I am wondering whether the little dog is almost too black; but I think it is a better likeness, I am glad that you stopped the others.

I could see they were bad when I borrowed her again on Saturday.

I find the smooth paper much pleasanter for the pen & ink, I will get on with them as quickly as I can.

I remain yrs sincerely
Beatrix Potter

If they want still *more* doing to them – send them back & I will alter that oven after all.

To Norman Warne

June 6th 05
2, Bolton Gardens,
South Kensington. S.W.

Dear Mr Warne,

I have altered the oven as it will save a good many corrections, I did a good deal to the cat but she still is looking at the top one. I don't think it signifies as she talks about both ovens.

I have been correcting the text of 'Mrs Tiggywinkle', I thought I would bring it on Thursday afternoon if convenient, together with some of the pen & inks [for *The Pie and the Patty-Pan*].

I am not going away until after Whitsuntide, but probably you are;? I ought to get them finished soon. I don't think I have ever seriously considered the state of the *pie*, but I think the *book* runs some risk of being over-cooked if it goes on much longer! I am sorry about the little dog's nose. I saw it was too sharp, I think I have got it right.

I was intending to explain the ovens by saying the middle handle is very stiff so that Duchess concludes it is a sham, – like the lowest. I think only 2 pages want changing, I think it will come right.

With kind regards believe me yrs sincerely
Beatrix Potter

There is no clue as to when (or why) the decision was taken to produce MRS. TIGGY-WINKLE *in the* PETER RABBIT *format after all. The original illustrations are in the larger size but the published volume has always been a little book. It was apparently thought necessary to consider a companion story in the same format, even though work was proceeding with the larger* THE PIE AND THE PATTY-PAN.

To Norman Warne

June 6th 05
2, Bolton Gardens,
South Kensington. S.W.

Dear Mr Warne,

I had intended bringing some more drawings today, but find I shall not be able to bring them before you leave. But I think they look all right, & that you would like them; I will get the book well on before you come back.

I must not have more alterations than I can help – I find that white paint which I was recommended to use turns brown! I have been to Rowney's, they are quite un-ashamed, & say it is only meant for temporary use. I'm afraid the Christmas tree is not worth a frame, I will not use the paint again.

I will rub up one or two of the other old stories before you come back, to choose from – I think we ought certainly to have another as well as 'Mrs Tiggy'.

I remain yrs sincerely
Beatrix Potter

Title-page drawing for The Tale of Mrs. Tiggy-Winkle

To Norman Warne

June 8th 05
2, Bolton Gardens,
South Kensington. S.W

Dear Mr Warne,

I do not think that rhyme is right grammar [in *Mrs. Tiggy-Winkle*] – it is the 'no' that throws it out –

119

If it were
"Smooth & hot – red rusty spot never here be seen – oh!"
that would be all right.

She is supposed to be exorcising spots and iron stains, same as Lady Macbeth(!), the verb is imperative, and apparently it is not reasonable to use 'no' with a vocative noun. It is a contradiction to address 'no spot!' I am afraid this is rather muddled; I used to known my Latin grammar but it has faded. [The change was made.]

I hope that you will have a pleasant holiday & fine weather, & I remain yrs sincerely

Beatrix Potter

I wish another book could be planned out before the summer, if we are going on with them, I always feel very much lost when they are finished.

To Norman Warne

2, Bolton Gardens,
South Kensington. S.W.
June 20th 05

Dear Mr Warne,

The pincushion is a splendid idea, I should like to begin one at once – all the more so because I ought to be doing something else – as you very properly remark!

It would be most pleasing to use large black pins for the eyes and nose. Mrs Tig is scattering pins all over the place, she moults about a third of them every season, they are simply stiff hairs. Perhaps I can try a model some evening, I cannot draw beyond a certain time. I shall have to do some joinering too before going into the country.

The brown coat looks much better [for Lucie], I am doing the extra piggy just now.

Miss Woodward can go on Friday, she thinks we had better leave S. Kensington at 4 & meet you at Swan St at 20 to 5, if that is not too early, we would go to Westminster Bridge & take a cab, I should think it would take us less than $\frac{3}{4}$ of an hour. [The offices of Edmund Evans, the printers of Beatrix's books, were in Swan Street.]

I am so very much looking forward to it, I am very much obliged to you.

I remain yrs sincerely
Beatrix Potter

I wish I had drawn the child better; I feel sure I could get into the way of it, only it is too much of a hurry.

To Norman Warne
June 26th 05
2, Bolton Gardens,
South Kensington. S.W.

Dear Mr Warne,

I will bring the drawings and pincushion tomorrow (Tuesday) afternoon to see if you have come back.

I did not go to the printers last Friday. I thought that perhaps there might be another chance?

It is Hunca Munca's travelling box that is shaky, it seems a shame to ask for joinering when it is such fine evenings, but perhaps it would not take so long to mend, I have so very much pleasure from her other little house.

I was sorry to hear of your loss; for I shall miss my own old aunt sadly in Wales.

I am afraid the drawings are not yet quite right, but there will be time for one more try, and you have got one of them that still wants correcting.

I remain yours sincerely
Beatrix Potter

I do so *hate* finishing books, I would like to go on with them for years.

To Norman Warne
2, Bolton Gardens,
July 2nd 05

Dear Mr Warne,

The proofs [of *The Pie and the Patty-Pan*] are startling in colour, but I think it will make all the difference when they are printed with Mr Evans' blue, especially the plants.

I enclose the remainder of Tiggy, regretfully; I began that story in Aug. 86, & I am just beginning to be able to do it – and without undue 'slaving'! What saith the proverb; "a spaniel, a woman, and a walnut tree – the more you beat them – the better they be"?

There was one of the Ap. Dap. rhymes that would want little faces; you did not mark it, but I think it might be pretty – "Nid Nid Noddy, we stand in a ring", I meant it for mushrooms dancing in the moonlight with little faces peeping underneath their caps.

I will try to sketch out some ideas, perhaps you would let me know when you are back in August & able to consider them.

Hoping you will have good weather in the north, believe me yrs sincerely

Beatrix Potter

I think my parents have almost decided to go to Keswick again this summer, so I would go on with the rhymes.

To Norman Warne   2, Bolton Gdns,
                                                   S.W.
                                                   July 4th 05

Dear Mr Warne,

I am very glad you liked the remaining drawings, if the book prints well it will be my next favourite to the 'Tailor'.

I expect we shall go north about 20th but have not yet heard definitely if the house is still to let.

I met a small child yesterday who smiled at me from under an immense mushroom hat! It was just exactly like.

I am half hoping to get a holiday to Painswick near Stroud next week, I could do some good sketching there.

I remain yrs sincerely
Beatrix Potter

I fancy your reading of the proverb is right!

To Norman Warne   July 21st 05
                                                   2, Bolton Gardens,
                                                   South Kensington. S.W.

Dear Mr Warne,

I shall be glad to call at Bedford St tomorrow morning, I do not understand the *two* dummy books of "Applely [sic] Dapply", and as there seems little chance of my coming to town in Aug. – I should be glad if you can look at them tomorrow.

I went to Islington yesterday and saw the wallpaper printing, it was very interesting.

I am sorry you have had toothache & the dentist, it is horrid in hot weather.

I have made a little doll of poor Hunca Munca, I cannot forgive myself for letting her tumble. I do so miss her. She fell off the chandelier, she managed to stagger up the staircase into your little house, but she died in my hand about 10 minutes after. I think if I had broken my own neck it would have saved a deal of trouble.

I should like to get some new work fixed before going away to Wales. I am feeling all right for work, but very worried.

I remain yrs sincerely
Beatrix Potter

[To Norman Warne]   July 25th 05
                                     2, Bolton Gardens,
                                     South Kensington. S.W.

Dear Mr Warne,

I am rather staggered with the blocks [of *Mrs. Tiggy-Winkle*] I confess. Please ask Hentschell's [sic] – civilly but *firmly* – to take the trouble
to rub down the spottyness as much as they can.

You say there is hardly time to re-engrave them, & I think there is
another difficulty – the weather. I quite believe it is true that it is the
heat, now that I study them. I have seen my brother's copperplate
etchings go exactly the same way, especially if using a mixture of
hydrochloric & nitric acid. I think H.Cl. feels the heat most & they split.

There is one comfort, they will all look much better with the lighter
blue.

It is unlucky about the child's face for I thought I had got it pretty
good at last, but no doubt much rubbed & laboured.

                                     I remain yrs sincerely
                                     Beatrix Potter

Address after Thursday morning.
    Hafod-y-Bryn
    Llanbedr
    Merionethshire.
I think the cheque had better wait till I come back in the autumn.
    pps 77 [55] & 26 [20] are worst but the originals are not very good.
    I might have put more lights but I think they are already too spotty;
what they want is the ink spots rubbing down. They are not so bad as
one gets used to them.

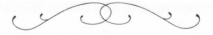

On 25 July Beatrix received a letter from Norman Warne proposing
marriage – and she accepted. The Potters were horrified, in particular
Beatrix's mother, for after all Norman was 'in trade', and even though
Beatrix was now thirty-nine, it was not usual for a young lady to go
against her parents' wishes. Beatrix, however, was determined to marry
Norman and she agreed to a compromise. She would wear his ring but
there would be no announcement and the engagement would be kept a
secret from all but the immediate families.

For some years Beatrix had been accepted warmly into the Warne family circle, visiting Norman's widowed mother and his sister, Millie, with whom he lived in Bedford Square, and even attending one or two of the large family parties there. But her engagement to Norman was not something Beatrix wished to discuss, as she made clear when she heard that, as Norman was ill, she would be seeing Harold on her next visit to the office.

To Harold Warne

51 Minster Road
West Hampstead
N.W.
July 30th 05

Dear Mr Warne,

I gave the larger contents of the parcel (dummy book, proofs etc) to your messenger on Wednesday night – I asked him to wait a few minutes, as it would be too late for parcel post. He said he was not going back to the office, but would take it with him next morning.

I should think it is probably at Bedford St, overlooked.

If it is lost, and there is any doubt about the man, I may mention I gave him a shilling; & I could get our caretaker to inquire [sic] at the next "hotel". I daresay it is an unjust suggestion; but it was a very hot night, & he may have left it somewhere.

It had my address on it anyhow.

I will call on Monday morning at the office; I shall bring Miss Florrie Hammond with me. You will not think me very cross if I say I would rather *not* talk much *yet* about that business? though I am *very glad* you have been told.

I do trust that your brother is not going to be very ill, I got scared before he went to Manchester, wondering if he had been drinking bad water.

I shall be able to ask you after his health, as Miss Florrie is not quite "all there" & stone-deaf!

It is a very awkward way of happening; I think he is going a little too fast now that he has started; but I trust it may come right in the end.

Thanking you for all your kindness,

believe me yrs sincerely
Beatrix Potter

Norman's health deteriorated rapidly and a month later he was still very ill. On 25 August he died of pernicious anaemia in his home at 8 Bedford Square. He was thirty-seven years old. He was buried in Highgate Cemetery four days later and, in her grief, Beatrix fled to her uncle's house, Gwaynynog, in North Wales where she surrounded herself with work. THE TALE OF MRS. TIGGY-WINKLE *was scheduled for publication in late September.*

The walled garden at Gwaynynog in pencil and watercolour

To Harold Warne

Sept 5th 05
Gwaynynog,
Nr Denbigh,
N.W. [North Wales]

Dear Mr Warne,

The proof sheet arrived this morning [the *Mrs. Tiggy-Winkle* illustrations had been reproofed], and I like it very much on the whole – if anything I think one or two figures are a trifle too blue – the last one of the hedgehog running away and the one of the spring might have had more yellow so as to give a more grass green effect.

But the general effect is *very much* better than that of the first trial proofs that my dear old man was so vexed with. It will be a trying thing to come for the first time to the office, but there is no help for it. I have begun sketching again; I am badly behindhand with my stock of summer work but I shall be able to make it up if there is a fine autumn.

We had thought of doing the larger half-crown book of verses "Applely [sic] Dapply" & the frog "Mr Jeremy Fisher" to carry on the series of little ones. I know some people don't like frogs! but I think I had convinced Norman that I could make it a really pretty book with a good many flowers & water plants for backgrounds. That book would be easy & plain sailing.

The larger book he made two dummies for, to make out size & number of pages. The one I have here is wrong; the second copy he *thought* was right, but he wanted to look it over again, as it had been made some time since, and he couldn't get his head clear about it that last Saturday. It was a sort of creamy buff colour with an inlet cut out of Benjamin Bunny on the back. I cannot quite remember whether I left it with him at the office? or whether it is at Bolton Gardens. There is no hurry about it, what I have to do first is to sketch; & I think I will also plan out the frog-book.

I am moving from this terrible address on Saturday to lodgings, I will send the new address in a day or two to the office. I think, unless anything went wrong at home, I shall stay away 2 months; but I shall want to come to London in the middle of the time to get the projected new books looked over, and to see dear Millie again. I feel as if my work and your kindness will be my greatest comfort.

It is lucky Mr Herring [the Warne production manager] knows about the printing; we shall have to manage them somehow amongst us & keep up the standard of work.

Thanking you very much for all yr kindness,

believe me yrs very sincerely
Beatrix Potter

To Winifred Warne

Gwaynynog
nr Denbigh.

Sept 6th 05

My dear Winifred,

Would you like a letter from the "Peter Rabbit Lady?" I want to tell you all about my 2 bunnies. I have got them with me here.

They are called Josey and Mopsy; Josey is a dear rabbit, she is so tame; although she is only a common wild one, who lived in a rabbit hole under a hedge. A boy caught her when she was quite a baby, she could sit in my hand. She is 3 years old now.

127

The other rabbit Mopsy
is quite young, but it is
frightened and silly; I am not quite
sure whether I shall keep it; perhaps
I shall take it into the wood and let
it run away down a rabbit hole.
    We picked such lots of mushrooms
yesterday, my cousin and I and
the gardener.
We looked out after breakfast and we
saw a naughty old man with a
basket, & a little girl with a black
            shawl quite full
        of mushrooms.
        So we ran out in
a great hurry to get some before they were

all stolen. I am going to put a picture of mushrooms in a book. I have got my hedgehog here with the too. She enjoys going by train, she is always very hungry. When she is on a journey. I carry her in a little basket and the bunnies in a small wooden box, I don't take any tickets for them. My hedgehog Mrs Tiggy-winkle is a great traveller, I don't know how many journeys she has n't done. The next journey will be quite a short one, I think I am going to

the sea-side on Saturday.
I wonder if I shall
find any crabs and shells and shrimps.
Mrs Tiggy-winkle won't eat shrimps; I
think it is very silly of her,
she will eat worms
and beetles, and I
am sure that shrimps would be
much nicer.   I think you must
ask Mrs Tiggy-winkle to tea when she
comes back to London later on, she
will drink milk (& any thing)
out of a doll's
tea-cup!
    With a great many kisses,
from your loving friend
    × × Beatrix Potter.

Fruing Warne's wife, Mary, thought that Beatrix might like to have a photograph of Norman's nieces, Winifred and Eveline.

To Mrs Fruing Warne   8 Bedford Square
                                                     Sept 26th 05

Dear Mrs Warne,

Thank you so much for the sweet photograph of Winifred and her little sister. I should have liked it and admired it even if they had been strangers, but I have heard Norman talk so often about the children that they seem like little friends.

I am going back to north Wales tomorrow, and afterwards to the Lakes for sketching, which has got sadly neglected this summer. I hope there is a chance of a fine October after so much damp weather.

I expect I shall get back to London about the end of October, I will write to you as soon as I get back and ask when I may come over to lunch. I cannot tell you how grateful I have felt for the kindness of all of you, it has been a real comfort & pleasure to stay in this house [with Norman's mother and sister].

I shall be amused to introduce "Mrs Tiggy" to Winifred; Louie [Harold Warne's daughter] has seen her here, she didn't make much remark at the time, but seems to have had plenty to say about it when she got home.

I hope I shall write Winifred lots of letters, it is much more satisfactory to address a real live child; I often think that that was the secret of the success of Peter Rabbit, it was written to a child – not made to order.

Millie & I went up to Highgate yesterday, the stone is put back quite neatly again; it seems to want something planting at the back, there is much untidy trampled earth where the hawthorn was cut down. I don't believe grass will ever grow well under the fir tree, I was wondering whether white Japanese anemonies [sic] would grow where it is rather shaded, Millie says you have them in your garden & know their habits.

I think I never saw a better photograph of a baby, it is a delightfully pretty group.

I remain yrs sincerely
Beatrix Potter

After seventeen summers in the Lake District the Potter family had all grown to love the area deeply. Beatrix had determined on her first visit to Sawrey in 1896 that she would one day own some land there and at last she had achieved it. Earlier in the summer, at about the time of her engagement to Norman Warne, she had negotiated the purchase of a working farm in the village of Near Sawrey, sinking into it all her savings. Hill Top Farm stood behind the village inn, The Tower Bank Arms, under the shelter of a small hill. The farm house was occupied by the farm manager, John Cannon, his wife and their two children, Ralph and Betsy, and Beatrix had asked them to stay on to look after the farm for her.

An unfinished pen-and-ink drawing of Hill Top before alteration

As Hill Top was not large enough to accommodate Beatrix too on her increasingly frequent visits to Sawrey, she decided to build new rooms on to the side of the house for the Cannons. While the building was in hand Beatrix kept an eye on things from Belle Green, where she took lodgings with the Satterthwaites, the Sawrey blacksmith and his wife.

To Harold Warne

Belle Green
Sawrey
Lancs.
Oct 10th 05

Dear Mr Warne,

Thank you very much for your letter, the parcel of books, *and* the cheque. The latter is acceptable, and will, I hope, inspire the natives with rather more respect for me; I will pay it in on Friday.

My purchase seems to be regarded as a huge joke; I have been going over my hill with a tape measure.

I had 6 copies 1/-, of Tiggy, so the two cloths make up the right number I think? and I shall be owing you for this extra half dozen.

I am so glad to hear the book is such a great success, I did not quite expect it. [A reprint was already in hand.]

If the Pie is coming out on 15th I conclude there is no time to get an endpaper design done – unless Mr Stokoe has already designed one. [W.J. Stokoe was Warne's resident artist.]

I do not mind one way or another; I had begun to scribble something but it looks a bit stiff.

I believe one of those copies at Bedford Square was meant for me but I got confused about it and did not bring it away, so I had no copy.

I think both the covers are very pretty colours.

Tell Louie there is a little dog called "Midge" in this cottage (cousin to Duchess); also a cat; and they are such friends they sit in the sun on the doorstep & the cat washes the dog's face & ruffle!

I think the account is quite correct, I enclose the receipt and with many thanks believe me

yrs sincerely
Beatrix Potter

P.S. It is most lovely autumn weather, I shall try to stop till end of month if I am not sent for.

To Millie Warne

Hill Top Farm
Sawrey
Ambleside
Oct 14. 05

My dear Millie

I was afraid there was very little chance of your coming, I should think you will feel busy. Perhaps it is well that you are taken up with something, even though it is not the most cheerful occupation. There is nothing like work! I have been scuffling about since 6.15 in spite of your injunctions but I am driven indoors by an early sunset; & the moon seems to have deserted suddenly. It is fine, but very thick. I went to Hawkshead in the trap this morning, the lake looked very pretty, as smooth as glass & numbers of black sea-ducks swimming & diving. The colours are not so fine as usual, the leaves seem to be dropping straight down, without a wind. I found it very hot travelling on Monday, there was a fog when I got near the coast. I got in just at dark, it was very pretty driving through the woods but not a very nice road after dark. However it was lucky I came by Ulverston, for the ferry boat was off for repairs, which I was not aware of!

The pigs are mostly sold – at what drapers call a "sacrifice"; they seem to me to have devoured most of my potatoes before their departure.

I was extremely amused during my drive in the trap, he kept pointing out cottages "Do you see that house, they've bought one pig! Do you see yon, they've bought 2 pigs!". The whole district is planted out with my pigs; but we still take an interest in them because if they grow well we shall "get a name for pigs". Such is fame!

We took the scales to the police station, there was a notice out that every body who traded was to send in their weights & measures to be tested. There was crowds of scales so we left them; & horrible to relate they have been returned with a notice that they are out of register! Fortunately I have been cheating myself, the dish that held the butter had some enamel chipped off it, so we have been selling about ½ ounce over the pound. If it had been the other way round I should probably have been fined. There is a new policeman last week. The garden is very overgrown & untidy, I hope next time you come it will be straighter, I have got the quarryman making walks & beds, it would not have been work for a visitor! but it will be a great pleasure to show you the result some day.

With love yrs aff
Beatrix Potter

To Winifred Warne

Dec 15 05.

Dear Winifred,

This is all that is to be seen of Mrs Tiggy today! She went to sleep on Wednesday night and I don't expect her to wake

up till Sunday. Did
you ever hear any thing so
lazy? She sleeps for 4
days at a time!

When I touch her she
snores very loud, and curls

herself up tighter.
When she wakes up she
is very lively and dreadfully
hungry, and rather weak
on her legs.

I have been drawing a
frog today with a fishing

rod, I think it is going to be a funny book.

I wish I could come and see you but I have got a cold, and a head-ache, and some nasty medicine! yrs. aff. Beatrix Potter.

To Millie Warne

14 Brock St
Bath
Feb 1st 06

My dear Millie,

You will be surprised to see where I am; and I don't exactly know why I came, except that it was kind of my aunt to ask me and I had never seen Bath & I thought it was an opportunity. Uncle Harry Roscoe is taking baths for gout, & my cousin [Dora Roscoe] went back to town for the week end, so I have got her bed till Monday. I came this morning. I have been to the pump room, & drunk a glass of hot water which I thought extremely dear at 2d as it had no particular taste & there were gallons & gallons coming up & bubbling over. It has not made me ill yet! but I am wishing I had not come. If I had waited & gone to stay with them at [their home in] Horsley it would have been more sensible, because I could have gone to Surbiton on the way back.

I went to St George's on Sunday, I did not expect you as it was so fine, there was a beautiful anthem & a fine sermon. I saw Mrs Peacock & her companion coming down Bloomsbury St, I did not see if she came out from no 8.

I find the names of the streets rather melancholy here, do you remember Miss Austin's [sic] "Persuasion" with all the scenes & streets in Bath? It was always my favourite and I read the end part of it again last July, on the 26th the day after I got Norman's letter. I thought my story had come right with patience & waiting like Anne Eliott's [sic] did. There was a concert going on this afternoon at the pump room, I kept thinking about the book. Uncle Harry is very deaf & rather tottery on his feet, I was glad to get him out of the Roman pavements & cellars, I went a nice walk up the hill afterwards.

I am sorry to say I am upset about poor Tiggy, she hasn't seemed well the last fortnight, & has begun to be sick, & she is so thin. I am going to try some physic but I am a little afraid that the long course of unnatural diet & indoor life is beginning to tell on her. It is a wonder she has lasted so long. One gets very fond of a little animal I hope she will either get well or go quickly. These lodgings are very comfortable & a fine view. With love to your Mother believe me dear Millie,

yrs aff
Beatrix Potter

To Millie Warne

Belle Green
Sawrey
Lancs
April 5th 06

My dear Millie,

I had quite a hot dusty journey, I arrived at 5 and did some shopping in Windermere, and was out walking about till nearly bed time. It keeps light longer up here. There is very little sign of spring except lambs & daffodils, the country is dried up.

I thought my property was looking extremely ugly when I arrived I was quite glad you weren't there! The new works though doubtless an improvement are painfully *new*. Instead of the old winding road – with a tumble down wall covered with polypody – there is a straight wide road & a very bare wall. Also heaps of soil everywhere & new railings, they would show less if they were tarred. Things very soon become moss grown at the Lakes, it will mend itself in a year or two. Some work has been done all wrong, that I am a little vexed with. I started a man filling up one corner in the garden to make a flat lawn. I believe the word "tennis" *was* mentioned but I have never played it, so it conveyed nothing particular to my mind. I could not think why he was taking such a time & now I discover a thing big enough for playing football! half the garden. I was just in time to stop him sowing it today, I have told the farmer to plant potatos [sic] all over it this season, as I don't feel inclined to pay any more wages at present for altering it. It reminds me of the confusion about making colour-blocks one third, smaller. The lawn is ⅔s too big! The little fruit trees are going to flower well, the first shower of rain will bring things out.

I have had an amusing afternoon thoroughly exploring the house. It really is delightful if the rats could be stopped out! There is one wall 4ft thick with a staircase inside it, I never saw such a place for hide & seek, & funny cupboards & closets. The beds seem all right, she has had a fire once a week.

"Tabitha Twitchit" is so extremely pleased to see me, I am afraid she is pleased *not* to see the hedgehog, which she disliked. She is an ugly cat compared to your Miss Giffy. She is fond of meat too, but I shouldn't think she gets much.

I shall stay here till Tuesday I think. I find I can get into a through carriage from Crewe to Brighton. I hope this warm weather will last for you to get to Broadstairs. With much love to your Mother & you believe me.

Yrs aff.
Beatrix Potter

I have not seen Joseph [Joseph Taylor, a tenant on her land]. I have written to him to come up.

I shall tell Mrs S. [Satterthwaite] to reserve the lodgings. It will be delightful to have you up here at the beginning of May; it is like summer today & the air is so pleasant.

Beatrix had spent the first half of the year working on her next book, THE TALE OF MR JEREMY FISHER, *and it was due to be published any day. Now she was planning three simple stories for very young children, to be produced in panoramic rather than in book form.* THE STORY OF MISS MOPPET *and* THE STORY OF A FIERCE BAD RABBIT *were selected for publication first, with* THE SLY OLD CAT *to follow the next year.* A FIERCE BAD RABBIT *had been specially written for Harold Warne's daughter, Louie, when she had asked for a story about a really naughty rabbit as she thought Peter was too good. Beatrix also had another story in mind for the little books series, this time about a kitten called Tom.*

To Millie Warne

Sawrey
Lancs
July 18th 06

My dear Millie,

Thank you very much for your letter which I was very glad to get, I should be glad if you can find time to write occasionally – even if there isn't much news to write about, it is cheering! I am going through a most *awfully* wet evening, & the day's newspaper has missed post! I don't know what has happened to the weather, but Mrs Satterthwaite has quite made up her mind that it is St Swithin, so we are to have 30 days of it.

Most of the Hill Top hay is safe in the barn; but a great deal round the village is still out. I should hope that tonight's downpour may be the end of it, in spite of St S. It is most provoking for me, as it brings more cold in my head, but I am getting so fat & feel so much better that I hope I shall soon be clear of it. It is nothing to signify now, & if it does not quite go away I must try the seaside in August. Miss [Gertrude] Woodward has had to go back to London today but I am expecting someone else either Sat. or Monday. In the meantime I have borrowed a kitten & I am rather glad of the opportunity of working at the drawings. It is very young & pretty and a most fearful pickle. One of the mason's [sic] brought it from Windermere.

I had such a surprise on the road this afternoon, someone overtook me on a bicycle, & proved to be Joseph Taylor, extremely jolly & amiable. He pulled out a bag of money & paid his rent £2.10. I never expected to see the money! He seemed to consider it a great joke.

I found a swarm of bees on Sunday & caught them, (it isn't quite so valiant as it sounds!) they were lying on the grass near the quarry, we think they had been out all night, & blown out of a tree; they were very numbed, but are all right now & a fine swarm. No one in the village has lost them, & I don't mean to inquire further afield! I have bought a box-hive & Satterthwaite is fixing it up for me. I borrowed a straw "skep" to catch them in, & put it down over them.

Ees bridge at the bottom of Esthwaite is being pulled down, I have got some pretty wall-rue fern to plant in the garden wall. It is a pity to see it pulled about, I like old walls.

It is fine this morning (Thursday . . . [incomplete]

To Millie Warne   Lingholme
                                          Keswick.
                                          Aug 5th(?) Sunday [1906]
My dear Millie,

I had a presentiment too that our letters would cross so I waited; also I was very busy at the last. I came here on Friday, I suppose it is 20 miles "as the crow flies" – or the "ravens" I should say, for they cross over the mountains.

It took me 5 hours; and at the first junction the porters declined to put in the luggage because the train was full. There was a Windermere lady in the carriage who was going to Scarborough, I should think she won't get her box till Tuesday! I had to wait some time at the second change, & mine came up by a relief train & overtook me.

I was very much taken up by the quarry; I have got an order for stone for rebuilding a bridge, I don't think I shall make much profit, not being there to look after things, but I shall like to see my stone in the bridge. I have hired a very good quarry man & insured him in case of accidents; but it is an easy one to work. It took a good deal of arranging though it is not a big job. I am wishing most heartily that I was back at Sawrey, but I suppose I shall scramble along here for a bit, at all events I must get some drawing done, that kitten book has been sadly neglected.

I am up aloft with my drawing etc. in one of the attics, I thought there might be more air, but there is such a wind I think I shall be blown out. It is a curious (& unpleasant) place for atmosphere, very stuffy & at the same time very windy; draughts of wind between the mountains & a draughty house. I miss the sheltered open air & the gardening, I think I might start weeding here! but it might be an uncivil reflection on the gardener, the weeds are awful! There are some pretty roses, I wonder if they would carry. My parents seem very well, & my brother is coming over this next week. I almost wish I had stayed away longer, but was perplexed what to do; & Mrs Satterthwaite had got some other boarders, very inoffensive but rather crowded in the front of the house, so I thought I had better come away. I think I must go over again before the mason finishes to make sure the work is all right; also I don't want to be at home at the end of this month. My cousin at Windermere [Edith Gaddum] would have me, I have been so uncertain of my movements that I could not ask Mrs S. to reserve the rooms at this busy season. How very awkward for Edith [Stephens, Millie's sister] about . . . [incomplete]

To Millie Warne   Sawrey
                                                   Ambleside
                                                   Sept 6th 06

My dear Millie,
    There was some rain here last night, followed by a fine cool day. I planted the roots of "London pride" last night as soon as I arrived, and they are looking as though they quite enjoyed the change of climate.
    I have been planting hard all day – thanks to a very well meant but slightly ill-timed present of saxifrage from Mrs Taylor at the corner cottage. She brought out a large newspaper full! it is not all planted yet. I daresay it will have a better chance of living in this damp climate; but it is rather early. It seemed a coincidence when we had been talking about saxifrage; I think the sort up here is longer in the stalk, more suitable for a rockery than for a flat surface.
    The plumber had been over here while I was in London & put up a pipe at the opposite end of the kitchen to where I wanted it. I felt rather in despair about him last night, but he reappeared this afternoon in a more reasonable state of mind and took it down again. Iron pipes seem to screw & unscrew very easily, which is fortunate under the circumstances.
    This place looks so green & pleasant compared to the Midlands & south country. I think it is worst about Watford; some of the elm trees were quite yellow, and the cows were being fed with hay in the fields.
    I slept very sound after my journey, and I feel very sleepy again tonight.
    I am sure you will enjoy sea air after that hot weather; I hope you will get away for a change, or it will seem a long winter. I did so much enjoy staying with you and seeing you all again. Will you write to me at Lingholme next, I shall be going there on Saturday & always glad of a letter when you have time.
                                    With much love yrs aff.
                                    Beatrix Potter

In the early 1900s Beatrix varied her picture letters to children with 'miniature letters', each one written on a small scrap of paper and then folded to represent an envelope. Often there were tiny stamps above the address drawn in red crayon. Some of the letters were addressed to the children themselves – 'Dear Miss Kitty [Hadfield]' or 'Dear Mr Jackie [Ripley]' – and signed by one of the characters from the little books – 'The Tailor' or 'Peter Rabbit'; others were written as from one character to another – 'Dear Cousin Tabitha' from 'Yr aff. cousin Ribby' or 'Dear Mrs Ribby' from 'Yr sincere friend, Rebeccah Puddleduck'. The letters were posted in a miniature mail bag made by Beatrix with 'G.P.O.' stitched on the front, or in a bright red enamelled tin post-box. The earliest miniature letter so far discovered is dated 1905, the latest 1912.

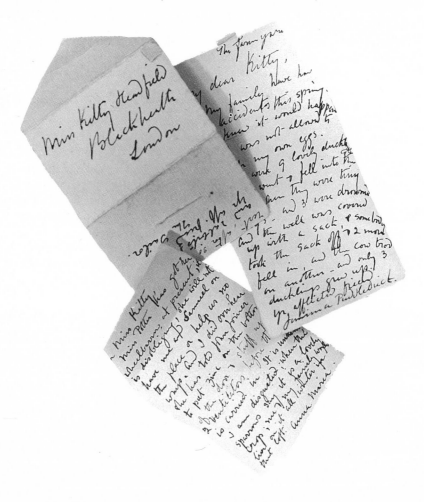

To Harold Warne

Lingholme
Keswick
Sept 19th 06

Dear Mr Warne,

I have made one or two marks on the proof [of *The Story of A Fierce Bad Rabbit*]; and I should think it would look better to print Rabbit with a capital – as in Mouse [in *The Story of Miss Moppet*]?

The disputed footstool or buffet might just as well be left out.

I have not altered the gun much, I have thickened the barrel. After looking at the live gamekeeper I conclude that the stock *would* show when the gun was pointed so low. I took out the big nose, then put it back, I think it is better to treat it as a sort of cariacature [sic] [*see Plate 8*].

I am rather afraid of making the figures wooden with trying to improve them.

I remain yrs sincerely
Beatrix Potter

Early pencil and pen-and-ink sketch for The Story of A Fierce Bad Rabbit

To Millie Warne

Belle Green
Sawrey
Ambleside
Sept 30th 06

My dear Millie,

It has been most lovely autumn weather for the last 10 days. I hope you are having the same at Bournemouth. One expects it to break down any day, there is generally a storm of wind & rain during the first few days of October. I am extremely interested in the subject, because what is called locally the "rigging" is not on the top of my roof, it is the coping that holds on the slates at the ridge; if the slates blow off the rain will come in, & spoil the new plaster, so I hope it will keep fine a few days longer.

I have got a large bed in the garden prepared by digging. I am going to the nursery at Windermere this week to choose some bushes; I am being inundated with offers of plants! It is very kind of people; and as it really is the right time to thin & replant, I don't feel such a robber of the village gardens. There is a quarry-man who lives on the road to the ferry who has got some most splendid phloxes, they will look nice between the laurels while the laurels are small. I shall plant the lilies between the azaleas. I have got a saxifrage here that would be just what you want, but I do not know its variety name. I will try to find out – my cousin gave me some bits, it was planted in a pot about this much in August & in that short time it has completely covered the soil in the top of the pot like small moss. I might as well bring one of the pots back with me for you to look at. I have been very busy planting cuttings of rock plants on the top of the garden wall – I have got cuttings of "white" rock which have crimson & purple flowers. I wonder if I shall ever get it to grow as well as Satterthwaite's.

The little black dogs here have each got puppies, but they are at present too young to be amusing. Mrs S. has got a new kitten to replace T. Twitchit but it is rather wild, I don't know if she will keep it. Someone asked me this morning "if I was still wanting a *tiger*?"!

A startling question but quite matter of fact; they call barren cats – what I should call tabby – is "tiger" up here.

I hear that Jo Taylor is having a furious quarrel with somebody else, lawyer's letters etc. I have not happened to see the old person, I shall ask him all about it if I do. There are several rows going on! but I am not in any of them at present – though much inclined! I think I shall attack the county council about manure, I am entitled to all the road sweepings along my piece, & their old man is using it to fill up holes, which is both illegal & nasty. The carrier brought a new pump yesterday & broke the handle in putting it down. I don't know whether it is the fault of the pump or the man, but it is likely to lead to argument.

The first thing I did when I arrived was to go through the back kitchen ceiling, I don't think I ran any risk, it went down wholesale so it was not scratchy to my stockings, & the rafters were too near together to permit my slipping through. The joiner & plasterer were much alarmed & hauled me out. I was very much amused. It was a very bad ceiling, I was intending to have it patched up so it did not matter.

Cannon has bought 16 ewes, so there will be lambs next spring. He is busy now bringing down fern from the moor to use as bedding, he has cut it about a mile off up the lane behind Belle Green, it is a rough road to bring it down. I think I will go up next time with the cart & help the children to rake it, it is such nice dry crackly fern.

I am alone at present but someone is coming on Wed. a sort of nurse-attendant to that rheumatic old governess that I went to see. Miss Hammond is no better; but she said her nurse really must have a holiday, so I was glad to invite her here, she is a nice quiet woman. I am sorry to hear of the colds at Surbiton – a great many people have had them; There has been an epidemic of "squinskies"!? at Bowness – either quinzies or mumps! Mine was most satisfactory & short. I have had to give up my teeth, it is like Edith's case, they were not got quite right before I left town.

I hope you are all enjoying your holiday. I remain with much love

yrs aff.

Beatrix Potter

They have had the harvest festival at Sawrey church it was prettily decorated.

To Millie Warne   Sawrey
                                                  Ambleside
                                                  Oct 4th 06

My dear Millie,

We seem to have got into a regular habit of crossing letters! I won't write on *Sundays* as it seems to be your day – perhaps you will be writing across this to say you will avoid writing that day too!

I hope you had a dry journey yesterday; I think you had, as Nurse Bond said it was fine in London. Today has broken down dismally wet, of course as soon as I have a visitor. We got a walk before it began to rain, we went along the other side of Esthwaite & looked at the charcoal burning in the wood, such funny mounds, banked up with turf, like a smouldering volcano. It is spoilt if it bursts into flame. It is taken away in sacks to the gunpowder works.

I suppose you have still got Aunt Dumarecq at Primrose Hill? [Aunt Dumarecq was old Mrs Louisa Warne's sister, who lived in Jersey and sometimes came to stay with Millie and her mother when they moved from Bedford Square to 30 Primrose Hill Road, to be near Harold and his family who lived at number 22.] You did not mention that she had gone back to Ilfracombe, I sometimes think about the 'Heavenly twins' in their 4 post feather bed! Give them my love and tell them I shall be *very* glad to see them again. But I am inclined to stop here for a good visit as I feel so very well, & eating so much I am almost ashamed of my appetite. Moreover I am absorbed in gardening. I am in course of putting liquid manure on the apple trees!! It is a most interesting performance with a long scoop.

There will be some more to be had tomorrow after this rain; it does not smell particularly. The apples on the old trees prove to be very good cookers, we have had some for dinner.

I think the road people are going to buy a quantity of stone for road mending. The rats have come back in great force, 2 big ones were trapped in the shed here, besides turning out a nest of 8 baby rats in the cucumber frame opposite the door. They are getting at the corn at the farm, Mrs Cannon calmly announced that she should get 4 or 5 cats! imagine my feelings; but I daresay they will live in the outbuildings. The plumber has nearly finished, he seems to have done his work well.

I chose some delightful bushes yesterday, lilac, syringa, rhodondendrons [sic], & a variety of others – including a red fuchsia, they say it will grow out of doors here all winter.

Yrs aff.
Beatrix Potter

To Millie Warne

Sawrey
Ambleside
Oct 12th 06

My dear Millie,

I think we have avoided crossing this time; and it really doesn't much signify, when we are only giving each other the news – not requiring an answer. My news is all gardening at present, & supplies. I went to see an old lady at Windermere, & impudently took a large basket & trowel with me. She had the most untidy overgrown garden I ever saw. I got nice things in handfuls without any shame, amongst others a bundle of lavender slips, if they "strike" they will be enough for a lavender hedge; and another bundle of violet suckers, I am going to set some of them in the orchard. My cousin at Windermere sent a hamper of big roots, rather coarse things but they will do nicely amongst the shrubs and there were some nice things amongst them, Japanese anemones & sweet williams.

Mrs Satterthwaite says stolen plants always grow, I stole some 'honesty' yesterday, it was put to be burnt in a heap of garden refuse! I have had something out of nearly every garden in the village.

I can't remember whether I have written to you since lighting the library fire, it was a great excitement. I laid the fire & lit it myself & it went straight up directly & gives a great heat. It is an old fashioned high hob pattern.

I think they are much pleasanter, but I felt anxious about smoking. The plaster has been drying for some time; I am very glad to have got the mattresses up there, it was not at all fit for beds in that downstairs parlour but they do not seem to have taken any harm. The cats have not arrived yet, but Mrs Cannon has seen a rat sitting up eating its dinner under the kitchen table in the middle of the afternoon. We are putting zinc on the bottoms of the doors – that & cement skirtings will puzzle them.

The weather is rather rough & unsettled; it is a little colder today, if it comes frosty it will probably be finer. There are quantities of blackberries still. The trees are turning colour but many leaves are coming off green. I hope your cold hasn't been much, mind you don't get a cough like last spring – but I think that was some special epidemic, for every one had it. I keep very well.

With much love yrs aff.
Beatrix Potter

I have planted Mr Dipnalls lilies most carefully, in a mixture of sand, old mortar & peat. I ought to do well with lilies, having a supply of black peat soil.

THE STORY OF A FIERCE BAD RABBIT *and* THE STORY OF MISS MOPPET *were published in November, each panorama in a wallet tied with ribbon.*

For Christmas 1906 Beatrix gave Winifred Warne an illustrated story, called THE ROLY-POLY PUDDING, *which featured her pet white rat, Samuel Whiskers, who with his wife, Anna Maria, captured poor Tom Kitten.* THE ROLY-POLY PUDDING *(later renamed* THE TALE OF SAMUEL WHISKERS) *was chosen to be the companion volume to* TOM KITTEN *for publication the following Christmas. Both books were to be set very clearly in Beatrix's beloved Hill Top and in the village of Sawrey.*

To Harold Warne

55 Eversfield Place
Hastings
Feb 9th 07

Dear Mr Warne,

"*Nearly* all" won't do! [in the text of *Tom Kitten*] because I have drawn Thomas already with *nothing*! That would not signify; I could gum something over but there are not many garments for Mr Drake to dress himself in; and it would give the story a new & criminal aspect if he forcibly took off & *stole* Tom's trousers!

We might have it this way – which is more like the original – "Come! Mr D," said Moppet – "Come and help us to dress him! Come and button up Tom!"

"Him" would be all right, as "Tom"'s name occurs in the previous sentence.

I am so very sorry to hear of your anxiety about Bobbie; but one often hears of alarms about schoolboys, and then they are better again in no time and no more about it.

But it must be an uncomfortable feeling to be guardian of an only child whose parents are so far off.

Tell Louie I shall have to teach her kitten manners. I was scratched fearfully by the original manx Tom. I had to whip him.

It is raining here today. I wonder if you and Alice [Harold's wife] are at Eastbourne, I hope you haven't found it necessary to go.

Yrs sincerely
Beatrix Potter

To Harold Warne

June 9th 07
2, Bolton Gardens,
South Kensington. S.W.

Dear Mr Warne,

There are still 4 ducks, I had hoped to finish them last week but for the showery weather. I hope you will like them, I think myself that they will lighten up the book. I hope to bring the remaining 4 in a few days, if I get to Putney [where she was sketching the ducks] again tomorrow.

It is a refreshment to do some outdoor sketching again. I am beginning to have doubts about finishing the "Roly Poly pudding", I think it was a mistake to be working at *books* last August, it has caused me to be behindhand all this season because I had not laid in any supply of sketches last season, I must not make the same mistake again.

Unless I were able to finish it comfortably in July, I think you must not count upon it.

I remain yrs sincerely
Beatrix Potter

Studies in pencil and wash

To Louie Warne

Hill Top Farm
Sawrey
July 8th 07

My dear little Louie,

I was so pleased with your letter, you are a grand scholar! I must be very careful with my spelling when I write to you.

I have got two lovely pigs, one is a little bigger than the other, she is very fat and black with a very turned up nose and the fattest cheeks I ever saw; she likes being tickled under the chin, she is a very friendly pig. I call her Aunt Susan. I call the smaller pig Dorcas; she is not so tame, she runs round & round the pig-stye and if I catch her by the ear she squaels [sic]. But Aunt Susan is so tame I have to kick her when she wants to nibble my galoshes. They have both got rings in their noses to prevent them from digging holes in the field, but at present they are shut up in their little house because the field is so wet. It rains every day – whatever shall we do for hay! There is a little bit cut and it is sopping wet.

When I lie in bed I can see a hill of green grass opposite the window about as high as Primrose Hill, and when the sheep walk across there is a crooked pane of glass that makes them like this and the hens are all wrong too; it is a very funny house. It would be a beautiful house for playing hide & seek, I think there are 13 wall cupbards [sic]; some of them are quite big rooms, quite dark.

There are 6 cows, they have got funny names, the best cow is called "Kitchen", I watched her being milked tonight, such a big bucketful. There is another cow called "White stockings" because she has white legs, and another called "Garnett"; and calves called Rose, & Norah & Blossom.

I remain yours affectionately
Beatrix Potter

To Harold Warne

Lingholme
Keswick
Aug 24th 07

Dear Mr Warne,

I am much pleased with "Tom Kitten". Some of the pictures are very bad, but the book as a whole is passable, and the ducks help it out.

I think Mr Stokoe's end-paper [for *The Roly-Poly Pudding*] is a good match for the cover design and I like it better than plain ends for a book of that size. I suppose the new endpaper for the small series is not wanted yet? I think you have the originals when it is wanted.

It is a fine day at last, I am going out to sketch.

I remain yrs sincerely
Beatrix Potter

I will keep the copies of the new book private till Sept. 3rd [*Tom Kitten* was to be published on that day without a companion volume, as *The Roly-Poly Pudding* would not be finished in time].

One of The Roly-Poly Pudding *endpapers*

Warne had plans to seek French and German publishers for PETER
RABBIT, *offering them texts already translated.*

[To Harold Warne]   Gwaynynog,
                                                    Nr. Denbigh,
                                                    Sept 13 1907
Dear Mr Warne,
    I received the parcels just before leaving this morning. That French is
choke full of mistakes both in spelling & grammar, I daresay it is the
English type-writer's slip-shod reading of the MSS.; but we shall have to
have the proof sheets read very carefully.
    I don't think it is nearly such a good rendering as the German; it is too
English and rather *flat* for French. I should think a French person would
tell the story in the present tense with many exclamation marks. I will
ask my cousin to read it over.
    I think the proof sheet of blocks for Peter are very good indeed; & so
very well printed. The first few copies of Tom Kitten have been a little
smudgy.
    I have got here pretty comfortably, after much catching of trains. I
think I shall be here till Wednesday or Thursday, if the German comes
to hand.
    I am very glad to hear you are all well, it will be pleasant to see you
all again in about a fortnight.
    I find my old uncle looking very feeble & rather ill, which is
melancholy, for he is quite alone with servants.

                                                    yrs sincerely
                                                    Beatrix Potter

To Millie Warne   Hill Top Farm
                                                    Sawrey
                                                    Ambleside
                                                    Oct 6th 07
My dear Millie,
    I came here last Tuesday and have been exceedingly busy – also a
little upset the first few days about the death of a very nice woman in the
village, the wife of a man who works for me, at the quarry.
    The weather has broken down, but it was a perfect day on Friday, the
little lake was like a looking glass. I think a still autumn day is almost the
most beautiful time of year, but when there are such heavy hoar frosts
at night it is always a chance whether the sun conquers the mist, or
whether it turns to rain.
    I have got some nice little chickens, the month of fine weather has

given them a good start. I have been discussing salt butter with Mrs Cannon, they don't seem to use it in this country, but I think it ought to answer; it is quite time that butter went up, it is still only 1/1 or 1/2 a pound.

I have done some gardening but no sketching or photographing yet! I don't know how I shall tear myself away in a fortnight. Another room has been got straight, the front kitchen – or hall – as I call it. I have not meddled with the fireplace, I don't dislike it, and besides it is wanted for the next book [*The Roly-Poly Pudding*]. I have got a pretty dresser with plates on it & some old fashioned chairs; & a warming pan that belonged to my grandmother; & Mr Warne's bellows which look well. The new barn is very satisfactory, I have come just in time to see the finishing & fittings, there is a large loft above & a stable for calves & bullocks below. The farm has done very well.

There are much colds about, if I don't catch one I shall be surprised; but every one is bound to have one cold in autumn. With love to your Mother and Aunt,

yrs aff
Beatrix Potter

From The Roly-Poly Pudding

To Millie Warne

2 Bolton Gardens
Jan 2nd 08.

My dear Millie,

I rather reproach myself that I haven't written to wish you a happy new year! but you have not written either, and it is not too late within the first week to be seasonable.

Did you ever feel such horrid weather? but I feel much obliged to it for keeping off just over Christmas, you would get home comfortably from Surbiton before the wind began to blow. I enjoyed my Christmas afternoon at 30 [Primrose Hill Road] very much and they sent me home most comfortably & carefully. I have had a cold since, but I am sure I did not catch it on that occasion. I fancy it has been nothing but the wind & I was feeling rather run down. I am all right again but rather hoarse so I will wait a little longer before coming up to see you. I had the doctor as I was nervous about getting bronchitis, & I thought I would be better of a tonic, he made very little about it.

I have got a lot of drawing done, & some mending and a swarm of letters. There have not been so many Christmas cards from unknown infants this year, thank goodness! they are very kindly meant but rather a nuisance. Mary [Warne] has sent me such a pretty photograph of the little boy [Norman, a brother for Winifred and Eveline, had been born in August 1906], he looks a very fine child and so handsome. I must really get over there to see him next time there is any good weather.

I have been examining the blue comforter, I can't think how your mother managed to do it without seeing. I hope she is very well & keeping warm.

With love & best wishes for the New Year,

from yrs aff.
Beatrix Potter

Winifred, Eveline and Norman Warne in 1906

The licensing of the characters from Beatrix's books for use on wallpaper and china, or as dolls and so on was growing apace and generating increasing royalties. Beatrix was consulted by Warne at every stage.

To Harold Warne　　　　　　　　　　2 Bolton Gardens
　　　　　　　　　　　　　　　　　　SW
　　　　　　　　　　　　　　　　　　Jan 18th 08

Dear Mr Warne,

I enclose receipts for the three cheques, for which I am much obliged.

I have been thinking about that china agreement, it is rather an awkwardly worded document. I think the words 'all earthenware' would prevent me from offering the statuettes to other firms, and I should not care to offer them to the German people. I hope you will be able to get rid of them.

But if you decide to let them go on making *tea-sets* – with a promise of *improvement* – I should think the agreement had better be written out again? in a less wholesale style? The agreement with Hughes seems a much better model.

I have made a great many little figures, some of them are good.

　　　　　　　　　　　　　　I remain with thanks yrs sincerely
　　　　　　　　　　　　　　　　　　　　Beatrix Potter

Beatrix was at last making progress with THE ROLY-POLY PUDDING, *which was to have an even larger page size than* THE PIE AND THE PATTY-PAN. *Like that book it would have black-and-white line illustrations, as well as full colour plates. Its companion, a new little book, was to be a tale about Jemima, a duck at Hill Top Farm who battled to be allowed to hatch her own eggs away from the farm.*

To Harold Warne　　　　　　　　　　2 Bolton Gardens
　　　　　　　　　　　　　　　　　　Feb 27. 08

Dear Mr Warne,

I am sorry to say I don't like the cover [of *The Roly-Poly Pudding*] at all.

You & Fruing are fond of that subject – but look at it across the room; it would never show in a shop window, or sell the book.

I think it would be very much safer to follow the Peter Rabbit style of cover, which has been a success. This is after the style of Patty pan which was a relative failure.

The scroll is very pretty – a little too fine. The whole effect is too finicking for the size of book – especially for a childs book.

You will find Peter's figure is more than $\frac{1}{3}$ height of his book. These are under $\frac{1}{6}$, & they are complicated by accessories in background. I could introduce the rolling pin with the rat.

I don't think that objects *naturally* drawn in gold fit in with conventional designs.

I objected to the cloth case of the Patty pan for the same reason.

I hope Mr Stokoe will not be vexed, he has drawn it so beautifully, but I don't think it is an effective cover and it is top heavy & too near top & bottom.

I am sorry to be obstinate but I positively object to that scattered 3-figure subject.

yrs sincerely
Beatrix Potter

Why not use that subject for the frontispiece?

*Pen-and-ink and pencil sketch for one of the illustrations
in* The Roly-Poly Pudding

[To Harold Warne]   Hill Top Farm
                                                           Sawrey
                                                           Ambleside
                                                           March 12th 08

Dear Mr Warne,

I return the proofs [of *The Tale of Jemima Puddle-Duck*] which are much improved. The only thing I am disappointed with is p. 34 [26]. I should very much prefer the ?s after the indeeds. – or at all events after the second one. There are too many !s – besides not carrying out the conversation so well.

Surely *any* word – or words, can be used with a note of interogation [sic], especially adverbs. Many people have a trick of interjecting words like really? or ah? or indeed? while listening to a long account. I think if you looked at a conversational novel – such as Dickens's, you would find some funny grammar; it takes the spice out of reported conversations, if they require to be written down according to Lindley Murray.

It is beautiful frosty weather, I have got some sketching done.

Would you prefer to alter the second indeed to "really?" or take it out altogether? there are too many exclamations, the fox is not meant to be excited in manner.

                                                    yrs sincerely
                                                    Beatrix Potter

To Harold Warne   Stock Park,
                                                           Lake Side,
                                                           Ulverston.
                                                           July 29th 08

Dear Mr Warne,

I am writing to apologise for having sent the last drawings [for *The Roly-Poly Pudding*] directed to Mr. Herring. I had understood you were going to Swanage *last Saturday.*

There is a gentleman from Vienna staying with some of my neighbours at Sawrey (his wife relations). He seems an intelligent brisk person, has small boy who is an admirer of P. Rabbit, which he wishes to translate & find a publisher for. I told him the translation was effected & that I was perfectly sick tired of waiting for a German publisher.

I said nothing could be done at present, because you were trying to arrange with a publisher at Berlin. If that comes to nothing, could we try whether anything can be done through this gentleman? Would the Berlin man include Vienna?

Do not worry about it now before your holiday, but I do hope in the autumn you will find time to think of it; and also get rid of those china people. His name is Dr Erick Pistor secretär steller [sic] der Handelskammer – Wien I take it he is some sort of official at the Chamber of Commerce.

The weather is pleasant now. I am still feeling rather tired – also *very old* since Millie misguidedly reminded me of my birthday which I had forgotten! [She was forty-two the previous day.]

With love to the children

I remain yours sincerely
Beatrix Potter

To Harold Warne   Stock Park,
                                                 Lake Side,
                                                 Ulverston.
                                                 Aug 13th 08

Dear Mr Warne,

I think the proofs of the line drawings [for *The Roly-Poly Pudding*] are passable. Apparently some of my ink work is too fine, the lines break.

I don't think it will be noticed.

I have found "Anna Maria" rather a difficulty throughout the book as I intended her to be thin & ugly; but the 2 you returned are rather bad. The lettering on the bookplate is just what I wanted it to be.

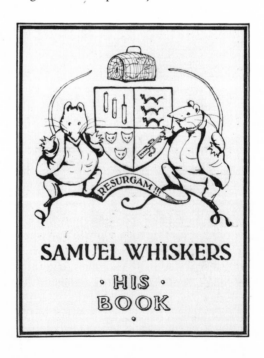

If it is a matter of necessity to put the dedication so near the story – ought not the former to be printed in italics or something? It will read in with the rest otherwise – for I don't think there is room – or need – for a heading on the first page.

I remain yrs sincerely
Beatrix Potter

If Mr Fruing Warne is in London I should be rather glad of a small cheque by end of August.

The sample page looks well.

The dedication reads, 'In Remembrance of "Sammy", The Intelligent pink-eyed Representative of a Persecuted (but Irrepressible) Race   An Affectionate little Friend, and a most accomplished thief'.

[To Harold Warne]   Sawrey
                                                                    Ambleside
                                                                    Aug 17th 08

Dear Mr Warne,

I have been a little worried about some work I have started here, laying on water.

Could I depend on having £50 end of this month, £50 in October and some more by Christmas?

Perhaps the question is not necessary; but I had understood there would be some sent in July – which didn't come, & I got rather anxious.

There was not the least need to have done the job this summer if I had known.

I do not in the least mind waiting for money, *if* I know beforehand. I should like to know what I have, to spend this autumn, without being rash.

The place is not at all expensive to keep going, but there is still ample opportunity to lay out the garden & surroundings.

It is beautiful hot weather again, almost too dry, in a country where there is no corn to consider.

The cattle would be glad of rain & green grass.

There are 8 jolly little pigs, which brings the swine up to 14 head! Some little pig will have to go to market.

The waterworks will probably cost about £50, with pipes & labour.

I am hoping to stay here till Saturday.

I remain yrs sincerely
Beatrix Potter

Is J P. Duck out? I should like a dozen.

THE TALE OF JEMIMA PUDDLE-DUCK *was published in August and* THE
ROLY-POLY PUDDING *scheduled for October.*

[To Harold Warne]

Hill Top Farm
Sawrey
Ambleside
Aug 22nd 08

Dear Mr Warne,

I am much obliged for the cheque and the parcel of books which
both came by first post this morning.

The books [*Jemima Puddle-Duck*] look very nice, I am glad it is being
ordered well. I don't think it is as good a story as it ought to be; but
Rolly Poly [sic] is better.

I have had such a pleasant week here, the garden is very pretty, &
there has been some welcome rain. The weather has been delightful this
summer. I hope you enjoyed Swanage. Almost the last thing your Mother
said to me, she said she should like to go there again "if she lived".

I am going back to Lakeside tonight.

I think the 1/6 duck cover is the prettiest we have had.

With many thanks for the money & your letter.

I remain yrs sincerely
Beatrix Potter

[To Harold Warne]

2 Bolton Gardens
Tuesday evening.
[September 1908]

Dear Mr Warne,

I should like "pink-eyed" to stand, as "Sammy" was an albino. I think
it is sufficiently clear that the dedication [in *The Roly-Poly Pudding*] is
to an actual pet rat, and "Mr Samuel Whiskers" is never called "Sammy"
in the book.

I have been looking for "scutter" in Halliwell Phillips' [sic] Archaic
words & I cannot find it, rather to my surprise. I think it is common
Lancashire & probably good Anglo Saxon. There is another form of it
"scat" = or "scatter"; & "*scut*" is a common name for "*tail*" of small
animals. Rabbits or Hare's tails are generally called scuts.

If you really want to change it I would have *scurried* rather than
scuttle. "Scuttered" appears on p. 69 [49] of the immortal Peter Rabbit
which is a classic! ['Scuttered' was retained in *The Roly-Poly Pudding*.]

It is rather interesting to come across many old words in common
use; for instance "water-logged" is a word you would find in any
dictionary – but until I began to undertake field drains I didn't realize

that it is a sort of double past-participle of a verb, to "lig"; water always 'ligs' in drains at Sawrey.

If you want to pick holes – has anybody noticed the embarrassing fact that the foxywhiskered gentleman appears *without his knickerbockers* on p. 38 [28] of J. Pdk?

The sheet looks very well by gas light. I will return them tomorrow. I am occupied in putting back most of the Q/S. [i.e. deletions] Has Mr Step been trying this hand at it again? [Edward Step was Warne's reader and editor for many years, and a notable naturalist.]

Some of the sentences do want improvement but not in the way that has been suggested.

I remain yrs sincerely
Beatrix Potter

Detail from pencil sketches

Beatrix was anxious to start a new book. She had one story she had written the previous year about a dove, another about a family of rabbits who ate too much lettuce called THE FLOPSY BUNNIES, *and then there was the story she was planning to give Louie for Christmas about a dog and a cat who kept a shop.*

[To Harold Warne]   Nov 17. 08
                                                     2, Bolton Gardens,
                                                     South Kensington. S.W.
Dear Mr Warne,

I have been talking to the Bank about the money for buying a field [in Sawrey].

I may take it I can have a cheque for £100 *last week* November and a small cheque *early* December?

This is only a memorandum, I think it is according to what you said.

I shall pay part of the price on Dec 1st and there will remain to pay in the future a sum of £300 at 4%, which need not cause any anxiety as the books are doing so well.

I should like a copy of that book of Mr Dulac's [*Lyrics Pathetic and Humorous from A–Z*, published by Warne that year]. I have been thinking a good deal about it, it is remarkably good. There are some drawings of his in Nov. Studio which are just as *un*pleasing; but probably the Editor picked them out for the very reason that they are eccentric and unlovely in the style of Mr Rackham.

I shall be coming down presently to the office to bring some of these new little figures I have made.

I think I will bring them down tomorrow morning. If you are out I will just leave them.

                                                     I remain yrs sincerely
                                                     Beatrix Potter

No answer required

To Harold Warne   2 Bolton Gdns
                                                     Nov 18. 08
Dear Mr Warne,

I am sending this [the text of *The Faithful Dove*] to Primrose Hill in case you care to try it on the children. It seems to me to be more like The Tailor – older and sentimental. If it went into print, the name 'Vidler' – or Viddler – would perhaps have to come out.

It tickled my fancy – but *the* "Mr Vidler" in Rye is a respectable citizen & brewer, several times mayor!

It could be changed to *Tiddler*, (Thomas of silver & gold). [In the published text it is Tidler.]

I have plenty of sketches & photographs of Rye, & it is a lovely background, but there would be great repetition in a *large* number of illustrations.

It seems to me to run to 3 or 4 little pen & ink sketches of the old houses, with birds on a small scale; & perhaps one large coloured drawing.

You will notice it is about a chimney & laying eggs. It was made before Roly Poly and Jemima.

It is an objection. The story has been lying about a long time, & so have several others.

I should like to get rid of some one of them. When a thing is once printed I dismiss it from my dreams! & don't care what becomes of the reviewers. But an accumulation of half finished ideas is bothersome.

I remain yrs sincerely
Beatrix Potter

Queer thing it is that I cannot spell chimn*e*y; I trust it is not a sign of incipient lunacy!

To Harold Warne
Hill Top Farm
Sawrey
Ambleside
Dec 15th 08

Dear Mr Warne,

The weather has taken up very fine & frosty, so I am staying on a bit – till end of the week.

I hope the Roly Poly is going well, it seemed to be liked here.

I have sent a copy to that Austrian gentleman Dr *Pistor* who was staying in Sawrey last summer. I don't know if I mentioned his name, I think it is just possible he may write to you about the German edition [of *Peter Rabbit*] – he was so much interested in the matter that I sent him a printed slip of that German text that you had printed. I thought there were one or two mistakes in it, & wanted correcting before anything more was done with it.

I am short of note paper!

I remain yrs sincerely
Beatrix Potter

P.S. I have bought a most beautiful cow from another old woman. She gave me a shilling for luck!

The farm is doing very well, but he [John Cannon] has gone & spent all the pig money in buying sheep.

I should be glad of another bit of money presently. I have now got 10 cows, & 31 sheep.

I think it would be best to send me a cheque here postdated – say for Dec 12th or 14th? £50 or £60 would carry me on here for a good while, & pay some bills.

To Harold Warne   Meadhurst
                                                            Sidmouth
                                                            Dec 22nd 08

Dear Mr Warne,

I do not think this German is quite so spirited as Fraulein bridge's [sic]. It is *better German*; she had got a little Englishy with living in Wales, which sounds Irish! I would rather have that old translation of the two. I have not had any answer yet from Dr Pistor, if he would send the proof back corrected, it would be better than this. I send Louie's Christmas book to you to read first [*Ginger and Pickles*]! Best wishes to all for a Merry Christmas

                                                            from yrs aff
                                                            Beatrix Potter

The book is scribbly, I did all the pictures in 24 hours.

To Winifred Warne   Meadhurst
                                                            Sidmouth
                                                            Dec 29 08

Dear Winifred,

I said last Christmas I was afraid I should see a great deal more of Mr Samuel Whiskers; but I am glad to tell you he is still living at Farmer Potatoes'. He only comes now and then up to Hill Top Farm. He never came near the place for months, because we had a wonderful clever black cat, called Smutty. She was such a good rat-catcher! But alas poor Smutty went for a walk one night and she did not come home again, I am afraid she met a bad man with a gun, early in the morning. We have 3 of her children & some grandchildren, swarms of cats! I say they are to be all kept for a little while, till we see which is the cleverest. There is one little gray kitten that is very sharp, it stands up & fluffs itself out and scratches great big Kep [Beatrix's collie]! No sooner had Smutty disappeared than there began to be swarms of mice! And one evening there was a visit from Mr Whiskers! I was sitting very quiet before the fire in the library reading a book, and I heard someone pitter patter along the passage, & then someone scratched at the outside of the library door. I thought it was the puppy or the kitten so I took no notice. But next morning we discovered that Mr Whiskers had been in the house! We could not find him anywhere, so we think he had got in – and out again – by squeezing under a door. He had stolen the very oddest thing! There is a sort of large cupboard or closet where I do my photographing, it is papered inside with rather a pretty green & gold paper; and Samuel had torn off strips of paper all round the closet as high as he could reach up like this –

I could see the marks of his little teeth! Every scrap was taken away.

I wonder what in the world he wanted it for? I think Anna Maria must have been there, with him, to help. And I think she must have wanted to paper her best sitting room!

I only wonder she did not take the paste brush, which was on a shelf in the closet. Perhaps she intended coming back for the brush next night.

If she did, she was disappointed, for I asked John Joiner to make a heavy hard plank of wood, to fit into the opening under the door; and it seems to keep out Mr & Mrs Whiskers.

My fingers are so cold I can't draw!
With love to you & Eveline & Baby from yrs aff
Beatrix Potter

167

To F. Warne & Co.   Meadhurst
                                                     Sidmouth
                                                     Jan 9. 09

Dear Mr Warne,

   I am much obliged to you for the cheques for £50 and £3.15 received
last night. There was only one receipt slip, which I enclose. I shall be
coming home on Wednesday and I will call in shortly. I have done a
great deal of the Fl. Bs [*The Flopsy Bunnies*], but not many drawings are
quite finished yet.

                              I remain with thanks yrs sincerely
                                                     Beatrix Potter

[To Harold Warne]   2 Bolton Gdns
                                                     Feb 5. 09

Dear Mr Warne

   I had intended to propose coming tomorrow to catch you when you
came home; but I am going to a funeral service instead – an old servant
(retired from work) – & think I had better call at the office Monday
morning to see if the papers are done at last.

   Sometime there ought to be some agreements typed. I believe
Puddleduck was the last, so Roly Poly & the Flopsy Bunnies could be
signed together.

   I have not finished the F Bs, I have been doing the other [*Ginger and
Pickles*] for a change; also I want to get the large drawings planned
before I next go to Sawrey (which depends on weather).

                                                     yrs sincerely
                                                     Beatrix Potter

Do not trouble to send proof of [the text of] F. Bunnies, I can see it
when I call if it has come.

THE TALE OF THE FLOPSY BUNNIES *was published in July as a little book.*
GINGER AND PICKLES *would match* THE PIE AND THE PATTY-PAN *format and
have line drawings as well as colour plates. That book was scheduled
for October.*

[To Harold Warne]   Broad Leys
                                                        Windermere
                                                        Aug 4th 09

Dear Mr Warne,

I am agreeably surprised with the proofs [of *Ginger and Pickles*], following your letter. They are *strong*; but we complained that the last book was weak.

The green drawing of Pickles with the gun is spotty, but it will be all right with Mr Evans's blue. Same applies to the dormouse green subject.

The only 2 *I* think over heavy are the Hedgehog buying soap, & the kittens looking in at window. Possibly the cover inlet is dark, but an excellent colour.

I really think – if not uncivil to say so – you get things on your nerves at this time of year; these blocks are quite good!

I will keep the line proof a little, as it is useful; I think it will do.

I am sending some more pen & inks, in this parcel. If there are any you don't like please *send them back soon* as I want to get finished: There are about 4 more wanting, & I will go over the text carefully.

I remain yrs sincerely

Beatrix Potter

To Harold Warne   Hill Top Farm (till Saturday)
                                                  Sawrey
                                                  Ambleside
                                                  Aug 16th 09

Dear Mr Warne,

There are still 2 pen & inks wanting, it is always an effort to screw out the last!

I think the type should be set up soon as we shall require a carefully placed dummy for America.

I do not know what you will say to this dedication? In a way – it ought to be Louie's book, but she can look forward; I sometimes think poor old John Taylor is keeping alive to see this one printed, I should rather like to put his name in if you don't object?

I remain yrs sincerely

Beatrix Potter

The cuts still missing are p29–41 [34–49].

With regard to Ginger reading the letter there was a pretty good sketch in the original book, I do not know whether this is better or worse?

My rates & taxes don't come in one envelope, does it matter?

The dedication reads, 'With very kind regards to old Mr. John Taylor, who "thinks he might pass as a Dormouse!" (Three years in bed and never a grumble!)'. John Taylor owned the village shop in Sawrey when Beatrix first knew it.

[To Harold Warne]   Broad Leys
                                                      Windermere
                                                      Aug 20th 09

Dear Mr Warne,

I should like "little small" to stand, I have several times used piled up adjectives.

I don't think there is anything wrong with p. 20 [25]. The contradiction of Ginger eating a haddock instead of a biscuit was intentional.

I suppose Mr Leadbitter [sic] will edit the American text, he will no doubt change the coinage – "halfpenny" etc. [P. C. Leadbeater ran Frederick Warne in New York for forty years.]

I don't know whether they require dog licenses [sic] in America.

I have looked it over very carefully – cork for cook p7 [11] is the only misprint I can find.

                                                      yrs sincerely
                                                      Beatrix Potter

Meanwhile Beatrix was buying another farm in Sawrey, Castle Farm. In all her property dealings she took the advice of William Heelis, a partner in the local firm of solicitors, W. H. Heelis & Son, Hawkshead.

To Harold Warne   Broad Leys
                                                      Windermere
                                                      Sept 11th 09

Dear Mr Warne,

Can I have another cheque? If convenient I should like £40 to pay into the country bank this next week; and after I get back to London £100 to pay the London bank to get rid of part of the loan for my new fields.

The weather has been rather better lately; I expect to go back to Bolton Gdns Sept 23rd.

Old "John Dormouse" was given up last Wednesday, but is now extremely lively, smoking his pipe in bed. Let me have a copy for him as soon as there is one to spare & ready.

Are you pasting up the dummy? Have you got the pictures right places.

I hope the Flopsy Bunnies is doing well, there are various opinions about it.

I remain yrs sincerely
Beatrix Potter

To Millie Warne

Hill Top Farm
Sawrey
Ambleside
Nov 17th 09

My dear Millie,

I have been enjoying all sorts of weather; first of all a most furious gale, and then the hardest frost I ever felt here, 14 degrees on the grass. There has been skating on some of the smaller ponds these two days, but I think it is thawing tonight. It has been glorious weather but I shall be rather glad of a thaw as the garden has been as hard as iron. I managed to get some fruit trees moved today.

The colours are most lovely in the sunshine, all the leaves are off the trees, but the copse wood and fern on the hills keep their colour all winter. The sunrise & sunset – 8 and 4 oclock [sic] have been a sight. The woods look crimson. I managed to do some sketching yesterday in a sheltered place [see Plate 6], & I hope to do some more tomorrow, if the thaw does not bring rain. As usual I have been busy, looking after drains, quarry etc. This morning I went to Hawkshead in the trap to see about the fire insurances which wanted re-arranging. It was pleasant driving, for a short drive, too cold to go far.

There are two remarkable "Persian" kittens – (they called them "Prussians" here!) I wondered where in the world they came from, but they seem to be the property of our farm cat who is perfectly smooth. The other parent is "Ginger", alias "Tommy Bunckle", a bright yellow cat with *short* hair belonging to Mrs Bunckle the schoolmistress. I suppose their long hair will come off, at present they are like little muffs. They are living in the hay loft and are rather wild.

The white chickens are getting into their full feather now. I have kept the pullets – about 20– they are very pretty birds, and I hope they will be good layers. One of the two hens I brought from Sidmouth is the best layer we have ever had, she has had two holidays of ten days; she had laid month after month since February last. She always gets over the fence and lays her egg in the garden, in a hole in the wall.

The "Ginger & Pickle" book has been causing amusement, it has got a good many views which can be recognized in the village which is what they like, they are all quite jealous of each others houses & cats getting into a book. I have been entreated to draw a cat aged 20 "with no teeth", its owner seemed to think the "no teeth" was a curiosity & attraction! I should think the poor old thing must be rather worn out.

The two biggest little pigs have been sold, which takes away from the completeness of the family group. But they have fetched a good price, and their appetites were fearful – 5 meals a day and not satisfied.

I have no particular plans of coming back, if I am not required at home & the weather keeps fine I may stop another week.

I remain with love yrs aff

Beatrix Potter

To Harold Warne

2 Bolton Gdns
Dec 20th 09

Dear Mr Warne,

I am sorry to bother you again for more Ginger, but my Christmas presents have been driven to fall back upon them & *farm produce*! because I have not been able to shop.

I have been out a little in the sun today, I am all right except my throat.

I think the next two books look promising [*The Tale of Mrs. Tittlemouse* and *Pigling Bland*]. I have got them planned out, but no drawings finished yet.

Excuse me mentioning it but for goodness sake don't give me anything *big* [for Christmas]! The log scuttle has been much admired but it was the last straw for squeezing in. I know you always leave your shopping to the last, if you don't know what to get I should much appreciate a book, is not there a book of Irish poetry just published by the Oxford U. press called the Dublin Anthology, I don't think it would harm me, though doubtless full of treason.

I wish Frue would give me a book about pruning roses; there is nothing like being candid. You will receive pork, killed today Monday, & very small.

I remain yrs sincerely

Beatrix Potter

Among Beatrix's many fans was a small girl in New Zealand called Louisa Ferguson whose mother, two years before, had sent Beatrix a photograph of her daughter. Beatrix answered most of her fan letters but particularly those from overseas, and she kept a gallery of photographs of her readers on the wall in the parlour at Hill Top. Now Louisa had sent her a present.

To Louisa Ferguson

Jan 8. 1910
Sawrey
Ambleside

Dear Louisa Ferguson

You will think I am *very naughty* – I have never written to thank you for that lovely pen holder. It came just when I was starting on a journey. I think it is beautiful, and such a length. We have greenish agates that are made into brooches but they are only little pebbles.

Now I am sending you a a [sic] new book to make up amends – It was not ready in time for Christmas in New Zealand, so I don't think you have got it. [*Ginger and Pickles*]

It was all drawn in the village near my farm house, and the village shop is there.

Only poor old "John Dormouse" is dead – just before the book was finished – I was so sorry I could not give him a copy before he died. He was such a funny old man; I thought he might be offended if I made fun of him, so I said I would only draw his shop & not him.

And then he said I had drawn his son John in another book [*The Roly-Poly Pudding*], with a saw and wagging his tail! and old John felt jealous of young John. So I said how could I draw him if he would not get up? and he considered for several days, and then sent "his respects, and thinks he might pass as a dormouse!" It is considered very like him. Also it is very much like our "Timothy Baker" but he is not quite so well liked, so everybody is laughing. I think I shall put *myself* in the next book, it will be about pigs; I shall put in me walking about with my old "Goosey" sow, she is such a pet.

I am so busy over the Election my fingers are quite stiff with drawing "posters".

Yr aff friend
Beatrix Potter

The posters were part of a Unionist campaign for tariff reform which was to be an important issue at the forthcoming election. Beatrix felt passionately against Free Trade, having failed to find a British manufacturer for her Peter Rabbit doll and then seeing the shops filled with a cheap (and unauthorized) German version. She prepared a number of posters, some featuring a doll made in Camberwell leaning against a gravestone marking the death of the South London Toy Trade 'killed by Free Trade with Germany', posters which Beatrix called her 'Camberwell Beauties'. Others were headed by a picture of Peter Rabbit 'Made in Germany', followed by a note that German ships were being built on the profits of German trade with England. Every poster was drawn and coloured by hand and Beatrix reported, 'I must have made sixty' (see Plate 9).

The posters were supported by a leaflet about tariff reform which Warne arranged to be printed by Martin, Hood & Larkin. Warne then suggested to Beatrix that Peter Rabbit might be used in the campaign which was being broadened to include the protection of printing and publishing copyright.

[To Harold Warne]

Jan 8 1910
2, Bolton Gardens,
South Kensington, S.W.

Dear Mr Warne,

I should object *most strongly* to send a letter to the "Times" or print a pamphlet of "Peter R. on politics". It would savour of advt; and don't you see it would do the thing *you* dislike = drag the little book into radical politics.

I have never mentioned its name in the letter. I don't think the technicalities of copyright are possible to explain to joiners etc I think what I have now altered it to, is clearer; I think yours had too much repetition.

I have sent off about 2 dozen Camberwell beauties so excuse my writing. I did not send any Peters; but I have not an atom of affection for that doll, you know I have had no money from him for 2 years – I have had enough & more than I ever expected; but I consider him done with!

If you could arrange possibly to get me 100 copies of the amended version [of the letter] printed, say by Tuesday night's post – to Sawrey – I should be very much obliged.

There is no one up there who would buy it [*Peter Rabbit*] more, or less, by politics, & no one ever thinks of politics over child's books.

I have cut off Tom Dixon, as being too personal for use in Windermere.

My fingers are rather stiff. I am going to Sawrey Monday morning to Saturday.

Do get me the printed copies if you can, my fingers are tired of writing.

The abrupteness [sic] was intentional, I can cut it in two.

yrs truly
H B Potter

I intend to draw pigs there – unless I am forced to copy my letter by hand!

Let that paragraph end at British wages; it is better to drop your sentence than spoil a good tag end.

To Harold Warne

2 Bolton Gardens
Jan 20th 1910

Dear Mr Warne

I am ashamed to have overlooked this bill for a month.

I am much rejoiced to see the results of the neighbouring Windermere & Kendal elections.

I promise faithfully to return to pigs & mice next week.

I have received an invitation from a leading Kendal tradesman to "address a meeting", but I shall have no difficulty in resisting that temptation! Especially as they have won without me.

What a funny mistake about Wandsworth.

yrs sincerely
Beatrix Potter

The tariff and copyright campaigns were followed by another concerning the Liberal Government's horse census. Beatrix approached the printers of PETER RABBIT *to produce her new leaflet, which she proposed to sign* 'North Country Farmer'.

To Messrs Edmund Evans

Feb 28 1910
2 Bolton Gardens,
South Kensington, S.W.

Dear Mr Evans,

If there is another election directly – something in a *fresh style* might be acceptable!

I am fast indoors. I wonder if you would be so kind as to get line blocks from these, for me?

I want to do some leaflets about size of enclosed sample – (That other leaflet was very awkward size for envelopes)

Has your firm given up letterpress printing? (re. P. Rabbit). I had intended to ask if you would print these horses? I am in a curious difficulty about Messrs M.H. & Larkin. They liked the Tariff leaflet, & put their name & address on it (which is *necessary* if a paper is used by an *official canvasser in an election*). Then I wanted another which they printed, but *without* their name.

They had a reasonable reason, they seem to do some printing for a Govt department.

It is useless to talk to farmers about *dolls*. But if there *is* a subject which enrages us – it is meddling with our horses! (*I* am a one horse farmer, amongst other trades). This last autumn we filled in an innocent looking paper, handed by the country police, for a horse census. Everybody thought it foreshadowed a most welcome scheme for subsidising *army remounts*.

Last week it came out under cross questioning in the House of Commons that we have rendered our horses liable to requisition in case of necessity during war.

I am as loyal as most people; nobody likes to be tricked. What the Unionists have advocated for a long time is a proper system of reserve horses, earmarked & registered for a very small retaining fee. I would willingly keep a yeomanry horse. But to seize the very scanty present stock would bring agriculture to a standstill. Even at a fair price it would be exasperating. There have already been indignant letters in Saturday's "Field", from gentlemen afraid of losing their hunters.

Capt. Bagshot is strong about it in Westmoreland [sic].

Of course I could not ask anybody to print anything they did not like on reading it over. I have not quite corrected my letter yet, might I send it you? I should sign it "N. Lancs", as a female farmer is silly on paper; though well informed, being in a neighbourhood much devoted to horse breeding, *when it paid*.

Yrs truly
H. B. Potter

To Harold Warne   2 Bolton Gardens
                                                   March 7. 10

Dear Mr Warne,

I am posting these drawings [for *The Tale of Mrs. Tittlemouse*] as I
do not think I could bring them to the office tomorrow, I am a good
deal worried about a cousin who is coming to London to have an
operation at a hospital.

I rather expect you will think that one or two of these drawings want
working up still.

I have brought the *moss* forward in the spider plate. I don't think its
eye could have showed before, but it is always better to alter any point
that perplexes anybody. The last page but one was the missing plate, (the
dancers).

If I go away I will send word, my plans have been disarranged, first
with a cold, & then with this cousin's illness.

I wonder if the Leipzig fair is over? Fru said some one he knew was
going, who might casually inquire the *wholesale* price of those rabbit
dolls, I have a great curiosity to know.

I am very sorry to hear that the little girls have caught *it* [whooping
cough] after all, I hope it is not severe? It does pull children down if they
have it badly.

                                                   I remain yrs sincerely
                                                   Beatrix Potter

If any of them want more work, please send them back *this* week; I
mean to say if I am away *next* week I shall not want to be doing them at
Sawrey.

From The Tale of Mrs.
Tittlemouse

The horse leaflet was joined by yet another, this time addressed to printers. It concerned the protection of copyright overseas and foreign import restrictions.

To Mr E. Wilfred Evans   March 8th 10
[Edmund Evans Ltd]   2, Bolton Gardens,
Racquet Court Press   South Kensington, S.W.

Dear Mr Evans,

I think the leaflet reads rather well; I have made two corrections.

It is not inexact to say that we cut *"prices"*, but the matter is a little complicated by the fact that the American importer is a branch of the English exporter.

I think you had better print 2,000 of the leaflets (but send me only 500 of them to this address), and I will try – (as soon as I have some more copies) whether I can place any large packets of them with any association who would distribute them.

Of course if *you* think more than 2,000 could be used, *I* am quite willing to pay for more.

I intend to try the dump shop people; Mr Dunn who had charge of the Chelsea dump shop was very civil; after snubs elsewhere. I cannot stand official Tories; they will never do any good with Lancashire folks. I can get addresses of London printers from the P.O. directory, but I wish I could get it to *Lancashire, Glasgow & Edinboro*.

It looks as if the Govt were being gradually squeezed about the remount question; but the unionists ought to get the credit if anything is done.

I have had a letter (substantially the same) in several country papers, so I don't think it too strong?

If there were anything you disliked printing it might be the sentence about the policeman! It really was a very mean trick.

The little cuts will do nicely.

My writing takes more space than I expected. If there is not room for the hay-cart – leave it out. I like the way the printers leaflet has been set up.

I remain yrs sincerely
Beatrix Potter

It must not be let out the horse leaflet is written by a *female*. I should give it away as being written by a small farmer in Lancashire.

To Harold Warne   2 Bolton Gdns
                                                  March 21. 10

Dear Mr Warne,

I am sorry for the delay; and I have not done the pen & ink yet for the title [the title-page of *Mrs. Tittlemouse*], I will send it soon. I can alter the text, when I get proofs; I am inclined to keep in the *"slaters"* [the generic word for wood lice] but will erase the offensive word "wood *lice*!!" [The final text reads 'creepy-crawly people'.]

I had 3 hard working days at Sawrey but could do no sketching.

I am going to S. Devon tomorrow for Easter. I had better write you my address for proofs; we are going to the Royal Hotel, Teignmouth, but please do not address there, as I think we are more likely to move into apartments either in Teignmouth or Dawlish, as my parents are more comfortable in quiet rooms.

I have been over busy lately, I could not go to see Millie.

I hope the whooping cough is getting well.

                                                  yrs sincerely
                                                  Beatrix Potter

Whenever are they going to collect income tax? I have paid it in Lancashire.

Mr Evans is very civilly printing the printers leaflet gratis. I did not think that first leaflet was suitable for London.

To Harold Warne   2 Bolton Gardens S.W.
                                                  April 22. 10

Dear Mr Warne,

Will you be good enough to inform Mr Hughes whether you agree to his proposition about royalty upon the doll rabbit?

He offers ½ royalty (½ previous amount), to run from the last settling up & continue so long as the rabbit has a fair sale.

Taking various things into consideration I said I was satisfied with his offer; but I did not think I could give a definite answer, as you act (?) for me in the matter.

I should very much prefer to manage the dolls myself, in future.

Possibly Mr Hughes may be mistaken in saying he has been unable to obtain any answer from you for more than a year.

His address is now 90 Goswell Rd.

                                                  I remain yrs sincerely
                                                  Beatrix Potter

I must ask you *not to make any fresh arrangements* without letting me know, I am seriously provoked about things being in such a muddle.

To Harold Warne   April 23. 10
                                                   2, Bolton Gardens,
                                                   South Kensington, S.W.

Dear Mr Warne,

I am obliged for your letter. I made *no* complaint about the management of my books, and I am sorry you have given yourself the trouble of writing an enormous letter on a Saturday.

You are incorrigible as a correspondent!

Why in the world should I come & go through the American arrangements about Mrs T. when I never referred to her at all, & when you are busy?

I did not like Hughes, & if he did wrong – that was then more reason for giving him a short decided answer at once. I think it would be better to employ a clerk sometimes; rather than always want to do it yourself when you are busy (which you undeniably are).

It has made all the difference since it has been agreed that Mr Herring should write me one line, when there [is] anything concerning proofs etc.

I am very much obliged for the parcel of accounts received last night. It is always interesting to see the number of copies sold, I particularly felt curious about the Roly Poly pudding.

To return to the matter of Hughes – I am of opinion that the matter has in a sense "gone by default", having been slipped over so long; & the shops being full of imitation rabbit dolls – which it is now very late to object to. I certainly should *not* myself choose to employ him again over another doll; he is strongly pro German & has *no desire* to save English patents.

At same time when he & his clerk inform me separately that they have found it difficult to get letters answered – I did not disbelieve them.

Everybody knows you have been busy.

I shall not be able to come to the office for several days, I am sorry; but so far as Mrs Tittlemouse is concerned I am sure there is no more to say about her – except to give her a good wish & hope she may do as well as the others.

I hope the children are having nice weather at Folkstone.

I remain yrs sincerely
Beatrix Potter

To Messrs Curtis Brown & Massie   June 30. 10
[New York]   Chandos House,
        Bedford Street,
        Strand, W.C.

Dear Sir,

I am obliged to you for your letter, but as Messrs F Warne & Co have a branch office in New York, I find it more convenient to do all business through them.

I should not choose to employ another agent.

I remain yrs truly
Beatrix Potter

To Harold Warne   (Stroud)
        2 Bolton Gardens
        SW
        June 30. 10

Dear Mr Warne,

I am delighted with the bound copies of "Mrs Tittlemouse", the buff copy is the prettiest colour, though it may not keep so clean.

I think it should prove popular with little girls.

I have replied to that agent, that your firm has an office in New York, therefore I prefer to do business through it.

With regard to pig book [*Pigling Bland*], I have done the few drawings – which are already commenced – upon the same plan & size as the *Ginger* & *Pickles*.

Is that a definite *fixed scheme*?

I mean to say – if you could save anything in the cost of production by cutting down the number of coloured plates – it ought to be considered *beforehand*, as I like to know where the coloured incident falls in the story. There is no use drawing a coloured picture for a page that ought to be black & white.

The *size* ought decidedly to be the same as *Ginger*.

No doubt Mr Herring could answer the question, 'whether it is a convenient economical sheet?

My recollection is that it was inconveniently big.

I don't believe people count the number of plates.

I shall be returning to London either tomorrow or Saturday.

yrs sincerely
Beatrix Potter

BEATRIX POTTER'S LETTERSment>

THE TALE OF MRS. TITTLEMOUSE *was published in July.* THE TALE OF PIGLING BLAND *was not yet finished and it was starting to look as though it could not be ready for this year.*

To Harold Warne

July 15th 10
2, Bolton Gardens,
South Kensington. S.W.

Dear Mr Warne,

I have posted the cheque tonight to the Windermere bank, I have not got a printed receipt to send to you.

I have been thinking about the pig book, I am strongly in favour of charging 1/6 for it [instead of the usual 1/-]. The price of these books is not so much stereotyped as that of the "Peter Rabbits".

No doubt the shops might remonstrate; but it would enable you to give them their extravagant discount comfortably.

I cannot help thinking you set too much store on these enormous sales; it is painfully like Ginger & Pickles – "the sales were enormous, *but* etc!"

I do not see any advantage of having immense sales without a fair profit – if Harrod's [sic] for instance would not pay 9d, for my part I would have let Harrods go without it.

The sales go up year by year; but I would be quite content to see them considerably drawn in, if there were less anxiety about the money.

To change the subject. I saw a Camberwell Beauty in Kew Gdns yesterday. It was very nearly caught by a tomtit. It was like the upper specimen on your plate with a lightish border.

I remain yrs sincerely
Beatrix Potter

Title-page drawing for The Tale of Mrs. Tittlemouse

182

To Millie Warne   [Windermere]
                                                   Aug 23rd 10

My dear Milly [sic],

I was wondering whether you had got off on your own Country Holiday, after many good works in Drury Lane you have earned it! You seem to have been all scattered about, except Mr Warne – who looked as if he wanted a change more than anybody, it is to be hoped he will get away somehow.

My second book won't hinder him, alas – I cannot screw anything out of my head at present! I have done a little sketching when it does not rain, and I spent a very wet hour *inside* the pig stye drawing the pig. It tries to nibble my boots, which is interrupting.

I don't think it ever answers to try & finish a book in summer, it makes me short of material afterwards if I do not sketch.

The weather has been very dull, and this last weekend very wet. It began to rain on Thursday afternoon, (during the Grasmere games) and scarcely stopped until Monday. The lake has risen nearly a yard, & my poor field of oats has been beaten quite flat. It will be very troublesome to cut, it cannot be done with the machine. I don't think it is spoilt yet, but the rain came on again today which was disappointing.

I shall try to get over again tomorrow and stop a night or two. I don't like leaving my parents for any length of time, they are both very well in health, but they do not like this place so they feel inclined to be dull here. It is a fine view, but *such* a hill!

My garden has come up a perfect forest of groundsel since the rain; it is easy to pull up, which is a blessing. *I* have got 3 bunch of grapes too! but I doubt if they will ever ripen out of doors. There are quantities of apples, very few pears, & plums. And the holyhocks [sic] have been very good this year, they were about 12 to 14 feet high before the storm.

I expect we shall go back to Bolton Gdns about Sept 14 or 15. I shall come home at the same time, it is scarcely fit to send them alone; perhaps I may come back again later on in the autumn. With love to you & Edith

                                                   I remain yrs aff
                                                   Beatrix Potter

From the first edition of The Fairy Caravan

Elizabeth (Bessie) Hadfield was another of Beatrix's New Zealand fans. She had come to London the previous year with her young children and her husband, who was having treatment for cancer, and they stayed in Blackheath, in south-east London. Her husband was to die soon after their return to New Zealand but Beatrix kept in touch with Bessie and the children, and for Kitty and Hilda Hadfield she wrote a story, THE FAIRY IN THE OAK. *In 1929 it was rewritten as the last chapter of* THE FAIRY CARAVAN.

To Elizabeth Hadfield

2 Bolton Gardens
South Kensington SW.
Sept. 28th 10

Dear Mrs Hadfield,

There is a picture of china in this old first edition of the Tailor which was left out of the reprint, perhaps you would like to have it.

'Peter' & the tailor were printed for myself before my books began to be published. I have always liked this old edition.

The china was borrowed from the cobbler's wife at Sawrey, it had been in her mother's family, some of it was very old, especially the cup without a handle, beside the lady-mouse. One with a pattern inside the rim was a good one, they were not marked but looked like Bristol china.

I wish I had not had to keep the children at "arms length", I am not generally so severely distant with them!

I did enjoy my visit to you, it does one good to see anybody come through a time of trial with faith and courage.

I do not know how to talk religion or write it in my books but I can see when faith is there. I hope some day you will write and tell me that you have had a very happy journey home to New Zealand.

With kind regards to you and your husband, and best wishes

from yours sincerely
Beatrix Potter

To Millie Warne

Hill Top Farm
Sawrey
Oct 9th 10

My dear Millie,

I have been very undecided in my movements, & finally came off here at very short notice. My brother came home, and thought I had better take a holiday(?) while I could get away. My father has been very complaining again, but I really do not believe that there is anything the matter with him except muscular pain on the outside. He is going about again as usual, so unless I am sent for I shall stay a little longer, there is a very great deal to do. I have been doing some sketching today – Sunday – but it was rather cold. The woods are lovely when the sun comes out. I have got a man digging in the garden & I replant after him. I wonder if you have room for any phlox, it is the time of year for dividing herbaceous plants, mine have all grown into a tangle.

The farm business is mostly sheep sales – buying – and selling – which is a difficult matter. Nobody seems to want mutton now, I suspect we eat more 'Canterbury lamb' than we are aware of. There is actually a frozen meat butcher started at Windermere selling mutton at 6½d.

I have got some white pullets which amuse me, they are such pets they will all try to jump on my knee at once if I sit on the doorstep, and two or three will allow me to pick them up & stroke them like a parrot. Their feet are rather dirty. There are 7 little chickens hatched last week, they are enjoying the fine weather while it lasts. I hope I may be able to stop till the end of the week, I was much wanting a change, it has been rather a trying season.

I was pleased the butter did well at the Dairy Show, it was "commended" with 90 marks; the 1st prize had 97, so it was quite in the running for a prize another year.

I remain yrs aff.
Beatrix Potter

Pencil and Pen-and-ink sketch for The Fairy Caravan

*Louisa Ferguson, to whom Beatrix had written to thank for the pen-
holder present from New Zealand in January, had unexpectedly died.*

To Mrs William Ferguson

Hill Top Farm
Sawrey
Ambleside
Oct 12. 10

Dear Mrs Ferguson,

I scarcely know how to write to you in your terrible trouble. One can
only hope that you are given strength and patience. Dear child – she has
been taken away from a world of troubles – troubles which it is useless
to question or try to understand. I heard you are not very strong, it
makes the loss greater.

I made acquaintance with Mrs Hadfield from Wellington and I asked
her about Louisa – indeed that was the beginning of it – for without that
inquiry I don't suppose we should have done more than exchange two
letters; but she wrote so pleasantly about you that I thought I would like
to see her and send a message to New Zealand. It does seem so strange
that when we were talking about Louisa, it was all over.

I was very much shocked when I heard from Mrs Hadfield last night.
She had evidently had the paper by the same mail, my copy came this
morning forwarded from the publishers' office.

I had the child's nice little letter and the photographs last August, I
had been intending to answer when I got back to London, & could send
her a doll & a new book. And now it is too late. I think I have little
friends all over the world, I am glad if my books have given her pleasure.
Her little grass bag is hanging up in the house-place here, my house-
keeper (the farmer's wife) was so sorry when I told her. We have a
handful of children in this house – but not one to spare; and to think
that you have lost your one little ewe lamb is dreadful. I hope she did
not suffer much. With sincere sympathy for you and your husband

believe me yours sincerely
Beatrix Potter

Beatrix had put PIGLING BLAND *aside altogether while she worked on* PETER RABBIT'S PAINTING BOOK, *which was based on one she had made for Louie Warne a few years earlier featuring the animals at Hill Top. She was also well into a new story,* THE TALE OF TIMMY TIPTOES.

To Harold Warne   Lindeth Howe
                                                   Windermere
                                                   July 27. 11
Dear Mr Warne,

I am sending 12 drawings [for *Timmy Tiptoes*], I have kept back some of the earlier finished as patterns for the *squirrel colour*. I have all the plates sketched except two or three.

I think I can do some good ones for the finish.

I have compressed the words in the earlier pages; but it seems unavoidable to have a good deal of *nuts*.

The songs of the little birds will be easier to judge as to spelling when one sees it in type.

I forgot to ask you about the dedication – should you approve of this one? ['For many unknown little friends, including Monica'] I do not know the child; she is the school friend of a little cousin, who asked for it as a favour, and the name took my fancy.

I think Louie is rather ill used in not having had her name on a book; but she has got too big for these little books now.

The haymaking is finished prosperously, (except a few trimmings) it has been hot work; I hope there is now some prospect of rain.

I go backwards & forwards, it will be best to send the July cheque to this address.

Please cut the mounts any way convenient.

                                                   yrs sincerely
                                                   Beatrix Potter

You did not send the 3 extra painting books, but I find I have plenty left, I had packed them in "advance luggage".

To Fruing Warne

Hill Top Farm
Sawrey
Ambleside
Aug 9th 11

Dear Mr Fru,

As Mr [Harold] Warne is in Jersey, perhaps you are in charge – (though I hope for your own sakes that you are all away at the seaside! 82 in shade here on the hills).

Would you mind telling me – without sentiment – & I trust without the slightest irritation – does FW&Co mean to pay the first installment of the 1910 royalties in *Aug* or *Sept*? The winding up cheque of the 1909 royalties was July 29th (nominally) (paid in Aug 5th).

I am *not* short. I am *not* of opinion that the circulation of the books is smaller than it ought to be, or any other of Mr Warne's etcs. His letters are enough to drive anybody mad. I only want to know as a matter of banking arrangements whether the next cheque is going to be inside August, or whether it means Sept 15th. You had better *not* tell him I wrote; it is very annoying that he always thinks I am complaining about the *amount* of the money, whenever I ask about the *date*. I think the books sell & pay more than enough. The difficulty of getting cheques at the time promised has sometimes rather perplexed and alarmed me; but that is not the same thing, as he tries to make out.

There was a deluge of rain last Saturday, which was fortunate as water was getting scarce. Now it is as hot as ever, we intend to begin harvest on Friday. I have had extra good crops of everything – but much fruit fell off with the drought. I will send the rest of squirrels this weekend.

Yrs sincerely
Beatrix Potter

THE TALE OF TIMMY TIPTOES *and* PETER RABBIT'S PAINTING BOOK *were published in October.*

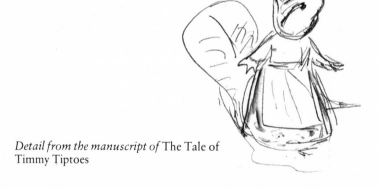

Detail from the manuscript of The Tale of Timmy Tiptoes

To Harold Warne   Nov 18 11
                                                 2 Bolton Gdns

Dear Mr Warne

I had thought of coming up to Primrose Hill but it seems to be wetter than ever.

I think this story is amusing [*The Tale of Mr. Tod*]; its principal defect is imitation of "Uncle Remus". It is no draw-back for children, because they cannot read the negro dialect. I hardly think the publishers could object to it? I wrote it some time ago, I have copied it out again lately.

It would make pretty pictures, the situation of Mr Tod's house is fine, & the moonlight would be weird.

I shall be coming to the office, I am wanting a few books.

I remain yrs sincerely
Beatrix Potter

[To Harold Warne]   2 Bolton Gardens
                                                Nov 20. 11

Dear Mr Warne

I will come *Tuesday* morning, it is no good saying "weather permitting" I have got a new waterproof.

'Tod' is surely a very common name for fox? It is probably Saxon, it was the word in ordinary use in Scotland a few years ago, probably is still amongst country people. In the same way "brock" or "gray" is the country name for badger. I should call them "brocks" – both names are used in Westmoreland [sic]. "Brockholes", "Graythwaite" are examples of place names; also Broxbourne and Brockhampton.

I suppose birthday books are very popular, I have always had an unreasoning aversion to them – one day is same as another. I remember having birthdays as a child, and I remember ungratefully getting rid of a Kate Greenaway birthday book.

I remain yrs sincerely
Beatrix Potter

"Hey quoth the Tod
    its a braw bright night!
The wind's in the west
    and the moon shines bright"

Mean to say you never heard that?

The text for THE TALE OF MR. TOD *was longer and denser than for any of Beatrix's previous books and she felt no longer able to provide as many colour illustrations as before. Warne therefore suggested that* MR. TOD *should have a different format and be published not as a 'Peter Rabbit Book' but as the first in an entirely new series.*

[To Harold Warne]   Tuesday afternoon
                                                      Nov. 21st 11

Dear Mr Warne,

It is puzzling. If I were left to my own devices – I believe I should make those books exactly the same size, only a little thicker; and I should call them "The Peter Rabbit books" New Series.

Do you really think the advantage of an intirely [sic] fresh series will make up for the loss of the "Peter Rabbit book" name?

If that series had been falling off *in sales* there would be a reason for changing. But I understand the only reason for making a change is that *I* find it so difficult to continue to make "fresh" short stories.

It all turns on whether the shops would give the 1/– for a book with fewer pictures. I feel convinced that children would prefer the same familiar size, and as little change as may be.

My plan would have less risk of injuring the old "Peter Rabbits".

I don't want to be obstinate, – only to ask you to think it over again. Could you not ask the travellers whether they think 2 independent series is best; or the same with variations?

                                                      I remain yrs sincerely
                                                      Beatrix Potter

I enclose the receipt with thanks, I will put it through at the weekend – for Monday.

Many of Rupert Potter's friends were politicians (his father had been Liberal M.P. for Carlisle) and all her life Beatrix was politically alert. Now she had seen a new piece of legislation upon which she felt she must comment.

[Draft letter]

Sir,

Grandmotherly legislation

Under the amended law for the protection of animals it has become illegal for a "child" under 16 years of age to be present at the slaughter and cutting up of carcases. It is unwise to allow little children of 4 or 5 years old to be present at a pig-killing. There have once or twice been serious accidents, where they have tried to imitate the scene in play. But – do our rulers seriously maintain that a farm-lad of 15½ years must not assist at the cutting up? One of the interesting reminiscences of my early years is the memory of helping to scrape the smiling countenance of my own grandmother's deceased pig, with scalding water and the sharp-edged bottom of a brass candle-stick. Pan lids were also in request. Lord Rosebery is right. The present generation is being reared upon tea – and slops.

Yrs XYZ

Paragraph 7 of the First Schedule of the Protection of Animals Act, 1911 *reads: 'No person who is under the age of sixteen years shall be admitted to, or permitted to remain in, the knacker's yard during the process of slaughtering or of cutting up the carcase of any animal.' The penalty for failing to comply with the regulation was a fine 'not exceeding ten pounds'. The Act received the Royal Assent on 18 August 1911 and came into effect on 1 January 1912. There is no record that Beatrix's draft letter was ever published.*

Detail from a pencil drawing

To Millie Warne

Hill Top Farm
Sawrey
Ambleside
Dec 13th 11

My dear Milly [sic],

I am so glad to hear that you have got your purse & *key*, it is much pleasanter to feel there is an honest shopman in the case – instead of a pocket pulled inside out!

I never have had my pocket picked, and I am sure it would hurt my feelings if I had to remember such an indignity.

I too once dropped a purse, on the platform at the Temple station; I had put it through the slip of my skirt, instead of into the back pocket. I found out when I got *back* to the station in a cab, which I wanted to pay, & when I got downstairs & mentioned it (quite casually & hopelessly) to the ticket collector, he asked for a description & produced it from the lost property; so *my* anxiety only lasted 5 minutes and I was able to pay the cabby. It had been found by a Wimbledon-address gentleman.

I came here suddenly on Tuesday as it was fine. It would have been impossible to get over yesterday as the lake was too rough. But today is mild & pleasant – except for two noises. One very sad & dreadful noise after breakfast which we guessed was the Black Beck gunpowder works. There is a rumour tonight that 2 men are killed; a mercy if no more. It is about 10 miles off; it shook the ground here. The other disturbance moved me to bad language. There is a beastly fly-swimming spluttering aeroplane careering up & down over Windermere; it makes a noise like 10 million bluebottles. It is an irritating noise here, a mile off; it must be horrible in Bowness. It seemed to be flying very well; but I am extremely sorry it has succeeded, if others are built – or indeed this one – [it] will very much spoil the Lake. It has been buzzing up & down for hours today, and it has already caused a horse to bolt & smashed a tradesman's cart.

I am busy planting shrubs, it is very dirty. *I* thought the rabbit shop was rather nice, I'm glad you like it.

Yours aff HBP

[Published 13 Jan 1912]
To The Editor of *Country Life*. WINDERMERE AND THE HYDROPLANE

Sir, – "Att the fferry boate on the King's hye way, time out of mind itt hath been ussed and Accustomed that the parties to these presents and all others ... passe repasse & travell over Windermer Watter." Thus says an old deed, quoted in Mr. Swainson Cowper's "History of Hawkshead." It is an agreement, dated April 13th, 1670, between the fishers and ferriers of the "highest, middle and lowest cubles." The ferries at Miller Ground and Rawlinson Nab are coble boats yet, and little used. But the middle boat – Windermere horse-ferry – continues to be the connecting link for all road traffic between the Kendal district of Westmorland and that northern part of Furness which lies between Windermere Lake and the eastern shore of Coniston. For dwellers "beside the road from Hawkshead to the Great Boate" the ferry is the sole means of access for horsed vehicles on the way to town, to station and to Kendal Market. The present ferry-boat is worked by a small engine and flywheel, along a wire cable. Tourists on the steamers notice the ramshackle, picturesque boat, heavy laden with the Coniston four-horsed coach and char-à-banc, or with carrier's tilt cart and bustling motor, or homely toppling loads of oak bark and hooper's swills, or droves of sheep and cattle. Farm-carts go down and across with sacks of wool and bark and faggots; they struggle homewards with loads of coal. Everyone uses the ferry. On calm summer waters no voyage is more cheerful and pleasant than this crossing of Windermere. Those who live to the west can tell another tale of winter nights, when the ferry cannot cross in the teeth of the wind. Then the home-coming carriers are storm-stayed at Bowness, and the Crier of Claife calls in vain for the ferry-man. For the most part we accept these interruptions as a dispensation of Providence – and the climate. There has been no serious accident since October 19th, 1635, when forty-seven persons and eleven horses were drowned at once. A crowd of market folk and a wedding party were returning from Hawkshead. "The great Boate upon Windermeer water sunck about sun-setting." But danger, turmoil and possible pecuniary damage in calm weather at the hand of fellow-man are another matter altogether. Our peaceful lake is disturbed by the presence of a hydroplane. We are threatened with the prospect of an aeroplane factory at Cockshott Point, between Bowness Bay and the Ferry Nab, and with the completion of five more machines before next summer. The existing machine flies up and down in the trough of the hills; it turns at either end of the lake and comes back. It flies at a comparatively low level; the noise of its propeller resembles millions of blue-bottles, plus a steam threshing engine. Horses upon land may possibly become accustomed to it, but it is doubtful whether they will ever stand quietly as it swoops over their heads while on the boat. If they back while on the water, there will be an accident. When the machines become numerous there will be danger of actual collision. It seems deplorable that this beautiful lake should be turned into another Brooklands or Hendon. The Ferry and Cockshott lie between Belle Isle and Storrs Point – that Storrs where Wordsworth, Scott, Canning and Christopher North embarked upon the lake with their host, Mr. Bolton. We are sometimes told that England is being left behind by other nations in the race for the conquest of the air. But, surely, the proper place for testing hydroplanes is over the sea, rather than over an inland lake? A more inappropriate place for experimenting with flying machines could scarcely be chosen. The noise is confined by the hills:

> "echoes
> Redoubled and redoubled; concourse wild."

But the first consideration should be given to the question of danger to existing traffic – the traffic of steamers, yachts, row-boats and Windermere Ferry. – BEATRIX POTTER

The flying boat on Windermere had given Beatrix fuel for another campaign – to get it stopped. She drew up a petition and approached everyone she could think of for a signature. Publishers were an obvious target as she felt that by now they ought to know the name 'Beatrix Potter'. Farmers were another body of people she could call on for help but for them, perhaps, it would be better if she were thought to be a man.

194

To Harold Warne

2 Bolton Gardens
S.W.
Jan 27. 12

Dear Mr Warne,

I hope you do not mind my having given c/o F.W rather often this week? I wrote to two or three publishers & literary people – and you know we agreed that I am an addressless person in London.

Not that I find the precaution very necessary; I am amused & *not* sorry to find myself so completely unknown.

I can really do better as H B Potter, *farmer*. I have got 14 firms in a row, signing the petition.

I am obliged to confess the aristocrats won't sign – the great Mr Murray declines to "commit himself to an opinion" – and others like Arnold, Black, Longmans, Methuen took no interest. Mr Fisher Unwin was very civil in giving me a list of names. I know Mrs Cobden Unwin; I find radicals much more willing than conservatives; which may be a good omen. Also, the religious firms will sign, because of Keswick Convention.

The canvas will have to be finished this week Feb 3rd I mean I may go to Sawrey anytime after Tuesday; it is better weather now – but my plans are complicated by an appointment with the district surveyor about water tanks & pipes. I missed him last time.

I will be sure to get some sketching if it is better weather; in fact I want some indoors, for the kitchen [in *Mr. Tod*].

I remain yrs sincerely
Beatrix Potter

I got that Country Life Signature and another paragraph, I think he is short of copy!

I think the most striking list is 34 doctors & nurses at the London Hospital, of whom 31 have visited the Lakes, collected by a nurse who had been to Sawrey.

The campaign was entirely successful. The plans for the aeroplane factory were abandoned and before the year was out the planes had left Windermere.

[To Harold Warne]
Hill Top Farm
Sawrey
Ambleside
Feb 3. 12

Dear Mr Warne,

I am much obliged to you for the cheque which I will pay in on Monday.

Conditions are Alpine – 24 degrees of frost last night, but hot sun today. It is warm enough to sit out, where sheltered. The only thing I draw the line at is *washing*; a pot of goose grease is in great request!!

I was amused about Nellie Oliver's 'scholastic profession' – she is one of the infant teachers in a school started 40 years ago by my Grandmother Mrs Leech of Gorse Hall for the children of the mill hands. It grew into a fine school, but the board of education have been at them, with their absurd building regulations.

As there seemed no one left of the family, I promised to open the bazaar.

I quite expected they would want *books*, but found it would be *gratis*! I think they could sell a large number. Do you think you could let them have rather a liberal discount (of course they must charge 1/ nett) & let me make up the usual wholesale price – say let them have them at 7d?

The hydrop. seems to be stopped with ice at present. Tobogganing is in progress, but it looks bumpy.

I remain yrs sincerely
Beatrix Potter

[To Harold Warne]
Hill Top Farm
Sawrey
Ambleside
April. 4. 12

Dear Mr Warne,

I came away on Tuesday morning & arrived at Windermere 3½ hrs late, too late for the ferry – so had to sleep on the other side.

The country doesn't show much sign of spring yet, but I quite hope to get on with the backgrounds of the drawings [for *Mr. Tod*]. Yesterday was very fine, but I spent it at the selling off of an unlucky (& deserving) neighbour, there is universal trouble with this [coal] strike, nobody had come to the sale from outside driving distance.

I am supposed to be going back next Thursday – if I can get.

I am very pleased to hear that the roof of the hydro hangar has blown in, & smashed two machines. But they will be repaired. I hear one broke down & actually blocked the ferry the other day. It is quite monstrous to allow them in such an unsuitable place.

The weather today is very mild.

I remain yrs sincerely
H. B. Potter

Quantity of lambs – nearly all twins. But the pig has only six pink cherubs.

A preliminary drawing in sepia pen-and-ink for The Tale of Mr. Tod

[To Harold Warne]   2 Bolton Gardens
                                                     June 11. 12

Dear Mr Warne,

I intirely [sic] forgot to ask you this morning whether you – (or Mrs Grundy) object to the name of Bull Banks [where Mr. Tod had an earth]?

One thinks nothing about bulls and tups in the farming world; but after you objected to cigars it occurred to me to wonder.

'Bull Banks' is a fine-sounding name, but I could just as well call it 'Oatmeal crag'.

I wonder whether the Ladies Journal would print the small blocks too? If they did *not*, that would make the reprint more interesting; and would give more time to finish pen & inks.

I take it the colour blocks (& especially cover) are required *first*.

yrs sincerely
Beatrix Potter

I *enclose six.*

197

Warne's earlier suggestion of a new format for MR. TOD *had been dropped and the book was to be published with a page size to match the other little books, though it would have a more elaborate binding with a rounded and decorated spine. As Beatrix had suggested in her letter the previous November* MR. TOD *was to be advertised as the first in 'The Peter Rabbit Books, Series II, New Style'. Warne sent Beatrix a copy of their planned advertisement / poster for her approval.*

[To Harold Warne]
Broad Leys
Windermere
July 14. 12

Dear Mr Warne,

I am much pleased with the poster, I think the new plan is intirely [sic] satisfactory.

It ought to have gone back by return, but I was out before post came in & only saw it at night.

About your slip [with suggested changes to the opening of *Mr. Tod*] I am completely puzzled, I *had* thought you objected to "disagreeable".

I cannot say I like the samples, they are too conversational. I don't like "young" readers.

I am inclined to stick to this

"I have made many (or several) books about well behaved people. Now, for a change, I am going to make a story about two disagreeable people, called Tommy Brock & Mr Tod."

I cannot think what you are driving at, "this time" is no improvement on "now". Can it be that you think the making of many books is too Biblical – but I had no 'many' before.

If it were not impertinent to lecture ones publisher – you are a great deal too much afraid of the public for whom I have never cared one tuppenny-button. I am *sure* that it is that attitude of mind which has enabled me to keep up the series. Most people, after one success, are so cringingly afraid of doing less well that they rub all the edge off their subsequent work.

I have always thought the opening paragraph distinctly *good*, because it gets away from 'once upon a time'.

The book will be getting late.

The dock strike will have been a great upset to business. I heard one queer story about it from the wife of a Sunderland Skipper. The Germans have been buying all the steam coal that could not go to London.

I remain yrs sincerely
Beatrix Potter

To Millie Warne

Broad Leys,
Windermere
Aug 22. 12

My dear Milly [sic],

I wonder whether you are any less wet in London, I don't know when I remember such a summer! but it seems to be slipping away very fast – unless we are able to extend our tenancy here, it will be over in another three weeks. I daresay September may be better.

My hay was nearly all got in before the rain, but it is sad to see other peoples haycocks rotting. I go over to the farm three or four times a week, and get caught in the rain coming back. Today I came by road instead of by steamer, in state, in the farm gig with a swill tub on the back seat. We have rather a crowd of little pigs, as the markets have been inconvenienced by police orders. [There was a serious outbreak of foot and mouth disease.] Fortunately my farm is outside the area where cattle cannot be moved. I have just got out a nice hatch of 14 little chickens in the incubator.

I have done no sketching – alas – partly the weather, & partly fatigue. I have kept very well & managed the going backwards & forwards; but it takes it out of me.

The hydroplanes have scarcely shown themselves this last month; during the first fine fortnight they were very objectionable, they make such a racket, & actually rush about in Bowness Bay amongst the boats, but I am glad to hear there is going to be a government inquiry about them, so I hope there will be some regulations.

I heard from a cousin in Devonshire that she has had such fine sweetpeas from Mr Dipnall's seed. I find the birds take them at Sawrey. It is a grand season for cabbages! the caterpillars are all drowned. There has been a disturbed week at Sawrey, first a man tried for stealing a purse, & then another young married man fatally kicked by a horse. The wife is left with 3 little children; he was a bad husband, but somehow that seems to make it more shocking. I think it is a comfort to have pleasant memories, if nothing else.

I remain with love yrs aff.
Beatrix Potter

THE TALE OF MR. TOD, *published in October, was the first of the little books to have both black-and-white drawings and colour plates. There were new end-papers drawn by Beatrix, a picture of Samuel Whiskers pasting up a poster listing the earlier books in the series, watched by a group of the characters from them* [see Plate 11].

To Harold Warne

2, Bolton Gardens,
South Kensington, S.W.
Oct 9. 12

Dear Mr Warne,

I am much obliged for the new books [finished copies of *Mr. Tod*]. The black and white pages I like very much; & the coloured plates seem stronger than of late years. The cross ways plates look best; the uprights are rather uncomfortable with the tallness of the opposite block of type.

I think the endpapers spoil the book; to my candid thinking, they are perfectly horrid – too big, and rather commonplace – I wonder if I could have some bound, for myself, with plain white – or marbled ends? I should think Liberty's won't like them. It is a pity; without one or two drawbacks – it would have been a remarkably pretty little book. It is naturally difficult when starting a new pattern – to tell how it will come out; and it has been rather a rush.

I came back on Tuesday, bringing my little dairy maid with me for a few days to see the Islington show. We have had no success, but fairly high marks. Five solid hours have I spent there today! Tomorrow we will do the Zoo.

Let me know if I could have some bound plain? to give away. I don't object, commercially, if the travellers & shops know no better & like them, but they offend my own pleasure in the book completely! they are just like the field advts along the railway lines.

It never struck me when I was doing it! I am ashamed of them.

I remain yrs sincerely
Beatrix Potter

Warne had failed to find publishers for the French and German translations in 1907 and now they proposed to publish some of the titles in French themselves. They asked two new translators to work on the texts which were then submitted to Beatrix. She chose the ones by Mlle Victorine Ballon, an infant school teacher from Honfleur, commenting that her French 'is just right – colloquial without being slangy'. Meanwhile Beatrix had been making her own translation of PETER and sent it to Mlle Ballon for correction, with the message that it was by 'une anglaise'. Beatrix and Victorine Ballon settled the final texts between them.

[To Harold Warne]
2 Bolton Gardens
S.W.
Nov. 11. 12

Dear Mr Warne,

The improved translation of Peter is very good and spirited.

I think Mrs Tiggy is perfectly charming in French. I hope you may decide to print *Peter, Jemima* & *Tiggy.*

The Famille Flopsaut is still my favourite of the rabbit series; but it is useless for a start as it is a sequel to Benjamin Bunny.

I wonder whether the printers will be able to follow Mlle Ballon's french handwriting – her capitals are puzzling – for instance if one had not heard the French dog-name – Médor – one might have thought it was an N.

I am going to Sawrey on Wednesday, for a week I expect; I could have wished it had not turned so cold. I have to judge trussed poultry at a local show.

I hope you may decide to go ahead with setting up the French.

I remain yrs sincerely,
Beatrix Potter

From The Tale of Mr. Tod

Harold Botcherby was six when he wrote to ask Beatrix about the outcome of the battle between Tommy Brock and Mr Tod. Harold grew up to be an artist himself, his work exhibited at the Royal Academy and at the Brook Street Gallery in London.

To Harold Botcherby

c/o Messrs F Warne & Co
15 Bedford St Strand
Feb. 17. 13

My dear Harold,

I have inquired about Mr Tod & Tommy Brock, & I am sorry to tell you they are still quarrelling. Mr Tod has been living in the willow till he was flooded out; at present he is in the stick house with a bad cold in his head. As for the end of the fight – Mr Tod had nearly half the hair pulled out of his brush (=tail) and 5 bad bites, especially one ear, which is scrumpled up, (like you sometimes see nasty old Tom Cat's ears) – The only misfortune to Tommy Brock – he had his jacket torn & lost one of his boots. So for a long time he went about with one of his feet bundled up in dirty rags, like an old beggar man. Then he found the boot in the quarry. There was a beetle in the boot and several slugs.

Tommy Brock ate them. He is a nasty person. He will go on living in Mr Tod's comfortable house till spring time – then he will move off into the woods & live out of doors – and Mr Tod will come back very cautiously – & there will need to be a big spring cleaning!

Love to you & little Sally & the Flopsy Bunnies from yr aff friend

Beatrix Potter

During the winter of 1912 Beatrix had accepted a proposal of marriage from her Lake District solicitor, William Heelis. Just as eight years earlier, when accepting Norman Warne's proposal, Beatrix was faced with parental disapproval. The stress of the continued arguments and battles of will was beginning to affect her health. The next two letters were written for her by another hand. In the second the postscript was added shakily by Beatrix.

To Harold Warne

2 Bolton Gardens
South Kensington
3.3.13

Dear Mr Warne

I did not receive any letter from you on Saturday, I am still at this address.

I have gone through the French proofs & will send one copy to the school mistress & suggest she might correct it in the Easter holidays.

The *printers* have made very few mistakes.

I have been resting on my back for a week as my heart has been rather disturbed by the Influenza. I am assured it will recover with quiet. My chest has been quite well for some time.

I remain yrs sincerely
H. B. Potter

To Harold Warne

2 Bolton Gardens
South Kensington
7.3.13

Dear Mr Warne

Thank you for your letter, I will attend to the matter (paying in) on Monday.

The doctor has just been & he is so much pleased with my progress that I am going to keep flat a few days longer.

My heart now feels quite comfortable.

Yours sincerely
H. B. Potter

Give my love to Alice & Milly [sic].

I have an elegant [?] story invented! but not written out complete yet. Posted French to Mlle.

To Harold Warne

Hill Top Farm
Sawrey
Ambleside
April 7. 13

Dear Mr Warne,

I enclose the pig story [*Pigling Bland*]. *I* think it is rather pretty; but cannot say how it may strike other people.

I think it is about same length as Mr Tod. I should keep it as short as I can, as I should prefer to have a less tall block of letter press opposite the colour-plates. Probably I shall not have time to do quite so many *pairs* of line blocks; so I think it will go in.

It should be printed on a strip [galley] & I will cut it up, I have a dummy book.

The sooner I have it the better, so as to see where the plates come.

Have you heard from Mlle Ballon? I wrote again to her. We really mustn't miss yet another season for French if it can be managed.

I am very glad to have got here, it is cold but bright; I am well but not able to walk up hill yet.

Shall you be sending the cheque this next weekend?

I remain yrs sincerely
H B Potter

[To Harold Warne]

Hill Top Farm
Sawrey
April 8. 13

Dear Mr Warne,

Mlle Ballon has sent back the proofs with profuse apologies for delay. She has been given some appointment which appears to be a general inspectorship of French Infants schools, says she will push the books, I should think she may be able to do so.

1 The second name 'Profichet', is another teacher who has assisted her in the translations.
2 I should think on the binding, for shortness – "Pierre Lapin par Beatrix Potter would be sufficient.
3 dedication of B. Bunny, she has omitted purposely; I agree –
4 Lapin*e*, a vulgar term of reproach & to be avoided!
5 'Mr' throughout instead of Monsieur.
6 Flops*au*t Trots*au*t – I thought all along it must be this.
7 She would like to see revised proof
8 Her new address is
    3 rue des Augustins
    à Lille Nord

I do not send you her letter as it is very long, very French and chiefly about the new appointment & French & English schools.

Excuse haste to catch post. She says – & I say – the proofs are very good, considering the difficulties of another language.

Yrs sincerely
H B Potter

To Harold Warne

Hill Top Farm
Sawrey
April 19. 13

Dear Mr Warne,

I do not know what excuse to make – except that it is the first time I have done such a thing. I remember I did not acknowledge by return & then I forgot intirely [sic] – the cheque is still by me. I will pay it in on Monday.

The weather has been extremely bad, & I have had a bilious turn, but I daresay I shall be better for that. I seem to take a long time to get strong again.

I have been drawing pigs, but cannot do much till I see where the plates fall in the letterpress.

The chickens are deplorable in the hail & rain – & the last ill-luck is that a rat has taken *10* fine turkey eggs last night. The silly hen was sitting calmly on nothing, Mr S. Whiskers having tunnelled underneath the coop, & removed the eggs down the hole!

I remain yrs sincerely
H B Potter

[To Harold Warne]

[?]
Ap. 25. 13

Dear Mr Warne,
Covers
  I think "Pierre Lapin" looks best, but not particular.
    "par" Beatrix Potter
    F W & *Cie*
(accent would not be printed over a *capital* letter, neither on cover or title page.)

"All rights reserved"
"Tous droits réservés"
I will ask Mlle Ballon about this.

I presume you will get the exact words for cpright notice from the French publishers.

The end = La Fin

The question of how many books [in translation] to start with is rather one for *you*.

Personally I should like to see the 5 launched at the same time – because myself I thought "Sophie Canétang" & "Poupette à l'épingle" are more pleasing than the rabbits; and I should think it might be an advantage for your traveller to be able to offer an assortment of these little books, *as they are said to be something* new in France. There may not be a stack of similar sized books for them to be added to, as in England.

The existing end-papers won't do, because of the English titles on the little vols. I don't see that the menagerie of animals is of much consequence.

I am inclined to redraw it very similar, only I will *leave the books out*. Supposing the French series catches on – we would not want to be constantly re-engraving a French endpaper. A paper with a lot of animals, but no exact books, would do, over & over again for a series. *Please send me an original endpaper* drawing, for size; I hope I remember rightly that I left it with Mr Herring.

I do hope I shall get the pig text soon, I am almost completely at a stand still till I know when the plates come.

I am glad to say I am getting much stronger. I was not very well last week but the weather has improved since.

I remain yrs sincerely
Beatrix Potter

Decidedly a new block for the Flopsy market garden scene [the lettered notice board from the early edition was removed altogether and replaced by a picture of Peter, *see Plate 10*] – & no reading on any endpaper or pictures. There is a picture of Mrs R. "licensed to sell etc", does it show enough to matter?

I have no copy of Benjamin Bunny.

[To Harold Warne]

Hill Top Farm
Sawrey
April 29. 13

Dear Mr Warne,

English words. I must redraw endpapers, front B. Bunny, (p. 14 [12] B.B. engrave out? [the sign over Old Mrs Rabbit's shop]) Tower Bank Arms (Jemima) is not so serious as upon the titlepage it is admitted to be an English book. "How Keld" [engraved on a stone beside the spring in the original *Mrs. Tiggy-Winkle*] is Norse for Hill Well, and brings inquiries occasionally. These two I will redraw, if I am not too sick of it. It is a pity it was not thought of last autumn, when I was inclined to clear off odd jobs. The market garden scene [in *Benjamin Bunny*] I must of course redraw.

P. Bland. My dummy *is* the old pattern, but I had noticed it & corrected the place of the plates.

Probably I may pad out the text a little; also it *is* solid.

I was anxious to get it shorter than Tod, because I consider it is for smaller children.

I will see how it cuts up.

I have the originals of the earlier books, as you say.

The weather is still very bad, it rains, and thunders for a variety, so that the temperature is never two days alike.

I seem to get on very slowly, I am decidedly stronger & look perfectly well, but I was completely stopped by a short hill on trying to walk to the next village this afternoon. I believe persevering slow exercise is the best cure, I do not think there is anything wrong with my heart now. I am always better on fine days when I can work in the garden.

I think I have a worse pen than yours!

I have written to Mdlle [sic] Ballon.

These drawings for the foreign edition are the first thing wanted.

I do not think the plates for the pig would take me long, if I am able to stay here & do them on the spot. I am quite sure I am best out of London, & as my parents have come to an hotel for a holiday (& spring cleaning) I hope they will be satisfied for me to stay here a little longer. I should be willing to come up for the books & dentist, but not to stay long. One of my front teeth is coming out!

yrs sincerely
Beatrix Potter

To Harold Warne

June 4. 13
Hill Top Farm
Sawrey Ambleside

Dear Mr Warne,

Thank you very much for cheque safely received, I will pay it into the Liverpool Bank on Saturday.

I know what you mean about the backgrounds, but I assure you I contemplate two or three "landscapey" – The country is at last looking lovely, & today is like summer.

I am feeling much stronger now, & very much interested in farming matters; today there is a promising hatch of turkeys – and John [Cannon] & I are seriously discussing the question of buying a pedigree bull calf!

We have a very handsome bull that was bred here, but being all short people we think 'Billy' will soon be too big for us to manage.

The farm & cattle are looking particularly well.

I will attend to the proofs.

I remain yrs sincerely
Beatrix Potter

To E. Wilfred Evans

Lindeth Howe
Windermere
July 10th 13

Dear Mr Evans,

I am much obliged to you for your letter. If I had been wanting to put away just now, I should have been much interested to have a small interest in your company [the printers of the little books], but anything I don't spend I am collecting at the bank against building another room or two onto my house – also friends of ours [Warne] are always sadly behindhand, I trust it is all right.

I must not talk of "behindhand" though, I can't think how I am to get this book [*Pigling Bland*] done in time. I took so very long to get over my illness, I had my heart bad for weeks & could do nothing. I am alright now; but it might have been wiser to give up the book, before they took orders for it.

I wanted to come to see the new works – I was only up in town 10 days at the end of June & I never managed to fit it in.

I will write & ask to come over, if I am back at Bolton Gardens in the autumn. At present I am with my parents who have taken this house for 2 months.

I remain with thanks yrs sincerely
Beatrix Potter

Beatrix's photograph of Mr. T. Preston and his son

From The Tale of Pigling Bland

To Harold Warne

Lindeth Howe
Windermere
July 25. 13

Dear Mr Warne,

I enclose 8 [illustrations for *Pigling Bland*] – probably some of them will want touching up. It is awkward working under difficulties. I fear the drawings may be worse for it.

The grocer and *horse* are carefully copied from a photograph – to the red-nosed party's great pride! I took the horse standing up hill, its head seemed big, I reduced it a little.

I have others begun.

I have a letter from Mr Farnell [a maker of stuffed toys], with another small payment. I said I was doing a book about a pig going to market; he

209

thinks it might do for a doll but says it is late for this year. I should think it might answer. I will not give him the name or anything beyond a very rough sketch – as I presume you would not like it at this stage?

I wonder if you will be sending another cheque before the August bank holiday.

The weather is fine. I have been plagued with toothache.

I remain yrs sincerely
Beatrix Potter

What Mr Farnell would like to see is the *cover*. I don't know to what extent you keep it close, on account of U.S.A. Has the French text progressed at all.

To Harold Warne

Lindeth Howe
Windermere
Sept 13. 13

Dear Mr Warne,

I am rather disturbed at that cheque not having come – is there going to be any delay in keeping to the plan of settling the 1912 account, & beginning to pay the 1913 account in October? I was a little puzzled last time because the cheque was £70 & you had mentioned paying it off in 80s.

I am not short but I am spending money on building, and I ought to cut my coat according to my cloth! When one knows there is money overdue one is tempted to spending. I know the money market is very awkward.

I suppose you have got all the black & whites?

In haste yrs sincerely in haste to catch morning post.
HB Potter

Rain here at last – much wanted. Love to Alice & the children.

[To Harold Warne]

Lindeth Howe
Windermere
Sept 16. 13

Dear Mr Warne

Thank you very much for the cheque received safely last night. I will pay it in at the end of this week.

I got the second copy of proof this morning. I find there is one bl & white cut too many – (it is obliged to come out at a certain part of book unfortunately.

I think this the best to omit [see below – it was left out].

I suppose the printers will place the cuts all right as to height of page & keep them much the same & about same as the *full type pages*.

I don't like the bl & whites so well without a border line, they are inclined to [be] untidy.

In haste to catch post at Sawrey

yrs sincerely
H B Potter

Expect to be back about end of next week. That binders strike sounds serious.

Gertrude Woodward was the daughter of Dr Henry Woodward, Keeper of Geology at the British Museum (South Kensington) and editor of THE GEOLOGICAL MAGAZINE. *She worked at the Natural History Museum and was an old acquaintance of Beatrix, helping her to find a printer for* PETER RABBIT *twelve years before.*

A.S.W. referred to in the following letter was Dr A. Smith Woodward, who had succeeded Henry Woodward as Keeper of Geology in 1901. He had been working with Charles Dawson on the recently discovered skull 'of Neanderthal man' from a quarry in Piltdown, and on 17 September THE TIMES *carried a report of his lecture to the British Association. He used the occasion to defend himself against criticism levelled at his reconstruction of the skull and to declare the discovery 'one of the links in the chain of the human race which had hitherto been missing'. (It was not until 1953, nine years after A.S.W.'s death, that the skull was revealed to be a fraud.)*

Beatrix meanwhile was preparing for her wedding which was to be in London at St Mary Abbot's, Kensington, on 15 October. Reluctant to see any more changes made to Hill Top, she and Willie had decided to live at Castle Farm in Castle Cottage, where an extension was being built.

To Miss Gertrude Woodward

2 Bolton Gardens
(in train)
Sept. 24. 13

My dear Gertrude,

Excuse pencil in train. I am coming back with my parents. The weather has been so lovely we have kept staying on by the week, & *I* was in no hurry to leave.

I agree with every word you say about the nurse, she left on Tuesday, *most* unwillingly; she was a somewhat tactless thick skinned person – quite unconscious of being in my mother's way! She had done more for him [Beatrix's father] than any doctor, & got him under her thumb. I can understand the irritation, but as you say – a servant without influence will be useless. He is so well I am in fear they may not get anybody. If we were not coming to a difficult change amongst the home servants – I might be tempted to bolt at once, while he is well & cheerful! I was feeling the going away very much, but William has actually been invited up for a weekend soon – they never say much but they cannot dislike him. Also there have been comic incidents this last week, including a wasp which got "inside everything" & must have made Wm lively for once! Also he has asserted himself upon the subject of hens & put down Mr Simpson our new neighbour, to the satisfaction of J.C. [Cannon]

The building was getting interesting at the Castle, it was tiresome to have to come away. The garden has been much spoilt by drought all summer. I considered about bringing plants, but as I was not coming direct from farm & not sure if you had taken over the garden – I decided to delay till next time. I hope I may go over in Oct. if only for a few days to see how the new rooms shape.

What a triumph for A.S.W!

Please give my kind regards to Dr Woodward [Gertrude's father]. My parents send theirs & my mother hopes to see you soon – they are nearly always in at 5 oclock tea, but I daresay I may see you first if I'm near S.K. museum.

I remain yrs aff.
Beatrix Potter

I only got rid of revised proofs [of *Pigling Bland*] last week; it is disgracefully late, it has been such a nuisance all summer.

Mary Clark is being turned out of her nice little cottage – but according to her hesitating manner – won't say if she will come to me. She would be so reliable as upper servant that it would be worth keeping a girl to help. She is not strong alone.

THE TALE OF PIGLING BLAND *was to be published in October.*

To Mrs Martin

Hill Top Farm
Sawrey
Oct 28. 13

Dear Mrs Martin,

I wonder whether you would mind telling me what [rent] you paid for the "Bungalow"? (of course that was in summer?) I'm sure Flemings must know what Mrs Hutchinson asks, but they are so densely ignorant that I have an amused suspicion, there may be an intention to "try it on"! We are very comfortable here, but it is too hard work for the farm women for any length of time, & the cottage is so far off ready – I thought I could manage at the Bungalow for a fortnight or so, to help the time on. It is a nice little house, but rather plain in winter. I have written to Mrs Hutchinson today. I am sorry to hear she is very unwell.

I am going to London this next week, Thursday, as my mother is changing servants. It is rather soon to have to leave the disconsolate Wm. People are sure to say we have quarrelled!

I remain yrs sincerely
Beatrix Heelis

To Margaret Hough

Hill Top Farm
Sawrey
Ambleside
Nov. 4. 13

My dear Margaret,

As I am in London now for a few days, and not likely to be in London at Christmas – I am taking the opportunity of posting off some copies of the new book, which has just come out. I hope you will like it, I'm afraid it was done in an awful hurry and scramble.

The portrait of two pigs arm in arm – looking at the sun-rise – is *not* a portrait of me & Mr Heelis, though it is a view of where we used to walk on Sunday afternoons! When I want to put William in a book – it will have to be as some very tall thin animal.

Thank you very much for your nice letter of congratulation, I think it was a good idea to send cake to several girls who have written to me – and you have done it regularly. If you ever come up to the Lakes – be sure & let me know, as I should be delighted to see you – I can't do much entertaining at the farm, with farm servants, but we can stand a good farmhouse tea – and I have often packed in little girls for a night or two if their relations were staying in the neighbourhood. I had two for a very jolly picnic last August – so remember the address if you are ever within reach.

With best wishes for the coming Christmas to you & John, believe me,

yrs aff.
Beatrix Heelis

214

Castle Cottage, photographed by Rupert Potter on 13 July 1912

To Barbara Buxton

Hill Top Farm
Sawrey
Ambleside
Dec 31. 13

My dear Barbara,

I was delighted with your nice little basket, it will certainly be useful – and constantly used. It will just do for holding card of darning worsted of various colours. Mr Heelis walks through the toes of his stockings so it is lucky I like darning!

It is surprising you could do the basket work so firmly – very creditable altogether.

I have never had time to write, as I went away to Appleby, to my new relations, for Christmas, now I am very busy writing letters & trying to tidy things up before going back to London to see my parents. I hope it will be fine tomorrow for the journey, the roads are very slippy but not much snow, & bright sun. Taps & pumps frozen this morning, we have got caught with no sacking on them.

I am hoping to get settled in the Castle Cottage soon – it has been in such an *awful mess*. The new rooms are nothing like built yet, & the old part has been all upset with breaking doors in the wall & taking out partitions.

Those front rooms, where you & Augusta slept are one long room now & the staircase is altered, & we are going to have a bathroom – in the course of time – I think workmen are very slow.

With love & wishing you a very happy New Year

I remain yrs aff.
Beatrix Heelis

Be sure to come & call when you are in the neighbourhood again, any time of day, perhaps I am oftenest to be found in the mornings.

215

To Harold Warne

Sawrey
Ambleside
Feb. 23. 14

Dear Mr Warne,

I think Tom Kitten in verse is considerable twaddle; but that was pretty much my opinion of the original.

I should think it is a fair sample of song words. I can't imagine what sort of tune it would go with, but I am so hopelessly without musical ear that I am not a good judge.

I do very much regret the *French* never came to anything; that was exceedingly well done.

I have not hammered out any name for the next book [the working title was *The Tale of Kitty-in-Boots*], but will do so as soon as I can. It is about a well-behaved prim black Kitty cat, who leads rather a double life, and goes out hunting with a little gun on moonlight nights, dressed up like puss in boots. As the gun is only a pop gun (which continually goes off,) the bag is neither large nor painful [*see Plate 12*].

Miss Kitty ends in a trap, loses one of her boots & a claw, which cures her of poaching. My husband undertakes to hold a gun properly, which was a defect in the [Fierce] Bad rabbit pictures.

I'm sorry to be behindhand, but I have inhabited 3 houses since marriage & been having altogether too much to attend to at once.

I remain yrs sincerely
H B Heelis

P.S. You may remember that Mme Liza Lehmann who *is* known as a successful composer wanted to do Peter, & *you objected!* some difficulty about her working for Novello (?) or Chappel (?)

Ipswich may be a musical centre but I never heard of it; I don't suppose Miss Lehmann's would have been any better, or worse, but I fancy she is in the running as a composer of songs, "popular" rather than specially good.

To Harold Warne
2, Bolton Gardens
South Kensington, S.W.
March 20. 14

Dear Mr Warne,

I had hoped to call at the office, but the weather, and the troubles here make it rather hopeless. I found my father a little weaker after my absence of 10 days, and he seems to have taken another step downhill these last two days.

I shall be more free when we get a second nurse, but I don't like to make an apptmt as I shall go back to Sawrey for a few days whenever there is a chance.

He may last a good while, but it is scarcely to be wished.

I have several drawings begun – perhaps rashly! – for this cat-story. I'm afraid it's all I can offer this spring – so make the best of it! It will *illustrate* very well, plenty of variety & I could do them quickly if I had the proof [of the text] to cut & *place*. The earlier part wants compressing, the later part goes better. Of course there is a question of the sentimental dislike of traps. I haven't much pity for poaching cats myself; but traps are ghastly if not looked at regularly. Still I don't think this story is extra harassing.

I'm sorry to hear of the chicken pox.

I remain yrs sincerely
Beatrix Heelis

The Mss is about same length as Mr Tod.

To Harold Warne
May 9th 14
2, Bolton Gardens,
South Kensington. S.W.

Dear Mr Warne,

I am sorry I have never been able to attend to business. When I tell you I have been here 8 times = 16 journeys since New Year, & that my fathers illness was dropsy from internal cancer – I think you will understand. He died very peacefully last evening. I do not think he ever had acute pain, but it has been rather a ghastly illness.

We are very thankful it is over, as we feared he might drag on for weeks longer – he went suddenly at the end.

I have ended with a sore throat, after a week of sitting up. Mr Heelis is coming tonight & we are going to an hotel across the road as that really will be the most rest.

I will let you know when I return to Sawrey. I suppose there would be another cheque sometime. I am still tinkering at the house! It had got as far as plastering when I left.

I hope you are all very well again, please send my love to Milly [sic] – I have so many letters to write

yrs sincerely
Beatrix Heelis

There had never been a case of cancer in the family; except one old female cousin – who recovered! I suppose he was just worn out. But I suppose they diagnose it more exactly in these times – if Sir Alfred Fripp had not tried to operate we should have called it dropsy.

To Harold Warne

Lindeth Howe
Windermere
July 12. 14

Dear Mr Warne

I am sorry to hear you have had influenza for I know what it means, and how over tired and worried you often look towards summer. I hope you are going to get a holiday? – business or no business! people can stick to work *too* long.

I have not been 'resting' as you suggest; I only wish I had been settled; we could not leave my mother quite alone, and the lady who is going to live with her could not come, but I hope she is coming on Thursday next.

We have been here 3 weeks already, and it means nothing but going backwards & forwards. I have tried to get on with the book [*Kitty-in-Boots*], but there are no plates finished yet. I cannot imagine how it can be done in time to be of much use in America. I am interested in the drawings again – in the sense of getting my mind on it, and feeling I could make something of it – if only I had time & opportunity.

I do wish I had got more done last winter before interruptions began, but I was a good deal damped by neither you nor Fruing seeming to care much for the story, and then it was too late to think about another. It is very difficult to keep up to a fixed level of success. I think I can make something of it, it has (mostly) good subjects for colour plates.

I don't think I shall be in town before Oct. I *hope* not, for the only chance of getting work done is to be let alone. I am much obliged for the cheque, I shall be interested to see the accounts. I can get along at present, the bank will advance if I get short over the building which has got to the stage of plumbers.

I wish you had been feeling more cheerful yourself – especially when I have to make excuses.

I remain with love to Alice & the children yrs sincerely

H. B. Heelis

To Harold Warne

Hill Top Farm
Sawrey
Ambleside
Aug 3. 14

Dear Mr Warne,

I am sorry the only help I can do is to forbear asking for any payments; things are so bad – I was half afraid to open your letter, thinking it might be a crash.

I have rather less than usual – than more, in hand – I have not touched any of my father's money yet – if that is what is in your mind. A very slow solicitor is gradually winding things up, and I only hope there is no trouble in dealing with the stocks – £12,000 had to be sold for duties & small legacies.

I can't think how business people will scramble through. I hear it is very bad in Manchester.

The crops are very good here; I feel nervous about the horses which are down in the police list, but at a pinch we can use cattle.

The soldiers are reported to be at Barrow docks & the viaduct, a few miles off – there are 2 battleships nearly built, one for "Turkey", at Vickers Maxims.

That is our nearest to the war at present, but there is no saying who or what may have to go.

All one can do at present is to forbear spending more than possible, & cut down some wood, as there is going to be no coal.

I do wish you would send me *the accounts some time*. I am completely at large about the position, & I filled in income tax at random; but no compunction about *that*, as I blame Ll.G. [Lloyd George] for the panic. Things were so bad they could not stand another straw.

Give my love to Millie and all of you. Try for a clever working partner with some money – you have such a good organisation, but you know you *are overworked* & in a muddle. What has become of all the little side shows we discussed last spring? note papers? almanacs?

Yrs sincerely

Beatrix Heelis

Britain declared war on Germany on 4 August.

*After her father's death Beatrix had brought her mother up to Sawrey
and installed her in a furnished house in the village with a companion.*

To Harold Warne   Sawrey,
                                                             Ambleside
                                                             Dec 16. 14

Dear Mr Warne,

I should be much obliged if these two parcels can be sent from the
office.

I wonder what sort of Christmas you are having; I *hope* less anxious,
but I fear everything must be very upset still – and although the news is
more satisfactory lately, one cannot see the end in sight yet. It seems a
long time since I heard any news of you, Milly [sic] had just let her house
when I heard last. The Belgians are stopped coming about here, for fear
of spies. I wonder what is to be done with them – apparently they *can*
work when allowed – there is a story of some who went down a
Whitehaven coal pit & earned 10/9 at one shift piece work, which
nearly produced a riot!

I have not been away from here since June; we are going for a few
days to Appleby [Willie's home] at Christmas. My mother is comfortably
settled here, & has been wonderfully contented through some truly
awful weather. November tried to make up our rain average which is
still a little in arrears, in spite of 11 inch in a month.

I don't want to come to London in cold weather without necessity, I
catch such bad colds there, whereas here I have only had one very small
one for months.

There have been sad losses amongst local officers – my husband's
nephew was alright in "the Venerable" enjoying the bombardment when
last heard of; his brother has gone to India. I suppose Alice has one or
two nephews with the fleet? There is a nice little porker to kill early in
January when I shall hope to post a bit of pork.

                                        With kind regards yours sincerely
                                                             Beatrix Heelis

*The Warne archive has no letters either to or from Beatrix between 16
December 1914 and 18 May 1915, but it is known that* THE TALE OF
KITTY-IN-BOOTS *was set up in type and the text pasted into a dummy
copy by Beatrix. However only one picture was finished, the frontispiece,
and the book was never published.*

To Harold Warne
Sawrey
Ambleside
May 18.15

Dear Mr Warne,

I wonder how you are getting on in these bad times? I am afraid business must be in a queer state from anything I can gather from Bowness tradespeople. I should rather like to hear – not with the least intention of pressing you, for I have luckily enough – but I have thought once or twice I must really say I don't like going on indefinitely without some sort of accounts, you did not send any statement as you talked of doing, after the New Year. The last I can lay my hand on is for 1911!! I think I have had one since then; but not for a long time. I am a healthy person, but think what it would look like for unbusiness if I happened to wind up. If it has got beyond keeping count of, it would be better to say so.

I do hope your nephews are all alive & unhurt – or not badly. Sometimes it is a relief to have them safe in hospital. Last summer's recruits are having their leave about here, the last we shall see of many a fine lad. It is a weary job. A whole family of distant cousins went down in the Lusitania, father, mother, six children & nurse.

I tried a little drawing in winter, but could not stick to it, also could not *see*, my eyes are gone so long sighted & not clear nearby. They are alright for general purposes, like poultry & outdoor work – I suppose I shall have to take to spectacles, but I had better get properly fitted in London – a place I have no wish to go to at present!

I have not heard from Millie for some time, but I think I owe her a letter.

I remain yrs sincerely
Beatrix Heelis

To Fruing Warne
Sawrey
Ambleside
Dec 18th.(?) 15

My dear Fruing,

I heard from Milly [sic] that you are a special constable. It may seem hard to bother you at such a time, but I am getting seriously perplexed about the accounts.

From what Harold said in his last letter, May 23rd, the accounts for 1913 (the year of Pigling Bland) were ready; but I have never had them.

I also should like a statement of the payments in the spring of 1914, as I do not know which season they were on account of, or exactly how we stand.

I promised not to ask the firm for payments while times were so difficult; but I think you will allow that the failure to send any statements at all is a trial of patience; and the overlapping and unpunctuality had begun *long before the war*.

I know how unwieldy the P.R statements had become. Your book keeping seems so elaborate & careful, I expect you could write them up to date with time – but if it *is* past unravelling, I think it would be better for someone to see you on my behalf and get at some compromise; and also make some new arrangement with the firm about the copyright.

You know the letter of the agreements is not being kept, they were assigned upon certain terms, and conditions.

You will be busy just now with the Christmas season – such as it is. If the matter of the accounts is not gone into satisfactorily by the end of January, I shall have to take some steps about it – not in any unfriendly spirit, but to put the matter on a more businesslike footing. For one thing I should instruct my London solicitor to alter my will; I cannot leave this muddle to go on accumulating. I am writing this without any consultation with my husband; for reasons which you may guess I feel a repugnance to his intervening in any business between me and your family.

I am not likely to be in London at present; and I confess if I were I have no inclination to call at the office, it results in nothing but talking. I have done no book this season; and I should not have sent it if I had.

I am not out of temper; I am very sorry for you all, in the struggle that you must be having. But I am tired of the muddle, and it is *not* all due to the war. Neither is it *all* due to Harold; I think it would have been courteous if *you* had sent a line of regret about the half yearly interest.

We are having a real "old fashioned" winter here, yesterday was our third heavy fall of snow – such drifts, I am glad it is now raining, on account of the sheep. But it has been pleasant weather, bright & cold. Somehow winter seems more appropriate to the sad times, than the glorious summer weather, though we were thankful to have it for getting the crops.

I hope you and yours are all well – (as I am) – the children will be getting quite grown up.

I remain yrs sincirely [sic]
Beatrix Heelis

There is no record of Fruing's reply, and Beatrix's next letter in the Warne file is not until 22 April 1916.

THE TIMES *of 7 March 1916 carried a report of the inaugural meeting of the Women's National Land Service, and was followed by an article urging farmers to release men to the war and to employ women in their place – but to pay them adequately.* THE TIMES *of 13 March carried a letter from Beatrix using the pseudonym 'A Woman Farmer'.*

10 March 1916
To the Editor of *The Times.* WOMEN ON THE LAND

Sir, – In your leader upon the employment of women you say that the chief step is the offer of adequate wages. The custom of employing women upon farms has never quite ceased in the north, but the supply of women is undoubtedly affected by the competition of munition work. I pass no opinion as to whether munition workers are extravagantly paid; I only know that farmers cannot compete with their wages. Three girls have gone from adjoining farms here; they expect to earn at least £2 wages per week. They are trained dairymaids and milkers, but totally inexperienced in mechanics. The present waste of skilled training is unfortunate. At one and the same time I was receiving from a Labour Exchange advice to take outside women on my farm; from another Labour Exchange requests for the character of my cowman's daughters for munitions; and my little general servant was being canvassed to go on the land (from which I should presumably have been removed to do the housework). I have worked on it for years and love it; but I still feel some sympathy with the perplexity of the farmers. Harm is being done by the ridiculous and vulgar photographs which appear in the Press. I am perfectly ready to employ the right sort of woman. French women and North country girls have found it possible to work in a short petticoat, and they have not required the theatrical attractions of uniform and armlet to induce them to do their duty.

Yours truly,
A Woman Farmer

To Miss E. L Choyce   Hill Top Sawrey
                                       March 15, 1916.
Dear Madam,
    Your letter reached me this morning. Do you mind telling me, are you a girl or middle-aged? I am fifty this year – very active and cheerful; but I am afraid I and my farm-housekeeper are both going to be overworked. I must explain at once that I don't depend on the farm for a living, so some people might not call it real 'war work'; but I have farmed my own land for ten years as a business (before and since

marriage) and I have got it into such good order it would be a pity to let it go down . . . [The original of this letter is missing. The punctuation here follows that of a previous transcription.]

This is between Windermere and Coniston; very pretty hilly country, but not wild like Keswick or Ullswater . . . My husband is a solicitor; as there are all sorts of people in the world I may say he is a very quiet gentleman, and I am a total abstainer! We have been two years married, no family. We live very quietly in a cottage separate from the old farmhouse; I have one young servant here. On the farm I have employed a family for ten years – John Cannon, cowman-foreman-shepherd; Mrs C., dairy woman, farm-housekeeper; Willie C., ploughman . . . My husband helps with the hay, but he is short-handed too.

I have poultry, orchard, flower garden, vegetables, no glass, help with heavy digging, cooking with the girl's assistance. Mrs C., I and this girl all help with hay, and I single turnips when I can find time . . .

It is best to speak straight out; the difficulty with a stranger woman is the boarding. I can see Mr Heelis doesn't want a lady living here. I don't think a lady would live comfortably (for either party) in the Cannons' back kitchen. There remains the front part of the farmhouse, which I used before I married, and which we still use for spare bedrooms, library, etc. . . . It is a lovely old house, in fact the furniture and old oak is so good I can only have a careful occupier . . . There are two doors through to the farm quarters, but it is complete in every way (except a fixed bath).

I don't go out much, haven't time; and the little town seems nothing but gossip and cards. I'm afraid our own special sin is not attending church regularly, not loving the nearest parson; and I was brought up a Dissenter . . . I am very downright, but I get on with everybody.

[Beatrix Heelis]

Your letter is very earnest: I wonder if you have a sense of humour?

Eleanor L. Choyce ('Louie') had been governess to Denys Lowson, now away at school. (Thirty-four years later he was Lord Mayor of London (1950–51) and raised to the baronetcy.) Miss Choyce went to work for Beatrix, living at Hill Top with her brother, Tom. They returned to Sawrey again to help during the Second World War. When Beatrix was preparing CECILY PARSLEY'S NURSERY RHYMES *for publication in 1922 Louie Choyce contributed one of the rhymes 'We have a little garden'. She wrote three verses but Beatrix used only the first. For Christmas 1942 Beatrix gave her a story she had written and illustrated which featured a Miss Louie Choyce, two Pekinese dogs called Chuleh and Tzuzee, and an umbrella with a duck's head handle.* THE CHINESE UMBRELLA *was never published.*

To Harold Warne   Battlebarrow House
                                                   Appleby
                                                   April 22. 16

Dear Mr Warne

Thank you very much for the cheque forwarded here; I note that you hope to be able to make up the accounts presently.

It must indeed be worrying times to carry on a complicated business. I am glad you are getting a holiday – though but a short one – and *cold*, if it is like here. With love to Alice & the girls

                                                   from yrs sincerely
                                                   Beatrix Heelis

To Harold Warne   Sawrey
                                                   Ambleside
                                                   June 12th. 16

Dear Mr Warne,

I quite agree that the price must rise. 1/3 is a broken sum; but you are the best judge whether it should be 1/3 or 1/6.

The wording of the agreements would require alteration; and I am going to take the opportunity of suggesting another change, which I have had seriously in my mind, and which I hope you will consider not unkindly after the circumstances of the last few years. I do not like the indefinite term of the assignment to F. W. & Co their heirs and assigns – in view of the uncertain future for all trade.

You could not help the circumstances, but you will admit I have been forbearing & patient; the agreements are virtually a dead letter.

It is unthinkable that I should ever quarrel with you & your family but if there were ever a reconstitution of your business in the uncertain future I think I ought not to be in that indefinitely tied up position, in view of my easyness in the past.

I think the folding books will make up well [*Miss Moppet* and *A Fierce Bad Rabbit* were to be put into the series format], I see you will require a little front – mouse or kitten. If [I] draw it rather large it could be reduced.

                                                   I remain yrs sincerely
                                                   Beatrix Heelis

I do hope Alice did not lose a nephew in that battle, I saw the name of 'Mack'.

PP.S. The rat in the area [*The Sly Old Cat*] was rather best of the 3 as far as I (dimly) remember. [It was not published in 1906 with the other two panoramic stories.]

To Harold Warne

Sawrey
Ambleside
July 6. 16

Dear Mr Warne,

I am much obliged for the cheques safely received this morning – also for the bundle of accounts which I do certainly agree are *unwieldy* – the part that is really interesting is the front page showing the various books at a glance; and the separate statement of accounts to show dates of payments. It must be most troublesome to type out; and it really isn't interesting to me to be told what stock was on hand at N. York at a date long ago. It shows wonderful book keeping.

(I am writing this in spectacles confusedly). I like the little book covers very much. I am keeping Nellie's little rat story [*The Sly Old Cat*, written for Nellie Warne in March 1906] a little longer, but it is perfectly out of the question to try to rush it through at this time of summer, and without knowing whether these glasses will do. I should have to redraw the pictures, and probably part trace them, to save the expression.

It is wonderful how Peter Rabbit keeps on selling.

I will have another search for the 1913 statement; but I think it may be at 2 Bolton Gardens.

I remain yrs sincerely
Beatrix Heelis

From The Sly Old Cat

Harold Warne sent Beatrix a number of recently published illustrated booklets by Ernest A. Aris which seemed to him to be too close to Beatrix's own books for comfort.

To Harold Warne   Sawrey
                                                   Ambleside
                                                   Aug 12. 16

Dear Mr Warne,

After a week's reflection I see daylight. You had better engage Mr E. A Aris to illustrate the "Sly Old Cat". His plagiarisms are unblushing, and his drawing excellent. If you showed him Nellie's little booklet I have little doubt that he would be sufficiently modest to copy the designs exactly, and do them really well. His mice have too large ears, he should be advised that rats have still smaller ears. He can draw cats much better than I can, and he would do the rats' clothing excellently. I wonder any self respecting publisher would publish such a crib of *the shape & idea*. The style of drawing is rather more cribbed from E. Dulac's than from mine. But I do not think it is actionable, and frankly it does not annoy me because it is good. But the stories are not so well written as might be, – poor grammar & rather slip shod, but nothing vulgar like "Harriet Hare".

I should be glad to hear what you think about it. I should think he would accept a sum down for a set of designs, certainly I would do the same & a moderate one rather than the cumbersome royalty, for the use of my name & the letter press. I have wished for a long time that you could find some second string – this man to my thinking is just what we want *if* he would draw to order & take suggestions – you will have to get used to the idea that my eyes are giving way, whether you like it or not – and if I managed to do yet another book it would not be that cat story – (though I think it really amusing) but I do not draw cats well, & I am away from that sort of background.

I am registering letter, as the original is enclosed.

Let me know what you do as I shall write to him about a dog I should like done & which I never could have drawn myself if you don't.

                                                   Yrs sincerely
                                                   Beatrix Heelis

parcel of cribs posted separately.

To Denys Lowson

[?]
Oct. 3.16

My dear Denys,

Your letter was a pleasing surprise! I perceive that "Choicey" has taught you to write good round hand; and to be a polite little gentleman, which is still more important! I wonder how many tiresome unknown children have bothered me with birthday books, and letters wanting answers etc and – would you believe it – not more than one in twenty ever writes again to say "thank you".

That awful big beast at the museum is like a bad dream; I once did dream about it; it was coming downstairs on crutches into the big hall of the museum, and I was unable to run away. I am glad there are none of them left alive in the world now. Probably they did last long enough for the earliest men to see, and that was the beginning of the tales about dragons. There was an enormous bird, much bigger than an ostrich which lived in New Zealand until quite recent times. And that odd looking bird called the Dodo really lived till 16??. (Choicey says she taught you dates, I have forgotten mine – except William The Conqueror 1066)

She will have a great deal to tell you about Tom Kittens house, and all our rabbits, and potatoes, & cats, & cows. I think you ought to come and see them some day when she is here again. I have heard so much about you, we would feel quite like old friends to start with.

I remain yours affectionately
Beatrix Heelis

To Millie Warne

Sawrey
Ambleside
Dec. 15. 16

My dear Milly [sic],

It is good of you to have written again! I have had it on my conscience that it was my turn, and overdue. I do seem to have so little time; & my writing time is after supper, with eyes that – like your legs – are beginning to feel anno domini. I am so very sorry to hear of your rheumatism, for one cannot blink the fact that it is very bad to cure completely, and a sad attendant of old age when old age really comes. I hardly know what 'legs' are, & seldom sit down except to meals. I have been sitting an unusual amount today, with a little old mad woman whose husband had gone a "cockshuhing", if you know what that is! = acting as beater at a shoot. Had it not been one of Mrs John's lunacies to always keep the blinds down – I might have got some letters written or some darning. She is harmless & amusing.

I shall be glad to get the turkeys safely off, & the horrid slaughter over, poor dears they are so tame and tractable, but they *do* eat. They are selling at 1/3 & 1/4 in feather. I have not had so much difficulty about sugar, because I buy farm stuffs – cattle cake & poultry foods from 3 grocers, so I wheedle a little sugar from each; and also Agnes Anne at the village shop, the original of Ginger & Pickles, supplies some very dirty stuff, though I did not know it was called black. She has done a very unkind thing – sold cream of tartar by mistake for salt petre, & Mr Heelis rubbed it on the hams. It discoloured them, but I hope it may not have done any harm, as the mistake was found out & the hams washed. The farm has done well with good crops in spite of the *very* wet season, but labour is a great anxiety. I found myself faced with the prospect of losing & changing all my four servants, but have got together a scratch crew somehow, & there is always the chance of hiring a soldier or some Germans! I am very glad indeed that there [is] a change of Govt. & some chance of common sense. I wonder if Fred [Millie's nephew, Frederick Warne Stephens, Edith's son] will keep clear, he didn't look strong enough. I am very glad to hear Alice keeps better, it must have been a sad shock & anxiety. I had a woman (lady) help last summer who is coming back, we expect rather a strenuous summer. Give my love to Edith & Jenny [Edith's daughter] and with much love & good wishes for Christmas & New Year.

> I remain yrs aff.
> Beatrix Heelis

PETER RABBIT'S PAINTING BOOK *was to be shortened and reissued. The 'surplus' plates were to be put with a number of new ones to make a companion volume,* TOM KITTEN'S PAINTING BOOK.

To Harold Warne

Sawrey
Dec 19. 16

Dear Mr Warne

I am rather ashamed of the easel [for the cover of *Tom Kitten's Painting Book*], could Mr Stokoe touch it up? It is an article I never used or possess, but the crooked lines are due to cold hands & bad light.

We have a deep snow, & the railway is blocked by a bad accident at Wigan – an uncheerful time. I cannot wish anyone a Merry Christmas – but may the New Year bring more cheerful times to all. Please give my love to Alice & the girls, I wrote to Milly [sic] last week. The books have come safe, I hope this reaches you alright.

> With kind regards yrs sincerely
> Beatrix Heelis

Canon Rawnsley's wife of thirty-eight years, Edith, had been ill and in great pain for three years before her death on 31 December 1916. Hardwicke Rawnsley himself was too ill with influenza to attend either her funeral or her memorial service. He made the immediate decision to retire as Vicar of Crosthwaite, after thirty-four years, announcing that he was unable to continue without the help of his wife.

To Canon Hardwicke Rawnsley
Sawrey
Ambleside
Feb 5. 17

Dear Canon Rawnsley,

I read that you are leaving Crosthwaite; perhaps you will be more at Grasmere; I hope we may sometimes meet, in happier times.

I am sure you will believe it was not carelessness that prevented my writing before with sympathy from us and my mother; we thought you were ill and overwhelmed with letters – and really, I did *not* know how to write. As one gets older I begin to understand how the human mind and memory works back. I remember Mrs Rawnsley so very clearly when we first knew you at Wray, and again at Keswick when Noel [Rawnsley] was a very small boy. I doubt if I had met her once in London since we left off going to Lingholme.

You can imagine what a shock it was to see her last summer – it seemed to me – *that* was the *real* – the cruelest death – death in life.

My mother keeps well, in spite of the cold weather. We are not shorthanded here, but it is a queer season for getting on with work. If the land had been already ploughed all over the country – this frost would have been invaluable.

With much sympathy, in which my husband & mother join.

I remain yrs sincerely
Beatrix Heelis

[To Harold Warne]   [?]
                                                          [?end Feb 1917]

Dear Mr Warne,

The plates [for *Tom Kitten's Painting Book*] have come out very well, I agree with the corrections, though some are so slight I should scarcely have marked them.

The cover is the least satisfactory because of the colour of the cat – (which was too dull in the *original*, partly the fault of the paper.) I should advise strengthening the red & yellow blocks; it would probably be necessary to reduce the *blue* in the cat's face. It will be no matter if it does come out a bit orangy [sic], it can pass for tortoiseshell. The easel is rather red, it wants more yellow. I like the cover colour.

Sorry I missed post yesterday – it goes earlier & I keep forgetting.

                                            With kind regards yrs truly
                                                          H B Heelis

Warmer today; but I have just turned up a big frozen lump in digging.

TOM KITTEN'S PAINTING BOOK *was to be published in June.*

To Harold Warne   Sawrey
                                                          Ambleside
                                                          March 19. 17

Dear Mr Warne,

I received the [china] duck safely this morning. It is a *very embarassing* [sic] *bird!* It is not bad, but compared with my *own* models it is rather commonplace – do not hurt the young lady's feelings by saying so.

Perhaps something might be arranged; but I should like to know a good deal more about the firm; and at first sight it is a very annoying thing to have happened.

You may remember the trouble that there was with a German firm? I have thought about it several times lately, and thought that at least one need not be bound by a German bargain, I had intended to make inquiries when next I came to London.

A good many of my figures got broken & others I left in town.

My friend is not working at Doulton's now, & I think the manager Mr Moris [sic] has retired. I did not care in particular about Doulton ware, but I was very vexed, at the time, that the German firm *could* hold the matter up.

The makers of this figure have got the technical skill of making a mould for a figure (I think this is a *moulded* figure – not a modelled?) but their colours are ugly, & the general turn out is based rather on the objectionable German chimney ornaments which everybody wants to oust.

The old Staffordshire ware figures were equally simple and had a very similar glaze, but they were works of art. One of my uncles had a good collection & I copied some in clay. I fancy they were quite cheap when originally made.

The Worcester people could do them, but probably not at a popular price.

Can you tell me more about this maker, do they go in for figures or what? I have no doubt it would *sell*, but it is almost as objectionable to me as those German plates!

I am very glad to hear you are getting on fairly well – it is a trying time. We have a wild day here, storms of sleet, & all day wet lambs before the fire – the third dead since breakfast has just expired! There is not an atom of grass & the hill flocks must be in a pitiable state. Mine being fed hay – yet they have no milk. The ploughman has got his calling up, in the very middle of ploughing, I'm afraid I am not in a particularly good temper. It may affect my opinion of Jemima, I will keep her a day or two, but she won't "grow upon me".

yrs sincerely
Beatrix Heelis

Pencil drawing of an old Staffordshire figure

That month Harold Warne was arrested as he was walking in Covent Garden with his brother, Fruing. He was charged before the Lord Mayor in the Mansion House with 'uttering a bill of exchange . . . knowing it to be forged', and on 26 April he was sentenced to eighteen months' imprisonment with hard labour for £20,000 bill forgeries.

For years Harold Warne had been transferring money from Frederick Warne and Company into the ailing family fishing business in Jersey. The publishing company was now in serious financial trouble, and it fell to the remaining Warne brother, Fruing, to rescue it. He turned at once to Beatrix, the creator of the company's most valuable assets – and the person to whom the company owed the most money. The merchandise needed to be sorted out and resuscitated and perhaps Beatrix could even be persuaded to do a new book?

To Fruing Warne

Sawrey
Ambleside
April 30. 17

Dear Mr Warne

I am obliged for the statements, I saw those for 1912.13 *at the office*; they now complete my set of copies. I always said to HEW. that I had not had them sent me.

I should strongly advise terminating formally the arrangements with Hughes – (German rabbit dolls) – and also with the China tea service, Levien. The china was very ugly, and the agreement was so worded that they seemed able to block arrangement with any other firm about *any sort* of china – i.e. my little statuette models. I wanted to try to get them copied some years ago, but Mr Warne said the previous agreement was a difficulty. (There was a china duck sent to me a few weeks ago, but I don't know who was the maker? It was not quite right colour, but *promising*). I wish I could get into touch with the people, the last letter I had from HEW was about it.

Hughes was always rather slippery. Latterly he had a fairly good excuse – that there were such swarms of rabbits – of all colours – in the market, that the copyright could scarcely be said to exist. I don't think he is worth bothering about, I doubt if you can get much out of him. At least if he *does* pay, *I* have not been hearing much about it! And I believe *I* owe the firm about six or seven shillings upon the duck which I set against it.

Jemima was produced by Mr J. K. Farnell, Alpha Works, Acton Hill; it was the only side show which I arranged personally and accounted for. It paid very well for several seasons, and I forwarded half the royalty to Mr Warne. I find his receipt for a sum of £9.0.5 Aug 25th 1911. The payments dwindled and in May 31st 1915 Mr Farnell forwarded a notice from the patent agent asking if the patent should be renewed at a cost of £1.5.0. I said it was not worth while; he sent two further payments of a few shillings.

In view of the interruption of the German toy trade I may have made a mistake, possibly the doll is selling again. My feeling was that Farnell had paid fairly, and sufficient, and that the doll was about played out.

I have had correspondence with him about other dolls, but they never came to anything, partly through delays at Bedford St. He is a good man to deal with; but it is a struggling trade; & at present upset with these semi charitable amateur toy makers. I think something should be made of the china.

With kind regards yrs sincerely
Beatrix Heelis

To Fruing Warne Sawrey
Ambleside
June 21. 17

Dear Fruing,

According to the proverb ½ a loaf is better than no bread, (and *such* bread too).

Would it be too shabby to put Appley Dapply into a booklet the size of Miss Moppet?

I find I could scrape together sufficient old drawings to fill one, they would require some inking up.

A few are in square edges, but in a mixed book, I think it would not signify?

The original idea of the book was a large one with *borders*, but it would mean large expensive plates, and more time & eyesight than I see my way to at present.

If you think this worth doing – you might send me either a blank book – or a copy of 'Moppet' with papers pasted over the pictures & I could scribble in outlines that would do for the travellers. I have just remembered with a shock that they used to start about July 1.

Why not type the rhymes & paste in?

I would do several pencil outline [sic] if you will supply pasted up blank books. I'm afraid this sounds very lazy, but you don't know what a scramble I live in; and the old drawings are some of them better than any I could do now, I suppose the larger ones would reduce all right.

I hope things are fairly cheerful with you.

I remain yrs sincerely
Beatrix Heelis

Rough design for a page of Appley Dapply's Nursery Rhymes

To stop the company's debtors foreclosing the Warne family had to raise money quickly. Harold's wife, Alice, was forced to sell everything, and Fruing sold his home in Surbiton and took his family to a small house near Richmond Park.

To Fruing Warne

Sawrey
Ambleside
June 28th 17

Dear Fruing,

Would it trouble you to leave this on your way to the Tube? I have bought things over the counter from a secondhand saddler's – a corner shop at the turn to the tube & to Covent Garden – but I *can't* remember their name.

Poor Alice's household goods are pathetic reading. It was only clouded by the business worries; at least to me it seemed such a very happy home.

Yes certainly I will keep the poor Doll house for you [Winifred's doll's house used for *The Two Bad Mice*], if you can manage to get it packed & sent off. I wish I knew anywhere in London to store it; but I don't like suggesting it to my mother, or writing to her caretakers at Bolton Gdns without her leave & knowledge. I don't think she ever noticed that horrid report in the Times [of Harold's conviction], and one doesn't want to start anyone asking questions gratuitously.

The only other way I can think of, if you find the house too awkward to pack would be to try to lend it to a children's hospital, which would be a kind and useful resting place. [The doll's house was sold to the family who lived next door to the Warnes and it has since been lost.]

I am very glad Milly has had the good luck to let her house, and without a regular sale.

It *is* dreadfully sad for you and Mary, I do feel sorry for you.

But when she gets over the wrench of leaving a pretty home – there will be less housekeeping in a smaller house.

I wonder if any of the old fashioned books of Dalziel engraving, illustrating rather goody goody poems were amongst yours? I rather think they were amongst Millie's, so they will remain with the family – as they ought.

I am very glad things are looking up. I hope Apply Dap [sic] will be in time to be useful, and that it will be as good a season as can be had during this war.

I do think the side lines [merchandise] should be organised against the end of the war – those Germans will never give in, & the British public *will* buy cheap foreign again if they can.

I remain yrs sincerely
Beatrix Heelis

Hay & thunder at present!

Fruing Warne's wife, Mary, suggested an alternative version of PETER RABBIT'S RACE GAME, *which Beatrix had sent to Norman Warne in December 1904 but which had never been made. Mary Warne's game differed in that it involved all the Potter characters rather than just Peter and Mr McGregor.*

Beatrix's husband, Willie, was the youngest of eleven children and there were a number of Heelis nieces and nephews to whom Beatrix could turn for advice on important matters.

To Fruing Warne

Sawrey
Ambleside
Sept 1. 17

Dear Mr Warne,

Mr Watts wants sitting on; I wonder if he really has got money out of all those names in his list.

I have tried both games with the little nieces and feel puzzled what to say. I like mine better because it is a game of skill and more like the book – but Mary's version might easily be the better seller, because it is more elaborate and *more like the games which do sell in toy fairs*; these children say they had played one very like it called "from Private to Field Marshall" [sic]. And I remember one with race horses at Harrods. That is the chief difference of the games; yours is a race between competitors, being separate books. I think the plan is good & beautifully drawn, but it would have been a much better game if it had all been confined to one book, & retained the exciting element of the book – i.e. Mr Macgregor [sic] check mating Peter. But mine is not elaborate enough & has the defect of Mr M. holding up the game. Dice throws combined with a choice of routes would make the best game. But I haven't either time or intellect to work it out, and I really don't much care; I get so very sick of both versions! The smaller niece preferred yours; but then the little wretch learnt how to throw sixes. I think you had better consult a toy firm & do what you like about it.

The pocket hdkercfs [handkerchiefs] is a very good idea. And also the children's stationery. I think simple figures are the best, without much background. Probably you can find enough on the covers, but if you want any picking out from the illustrations & redrawing without backgrounds I shall be glad to do it. I am very glad Appley [sic] is liked. They were better pictures than I have done for a long time.

I have made one rather good clay Peter; & got a modelling spoon since, which I was short of.

The weather is terrible. I am afraid it will mean food tickits [sic].

I will get the games to the post office next week, the girl can't take it with the bicycle.

yrs truly
H B Heelis

To Fruing Warne

Sawrey
Ambleside
Monday Sept 3rd 17

Dear Mr Warne,

I have sent the game back today by registered post – to the office.

I have not sent mine, for on thinking it over I believe yours is the more likely one – and I hope Mary will have a success with it next Christmas, and please consider it *hers* – Let her use any profit for Christmas presents.

With kind regards yrs sincerely
Beatrix Heelis

Pencil sketch for Appley Dapply's Nursery Rhymes

To Fruing Warne

Dear Mr Warne,

I am *very glad* to hear the new book [*Appley Dapply's Nursery Rhymes*, published in October] has caught on.

Yes, decidedly the hdkercfs is a good offer. As regards the pirated china it seems useless to follow them up, if you frighten them sufficiently to stop them, that is as much as is worth doing; and the sooner a reliable firm can be started on an authorised set – the better. I didn't mention it in writing to Grimswades [sic], but from what you tell me about their making china as well as earthenware I should think it would be an advantage to deal with them for all china & model reproductions.

Excuse haste, we have the threshing engine here.

Yours sincerely
H. B. Heelis

I quite think I can make up another book of rhymes for next year from remaining drawings.

I have got the best Peter model & will post him to Grimswades [sic] but I rather fancy they will require *wax* on account of cutting for moulds.

Ernest A. Aris had now published an illustrated booklet called THE
TREASURE SEEKERS *in which there featured a rabbit called Peter. Warne
asked Beatrix to allow them to protest.*

[To Fruing Warne]   Sawrey
                                                           Ambleside
                                                           Nov 10. 17

Dear Mr Warne,
   I most certainly object to entrusting "Peter Rabbit" to that
objectionable (but amusing) little bounder. But I do blame his publishers
more than himself; & if you are communicating with them, please keep
my married name out of it. He is (or was) a photographer's assistant, last
I heard of him he was called up much against his will & Mrs Arris [sic]
was "expecting" their first.
   He doesn't write a bad letter poor man, so artlessly conceited.
   He is not truthful, at least when "Mrs Heelis" asked him what he
would charge for illustrating a booklet in the style of "Jemima
Puddleduck" by "Beatrix Potter" – he had the effrontery to inform the
offended author that he had never seen that classic! If he has not – it is a
strange case of two (dis similar I hope) minds running in one groove. It is
a fact that he sent me a booklet which was rather like a story of mine
which had never been published. I don't know whether he will return
from the wars; but his publishers will find some one else to do dirty
work if he doesn't. He lived in Holloway, but had at one time been
employed in Windermere. I am sure he had no suspicion to the end of
our acquaintance. He seemed pleased with my humble scribbles & even
suggested that possibly we might 'colobrate' after the war.
   He is the sort of person who will do anything for a few pounds; I was
expecting an outbreak of his booklets this winter as he conceitedly said
he was overwhelmed with orders. I got 6 useful illustrations from him,
for a story [*The Oakmen*, never published] which I had made for a little
niece [Nancy Nicholson]. Mr Heelis has said several times I ought to
hurry up with it for fear Arris [sic] gets a story with these drawings out
before me. He never saw any Mss; at all events I can fight him on that
having got his letter selling originals & copyright. It would want
redrawing as the animals are not good.
   I await your parcel with anxious amusement, I'm afraid I don't take
Mr Arris [sic] very seriously. But his publishers are rogues.

                                                      yrs sincerely
                                                      H B Heelis

P.S. I advised your brother to go for the publishers, but to buy Arris [sic] out. For some reason Harold chose to be much offended. But I still think I was right – I took the man's measure correctly at all events, he works altogether for money, he was quite willing to redraw & colour the outlines of an unknown amateur. He is not quite a good enough artist. My feeling was that my eyes were failing & my hands getting stiff but I had still brains & ideas which I might get carried out by an assistant.

Also – do not be vexed with this – I was getting so annoyed & puzzled by H's prevarications – that I really think if the crisis had not come you might have seen a new book by a new author HBH & Arris [sic] – but it most certainly would have steered quite clear of FW.&Co's "Peter Rabbits". The copying is very dishonest on the part of the publishers, & in a less degree of the part of Arris [sic]. I think he is a bounder who doesn't quite understand.

I am sorry for Mrs Arris [sic].

To Fruing Warne   Sawrey
                                                         Nov 13. 17
Dear Mr Warne,
I am puzzled what to say about the book; it is not vulgar; or objectionable apart from "Peter" – I suppose the defence would be that all rabbits *are* called Peter now, which is pretty much the case – either Peter or Brer Rabbit.

It is not so clearly harmful as the books last year which were the size of mine.

I should advise remonstrating with the publisher & ask what else is coming out? perhaps worse.

In haste to catch post

                                                    yrs sincerely
                                                    H B Heelis

I hear from Grimswade's [sic] they have got my little figures – rather broken – she is going to try some smaller ones from that idea of size.

Beatrix had sent some small clay models of her characters to Grimwades Limited, Winton Potteries, Stoke-on-Trent, with a request that they consider manufacturing them.

*After receiving Warne's letter of protest Ernest Aris wrote directly to
Beatrix from the Bacteriological Laboratory in the Military Hospital,
Colchester, where he had been sent to work by the army. He hoped that
Mrs Heelis's earlier knowledge of his work would exonerate him from
any thoughts of plagiarism and he commented, 'I might add that I had
never heard of your book* PETER RABBIT *till now. It is probably one of
your early ones . . . Perhaps you would be kind enough to give me a
signed copy . . . It would be interesting to compare "the two Peters".'*

Draft letter to Ernest A. Aris   Nov 23 [1917]

Dear Sir,

In reply to your letter, I must say that I intirely [sic] agree with my
publishers and leave the matter in their hands. You refer to my knowledge
of your work. My opinion is this. Your work has considerable technical
facility and no originality. After having had several of your booklets
brought to my notice last year, I started a correspondence, in my own
married name, with two objects – to see what you would say – and to
obtain certain figure drawings, which I believed I could make use of.

You have written several statements in letters, which I have kept, and
I have obtained some useful drawings, for the copyright of which I have
paid.

It is quite possible I may some day wish to buy some more. But
without a good deal of explanation, I regret that I am unable to believe
that your statements are truthful. Coincidence has a long arm but there
are limits to coincidences.

I have often wondered whether you had gone to the front – I am glad
that your wife has been spared that anxiety, I hope she got safely through
her troubles.

I remain yrs truly

Fruing Warne drew up an agreement to safeguard Beatrix's interests in the event of the sale of Frederick Warne to another publisher.

To Fruing Warne

Nov 26. 17
Sawrey
Ambleside

Dear Mr Warne

I have taken a little while to read over & consider the agreements, and I am writing to ask whether you and Mr Wingfield [Harry Wingfield was financial adviser to F. Warne & Co.] would be willing to consider an alteration of clause 7 – and a memorandum of the new clause upon the paper relating to the other books.

To the effect that if at any time you – your heirs etc wished to dispose of the property in my books I should have an option of either agreeing to the proposed purchaser or of purchasing back the property at the price which that purchaser had offered?

If there had been a clause of that sort instead of Clause 7 – a very useless clause since the books are a success – I should have felt much less uncomfortable last spring. Your books are all of such an eminently respectable old fashioned nice sort – that it was perhaps unnecessary nervousness – I mean they would have gone to a nice firm had it been unfortunately necessary to make a fresh start. But it might have been very unpleasant to be handed over to strangers with no choice, or power of objecting.

If you do not agree to this in the case of the earlier books, I don't think it is worth while to make the alteration in the case of the last ones. I am content to agree to the fixed rate. I should be still more content to agree, with the altered clause. *You* would never raise the price unduly. An unscrupulous firm might increase their own share, charging say 2/ & pulling down the number sold by so doing. But it is not likely.

I will keep the papers till I hear what you think.

yrs sincerely
H B Heelis

To Fruing Warne

Sawrey
Ambleside
Dec 13th 17

Dear Mr Warne,

Does the word "separately" refer to separate booklets of the series or to the block of PR books as distinct from the rest of your stock? I'm not taking objection; only it is not quite clearly worded.

"If the publisher shall at any time hereafter wish to dispose of the copyrights & properties in the various books covered by the Agt or any of them? the Author shall have the option of purchasing such copyrights & properties at the price offered by the purchaser, or at a sum to be mutually agreed, provided such option does not interfere with the disposal by the P. of his business *as a whole*, etc.

I do not see the slightest objection to the 3 days. I should in fact probably have an inkling if negociations [sic] for sale were going on, I suppose.

Especially as I feel sure that your feelings & mine about any possible purchasing firm would be identical.

Excuse haste, yrs sincerely
H. B. Heelis.

To Fruing Warne

Sawrey
Ambleside
Dec 19. 17

Dear Mr Warne,

I am much obliged for your letter and I return the papers for alteration. The [*Peter Rabbit*] handkercfs are wonderful [*see Plate 13*]! I feel sure they will have a good sale – of course the stitching at that price of 6d each must have limitations, but the boxes alone are enough to sell it.

I only hope the china will turn out as well. I can't post them back today as the P.O is closed, I expect you will want these at the office as samples.

Yours sincerely
H B Heelis

I can't wish anybody a very happy Christmas, but when things are worst they usually mend.

To Tom Harding

Hill Top Farm
Sawrey
Ambleside
Dec 21. 17

Dear Tom Harding,

"Better late than never!" You must have thought no answer was ever coming. When I tidied my desk today – or to be exact when I had a long *un*tidy search for a letter about sheep – I found yours. I get so many letters from boys and girls all over the world – especially from Australia & N. Zealand – that I put them in a bundle & answer if I can. As it happens *I* am partly indoors with a cold today, so I have a little time for writing.

I have a big farm and a very great deal to do, since the war, for my men left me, and now I have an old shepherd, 2 boys & 2 girls, which requires more looking after. Old "Kep" is dead. I have a black white dog, she is called "Fleet" – and I have a pony called Dolly, such a useful good little thing, my husband saw her in a gypsy cart and bought her for me to go about the farm, & she will carry sacks on her back, & cart turnips in the tub or sticks or anything. Then there are 3 horses, Diamond, Lady & Gipsy and I hope next spring Gipsy will have a nice foal. There are 14 cows, a lot of calves & young cattle, and 80 ewes & 40 young sheep & some pigs & 25 hens & 5 ducks, & there *were* 13 turkeys. But I am thankful to say they are killed except the hens. I do everything for the turkeys myself & I have had so much anxiety about foxes – a great big turkey was killed at the next farm last week, & in August a fox took 9 chickens & their mother hen, just outside the garden, I was vexed. The Drake – Mr Puddleduck is very handsome, he is brown fawn, Jemima & Rebeccah are white, Semolina is a comical little Indian runner. She made a very deep nest under a nut bush & sat on 11 eggs. She came running back to the house twice a day & running back to her nest in such a hurry after being fed, she came quacking into the kitchen if not fed at once. But alas – Semolina never turned her eggs. The bottom eggs were always stony cold, only the top ones hatched. I called the two children Tapioca & Sago. We have eaten Sago. It was rather dreadful & the stuffing disagreed with my conscience, but he & his father had begun to fight. I have lots of rabbits, Belgians – Old Benjamin & Cottontail are pets, but I'm afraid we do have rabbit pies of the young ones. Our cat is "Judy", there have been lots of Tom Kittens. Have you seen my new little book Appley Dapply? I must send you a copy if you have not got it. The pictures were done a long time ago – I have little time for painting now, & I have to wear spectacles.

With love & best wishes for Christmas

from your affectionate friend
"Beatrix Potter" (Mrs W Heelis)

Early pencil and pen-and-ink sketch for The Fairy Caravan

To Fruing Warne

Sawrey,
Ambleside
Feb 1. 18

Dear Mr Warne,

I have no wish to sell any of the originals – *personally* when they are no longer wanted by my family or yours I would sooner they went to some library, if thought worth keeping.

I had wondered the other day whether Mr Grimswade [sic] had been heard of. The question of food rather swamps all other plans at present! and you have the added trouble of these cruel raids.

Four of us have got through very nicely on 3½ lbs meat, with the char woman's 3 meals, and a rabbit & a pheasant.

But it does make some work, as the only chance is to do all the cooking oneself, including the hen's, & the sheep dog's! I presume the hens are now to be killed, as they are due to lay again. We are governed by idiots.

Yrs sincerely
H B Heelis

245

*Grimwades had agreed to try their hand at making the small figures
and then they requested permission to manufacture a range of nursery
plates, mugs and porridge bowls with a Potter figure transfer on each, a
suggestion to which Beatrix agreed.*

To Fruing Warne

Sawrey
Ambleside
Feb 26. 18

Dear Mr Warne

I am obliged for the copy of the agreement [with Grimwades], it
seems quite alright.

When I hear which they select, I will send those originals. I have not
had any letter yet from Miss Grimwade.

Do you think this mouse story would do [*Johnny Town-Mouse*]? It
makes pretty pictures, but not an indefinite number as there is not a great
deal of variety. Do you think it would go into an Ap. Daply [sic] size of
book, with rather more letter press? but the same number of colour
plates.

Of course I *am* lazy in wanting the smaller number; but there is the
question of getting them done. And also the expense of production.

A few years ago I amused myself by writing out several of Aesop's
fables, this is one that got rather longer than the others.

I remain yrs sincerely
H B Heelis

To Fruing Warne

Sawrey
Ambleside
March 18. 18

Dear Mr Warne,

Many thanks for your letter, the very handsome cheque & the
convenient dummy – which there is no getting away from. It will have
the same drawback & (the same advantage from a lazy standpoint) as the
Tittlemice which you have cut up for it – a good deal of repetition in
subject. I think it will make a pretty book. I had thought of the objection
to two "Timmys" [the other being *Timmy Tiptoes*]. I don't like Jimmy
Willie – besides the person exists. I am inclined to call it The Tale of
Johnny Town Mouse". "Johnny Town mouse was born in a cupboard,
but TW was born in a garden etc." The frontispiece might represent
Johnny – then we go on with Timmy Willy, & later Johnny is introduced
again.

I am surprised and pleased to hear that the books have done so well
in these bad times, I expect people want a cheerful present for children,

so they buy them. [*Appley Dapply's Nursery Rhymes* had sold out the first edition of 20,000 copies by the end of 1917.]

We are just starting the lambing here, in unusually favourable weather. I expect to get a few days holiday to Appleby at Easter which will freshen up my ideas, but I will try to send cover & front before then. At all events there is a plague of mice! we have pizened [sic] the rats.

Yours sincerely

H B Heelis

P.S. I am putting £500 into War Bonds & spending balance on a farmer's "float". They have gone & changed our market to Ulverston 17 miles off.

To Fruing Warne

Sawrey

Ambleside

May 4. 18

Dear Mr Warne,

I am sending you 6 drawings – in desperation – I simply *cannot* see to put colour in them. The coal cellar [p. 36] which I tried to work up, is the least satisfactory. I am doing them on card as I thought perhaps the life & expression (which I can still get in a sketch) might make up for sketchiness in direct work: rather than work up repeated copies as used to be my habit. The text comes out well; the cutting up I will revise, as I want to arrange a good few designs away from the direct mouse subject. It would have made a good book, with sight & cheerfulness to do it.

When the creditors meeting is fixed will you please send me a notice in good time, to post back to Mr Edwards to represent me? or else direct one straight to him, Messrs. Braikenridge & Edwards 16 Bartletts Buildings Holborn Circus, he will represent me, & strongly favour carrying on, and make a suggestion as to my share of indebtedness which I hope will be helpful. Only I want to say it must be clearly understood that 'H' never meddles again. I bear him no grudge, but I know & remember what a trial he has been, even to me, for many years.

I remain yrs sincerely

HB Heelis

I will post back the revise & some more drawings as soon as I can. Hope to finish *re* sowing turnips today! I couldn't see to draw any more, if no such thing as turnip fly existed.

To Fruing Warne

Sawrey,
Ambleside
May 6. 18

Dear Mr Warne

I can quite see that it is necessary to raise the price to 2/-, and I am sorry if any remark of mine has put you to loss or inconvenience by hesitating to alter the price – I was not thinking of *you* at all – only of strangers and in normal times; which seem very far off still.

I doubt whether certain class of things will ever be "cheap" again – or "reasonable"; for doubtless there will be cheap trash.

I do feel ashamed of my delay over the book, I have seemed so rushed lately, probably I will get more time to sit down after this week. I have just come in after a rough two hours search for some sheep & lambs with a boy – the old man being poorly. We got them; so that is done with.

They are beggars to ramble, these hill sheep. I got 2 back from Coniston last winter that were making tracks for Scawfell [sic] where they were born.

Somehow when one is up to the eyes in work with real live animals it makes one despise paper-book-animals – but I mustn't say that to my publisher!

The kitchen boiler has also collapsed & the plumber enlisted – such is life.

Yrs truly
H B Heelis

The pocket hdcfs seemed to me to be unprofitably cheap also. I am obliged for correspondence.

Detail from a page of animal pencil sketches

As well as passing on a request from a Swiss publisher for a German-language edition of her books, Fruing Warne asked Beatrix if she could come to London herself to discuss the reconstruction of the company.

To Fruing Warne

Sawrey
Ambleside
May 24. 18

Dear Mr Warne,

I received your letter this morning; I should be suspicious too about a German edition – though probably it is bona fide for *Switzerland*. They will have money to spend on picture books.

I was disappointed to gather that there is something causing you uneasiness, coming on the top of the very favourable trustee's report, received on Monday.

Surely upon that report the business *is* working itself round.

It is a very awkward time to leave home, can I not vote by proxy or letter? I personally am in no hurry for any dividend upon the arrears.

I hope you won't be killed by overwork; that seems to me to be the only argument in favour of amalgamation or taking over to another firm. I had hoped things were gradually mending, one can't hope for any sudden great improvement while this war lasts.

I am trying to get on with the book, I am ashamed to be so slow, & alas so bad to see colours now.

I remain yrs sincerely
H B Heelis

To Fruing Warne

Sawrey
June 12. 18

Dear Mr Warne,

I am sorry for the delay in sending these back; I will send the proofs too. J. T. Mouse. please alter which ever way will be least trouble. It does not look wrong either way. The proofs are very good, and I am pleased that they have printed up. Perhaps a little yellow, but that is better than too red, or too blue.

Mr Stokoe's touching up is perplexing. The *plates* dishes glasses etc I am most pleased with & obliged to him! also edges of vignettes – but he (and perhaps you) confuse *stippling* & colour. I doubt if he has added any *colour* (except a mauve carpet which I am spring cleaning); the worst of over stippling it generally processes muddy, whereas direct work can generally be trusted to print up. I am certain the skirting board mouse would have done so. I am keeping those two back, to put in some stronger touches which have got smoothed out. I had better mark on what I would like to have touched up, don't let him think I am otherwise than obliged for his help.

I remain yrs sincerely
H B Heelis

To Fruing Warne

Sawrey
Ambleside
July 2. 18

Dear Mr Warne,

The proof is satisfactory; there is only one misprint I can find "horses'" instead of "horse's" on p 15 [13]. I over looked it first time, it does not much matter.

I know you wanted the book finished by end of June; if you had been indignant I should not have been surprised.

I have been going through a hard time lately, first anxiety about Mr Heelis's [call-up] papers (fortunately grade 3), then my only brother died suddenly in Scotland at his farm after a few hours illness. What with the shock, the difficulty of getting to the funeral & back, & the number of letters I have had to write, since neither his widow nor my mother seemed able to write them – I am only just getting straight. On top of this we have had 2 boys ill with measles just when beginning hay so things have been a pretty muddle.

I cannot choose but turn out this afternoon to see if it is fit to cart, I will try to catch a "Timmy Willie", they chopped up a good many mouse nests with the machine.

I remain yrs sincerely
H B Heelis

I will try to post, some drawings with the proof tomorrow.

I got fitted with spectacles at Carlisle, that was something!

Detail from pencil studies

Hardwicke Rawnsley, now living in Grasmere and retired from Crosthwaite, was still chaplain to the King and Canon of Carlisle. On 1 June 1918 he had married an old family friend, Miss Eleanor Simpson.

Beatrix's brother, Bertram, had died of a cerebral haemorrhage in June at the age of forty-six.

To Canon Hardwicke Rawnsley

Sawrey
Ambleside
Sept 13. 18

Dear Canon Rawnsley

I am writing to express our sympathy with Mrs Rawnsley and you in your loss. These sudden calls are very merciful, but a shock. And hard to realize; I don't think I yet realize that Bertram is gone – in his prime, and in his usefulness.

He had such a fine farm; and although his nature – sensitive and like his father's – and patriotic & upright to a rare degree – made him feel the war very keenly – I do think he found true happiness in hard useful manual work. It is good to remember how much more cheerful & contented he had seemed towards the last. He had not painted lately, but he hoped & intended to take it up again "after the war". He is buried like the Grasmere folks in the bend of a stream – a flowery graveyard with a ruined ivy grown church and graves of the covenanters on the banks of Ale Water.

So your walk (& *Wms*) came to nought? As might have been expected by those who have had dealing with that party. Personally I employ George Gatey junior in my quarrels with Mr –. There was an occasion, of which I do not wish to be reminded, when the other party was employing W.H. Heelis & Son. I am afraid I was not very well pleased that Saturday you were over; but no more need be said!

Please tell Mrs Rawnsley that I wired before hearing the sad news, or should have wired differently.

Our corn is still out, alas; and if we had not hoped to be in it, there would still have been the impediment of relays of little nieces. The present ones are very lively.

I remain yrs sincerely
Beatrix Heelis

THE TALE OF JOHNNY TOWN-MOUSE *was to be published in December and Beatrix sent one of her early copies to Annie Moore, to whose children she had sent picture letters for so many years. This is the only known letter that survives from Beatrix to her last governess.*

To Mrs Anne Moore

Sawrey
Nov 26 18

Dear Mrs Moore

I *was* so glad to hear Eric is safe & all of you fairly thriving – except I am afraid yourself. You are over worked, that is all about it. So am I, but it is more of it out of doors, & healthy work. You say I didn't mention myself, I have kept very well this summer (I sometimes get pulled down with an attack of diarrhoea which this village experiences nearly every summer) I have managed to get a bit fatter. I'm afraid you are probably skin & bones for you were very thin last time I saw you.

I shall not have a turkey for you this Christmas but will send a pair of good sized cockerels. Turkeys were unlucky, only one pullet reared, after a chapter of accidents, ending with rats!

If you send me an almanac would you get one with at least 2 months on a side! This is very candid, but your last though very sweet was so diffuse & so sewed up with ribbons that the pages did *not* get turned regularly!!

Much love from yrs aff
H B Heelis

I had an awful scramble to do this little book. Old Dimond [sic] our farm horse is my favourite of the pictures [*see Plate 15*].

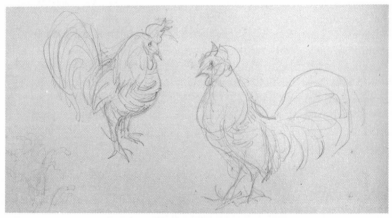

Pencil sketches for The Fairy Caravan

Beatrix offered to send a copy of JOHNNY TOWN-MOUSE *to Victorine Ballon, whose French translations of five of the earlier stories had been accepted and paid for – but never published – in 1912. Beatrix's letter brought a reply from Mlle. Ballon with the sad account of how all her books, including those by Beatrix (and the proofs of the translations), had been lost in the fire that resulted from the bombardment of Lille in October 1914. In 1916 she had been sent by 'the Boches' to work in Valenciennes, where she had been left to run the schools' inspectorate alone when her colleague was imprisoned and then sent to Germany for refusing to shake hands with a German officer. Now the war was over, Victorine Ballon was trying to restore her children's book collection and she was also anxious to find out the fate of her translations.*

To Fruing Warne

Sawrey
Ambleside
Dec 27. 18

Dear Mr Warne,

Many thanks for your kind letter and I heartily return your good wishes for the coming year. I had the printed statement and we thought it very satisfactory. I have been doing a little drawing to get my hand in, and I hope soon to send you a rough scheme for a new book. There exists also a nearly complete set of *old* designs for another rhyme book; but I gather from your remarks that it had better be kept in reserve, either for a second string, or for some season when I find myself unable to do a new book.

I received this most interesting letter from Mlle Ballon on Christmas Day = 6 days post. I am writing her at *Lille*, but I can't send her any books, being out of copies. (I should like some day to send her a complete set in recognition of her pluck!)

Perhaps you will forward to her what she requires now = Peter, Benjamin, Tiggy, Jemima, & the new mouse – also the proofs in French.

She seems to want her own written translations also – have you got them? I rather hope you *have*; as otherwise the later part of poupette is lost [*Poupette à L'Epingle – Mrs. Tiggy-Winkle*].

I have by me in my own handwriting copies of "Jeannot Lapin = B.B." La Famille Flopsaut" "Sophie Canétang" (very good).

It sounds as if the post might be rather unreliable in France.

I don't seem to have copied "poupette".

Her recollection is that no arrangement was made as to what she should receive, perhaps you could kindly approach this matter? She speaks of "works ready to be published", I don't know whether she is an authoress, and means "books"; or whether they were official reports drawn up by her, as inspector of schools.

If you have not Sophie Canétang [*Jemima Puddle-Duck*] I will copy it again, you would not want to print only rabbit books.

I think you would be able to sell a good many in England as French "readers" for children.

I should like to have Mlle Ballon's letter back, when you have done with it.

There are one or two "side show" suggestions I will write about another time. Evidently everything is held up still but as soon as makers of toys & smallware get to work it will be a time to move, before the Germans wire in. They will try to, sure.

With all good wishes yrs sincerely
H B Heelis

To Fruing Warne

Sawrey
Ambleside
Feb 28. 19

Dear Mr Warne

I am much obliged for the statement and cheque – you have indeed done well under trying circumstances – to judge by the difficulties in the country, I can't imagine how you "carry on" at all.

I am glad the new book [*Johnny Town-Mouse*] has done so well. I should think from the comparative figures the British infant is at length becoming satiated (or is it only provided with?) – "Peter Rabbit" – several of the others are in front of it this time.

I can't remember Tom Kitten's painting book? Was it the old book divided into two?

I have been thinking out a new book, nothing finished, as the light etc is all wrong for summer pictures, but I will send you a rough plan soon.

Have you ever thought of stencil plates? I had a nice letter from a small boy, he sent me a specimen, a sort of Japanese design stamped out of stiff shiny paper. I quite think Peter Rabbit could be adapted very well. Shall I draw a few? If stencil cutters exist now.

Things seem a long time settling down; people are in no hurry to work, that is the fact.

The influenza is very bad, we have escaped so far. I hope you will have another good season, and not too much worry.

I wish Grimwades would hurry up, if they would only get out samples it would be some gain.

With many thanks & kind regards   yrs sincerely
H B Heelis

No use talking to me about figures, I cannot do the simplest sum right.

Eight-year-old Neville Rowson and his sister Eileen, who was fourteen, had sent Beatrix decorated letters from Cheshire telling her how much they enjoyed her books.

To Neville Rowson   Hill Top Farm
                                                     March 6. 19

Dear Neville Rowson,

I must find time to thank you for your dear little letter – do you know I had 3 by that post? I'm afraid I don't find time to answer them all – I have so much to do – for I have a big farm and not so much help as before the war. I have cows and sheep and horses, and poultry – I look after the poultry & rabbits and pony and my own particular pet pig. She is called Sally, she follows me about the farm like a dog, through gates and along the road, and if she gets left behind, I call Sally! Sally! and she gallops. I am very fond of rabbits. I have big brown Belgian rabbits, and silver gray; and one rabbit is chocolate colour. I rather like spiders too, they are useful catching flies. I won't have them brushed away in summer, only when we do the spring whitewashing we have to sweep down their webs.

I am glad you saw the bunny family, popping in and out of their hole. Did you ever grunt to them?! Try saying umph! umph! in a very small voice; sometimes I have coaxed wild rabbits to answer me.

                              With love from yr aff friend
                                                  "Beatrix Potter"

To Eileen Rowson   Hill Top Farm
                                                     March 6. 19

My dear Eileen Rowson,

How nicely you have copied the little animals – (I was going to say anim*u*les, like my niece Nancy – bad habits are catching!) – I thought for a minute that the group was printed. My publishers had a plan to bring out a set of paper & envelopes for children; but everything has been delayed & thrown out of order by the war – dolls, china and all. You do seem to understand and enjoy the books!

Yes! it was the same policeman, a nasty German doll! The real Mrs Tiggy was a dear. I caught her & her brother Pricklepin when they were tiny little things; I let the little boy hedgehog run away in the autumn, but Mrs Tig lived in the house a long time. She was not a bit prickly with me, she used to lay her prickles flat back to be stroked. I seem able to tame any sort of animal; it is sometimes rather awkward on a farm, we cannot keep them out of the house, especially the Puddleducks, & turkeys. I am always afraid Sarah will get upstairs someday, she got into the dining room one day & nearly smashed the window with running her nose against it, while we were turning her out. She hates stopping in the pig stye! Chippy Hackee belonged to a cousin, I drew the bear at the Zoo [characters from *Timmy Tiptoes*] – now no more.

love from yr aff friend
Beatrix Potter

Detail from rough pencil studies

At last Warne's liabilities following the débâcle in 1917 had been sorted out and they were now offering their creditors: '13/- in the £, 4/6 of which will be in cash, 4/6 in Second Debentures @ 5¼%, and 4/- in Fully Paid Shares.' Beatrix was a major creditor and Fruing was anxious to have her approval of the offer. Her answer was written on two small and torn half-sheets of paper.

To Fruing Warne   Sawrey – Ambleside
                                                       April 10th 19

Dear Mr Warne,

   I have sent on the papers already, I think it seems a very reasonable arrangement – only hope it does not entail too much worry & work upon *you*. There is one question I might ask – (rather with reference to the *divd.*) are you wanting shares taken up by friends or not? I quite understand that part of the indebtedness to me will be paid in allotted shares, I was wondering if I should apply for any more.

   Excuse extreme famine of paper!

yrs sincerely
Beatrix Heelis

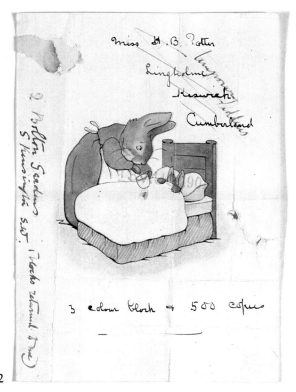

1 *Stereum hirsutum*, 5 January 1893 (see p. 18)

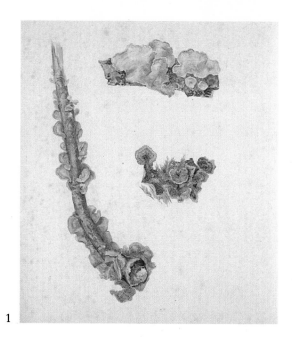

2 Proof of the frontispiece for the privately printed *The Tale of Peter Rabbit* (see p. 55)

3

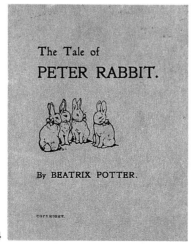

4

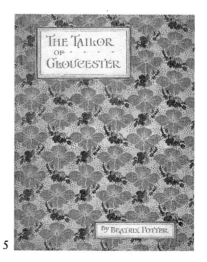

5

6

3 Endpaper for
*The Tale of
Squirrel Nutkin*
(see p. 72)

4 Cover of the
privately printed
*The Tale of Peter
Rabbit* (see p. 56)

5 De luxe edition
of *The Tailor of
Gloucester* (see
p. 74)

6 Wash and pencil
sketch inscribed
(*front*) 'Nov. 16
'09', (*verso*) 'Monk
Coniston Moor
[7.00 morn.] HB
Potter' (see p. 171)

7 Design for
Frederick Warne
1904–5 catalogue
cover (see p. 98)

7

8

8 Page 29 [23] of *The Story of A Fierce Bad Rabbit* (see p. 145)

9

9 Two of Beatrix's anti Free Trade posters (see p. 174)

10 Original
illustration for page
14 [12] of *The Tale of
The Flopsy Bunnies*
(see p. 206)

10

11

11 Endpaper for *The Tale of Mr. Tod* (see p. 200)

12

12 Study for the frontispiece of
Kitty-in-Boots (see p. 216)

13

13 Early *Peter Rabbit* merchandise (see p. 243)

14

14 Page 29 [23] of
*Appley Dapply's Nursery
Rhymes* (see p. 263)

15 Page 14 [12] of *The
Tale of Johnny Town-
Mouse* (see p. 252)

15

16 Illustration from the privately printed *The Tailor of Gloucester* (see p. 274)

16

17 The dust jacket for *Sister Anne* (see p. 352)

17

For many years Beatrix had, for her own amusement, illustrated a number of Aesop's FABLES, and she had also tried her hand at retelling them (JOHNNY TOWN-MOUSE had its origin in 'The Town Mouse and the Country Mouse'). Now she sent to Warne THE TALE OF JENNY CROW (or THE FOX AND CROW), a story that combined elements of at least five of the fables, saying 'I hope very much this may find favour? As I have (perhaps rashly!) started some of the pictures. Also crow shooting starts on Saturday so I have hopes of both models & pies.'

Fruing Warne was disappointed. He thought the story too confused and derivative: 'It is not Miss Potter, it is Aesop.' What he wanted to publish next was the 'very brilliant little MS in that Pigeon story'. Although Beatrix was fond of THE FAITHFUL DOVE she did not like the thought of spending time on the illustrations, 'I do bar the rather namby pamby pigeons for this season'. Fruing sensed trouble and suggested that he might visit Beatrix in Sawrey at the weekend 'to discuss matters'.

To Fruing Warne

Sawrey
Ambleside
May 29.19

Dear Mr. Warne,

Your letter reached me this morning & as it was dated 29th I thought it best to wire. We shall be away on Sunday next at my mother's [Mrs Potter was now living at Lindeth Howe, Windermere] & the next weekend – Whitweek end – away too.

I have no objection whatever to discussing business on a Sunday, but I can't help feeling that in this case it is no good and some risk of irritation! You do not realize that I have become more – rather than less obstinate as I grow older; and that you have no lever to make use of with me; beyond sympathy with you and the old firm, nothing else would induce me to go on at all. You see I am not short of money. I never have cared tuppence either for popularity or for the modern child; they are pampered & spoilt with too many toys & books. And when you infer that my originality is more precious than old Aesop's you *do* put your foot in it!

I'm not at all sure after this indecision & interruption that I could get Jenny Crow finished this year at all.

Don't you think this time as a stop gap you had better consider the other rhyme book like Ap. Dap? though also hoary favourites?

I will try & do you the pigeons some day, but this season I can't & *won't*; and at any time I fear it does not go well in the set, as the story is more in quantity than the picture subjects – it runs to no variety for a number of pictures; especially as I could not possibly "dress up" the pigeons. Some creatures lend themselves to "dressing up" (=clothes) but birds don't. . .

What are the other business matters? reduction of interest!? Out with it!

The thing that principally concerns & interests me at present is a bad drought, the crops are burnt up like August.

I am sorry to be so little encouraging but it is too far to come for no purpose but arguments without success.

I should have been drawing today but this has put me off; also the heat – very sticky.

yrs sincerely
H B Heelis

Char à banc descending high road opposite. Driver boy, "That's 'er 'ouse" – passengers "Hah? 'oo's?" (explanation by Tom), refreshing ignorance of P.R & on part of cargo who have obviously never read that book. Such is fame.

To Fruing Warne

Sawrey
Ambleside.
August 5th 19

Dear Mr Warne,

I am sending you three drawings, but whether they are any good or when the book can be finished I don't know – I can see nothing after staring at them for a bit.

I also send an idea for the cover, though I fear you did not take to the title of The Birds and Mr Tod [the new title for *Jenny Crow*]? The whole thing is rather a mess! I am not willing to get stronger glasses after only one year's wear. The oculist said there was nothing wrong with my eyes, beyond 53 years of rather unmerciful usage. They will last my time, I hope; but you must *not* count on my going on doing books of coloured illustrations. Find someone else.

I can't get any reply from Miss Grimwade, & the letter has not come back, last time she wrote she was having to do housework & nursing her mother, but that does not apply to the tea service though it prevented her from going on modelling figures.

I did part of the Jenny Crow drawings but when I got them out again they looked a bad colour.

I am very sorry not to have got more done, it is not for want of being worried with the feeling of being behindhand – if that is any satisfaction or expiation.

yrs sincerely
Beatrix Heelis

[To Fruing Warne]   · Sawrey
                                                       Ambleside
                                                       Nov. 3rd. 19

Dear Mr Warne,

I have not been ill. My charwoman's family have had measles, in relays; if I have neglected correspondence – it has not been through idleness! It is absolutely hopeless & impossible to finish books in summer. I will try and get one done by next spring. But I rather doubt the policy of going on with this one; I *did* begin it earlier than usual, but was put out of my course by your evidently not caring about it – otherwise I was in full swing to finish it last May – and even now I note you are asking for the *title* – I called it the "Tale of the Birds & Mr Tod" – was that unsatisfying? I think you had better send me back the three or four drawings which I forwarded in July, and when I see them altogether, I can consider what it looks like – I hardly remember which I have done.

With regard to Grimwades, you mentioned in an earlier letter that they could have done earthenware, but were unable to obtain some of the ingredients for china – would it not be worth while to let them try earthen ware first? I should think the same transfer-print engravings would answer for both – I mean to say they could do china tea sets afterwards, if they had started with earthenware mugs.

I had the enclosed correspondence about a Spanish translation, I told the lady I thought it was rather a hopeless time for getting things printed (What came of the French?) Her second letter shows more business aptitude than most of ones unknown correspondents; she seems to have considered out the matter of getting on to the market – "Harrods" describe themselves as "London & Buenos Aires" so they evidently have a branch there; it might be worth while to consult them?

We have all the crops in except turnips; and the pigs to kill; so things will be a little easier presently; provided I do not catch the measles myself. I am glad you are having a good season – apart from my misdeeds – which you will have to put up with sooner or later – for you don't suppose I shall be able to continue these d . . . d little books when I am dead and buried!! I am utterly tired of doing them, and my eyes are wearing out. I will try to do you one or two more for the good of the old firm; but it is quite time I had rest from them. Especially as there is still other work that I should like to finish for my own pleasure.

   I remain with kind regards and very moderate apologies yrs sincerely

                                                       Beatrix Heelis

Mary Isabel Warren, daughter of Sir Benjamin Brodie Bt, was the wife of Sir Thomas Herbert Warren. He was president of Magdalen College, Oxford and author of two volumes of verse.

To Lady Mary Isabel Warren   Sawrey
                                              Ambleside
                                              Dec 23rd 19

Dear Lady Warren –

Will you accept this original edition of the old Tailor of Gloucester – as I was told – in a very kind and too flattering letter – that you are fond of the little book?

It has always been my own favourite; and had the story fallen into more experienced hands I believe the result might have justified the praise of Mr John Masefield. I used to stay with some cousins on the edge of the Cotswolds, overlooking the vale of Severn; they told me the story of the tailor; and I added the mice & the old fashioned coats.

I have one or two other copies left – I wonder if Mr Masefield would accept one? I know I have in my mother's house in London a packet.

I would like to do two or three more stories like that, before my eyes give out completely – but it is the penalty of successful large sales that the publishers have plagued me to do "pot boilers" till I am sick of it!

The Tailor never caught on like the others, but he is far the best.

With kind regards & best wishes for Christmas to you & Sir Herbert Warren,

believe me yrs sincerely
Beatrix Heelis

Pencil study for The Tailor of Gloucester

To Fruing Warne
Sawrey
Ambleside
March 11. 20

Dear Mr Warne,

Thank you very much for the statement and cheque, you have had a very encouraging successful year, I am very glad indeed that the old firm is doing so well and righting itself.

I had a notice about stock that could be paid off; but unless it were going to be some advantage to you personally – I had no desire to part with any.

My preoccupation at present is a cold; I suppose I must make an effort to do a book this year; but it is very uphill work to do this Peter Rabbit pattern, there are too many plates – it is not the actual amount of work altogether – not chiefly even – it is the monotony of turning out 28 pictures of one subject.

I sent back to USA a little rhyme about a kitten, I wondered afterwards whether I did right to return it to the authoress, it was quite out of my line, but rather pretty.

Is the china ever coming out?

Enclosed is out of a Harrods catalogue I believe.

It is wonderful how the sales keep up; the figures are very interesting.
I remain with kind regards yrs sincerely
Beatrix Heelis

To Fruing Warne
Sawrey
Ambleside
May 7. 20

Dear Mr Warne

The Peter Rabbit piracy is indeed somewhat impudent [*Peter Rabbit Fold-A-Way Edition*, Reilly & Lee Co., Chicago, April 1920]; it is not very well done either, I seem to remember toy books to cut out when I was a child, but I think they were landscapes upon which I gummed cut out animals, with a bent foot-support.

I certainly should find it *easier* to do a Patty pan sized book – though I agree with the public, for once, in not thinking the pattern so attractive. Would you send me a dummy.

I'm afraid the only idea that has come to me yet is another cat, but I could introduce some other animals to make variety. I can't imagine how I am to find time to do it, but I suppose I must try.

I got out the half finished last year's book [*The Tale of the Birds and Mr Tod*] to look at; but alas I found such a very unenthusiastic letter put away with it . . . . I put all back in the wrapper.

We are nearly flooded out with endless rain – but the corn is sown, after a fashion.

I am keeping the fold book till I hear you want it back.

yrs sincerely
Beatrix Heelis

To Fruing Warne

Sawrey
Ambleside
June 12. 20

Dear Mr Warne

I think it is only honest to tell you that book is not getting on yet. The country is looking beautiful enough to give me inspiration; but I seem as if I can't screw it out, and my eyes are always tired. I am afraid you will be much vexed.

yrs sincerely
Beatrix Heelis

Fruing replied that he was disappointed but quite understood, 'Let it come as soon as you can, when you feel the inspiration.' The book was never finished.

Early study for Aesop's The Fox and Crow

The new firm of Frederick Warne & Company Limited had been registered on 25 May 1919 and just over a year later, on 25 August 1920, Harry Wingfield was appointed as Chairman and Fruing Warne as Managing Director. Fruing was about to visit the American branch of the firm in New York and he was hoping to be able to tell them there would be 'a new Potter' for 1921.

He also sent on to Beatrix a letter from The Gibson Dancing Academy requesting permission for their child pupils to give a single charity performance dressed as characters from the little books.

To Fruing Warne

Sawrey
Ambleside
Oct 12. 20

Dear Mr. Warne,

I had this perplexing letter forwarded by you, I have written to the lady to say I live so much out of the world I am unable to express any opinion on the matter. I know nothing about the people.

The samples of modern child that emerges from the hotels are positively indecent. I cannot bring myself to take the slightest interest in them. Perhaps it might be good for them to be dressed in skins, and act a book so hopelessly old fashioned as Peter Rabbit!

I have no book in hand alas! But it seems a pity, as several people have remarked, that some of my old miscellaneous drawings cannot be published. I always wanted Cecily Parsley's Nursery Rhymes as a companion volume to Appley [sic] Dapply – was she too much a failure to warrant it?

What became of the original Ap Ds? I have never heard of them since they went to America. And I considered the hedgehog was about the best drawing I ever made [*see Plate 14*]. Also J. T. Mouse never returned, did you ever get them back from the States?

Remember me to Mr Ledbetter [sic], I once met him & his wife at Bedford St. and I hope you have a successful & safe journey.

The crops are getting in well.

I will have a rummage in my portfolios. But they only cause me wonder, how I ever drew so much and well, while I could see.

I remain yrs sincerely
Beatrix Heelis

No lady at the turn of the century would venture outside without an elaborate and sizeable hat. The hats for the residents of Bolton Gardens had been delivered by two small children, Ivy and Jack Hunt, from their mother's millinery shop in Sloane Square, and Beatrix had come to know the children well. Mrs Hunt died when Ivy was only nine but Beatrix had kept in touch with the child through her Aunt Jessie. Ivy was now growing up and had recently followed her sister to Canada.

To Miss Wyatt

Sawrey
Ambleside
Nov. 15. 20

Dear Miss Wyatt,

I am ashamed of my delays in answering your kind letter about Ivy Hunt. I had one from the girl, written soon after her arrival in Galt – a happy letter – I do hope that she settles there. I am afraid she has given you a great deal of trouble, but you have the reward of having done of great kindness. And I do hope that the Canadian doctor is right, and that she will settle there and grow strong and sensible.

When I remember her poor pretty mother – dying as consumptives mercifully *do* die – quite cheerfully, and confident that someone would – under providence – look after her little orphans, it seems as though her touching faith has been justified.

I am afraid I have been able to do very little to help.

I wonder what you lent her? Will you let me enclose this £5 note; if the child is ever able to return the money to you, so much the better for her self respect and independence, and I am sure you would find some use for it in some other act of kindness.

I am sorry again I have no new little book; my eyes have failed very much; and somehow since the war I have never felt as if I could concentrate my attention on drawing, there is a great deal of work in the illustrations. It is much easier for me to attend to real live pigs & rabbits; and after all I have done about 30 books, so I have earned a holiday.

I have been much amused with two large litters of little pigs which I have been rearing this autumn.

With kind regards yrs sincerely
Beatrix Heelis
"Beatrix Potter"

To Mr Spedding Byers

Sawrey
Nov. 17. 20

Dear Mr Byers,

I have carefully considered your application for land to make a bowling green. You suggested a site in Crook Meadow; or another upon the southern side of the road, coming over the hill. I have never approved the taking of productive agricultural land for purposes of recreation; and two seasons of scarcity make the suggestion particularly ill timed. The land on the southern side is less useful; but the situation has no attraction for a bowling green. The game is not a warm game like football; it should be played in a sheltered garden amongst pleasant surroundings. Either site, enclosed in new railings, would be an eye sore. A bowling green is always more or less derelict in winter; and a good many public recreation grounds become untidy and desolate when the novelty wears off. However; there is no occasion to discuss that; as I am writing to tell you that I am not disposed to let any land for the purpose.

I remain yrs truly
H B Heelis

P.S. I may mention that Mr Heelis & I have sometimes in conversation discussed the suitability of the lower end of the Hill Top grass flat for a bowling green. It is no new idea. The stress of more useful work – and some knowledge of the labour of keeping a lawn in order – have hitherto prevented me from considering the subject very seriously. If I laid out a green there, I would willingly permit villagers, and resident summer visitors to play upon it. The space is not quite 40 yards wide; but the size is fair. It is sheltered and sunny; and above all – it has the advantage of being already enclosed in a garden. If the game proved to be a passing fancy, the green would revert to orchard grass. If on the other hand the bowling green proved to be a popular and permanent attraction, it would be easy to divide it from the Hill Top end of the grass flat by continuing a trellis and planting shrubs. I am inclined to consider the matter further, and discuss it with one or two people. It must be clearly understood that if I made a green, and permitted the green to be used, I should do so for the general advantage and enjoyment – not for the benefit of any one section of the community.

I remain yrs truly
H. B. Heelis

To Miss Wyatt
Sawrey
Ambleside
Nov. 27. 20

Dear Miss Wyatt,

Thank you so much for the print – a very good, broadly handled, sketch of a magnificent view. It has made me read again Wordsworth's sonnet "Earth has not anything to show more fair".

That is curious about the little nephew's mouse (by the way a sensibly informed child!)

I once had a mouse which must have been cross bred, but I can't remember where I got it. It was all brown except a white mark down its face. It was ferociously tame. I used to let it run about in the evenings & when I wanted to catch it I flapped a pocket handkcf. in the middle of the room – or rooms – when it would come out & fight, leaping at the hdcf.

I think I remember it was that same mouse which got into trouble with the authorities by biting out a circular hole in a sheet on my bed! I had many mouse friends in my youth. I was always catching & taming mice – the common wild ones are far more intelligent & amusing than the fancy variety. But strange to say mine never bred, in spite of having much liberty & comfortable nest boxes. White mice are too prolific; but "Hunca Munca" firmly refused to have any family. I have had several female brown mice but never a nest of young ones from tamed brown parents.

Thank you for the print.

Yrs sincerely
Beatrix Heelis

Fruing Warne meticulously forwarded to Beatrix all requests for interviews, and invitations to speak or to attend performances of her work. Much against personal publicity, Beatrix always refused.

To Fruing Warne
Sawrey
Ambleside
Jan 12. 21

Dear Mr Warne,

No thanks! The last thing you forwarded was a request for my photograph for the Sketch. I hope the performance will help a worthy object; but it ain't in my line to attend such functions.

We had a very jolly party last Saturday, commencing with infants at 2.30 and advancing through relays of uproar & refreshments to farm servants and dancing till 11; followed by the sweep! followed by influenza & headaches. It is much about, but only a mild type.

I had an idea the other day suggested by those beautiful illustrations of Mr Thorburn's [*British Birds* by Archibald Thorburn, published 1915–16]. Suppose I pulled the "Doves" [*The Faithful Dove*] together into workable shape – *not* Peter Rabbit shape – believe me it is *too much pigeon*, over & over, to make 28 illustrations. Suppose you could commission him to make & sell to you with copyright – about 4 pictures of doves in appropriate positions – I might screw out a half dozen more. If his name appeared with mine on the title page I should be proud to see it there.

You have got to understand sooner or later that my eyes are nothing like they used to be, and that persistent worrying me to strain them is not very kind. You cannot have forgotten your dear old Mother's pathetic "Can't see? can't see?" It is useless trying to have drawings of mine patched up by the worthy Mr Stokoe because he hasn't got it in him. The scamp Arris [sic] had! One thing about doves; no birds look well in clothes.

With best wishes for 1921.

yrs sincerely
Beatrix Heelis

portrait of the authoress not for publication in the "Sketch.

To Fruing Warne

Sawrey
Ambleside
March 4th 21

Dear Mr Warne

I must apologize for not answering sooner. I thought I ought to send the receipt by return and I expected to have time to answer next post; but have missed two. The amount is satisfactory, and the figures interesting. It looks as though the Americans have more money to spend, which is what one might expect. The American sales seem to maintain their level, I mean. Also the middle class who buy my books are hardest hit. I am glad there is prospect of the china; my information from local shops agreed that the firm were enterprising business people, in good trade; but for *earthen*-ware, rather than china.

I am sorry to tell you I have jibbed at the pigeons. I have never been good at birds; and whatever you say – I cannot see them in clothes – the story is sentimental, not comic. I did think at the time, that with the example of a good painter of birds, I might have done part – but probably you were right in saying Mr Thorburn would be too busy, and too big. I have got fresh glasses and can read better, but my eyes are not true for colours.

I would be glad if you would send me back the original drawings of J. Townmouse and of Apply [sic] Dapply – the latest and earliest. I want to compare them. I got hold of a copy of J. Tmouse lately, and it was so *atrocious*. I want to know how much of it is deterioration of skill and eyesight, and how much is bad printing! There is no satisfaction in blinding oneself to produce a book as bad as that.

I think I could probably make something out from my old drawings. But the ones I like best were done in imitation of Caldecott without stippling. I think that stippling up of drawings has been the mischief with my painting.

I am glad you take a cheerful view of trade in general; and delighted to hear that the old firm FW&Co is doing well, with a new lease of life. There is not much unemployment about here, but things have been very bad at Barrow; and there are Irish there, which is a certain amount of risk according to the police. We have kept well, except slight influenza at the New year.

With thanks and apologies!

yrs sincerely
H B Heelis

My stock of books is done.

To Fruing Warne

Sawrey
Ambleside
May 23. 21

Dear Mr Warne

Thank you very much for the French copies, especially "Jeannot" [*Jeannot Lapin - Benjamin Bunny*]. I had a sample of Peter in French, and in Dutch – no that was Jemima – some years ago you printed a few. I should think they ought to be a success. Benjamin is very comical and refreshing to the author, in another language.

It must be a fine sight to see London without smoke. I wonder how people manage, when there are no trees & sticks to pull at. It does not affect us here, with unlimited firewood. [The miners' strike (over pay) lasted from 1 April to 14 June.]

We have hot days & cold nights, but crops and fruit promise well so far, as there are thunder showers between times.

I have quite got over the influenza many thanks, but no better able to see for fine work; and large pictures are no easier I can assure you, I never was good at them. Are there no young ones coming on, who can take up the work?

I remain with kind regards yrs sincerely
Beatrix Heelis

To Fruing Warne

Sawrey
Ambleside
June 17th 21

Dear Mr Warne,

I should be very glad if the books would give pleasure to the blind children, as they have already done to the deaf & dumb. Will there be any attempt to draw an embossed figure? – say Peter running from Mr McGregor? I have seen a good deal of braille work, I do not think it would be difficult. I am quite willing for them to use the books.

We have an American neighbour & friend near Hawkshead, who has proved to us that Americans can be "educated & literary" – in fact Miss Rebeccah [sic] O [Owen] – is alarming! I shall be pleased to see Miss Moore. Also very pleased to see Winifred [Warne] 's book, a very good thing she is taking it up.

We are in the hay – very hot.

yrs sincerely
H B Heelis

Braille editions of six of the little books were published that year.

Warne had sent on to Beatrix a letter from Anne Carroll Moore, the Superintendent of Children's Work at the New York Public Library. Miss Moore was going to Grasmere for a holiday on her way back to the United States from France. There she had been visiting children's libraries, sponsored by the American Committee for Devastated France, and she had ordered fifty copies each of the French translations of PETER RABBIT *and* BENJAMIN BUNNY *to be sent to the library in Soissons. She was asking Warne if she could call on Beatrix in Sawrey – and unusually Beatrix agreed. Miss Moore was seldom parted from a wooden doll called Nicholas Knickerbocker, and the invitation was extended to him.*

To Anne Carroll Moore
Sawrey
Ambleside
June 24. 21

Dear Miss Moore

We shall be very glad to see you. Can you come to lunch on Monday? It is not long notice, but a pity to miss fine weather; and we have not much hay cut at present. I wonder how you will get here – if you can combine it with motoring it is easy, and you could combine it with a sideways excursion to Coniston, either going (or coming back) by Skelwith Bridge. We are 1½ miles south of Hawkshead and about same distance from Windermere Ferry. If you are coming by public conveyance the best way will be from Waterhead (Ambleside) pier to the Ferry pier.

My reason for these details is that our post town Ambleside is seven miles away, which is rather misleading, and I should not like to think of "Nicolas" [sic] hopping along the dusty roads. My husband will be at the Ambleside office, telephone 74 Ambleside, from 11 to 12.30 tomorrow morning, if you could call him up, it would be best, as we have no Sunday post. And if you fix to come by boat I would send down to the Ferry.

Excuse a scribble I have just come out of the hay – It is uncommonly warm!

Yours sincerely,
Beatrix Heelis

I like the French translations, it is like reading some one else's work – refreshing.

Anne Carroll Moore's visit was a great success and her encouragement was just the stimulus Beatrix needed to convince her that CECILY PARSLEY'S NURSERY RHYMES *should be her next book.*

To Fruing Warne

Sawrey
Ambleside
Aug. 5. 21

Dear Mr Warne,

I am ashamed to hear that I never acknowledged the parcel of originals, I have them safely – the old ones good – and "J.T.M." *bad*!

I can get together sufficient old drawings of Nursery Rhymes next winter, but *not* at this time of year. I thought it was safely too late for the current season when I showed them to Miss Moore. *I* very much enjoyed talking to her – and there have been some more Americans since. And visitors in prospect for all summer; which is cheerful, but fatiguing.

I have received Winifred's little book by same post as your letter. Thank you very much for sending it. I am very glad to see that you have got a young illustrator coming on who has the good taste and common sense to follow the old-fashioned road. These pictures give me far more pleasure than the modern bizarre style. She does light effects particularly well, the sexton 33p & 36p are my favourites. Tell her to study branches, the trees & bushes are a little weak for instance in p 15. I did so many careful botanical studies in my youth, it became easy for me to draw twigs. And little details like that add to the reality of a picture.

The blocks seem rather smudgy, but the printing is better than some of the recent rabbit books which are badly registered. She has done the human figures very well. The robin's tail is too short on the cover; but it is not a serious matter, the red breast is what counts.

I remain yrs sincerely
H. B. Heelis

P.S. Sorry I have no suitable photograph! – perhaps one of the children may snap shot me with the pigs.

Sylvester May Heelis (Sylvie) was Willie's niece, the daughter of his brother, Edward Alexander (Alec). She studied at the Royal College of Music and later worked as a secretary at the University of London, before retiring to Appleby in Westmorland where she was born. Sylvie wrote poetry (about which Beatrix was to be most complimentary when she was consulted in 1937) but now she was asking for advice about a story for children which featured a teasel called Prickuls.

To Sylvie Heelis

Sawrey
Ambleside
Sept 17. 21

My dear Sylvie,

I am used to "shocks" of this sort. It is a very nicely written little story with a pretty background. If any is left! I can remember "Old Kensington"; when the Hammersmith road was deep in summer dust & winter mud, under the high brick wall of Kensington Gardens – and half a dozen old 'knife-board' [double-bench] horse buses plied along it daily; and the guards blew a brass horn to summon up the old gentlemen going to their city offices. I have seen Jack in the Green and the sweeps & milk maids dancing on May day somewhere near Kensington Square; where there was a slum on the north side of the cabbage gardens that stretched down to Fulham; where Miss Thackeray's Dolly Vanborough and I walked with our nursemaids. We were matter of fact little people. We believed in fairies and the sweeps; but we did not see "little grey thoughts". Is that Maeterlinck, and understandable by the modern child?

I believe my books have succeeded by being absolutely matter of fact, & *thorough*. There is a little bit of vagueness – somethings and nobodies – in the commencement of your story. I should prefer Prickuls to explain himself as a teasle [sic]; & Uncle Willie & I cannot agree whether the parrot is alive or not? It comes out of no where. When you get to the little boy the story suddenly becomes precise. The flowers & bee part is pretty; not altogether new, but of a pleasantly old fashioned sort, of which we children-who-have-never-grown-up don't tire. I think water-colour would be more suitable than crayon because Prickuls & his friends are rather small people to portray in crayon, when it is a case of a group. It is alright for a single head. He is a weird person. You would have to find an illustrator who can do landscape, flowers and human boy. It makes pretty subjects but not altogether easy.

I should not (candidly) have chosen a teasle [sic] for a hero myself; but there is undoubtedly a taste for the grotesque; he might "catch on". You had better get your friend to make one or two illustrations & then try him on a publisher before making the lot. You don't know how the paper will fold etc. Plates are printed on one sheet & don't obligingly come exactly where an author wishes. I have always worked with a dummy book, paged & bound; it is one of the annoyances of illustrating profusely illustrated books like the P Rt. series that one has to grind out a lot of uninteresting subjects & leave out others that one would gladly do, *because* they do not fold into the sheet, or come opposite the right letterpress.

Now I must go & pick damsons; I am not through the crab jelly either. We are alone again, after lively holidays – You must come & stay with us some day, we would be so glad to have you.

I'm afraid this letter isn't over helpful. I can assure you of one thing, I should be only too delighted to see a successor. The illustrations are the trouble – nay *"trouble" is* the trouble. The modern art student can draw, and has had training I never had in schools; but nobody seems to have the nature study & painstaking behind the actual drawing. If you ever come here & see my thousands of old sketches you will understand better what I mean by "thorough".

Love from Uncle Willie & me – always glad to hear from you – especially in such an admirable legal legible handwriting.

yr aff aunt
Beatrix Heelis

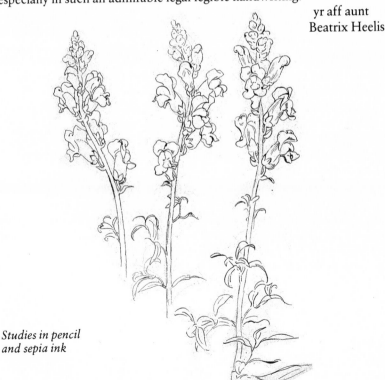

*Studies in pencil
and sepia ink*

Warne were planning a number of new editions and asked Beatrix to let them have the originals for THE TAILOR OF GLOUCESTER, MRS. TIGGY-WINKLE, JEMIMA PUDDLE-DUCK, THE FLOPSY BUNNIES *and* JEREMY FISHER. *Beatrix could find 'only 8 or 9' for* THE TAILOR OF GLOUCESTER *but she sent all she had, as well as some of the alternatives not used for the first edition.*

To Fruing Warne   Sawrey,
                                                             Ambleside.
                                                             March 2. 22

Dear Mr Warne

I enclose the receipt with apologies, very careless of me.

The china arrived safely yesterday. It is splendid – far better printed than modern editions of the books as regards true register – I wonder if they will maintain that standard.

I am glad they are going to be made in a larger size also, and the pieces sold separately – for instance mugs and porridge saucers will make nice presents, where people would not want to spend a guinea – (not that I think the set at all dear, as prices go, with experience of replacing breakages).

I quite approve of the earthenware. Their standard of printing & production is good; and earthenware is good enough for ordinary use. I think you should see what their mugs are like in earthenware (unless there is some special reason for confining earthenware to the colonial trade). Cottage children use mugs always.

I sent the drawings yesterday registered parcel. You will find an unmounted drawing of mice and china, very slightly differing from the published illustration and I think equally good.

One of the tailor letting out mice was not used in your edition [*see Plate 16*]; I like it better than the "little live gentleman mouse" which replaced it. But possibly you may think it too like one on p 29 [23].

I am returning the advt a very striking production and extravagantly produced – or at all events lavishly. It is ingenious and good but scarcely suitable to hang up in a private house, so back it shall go, not to be wasted.

With many thanks for the china

                                                        yrs sincerely
                                                        H. B. Heelis

Beatrix's first governess was a Miss Hammond and her niece, Margaret (Daisy) Hammond, had helped Beatrix to address the hundreds of envelopes sent out at the time of her tariff reform campaign. Now Beatrix had offered to let the next-door cottage for an initial six months to Daisy and the friend with whom she lived, Cecily Mills.

To Margaret (Daisy) Hammond

Sawrey
Ambleside
Ap. 1. 22

My dear Daisy

I am delighted that you and your friend have decided to come. I hardly know how to explain position of cottage, it is the front half of the old Castle Farmhouse which stands at top end of the village "street" – otherwise "Smithy Lane". It is end on towards the village, and looks across our drive & orchard. The back cottage, towards the lane, is let to a young married couple, superior farm class and quiet. The front cottage has a coal house door for convenience of carting coal to the back of the front house, but it is the understanding that – except for this convenience – the front & back are not on speaking terms. I have had experience of females sharing yards! I reserved the coal entrance right of way through the Bibby yard. It was a large rambling old house, in some respects better than this cottage, but this would have been more awkward to let, as it would have been between us and the fields.

I will send you an inventory of what I propose to put in, then you will be able to judge what is short. I want to ask if you have had experience of cooking with a Perfection Stove? parafin [sic] – I can either move an iron coal stove – a thing on legs with a chimney through the window, or I would stand a two burner perfection. There is no question which I would choose myself, parafin [sic] is so much less messy, and the oven heats in ten minutes. The iron stove is a very good oven, but puffs out when coal is being put in. The boiler will be behind the fireplace in the living room. I think it is a pity to put a kitchen fireplace in the *front* room, the plumber & the builder assure me there will be no difficulty or risk in putting a boiler flue, with damper, in the back of the fireplace.

I am glad to hear of Miss Wainwright, but she is a goose to take to spiritualism; it is sad stuff, and it works much mischief amongst unbalanced folk.

Is she still at same address. I have some drawings of hers on my conscience, never returned.

I must stop to catch post. I have had a very hard time with a favourite pig; she has pulled through, but we lost 5 out of 10 little pigs.

Yrs aff
Beatrix Heelis

Parafin [sic] stoves are easy to manage, only *servants* spoil them by letting things boil over into the wicks.

To Fruing Warne   Sawrey
                                               Friday [10 May 1922]

Dear Mr Warne,

I forgot to send the drawing for the cover [of *Cecily Parsley's Nursery Rhymes*]; & upon reflection I think it would be better to use it in outline on the title page, instead; as it is too much like Ap. Dap. cover figure. The wheelbarrow subject might be vignetted for cover as you suggest. I will recopy the returned guinea pigs, using some of the figures with a flower background, and supply a drawing of the pen inn to face the last verse "C.P. ran away etc", if you think this enclosed sketch would do. I don't know why – but I have never been able to imagine the dressed up rabbits coming to the inn door; it comes to my mind's eye deserted!

I would have got them done this week but I am plagued with visitors & poultry, & a bad drought.

Yrs sincerely
H. B. Heelis

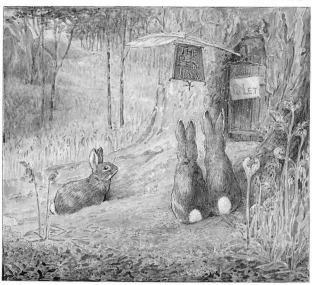

From Cecily Parsley's Nursery Rhymes

Willie Heelis was the youngest of eleven children, four girls and seven boys. When his brother, Arthur John, became ill, Beatrix and Willie were the only members of the family to help and they brought him from his home in the Rectory at Brougham to stay with them at Castle Cottage. Arthur John grew increasingly difficult and eccentric and when it became clear that he could never return to Brougham, Beatrix set about organizing the clearing of his house. She made sure that the rest of the family were kept informed, writing to Willie's sister Grace Nicholson, and to Sylvie, his niece.

To Grace Nicholson   Sawrey
                                                            June 29 '22

My dear Grace,

We went over to Brougham last Monday, getting there by 12.10, through Vale of St John. Thurnam & a man named Sharpe – appropriately named – had been & gone away! Ar. J. & I sat for about an hour upon the door step eating sandwiches; while Wm. inquired for the key. I tried all the windows; and A.J. derived some interest – I mustn't say satisfaction – from contemplating his successor's crops. We could not decide whether the "sowdown" had contained oats. I thought it had been what is called "nose bag". Arthur's sowing of wheat was good.

It would be disrespectful to describe their proceedings amongst the books. That place has a baneful effect upon A.J: he relapsed into helplessness. As for Wm. he started dipping into every book he picked up; as though he had never handled one before. They did do a little sorting.

It is obvious the main part are going to be carted here. There is plenty of room for them; but I hope the heavier series-s are going to be sold, as I hope that the books, & any furniture will not exceed the motor Ford lorry which can be sent from this village. It strikes me that most of A.J.'s relations are not inclined to store anything at all; apart from purchases for their own use.

I had difficulty in picking out anything to buy at sale for him. I avoided the box bed! Happily he did not mention it. The only things he would really say were a Madeira cane chair, and a writing desk; & two carpets Turkey and Persian large he did not want to be thrown away. I think Blanche [Willie's oldest sister] will buy the Turkey carpet, and as long as there is anyone bidding, it will not go cheap to a dealer; in fact it is likelier to go dear to Blanche. I very much wanted to get him a chair, but he would not pick out any, except he admitted using one which is desired by Jane [another of Willie's sisters]! Whether it is the only comfortable chair in the house, or whether he picked it because of Jane

– I cannot say! little bit of both ways perhaps. I did not put it on my list.

The set of Hepplewhite chairs ought to sell for a big price. I thought I had better buy the bookcase, to hold his better books; the others can go on the floor & on shelves in a closet at the farm. We brought away a dozen little pictures that he was fond of. It is a melancholy business. And how he must have been plundered. When we slept there eight years ago I helped the servant to get out sheets, there were quantities of linen.

He is much more sensible about things, though liable to turn "stupid" through edginess. He says if he is ever going to do any work again he ought to keep certain of the heavier theological books, which is quite sound. It seems that funny little man in the cocked hat is your grt grt grandfather [a stone statue still in the Heelis family]. A.J. said Alick [sic] was going to take it in, I should think he will when he understands.

W. & A.J. are going over again on Sunday aft. expecting to meet some of the family from Appleby. I don't intend to go. If I go again it will be to the sale. I hope the family will speak out clearly. It is a pity if the sale is disappointing, for instance through want of sufficient advertising – (there is a Preston dealer who would undoubtedly come after those chairs if he hears of them in time) and I can see that Wm. is burning to attend the sale & do a little "shoe horning"; but if he buys things with my cheque book against his own family it may be rather awkward afterwards.

The only articles I am really short of myself are a looking glass & a coal box! but I quite agree with Willie that it would be annoying to see things thrown away to a dealer, if there were only one local dealer there. The writing desk & cane chair I will buy in defiance of anybody. He is a curiosity; but one cannot help feeling very sorry for him.

It is very cold & showery here, I am glad we had not started hay.

yr aff sister
Beatrix Heelis

We had some tea cups and when I took them into the scullery to wash them there was no water, & I am sorry to say I left them dirty in a bowl in the sink.

The key is at Mr Lane's the Brougham gardener at lodge this end of avenue, we left it.

To Sylvie Heelis   Sawrey
                                                                  July 29 22

My dear Sylvie,

Mr Brown arrived quite smiling about 7.30, and unloaded safely! It was very kind of all of you to tie up the books; they would have run risk of slipping out, if they had been loose. He is going to pick up the remaining stuff at Brougham on Monday, & keep it at his warehouse till Thursday, which suits him for coming here again. He described an oak table, with book shelf underneath. Uncle Arthur says it belongs to a dictionary, which arrived yesterday, so it was alright to put it with the chairs etc, and he will bring it. Thank you very much for the trouble you took – all's well that ends well!

Uncle Arthur has had fish for dinner & he is coming downstairs to tea. I am rather curious to see what he will be like after this turn. It is a pity, of course, that it has pulled his strength down; but somehow I think he is better for it. The weather is against him, it is dangerous for chills; and exasperating for hay. We got 8 carts yesterday, but I have a lot out.

I think he is better in this sense – he dwells less continually on the past and on the future. My philosophy is to make the best of the present. *I* doubt if he will ever be fit for work; the first step in any case is to get him well, and more normal.

                              Love to you all from yr aff Aunt Beatrix

Uncle Willie has gone out fishing – or poaching; rather an odd performance, occasionally resulting in 1lb trouts.

From the manuscript of The Tale of Mr. Jeremy Fisher

To Fruing Warne

Sawrey
Nr Ambleside
Sept 28. 22

Dear Mr Warne

I am much pleased with the new book [*Cecily Parsley's Nursery Rhymes*], it is inevitable that the figures in some of the compositions must be very small.

The *blue* is rather dull, which affects *greens*; but we have always noticed this defect in proofs.

There should be a comma, missing on page 12.

I wonder whether it is a mistake to leave out that line in the Blind Mice,

They all run after the farmer's wife,

And she cut off their tails with a carving knife,

there is room for it, and it looks a bit incomplete without it. [It was restored.]

I remain yrs sincerely
H B Heelis

CECILY PARSLEY'S NURSERY RHYMES *was published in December 1922 and was well received. Warne were anxious to have a new book for the following year but Beatrix protested that 'as usual I cannot see. My drawing days are over'. Warne took the chance in the months that followed to sort out the merchandise, extending contracts and making completely new agreements.*

Beatrix and her cousin, Edith Gaddum, had for some years been working on both a Crompton and a Potter family tree, exchanging information unearthed from parish registers and from published genealogies. Their researches had traced the Crompton line back to The Rev. John Crompton, who had died in 1669, and the Potter line to Mr John Potter in the early 1700s.

To Edith Gaddum
Sawrey
June 8. 23

My dear Edith,

We have been asking for rain, and it has come! What *horrid* weather, it never gets any warmer.

I have had no time to do pedigrees lately, only I am sending you a copy of a paper which I have to return to Lizzie Badcock; she borrowed it from the aged Miss Potters who live in Earlscourt road.

I am rather glad to understand the Gerald Potter connection, though its ramifications are not of much interest to us. I am returning the letter about Camfield; my mother said with decision that she preferred to remember it as it was! She is very funny sometimes. I have been trying to obtain, by gift or purchase, the plainer set of double harness for use in the mowing, as our horses are light. She was not very willing because she may want to keep horses again if there were another war. When I suggested that all surviving horses would be taken, she said she would manage with a donkey. Which shows great spirit; not many of us care to contemplate another war.

We have been trying to talk business to her lately. She does not resent or dislike it, except that it distresses her to be unable to understand. I suggested that she should talk to your Willie [Edith's husband] who used to be her trustee. I do not think she will do so, as in the end she desired my Wm. to arrange as he liked; which is rather an uncomfortable feeling, inclining conscientious relations to *moderation*. If she ever does consult Willie Gaddum would he please try & explain what is meant by "capitalize". We wanted her to capitalize my allowance, (and a little more) She has been allowing me £300 a year. Willie suggested she should put £15,000 in my name. She has saved about £12,000 since she has been living at Lindeth How, the more she saves the worse becomes the supertax and the death duty. She sees that, and wishes to do something; but I am afraid she thinks that putting so much stock into my name would curtail her spending money.

She is not mean about money; it is simply that she cannot grasp large sums.

With regard to the magnificent allowance, I am luckily well off independently! so long as the books continue to sell. I was a little short during the war; but then there was not much opportunity for spending.

I am thinking of adding another room or two on the back of this house. I do not think we would ever want to move, – even with an increased allowance!

If she does transfer stock to me, Wm. says I would make a codicil leaving it back to her in case I died first. We had to deal with a considerable sum after Bertram died; his will, & my father's, and the Leech marriage settlement between them were such an awful muddle. Do you know half the Camfield furniture – books – pictures etc will go to Bertram's widow! a decent quiet woman, I do not doubt she will be alright to deal with; but it is odd. [Camfield Place, Hertfordshire, was the home of Beatrix's grandparents, Edmund and Jessie Potter.]

There is no occasion to say anything to my Mother unless she consults Mr Gaddum. I am glad to say she has stood this winter remarkably well, – much better than the winter before – As for me I have had lumbago, and I am feeling old.

I remain yr aff cousin
Beatrix Heelis

Beatrix's bedroom at Camfield Place

To Fruing Warne

Sawrey
nr Ambleside
Oct 7. 23

Dear Mr Warne,

You may remember some time ago a communication received from Mr Harcourt Williams husband of "Jean Sterling McKinly" about a simple Christmas play for children.

I had sometimes wondered what had become of the project. I have now received a typed rough copy of a scheme – The Tailor of Gloucester. The words would require amendment *before I would consent to its production*; but in the main, it is really charming. My point of view is this – of course I should not be responsible for any gag they introduced on the stage; but I know they print a book of words; because that other time they sent a book 'Beauty & the Beast'; pretty & harmless but *so* poorly written. Now the Tailor is my favourite book; and it is a story that I received one of the few compliments for that I value one halfpenny.

They have worked in slabs of my text; tacked together by pieces of their own words; good, poor, and absolute twaddle! I can correct it easily; often the mere position of a word makes all the difference in the balance of a sentence; and the Tailors talk to his "Simpkin, *dear*" just wants cutting out & rewriting. Also they have given the mice unsuitable names – one of them "Lady Golightly"!, which to the best of my recollection was in ancient days the rather equivocal name of a race horse. Otherwise the play is extremely proper, & there is only one bit of slang phrase. It is a pleasant reflection that my humble works have attained a large circulation without recourse to any slang at all.

I propose to return the copy to Mr Williams with my rough suggestions, and see *how he takes them*; referring him to you for business. They have left it late, they would have to hurry up, to get it ready for Christmas. Of course there would have to be a substantial royalty; but don't be so hard upon them as to stop the scheme. And I do hope you will appreciate my point of view; I care far more for the Tailor than for Peter, for instance. If they print a book of words I must be allowed to revise it. I have been pretty candid, but I hope he will take it alright. I am really charmed with the little play.

Yrs sincerely
H B Heelis

After a great deal of discussion and a protracted exchange of letters about Beatrix's work on the script, THE TAILOR OF GLOUCESTER *was finally staged and ran for four weeks at Steinway Hall in London.*

To Fruing Warne   Sawrey
                                                   Ambleside
                                                   Jan 9th 24

Dear Mr. Warne

I have had some correspondence with Sir Alfred Fripp – a friend of various links with the past – about helping the Invalid Children's Aid Association. He says it is his pet charity, there could not be a kinder one.

His committee are getting up a special appeal to the better-off children for pennies, and he wants the help of Peter Rabbit, with the use of a picture printed on the appeal.

I feel sure you will sympathize with the object; and I am advising him to consult you, as to how far the project can be carried without detriment to copyright. Up to a certain point there would be the advt.

I will not do anything without consulting you; and there is always my bad sight.

I suppose the idea would be an appeal by Peter Rabbit; I could do a letterpress leaflet & one or two black & whites if they could have had permission to use an old coloured illustration? But I doubt 3 colour is rather expensive in these days.

I should like to help them if I could. And I am wanting to raise some money for a local charity here; but I had rather a different scheme. Possibly they might be combined – at least I mean they might help me in a certain way, if I helped them.

                    I remain with kind regards yours sincerely
                                                   Beatrix Heelis

Warne offered to print off sheets of the small medallions from the covers of the little books and Beatrix suggested that they be used as stamps on a 'shilling card', with prizes offered when a certain number had been collected.

In its issue of 20 January 1924 THE ILLUSTRATED SUNDAY HERALD *carried an article by Sir J. Foster Frazer entitled 'Spite before Honour', in which he referred to Mrs Sidney Webb, 'whom many of us remember as the writer of children's books when she was Miss Beatrix Potter, sister of the wife of Lord Courtney'. Beatrice Webb's maiden name had indeed been Potter but she was not related to Beatrix.*

To Fruing Warne

Sawrey
Nr Ambleside
Jan 22. 24

Dear Mr Warne,

I enclose copy of letter which I am posting to the Editor of the Sunday Herald. I don't suppose the Herald circulates amongst the class who purchase my books, but Sir J. Foster Fraser [sic] may repeat it elsewhere.

I have often read, and appreciated, articles by him in local papers. It is a very old mistake, although the Christian names are spelled differently. I usually take no notice, as even the insult of being mistaken for Mrs S Webb is preferable to publicity.

But if the Webbs are going to become prominent along with our new rulers, the error had better be contradicted; for I do not think that nice old fashioned people who like my books would like them quite so much if they believed them to be of socialist origin.

I wonder if people have thought that play was Mrs Webb's?! Has it been a success do you think? I noticed that the fourth week was advertised.

Mr Heelis is much edified by the portraits of Mr & Mrs Webb on the front page of the Herald; he says it is adding insult to injury to suggest that Miss Beatrix Potter is married 'to such a little animal'! He thinks it wants stopping.

I should not like my real name to have to come out; if the thing unfortunately spreads I think the best contradiction would be to get photographed along with a favourite pig or cow and get it inserted in some more genteel newspaper!

I had lately a pig that continually stood on its hindlegs leaning over the pig stye, but it's hanging up, unphotographed & cured now.

Yrs truly
H B Heelis

What ever is Sir A Fripp driving at – he has some scheme that is going to bring in a deal of money but it never gets further than a mystery. His last letter had no stamp on it & cost 3d.

To Fruing Warne

Sawrey
Nr Ambleside
Feb. 6. 24

Dear Mr Warne

Bother Mrs Sidney Webb. Mr Heelis was asked in Ambleside yesterday whether his wife had married again.

I shall be glad to do the painting book [*Jemima Puddle-Duck's Painting Book*]. It is a pity Jemima was put into Tom Kitten's, but I will try to get in variety by a new picture or two. I think I shall be able to do these drawings easily with a quill pen; they are very much better than the illustrations in my later books.

I understand your feelings from the business point of view – but I doubt if I could ever explain *mine* to you. You as publishers like the Peter Rabbit series; naturally enough; and pressed me to go on with them after I was sick of them – there only were about 5 I ever cared about. The clay-faced paper & over-much-colour-illustrated has always been against my taste; but [a] new line might sell less well, and is not encouraged by you. I have always been too loyal to think of another publisher; but sometimes when I get hold of other peoples [sic] books I feel how pleasant (and expensive) it would be to be privately printed just as one liked without having to think of travellers & shops.

I remain yrs sincerely
Beatrix Heelis

Detail from the cover of Jemima Puddle-Duck's Painting Book

Beatrix had been approached by a Mr Tebbutt from THE DAILY GRAPHIC *asking if she would contribute drawings to the children's corner of the newspaper.*

The Tale of Johnny Town-Mouse *cover illustration*

To Fruing Warne

Sawrey
Nr Ambleside
March 3. 24

Dear Mr Warne,

Upon receiving this wire I thought it was a hoax – however there arrived a wandering taxi from Windermere containing the very image of Johnny Town mouse, walking stick, coat & all (except mercifully the bag). He had not come specially from London; had relations by marriage in Windermere. After half an hour's insinuating conversation he wandered back, leaving me to "think it over". I gave him your address.

I did not decidedly turn down the suggestion the first time he wrote; the second letter I did not answer at all, and thought the matter ended. I should like the job, apart from laziness; I hardly ever see the smaller 'dailys', (we take the Yorkshire Post & the Times) but any time when I have seen a chance copy of these papers that have a children's corner I have thought what a pity they are so poor – not vulgar, but rather commonplace.

I would only consider it even, on the terms that I did the words as well; & that it was at some future time when I could be three or four months ahead of the printing press. You have had sufficient experience of my slowness to judge whether that is ever very likely to happen!??! He says the Daily Graphic belongs to Cassells. I have always had a bit of prejudice against Cassells, I hardly know why; there were plenty of other publishers who refused Peter Rabbit as well as they. I described myself as much devoted to FW. & Co, and a share holder therein, (amount not mentioned!) He said Cassells might republish in book form, which I said was out of the question. He seemed to be pretty keen; and suggested he might be allowed to discuss it with you, on the line of the Graphic taking serial publication only. I am inclined to think it would be a good avt. I showed him the originals of Roly-Poly, the slighter pen & inks seem to be the sort of thing they want; in fact he became condescendingly enthusiastic and wanted to pocket one. I never saw a more laughable likeness. Myself in the character of Timmy Willie am smothered & drowned in a cold in my nose. But I am doing the painting book & I find I can still draw. I told him if I did think of doing it, I did not think any copyright characters from the P.R. books could properly be introduced, but he still persevered. He wants a year – Sundays & Bank holidays at £3.3.0 a day. It is a funny concern. I have a story alright a wandering interminable adventure with not much in it. Mr T. seemed surprised when he heard the circulation of our books; that is the pleasant thing about it, it has been done quietly & old fashioned like.

When will you want the drawings, I wish I had some *ducklings hatched*, they are so pretty, & they were not made enough of in the original pictures. There are none out yet; I have chickens hatched.

I remain yrs sincerely
Beatrix Heelis

It can hardly be a hoax with the Graphic paper heading?

To Fruing Warne
Sawrey
Ambleside
March 7. 24

Dear Mr Fruing

I guessed what would be in your letter before I opened it – it is going to snow editors! I shall be very pleased to see yourself again, and to discuss the mysterious business details; I have one or two things to ask about also.

If you are going to discuss drawing & bookbinding you are a rash man. Who is responsible for those horrible little things like crushed meat flies?! Is it you or Mr Stokoe that designs covers?

I have heard nothing more from Mr Tebbutt. His father in law seems to have been late registrar of births etc.

I do not know the present daily Graphic. The old original Graphic was a paper which good draughtsmen like Luke Fildes & Caldecott worked for.

I did not like Mr Tebbutt – and I am very unlikely to commit myself by any sort of rushing. If the project ever materialized at a future time it would not be like his idea; there would be more story & fewer pictures.

And I should want to know about the American rights. I was once approached by an American periodical.

I cannot do much of anything till I get some different glasses.

I will keep Fridays & Sats. free. It is a good hour's drive, I have no idea how the trains are. I am sorry I cannot offer to put you up in this house to sleep, we have a permanent invalid [Arthur John Heelis] in the spare room.

With kind regards yrs sincerely
Beatrix Heelis

[Copy of letter to Mr E. Tebbutt]   March 17. 24.
                                      Sawrey

Dear Sir

With reference to our conversation about drawings for the children's corner in the Daily Graphic, I have thought the matter over and seen a copy of the paper. I find that I have to stick to my opinion, written to you on Feb 15th. I regret that I cannot undertake to do the work. Thanking you for yr inquiry.

I remain yrs truly
Beatrix Heelis

The G. is neither better nor worse than others of the kind. I should not like to draw as badly as that! HBH

To 'Dulcie' [?]   Sawrey
                   Nr Ambleside
                   July 29. 24

My dear Dulcie,

I am going to answer your letter right away. It was naughty of me not to write. I really was sorry about poor dear "Puff". I am afraid white rats don't live long. Now I have got a white guinea pig. I call him 'Tuppenny', he is rather like a rat without a tail, he has the same kind of little pink hands and feet. He is a very talkative friendly person – only he *won't* let me touch him. He is in a small rabbit hutch with wire netting on the bottom and he nibbles the grass off short. Directly he hears my footsteps he begins to twitter like a little bird, but if I try to touch him – he rushes about his box. Perhaps he will get tame in time. I used to know 2 guinea pigs called Titwillow and the Sultan of Zanzibar, they belonged to a friend of mine and we used to pick them up & stroke them. Titwillow was a dear person and drank tea; the Sultan used to bite. I am disappointed with Tuppenny. Still it shows nice feelings to recognize my footstep! He knows who gives him bread & milk.

It is funny that you ask about a painting book! I have just finished a Jemima painting book, it has some of the old pictures in, and some new ones, I have drawn one of my sheep & her lambs in one picture. I really ought to do a sheep book or a guinea pig book, should not I?

I have got a new pair of spectacles, and I can see better again. First we must get in the hay & corn, it is such a horrid wet summer up here, all the time you had hot weather in London, we were in the mist, it comes from the mountains & the sea. Yes I have lots of flowers, I am very fond of my garden, it is a regular old fashioned farm garden, with a box hedge round the flower bed, and moss roses and pansies and black currants & strawberries and peas – and big sage bushes for Jemima, but onions always do badly. I have tall white bell flowers I am fond of, they are just going over, next there will be phlox; and last come the michaelmas daisies & chrysanthemums. Then soon after Christmas we have snowdrops, they grow wild and come up all over the garden & orchard, and in some of the woods.

I hope you will enjoy Wembley [the British Empire Exhibition], I don't think I am likely to see it – not this year anyway – The next entertainment up here will be the agricultural shows which is always great fun – you would never guess what I am going to show, a white bull, with a ring in his nose –
What a bad drawing, I have drawn him like a sheep. I shall also show some lambs and a cow.

These old cards are not much good if you collect sets, I found them just now in my desk.

Yours aff.
xx Beatrix Potter xx

Warne had arranged with Wall Paper Manufacturers Ltd (C. & J. G. Potter Branch) of Darwen, Lancashire, to produce a frieze 'introducing a few of the characters from three or four of your books'. The royalty would be 4½d per frieze with an expected sale of 10,000 friezes per annum.

To Fruing Warne   [?Sawrey]
                                                            Aug 8. 24

Dear Mr Warne

I am very glad to hear that you have been able to arrange the frieze, quite a satisfactory business. The design has not come to hand yet; we have a post, on a bicycle, who brings parcels when inclined.

Curious – the original Charles Potter was my grandfather's cousin & partner; but branched off into wall paper after a few years in the calico trade. I wonder whether Charles's grand daughter Juliet Potter is still alive. I haven't a London directory – does Mrs Stanhope still live at 64 Queen's Gate?

The subject of Christmas cards has lately been obtrusive. I was sorting old parcels & found a number of cards – and "valentines" – of fifty years ago. Those were worth keeping, Kate Greenaway, Story, Marks etc. Then a pleasant American friend from Boston passed through [Charles Hopkinson], and independently brought up a request for almanacs or old fashioned Christmas cards "Something to look out for every year". Then the P.R. Committee [of the Invalid Children's Aid Association] bring up the subject of a Christmas card or booklet to be used as a reward for collectors (my own suggestion that I should do something for the collectors). Could the ideas be combined to an extent that would make it worth while to produce a coloured block? It would almost *have* to be your copyright if it had Peter in it, and another season you might make use of it for ordinary sale. I should think it would be too late to bring out a Christmas card or almanac for shop purposes this season.

I remain with thanks for letter yrs sincerely,
                                                      Beatrix Heelis

Warne agreed 'to make any coloured block as an experiment' and to produce a Christmas card. They also asked Beatrix to consider preparing an almanac in the style of the one by Kate Greenaway that they issued with great success every year, possibly putting in it some of her pictures that had been used for greetings cards by Nister and by Hildesheimer & Faulkner in the 1880s.

To 'Dulcie' [?]

Sawrey
Nr Ambleside
April 18. 25

My dear Dulcie,

No more bunny books! I never seem to have time, and I cannot paint very well, with being obliged to wear strong spectacles. I drew a picture of Peter and Cottontail for the "Invalid Children", I would like you to have a copy of it, so I am sending you a collecting card, with the stamps stuck on ready. Will you put your name & address, and post it, and I hope they will send you the last year's Christmas card. I am not quite sure whether all the collectors get it, I think you will get one, in return for this many postage stamps.

Your Easter egg is very funny! No, I don't think it would have hatched any chickens! I have 3 hens sitting, and 2 turkeys on nests. The chickens will be rather late, but it has been such a cold spring it is better to wait for warm weather, there was a lot of snow on the hills yesterday. Today it is wet and cloudy, I hope it will turn warmer – we have 51 lambs. One sheep has 3, she is very proud of them. They look comical, there is a big one, a middle sized one, and a little teeny weeny that is always crying. I think it will have to have milk out of a bottle, as its big brothers get all its share as well as their own.

Tuppenny is quite well; but much annoyed by rats. His bread & milk disappeared so quickly, I wondered he did [not] bust up! one saucer after another. But it was not poor Tuppenny, it was a rat stealing it through a hole under the hutch. I have put wire netting now, and Tuppenny's appetite is quite reasonable & moderate. But the rats are nibbling the boards below the wire netting, they get any bread & milk that slops over. I have not got a big pig just now, I shall get one at the beginning of May, a neighbour has got a pig family coming on. Our cat has 2 kittens, striped & black.

Now I must stop & go out in a waterproof to feed hens. No I don't collect stamps, but I have kept some cigarette cards for you – somebody does smoke too many! It is not me; and it isn't Tuppenny. Old Mr Benjamin Bunny smoked rabbit tobacco, but he smoked a pipe.

I am sending you a Jemima painting book, it is the only new book for some time past.

I remain yr affectionate friend
'Beatrix Potter'

After discussing the programme for the coming year with their travellers, Warne came to Beatrix with the proposal that THE ROLY-POLY PUDDING *'to which we are not doing sufficient justice' should be reissued as a little book and the title changed to* THE TALE OF SAMUEL WHISKERS OR THE ROLY-POLY PUDDING.

In answer to a question from Beatrix about why W. H. Smith in Windermere had been unable to get stocks of her Christmas cards, Warne explained that there had been a bad strike in the book trade for the past two months over the low wages paid to packers and porters employed in publishing warehouses. The union at Smiths was supporting the strike by refusing to take work from the publishers involved.

To Fruing Warne

Sawrey
Nr Ambleside
Jan–8–9 [1926]

Dear Mr Warne

It is a very good idea to reprint Roly Poly in the uniform small size. The price & size of the book has prevented it from taking so well as it deserves. I note there will be 3 colour plates to drop out, 18 + cover reduced to 15 + cover. Certain plates will be less satisfactory to reduce than others – for instance John Joiner & the cat family p 58 [70]. will be on a small scale as regards the figures when reduced to the size which will cross a smaller page. Before I send the originals – would you think it worth while to cut up a copy of R. Poly into a dummy – you can do it in a *big* dummy book for your convenience – I only want to see where the plates come with reference to the text? There will be a good many to throw out and it might happen a little alteration would be well worth while. I might colour a subject which is at present black & white, or vice-versa.

There is one I do not like S Whkrs rolling the pin. And the cats ratcatching at the end of the book is uninteresting. The outside view of the old chimney with landscape is pretty, but I do not know how it would look on a smaller scale. I remember I put it in because there was such a string of sooty inside pictures. That part might be compressed a little. [The only thing left out of the new edition was the Samuel Whiskers book plate.]

It seems quite worth while to reprint the book.

I am still being asked for those cards, and several people have asked for the thin-paper-large-margin sort in order to have them framed. Could I have *4 doz cards and 4 doz unmounted copies.* and I am owing you for some already.

I was very much interested in the explanation about Smith's, of course it explains why fancy shops have been able to get supplies. The wages seem enormous already. It is taking a very long time for prices and wages to come to any sort of balanced scale.

We are too high for floods here, but it is very bad wild weather.

"John Joiner" has got to the pension age, there are not many deserve it so well. He has a mad wife, a little quaint old body not unlike "Anna Maria", he has had a sad time of it, but he would not put her away.

Since writing this letter our poor invalid Arthur Heelis has peacefully fallen asleep. It is a release for him & will be a relief when one gets used to it.

I remain yrs truly
H B Heelis

In 1924 Beatrix had added considerably to her property, buying the spectacularly-situated Troutbeck Park Farm, over 2,000 acres at the head of the Troutbeck Valley, near Windermere. The farm was in poor shape and the sheep on it riddled with fluke, but when the land was restored it would be the ideal place for the breeding of Herdwick sheep. This local, hardy breed thrive on the high fells and become 'heafed' to their own farm, so obviating the need for walls or fences. The acquisition of Troutbeck Park gave Beatrix an important place in Lake District farming.

Through her friendship with the late Hardwicke Rawnsley (who died in 1920), Beatrix had become closely interested in the work of the National Trust, of which he had been a founder member, and she had already made provision in her will for Troutbeck Park to go to the Trust. Willie Heelis, in his position as local solicitor specializing in land and property conveyancing, often had early knowledge of property coming on to the market and Beatrix felt she should alert the National Trust to anything of special interest. This letter is the first of an almost weekly exchange of letters between Beatrix and the Secretary of the National Trust over the next ten years.

To S. H. Hamer

Feb. 13th 26
Sawrey
nr Ambleside

Dear Mr Hamer

It seems possible that the property on the beck side of Rydal Road in Ambleside may be on sale later on, including the little old Bridge house perched on steps over the water. There is so little left of old Ambleside that the bridge house attracts more curiosity from visitors than it altogether deserves; it is not of much merit as architecture. Its preservation would certainly appeal to the town's people. Does it interest you at all? If so – it might be wise to make some inquiry *before* the sale planning matures. The back part of the site, over the beck is an untidy garage yard & motor builders premises; and a market garden further on; not a very fine use of a valuable town site. And so unattractive a background to the Bridge house as at present existing that I don't think its position & appearance would be any worse even if it were preserved in isolation – so to speak – in the foreground of a building scheme. The chances are that the site would be bought for a garage if it comes up for sale. I understand that the bridge house lets with 10 foot on either side; as a shoe makers shop. The beck is uninteresting; it is kept clean, according to bye laws, but it is the sort of stream that suggests pots & kettles & a rubbish dump. If some part of it were covered in, it would not matter – outside the 10 foot. I could not get a postcard this morning, but you probably remember the little house – this sort of thing – from memory.

Not beautiful; but it will be looked for, & missed, if it goes down. What usually happens in these cases is that the whole is sold, and a bit is tried for at great cost of buying back afterwards. The sentiment of the town would be for preserving it.

I remain yrs sincerely
H. B. Heelis

To S. H. Hamer   June 26. 26
                                                                 Sawrey
                                                                 nr Ambleside

Dear Mr Hamer,

I think it is wise to tell you how things are going on at Troutbeck Park. After very great trouble I have got out the unsatisfactory tenant. I have *not* relet the farm, because the land and the sheepstock are in such a derelict and unhealthy condition. Rather than have to straighten things for a complaining and disheartened new tenant – I prefer to have a free hand. It is a most lovely place and a fine farm, but until the mosses & drains are cleared, and the sheepstock is reclaimed by proper management – it is not fit to let at its former rent; and if let cheap it would go from bad to worse. I considered the question of planting – very extensive planting would spoil the landscape; and the Govt. grant for planting & fencing has been decreased. Anyhow I have refused applications to let this spring, telling people I intend to keep it in hand 2 years.

From the point of view of the Trust, the desirable prospect would be that I survive to get the farm on to a sound basis, and that I find a well chosen tenant. I have had experience of neglected land, and of sheep. But if I should happen to end while the farm is still in my hands I cannot disguise that I should be leaving a handful for my executors & and the Trust to deal with. Therefore I would like to make a few observations.

Tenants If the Trust happens to have the letting, please make every necessary reservation to preserve amenities, and remember that a good intelligent solvent tenant is preferable to a rack rent. Had I been letting I should have considered the application of E. L. Lucas, Skelsmergh, a man with a wider outlook than many, having been in Canada. But I should want to look at his present holding. *Herdwick men are untidy farmers.* I strongly turned down the application of Gregg Bros Troutbeck, intimate friends of the late tenant Mrs Leak, and jointly responsible for letting down bounds fences. Please bar out any goats; & limit the number of horses.

Sheepstock, number of "Landlord's stock". In my will I say "and together also with the Landlord's stock of sheep held with the said estate." I purposely did not specify the exact number because the suitable number has been a matter of discussion. At present I am minded to fix the number of "Landlord's stock sheep" at the number of 1100 sheep, viz 700 ewes, 180 twinters [two-winter sheep], 220 hoggs [male or female lambs before shearing], all to be pure bred heafed Herdwicks. I will leave a memorandum to that effect, but it is tiresome to put it formally in my will and perhaps find that the number is unsuitable when re-letting. Some tenants dislike a large tied stock. But there must always be a large landlord stock at the Park because the tops are not fenced. If a tenant got into debt and the sheep stock were depleted, the heaf would be stolen and lost.

I think 1100 is a reasonable number. The number which I took over from the Quarry Co. & Mrs Leak, and the number in excess which I shall be running while acting as my own tenant myself, has nothing to do with fixing this number 1100 for landlord's stock. While I farm myself I am in a dual capacity, which would split at my decease. The Trust would inherit the landlord part of me; & my executors the tenant part. Considering what the Park has cost me in money and care this winter – my executors ought to have every consideration and tenant privileges! For instance if they want the usual outgoing-tenant's-year rent-free, it would be a reasonable request. A sheep farm cannot be wound up at any chance time of year, instantly. It is a peculiarity of sheep farming that the early part of the year is all pay out; and the sales of wool & lambs & draft ewes [old ewes past their productive lives] are all in 3 or 4 autumn months. I am just running on the farm as grazing; no other live or deadstock except the 1100 sheep would go to the Trust.

House there is unfortunately no oak, except a floor, but I should like a few non fixtures – especially a cupboard 1667, and a heavy gatelegged table, to be considered as belonging to the house. It would be safe to 'let' them with the house, as Lakes housewives are accustomed to the care of old oak furniture.

Fencing. I have already done a great deal thanks to having larch plantations ready to thin at Sawrey. And I have planted 5 acres of larch at the Park for replacing present larch posts. No doubt walls are the ideal fence, but the cost of a *new* wall is prohibitive. An estate should always have a stock of larch coming on, no matter what sentimentalists may say against the tree. I should like to plant Scotch firs on Hall's Hill, before the house, and some oaks on the south slope of the Tongue & the Colt Park, but it is useless to plant specimen trees or groups without heavy fencing. I mention this because if I do not survive to do it – there will be ample posts when the new larch planting is ready to thin in about 10–12 years. It would be both ornamental & good shelter for stock to make a fairly large plantation – mostly Scotch fir, birch, & some larch, behind the Tongue near Dale Head Close.

If there were a good tenant there would still be a good deal of landlord's work. Especially looking after woods. There are nice young trees in the woods on the bank below the Kirkstone road, but they are worried by goats, & bad fences & neglect. The larger the estate – the more it is worth while to employ an estate workman, who should be a good dry waller and understand planting. It is a dream – or *was* – that I

297

wish all that corner of the district were a reservation, running back against the Haweswater land, bounded by the Kirkstone road. The land up the Kirkstone road from Brotherswater and in Wormdale is as nearly "plain" = unbeautiful as Lakes land can be, but with judicious planting it could be made interesting. But there is a flaw in that idea already. George Grizedale sold his farm last week. It runs up from Hartsop and joined Troutbeck Park. Two or three years ago some thousands of acres could have been bought cheap. I do not say it is very beautiful land but it seemed to me to be one of the few corners of the district not exploited; and curiously unspoilt & unknown to be so near railway stations.

To make the Park complete it will be necessary to buy the Poole's land, a long wedge lying between the Park and the land I have bought along the road. It is understood that the Poole's property will be on sale when the old woman dies; and I have completely cut it off from road frontages. Unless someone cuts in & buys it on purpose to screw up the price – it is of little value to anybody except the owners of Troutbeck Park. I should also like to buy a field of Miss Agnes Brown's, John Riggs, & Towneley's & some of Nick Wilson's, but they will have to wait & take their chance. I have got all the building sites except John Riggs' & I can trust him to wait till I can buy. I have had a good deal of worry and hard work with the Park but I have never for a moment regretted the purchase. Perhaps you will kindly put this letter on one side & keep it.

I remain yrs sincerely
Beatrix Heelis

Troutbeck Park Farm in the 1940s

The only new book from Beatrix since CECILY PARSLEY *in December 1922 had been* JEMIMA PUDDLE-DUCK'S PAINTING BOOK *in 1925. The new edition of* THE ROLY-POLY PUDDING (SAMUEL WHISKERS) *was ready for publication but there was nothing else in preparation. Warne once again decided to ask for a birthday book or almanac in the style of those by Kate Greenaway.*

To Fruing Warne

Sawrey
Nr Ambleside
Oct. 28. 26

Dear Mr. Warne

I must apologize for my forgetfulness in not writing to thank you for the copies of Samuel Whiskers, it makes a very pretty little book. I am agreeably surprised with the pictures, they have gained by the reduction, instead of becoming smudgy and confused as I feared. I hope it will be successful.

The Kate Greenaway pictures are very charming, as regards the coloured plates. The others seem snips & oddments, with rather poor words tacked to them. It would be a large order to make specially 365 miscellaneous aimless drawings. I should imagine that Miss Greenaway was a very prolific designer and had most of these little figures in her portfolio, and pieced out the number with some [that] can only be called *rubbish*, (see Feb 11th 24th 29th) It isn't worth drawing anything as feeble as the turnip on Jan 18th; the old woman Jan 20th is a contrast to it – excellent. I suppose there is a public for birthday books; there is no accounting.

I got a civil letter from "Nister's" successors, & paid them £2.2 for all rights; but Faulkeners [sic] were utterly stupid, refusing to sell back any rights. They rather "gave the show away" by saying it would take too much search – as they had thousands of old designs.

I think one might risk using old drawings, except some half dozen that I know for sure to have been published by them.

As a matter of fact – one such was the pair of rabbits under the umbrella with a different background; nobody seems to have remarked upon it.

I will look through my old drawings & see what I can find, but I have no stock of little figures to the number of Miss Greenaway's.

The nursery articles mentioned in your letter this morning sound quite a good idea. I wonder whether there is a crawling rug on the market? with cut out appliqué figures. I think they are not unknown.

I have never heard anything more of that objectionable woman with the tea cosies.

What became of the addresses of china makers that we got from the Burch Industry bureau. I heard some one could not get a tea set, but probably the retailers, Johnson Windermere was not anxious to send for a small consignment till near Christmas.

Yrs sincerely
Beatrix Heelis

To Fruing Warne   Sawrey
                                    Nr Ambleside
                                    Jan 13. 27

Dear Mr Warne,
 . . . I am making a start with the calendar [almanac]; I wish there were more light, I think I can make a good job of it, but I will not put in too many miscellaneous animals, in case there might be another later.

Yrs sincerely
H B Heelis

To Fruing Warne   Sawrey
                                    Nr Ambleside
                                    Feb. 20. 27

Dear Mr Warne,
I think it would be as well to get these 6 processed, as the three which are intirely [sic] new coloured seem so very *green*. I suppose peoples eyes alter as they get older. The colours seem difficult. I have others partly done, it requires 13. The difficulty amongst my old drawings is that too many are for the snowy months, having been Christmas designs, and also if a sequel were asked for it seems better to keep back some of the miscellaneous animals. Would your idea of a border be somewhat in the style of the title page ornament in Samuel Whiskers?

You will remember you sent a dummy with the umbrella rabbits pasted in? I thought them *very much* too large for the page, it could make a prettier book with good margins round the figures. The illustrations in Applely [sic] Dapply were very much mismanaged in that way, for instance the pig on page 42 [30] was a good page, but the mouse on p. 36 [26] is outsize, also compare 25 [21], too big. That sort of thing quite spoils my pleasure in a book. The size of the dummy book seems to call for drawings measuring not more than $3'' \times 2\frac{1}{2}''$ and not a jumble of sizes & shapes.

I remain yrs sincerely
Beatrix Heelis

To Fruing Warne

Sawrey
Nr Ambleside
March 2. 27

Dear Mr Warne,

The sales have kept up wonderfully, it is surprising that there should have been such a good year in spite of the strike. [The General Strike had lasted from 4 to 13 May the previous year.] Thank you very much for the cheque. I am glad to see the china is paying something.

With regard to the VR [on the letter-box in the almanac picture for February], I looked at various letter-boxes which are all marked that way as it is part of the original casting – if the London G.P.O. has new boxes for every reign it is a waste of money. I will keep all the drawings to the scale of those sent, for the almanac; they are near enough in size & shape.

I am afraid the 'invalid' is bigger. I will try to redraw it, but it is always a chance whether I can catch the expression a second time.

I am very glad to have had such a good year.

I remain yrs sincerely
H B Heelis

Illustration for February from Peter Rabbit's Almanac for 1929

With well over a thousand sheep at Troutbeck Park and the manager at Hill Top, William Mackereth, being more interested in cows than sheep, in November 1926 Beatrix had taken on a new shepherd, Tom Storey, whom she had lured away from a neighbouring farm with the promise of double wages. The following year, when William Mackereth retired, Beatrix moved Tom Storey to Hill Top to manage the farm there and to breed her favourite Herdwicks. At lambing time extra skilled hands were needed on both farms and every spring from 1926 for sixteen consecutive years Beatrix hired Joseph Moscrop - and his sheep dog. A bachelor just turned forty, Joe Moscrop came down from the Border Country where he lived with the family of his brother, Richard.

To Joseph Moscrop

Sawrey
nr Ambleside
April 2nd 27

Dear Joe Mosscrop [sic],

Are you at Allery Bar [his home in Allan Water]? I want to know your address when I write to tell you the lambing is on. There will be a rush when there is both lambs and *calves* - at present there is only calves, and a lot of folks messing about! the calves are healthy & good doers, but wrong colour. 1st black & white, next black, 3rd black, 4th muddy reddish grey from one of the best heifers; so I will have to change the bull. It is disappointing, and I am sorry about the bull, as he has done his work well, and he is a very quiet beast. It is an awkward spot to run a bull with the herd in summer; foot paths all over, and visitors roaming about.

The heifers are a surprise to me, there is no doubt they have been tied up before, they are very gentle in the shippon. I wish I had known earlier on; Hislop kept saying they were too wild to handle. Now we have very little manure as they have been fed on the hill side. There are no lambs yet at the Park - we have some a week old here. We have not made a good start as we had several lambed before due and the lambs did not live. I rather blame a dog, too rough.

I remain yrs truly
H. B. Heelis

I suppose it is same terms as last year, 4 weeks and bring your own quiet dog.

To Joseph Moscrop

Sawrey
nr Ambleside
April 12. 27

Dear Mr. Joseph,

I can match your name-sake's coat of many colours, as well as Jacob's lambs – there is a *yellow* calf today! They do look bonny, playing about like lambs. The poor little cow that had the calf bed out is still alive, the vet says there is a chance she may live, but she does not seem so well since Sunday. The calf was too big, had to be cut out.

I am wondering if there was some mistake, they were bought as hilling heifers, but this one has only 2 broad teeth, it was too young. There are 4 half bred lambs, they should be a week before the main crop. I hope you will be able to come next Monday April 18th without fail. I have asked Mrs Hislop to have the bed aired well. Hislop is in bed with a cold. The new man Tom Storey and Ted Wood were dressing and dipping hoggs. The wire netting is not up yet in hospital field. We will be glad to see you again, and Queenie's dog. The Leaks have ceased from troubling, I cannot make out whether they have given up the yoke, they have no sheep on – thank goodness!

Yrs sincerely
H B Heelis

Detail from a pencil sketch

Since her meeting with Anne Carroll Moore in 1921 Beatrix had been visited by a number of Americans, many of them children's librarians. Interest in the author of the Peter Rabbit books in the United States was growing, and at the end of 1925 Beatrix had received an enquiry for biographical details from THE HORN BOOK, *a prestigious magazine devoted to children's books and reading. Somewhat reluctantly Beatrix had sent them a note about herself. Now it was her turn to ask the editor and founder of* THE HORN BOOK, *Bertha Mahony (later Miller), for help. Her letter accompanied a packet of fifty original drawings, copied from four of the* PETER RABBIT *illustrations. The appeal was under the auspices of the National Trust and any contributions received would be listed as from 'friends in Boston'.*

To Miss Bertha Mahony

May 20. 27
Sawrey
nr Ambleside

Dear Miss Bertha Mahoney [sic],

Some months ago the HornBook contained a paragraph relating how the writer and illustrator of the "Peter Rabbit" books lived in the district of the Westmorland Lakes in the north of England.

Peter Rabbit is not begging for himself – and he offers something.

"Beatrix Potter" has very much at heart an appeal to raise a fund to save a strip of foreshore woodland and meadow [Cockshott Point], near [sic] risk of disfigurement Windermere Ferry, from immenent by extensive building and town extension.

So many nice kind Americans come through the Lake district on their tour, some of them ask after Peter Rabbit Do you think any of them would give a guinea (our £1.1.0) to help this fund, in return for an autographed drawing?

Alas! so many of our heirlooms – our pictures, our ancient books, even our old timbered houses – are crossing the Atlantic – would not American friends help to save a bit of our scenery?

It is only half-a-mile of Lake frontage; but it is right in the middle of the most beautiful part of Windermere; and it is near my home.

Yrs sincerely
"Beatrix Potter"

To Fruing Warne   Sawrey
                                                   May 21. 27

Dear Mr Warne

The Almanac is disappointing. The pages are over crowded and ill balanced. The borders not matched – the rabbit border facing the tree border. The cover especially is objectionable; I hope you will consent to do away with the line and the small-rabbit border – indeed if the book is to come out in this form, I am disinclined to take any further trouble with it. It will sell amongst toy book-sellers, who are people with no sense of style or taste; but it is disappointing to have taken such painful trouble, and to have an ill proportioned thing with no margins. The coloured drawings are too large – but it is impossible to explain balance & style to people, if they don't see it themselves.

Please let me know if this wretched sample is *final*? I know one thing; it is the first, and the last.

                                                   Yrs sincerely
                                                   Beatrix Potter

To Fruing Warne   May 27. 27
                                                   Sawrey
                                                   nr. Ambleside

Dear Mr Warne

I am glad to hear the book can be altered. I think it would be a good idea to have the light cover. It surely looks better without the border.

The reason – (so far as one can explain by reasons) the reason the rabbits and square line looks so badly opposite the coloured pictures is because the line ☐ has no relation to the size of the coloured picture, the sizes do not match, neither inside, nor same, nor outside. The tree design without a line goes better with the colour plates.

I have been puzzled all this time how you were going to cram a *legible* almanac-month inside so wide a border.

The colour plates are in the order of date intended. I should not think it would be advisable to have the almanacs any smaller print, and I suppose you want a border to them? otherwise just *A vignette* a plain thing about size of the colour plate would balance r better.

I will willingly make a vignette for the title page, & coloured ends. I have had absolutely no time this week.

                                                   Yrs sincerely
                                                   Beatrix Heelis

305

Warne did everything Beatrix asked and publication was postponed for another year. PETER RABBIT'S ALMANAC FOR 1929 *was published in September 1928. (The pictures from it are in the current edition of* MY PETER RABBIT DIARY.*)*

Among the Americans who visited Beatrix in 1927 were Mrs J. Templeman Coolidge and her young son, Henry.

To Mrs J. Templeman Coolidge   Sept 30th 27

My dear Mrs. Coolidge,

Everyone is happy and satisfied. Henry P. is pleased, and so am I – pleased to have given pleasure and drawings to such an appreciative friend of Peter Rabbit's, and such a very charming young boy.

And it is not unpleasing to receive such a substantial return this morning! I do feel very gratified to be able to help the Windermere fund.

Your interest in my surroundings will encourage me to try to work up my desultory chapters [later *The Fairy Caravan*] this winter. It is not easy to explain my feeling about publishing them on this side of the Atlantic. Do you know the old rhyme? "As I walked by myself, I talked by myself, and myself said to me –" I have always talked to myself (out loud too, which is an indiscreet slightly crazy habit, *not* to be imitated by Henry P.!) and I rather shrink from submitting the talkings to be pulled about by a matter of fact English publisher, or obtruded on my notice in the London Daily.

If they were printed in an American journal and looked silly in print and were considered foolishness, I needn't see them at all. But I must say the New Englanders who have drifted over to Hill Top Farm have been singularly sympathetic.

They appreciate the memories of old times, the simple country pleasures, – the homely beauty of the old farm house, the sublime beauty of the silent lonely hills – and – blessed folk – you are not afraid of being laughed at for sentimental.

I can quite believe that when Henry P. was a very very small white headed baby he may have been acquainted with fairies, like I was, if there are fairies in New England.

With very kind regards and thanks

yrs sincerely
Beatrix Heelis

By November Beatrix was able to tell her American friends that the Windermere fund had been a success. 'The land is safely purchased, and a dry gravel path is being made near the bank of the lake.'

To 'Dulcie' [?]
Sawrey
Nr Ambleside
Nov 18. 27

My dear Dulcie,

I am indeed grieved to hear of all the sad trouble that your mother and you have had to bear, it is terrible when one trouble comes after another. And nothing but time and patient resolution can deaden the painful memory of that great loss.

I'm sorry you bothered about the collecting card too! You should have sent it to me or to the secretary explaining that you couldn't finish it, of course you had to do something with it when people had given part of the stamps. I should think there are a lot of cards that don't get filled. It was not *my* idea; I always thought it had drawbacks, as a means of collecting.

Now I do hope you will keep warm and get strong again, there is so much illness with this bad weather. We have not had snow here, like there has been in Yorkshire & Scotland, which is fortunate as all farmers are very short of hay, and much of it is spoilt. It has been a wet summer, and the fine autumn came too late for haymaking.

My old guinea pig Tuppenny is dead, I should think from old age, he just got sleepy and eating less, and one morning I found him curled up in his hay bed – gone to sleep for good and all. Soon after that I had some American visitors to tea, and the young boy was very keen to give me 2 new guinea pigs – he said from Boston U.S.A.! – but fortunately he got them at Harrods which was a shorter journey. They are two lady pigs this time; Mrs Tuppenny who is lemon & white, exactly like the last one; and the other is a most peculiar colour, black with a yellow patch on its nose. It has to be called "Henry P." by special request. Mrs Tuppenny is *not* kind to Henry P. She had scratched a lot of hair off its back where it ought to have a tail; that was in the travelling box. I don't hear them fighting now; but Mrs Tuppenny has grown twice the size of the black one, so I think she steals its food, but it is warmer for them two in a cage.

Talking of tails, I saw a most curious sight the other day after heavy rain the hill sides are slippery, and I saw a neighbour's cow tobogganing as if she had been shot out of a gun – she *flew* down hill sitting on her tail. If she had not kept all her legs in front of her,

307

she would have broken her neck, but she finished on a flat piece of grass, sitting down

like a cat, just before she reached the river. I had a calf drowned in one of the floods, but that was with trying to wade across.

Our cat has reared a mischievous little black kitten in the barn, a regular little pickle, I have given it away. There are no puppies at present. Only calves and pigs; the lambs are grown up, and most of them sold at the fair.

Now I hope you will get quite strong again before Christmas comes.

Love from the guinea pigs and your aff. friend

Beatrix Potter

In August 1924 Charles Hopkinson, the Boston painter, had brought his wife and four daughters to visit Beatrix in Sawrey.

To Mrs Charles Hopkinson

Dec. 12. 27
[Castle Cottage
Sawrey
nr Ambleside]

[Dear Mrs Hopkinson]

I mislaid your address which has been supplied anew by your friend, Mrs. Coolidge, so I am able to send Christmas greetings to you and your family. Mrs. Coolidge came over twice while she was staying at Keswick; if you happen to meet Henry P. he will be able to tell you all about us, that boy doesn't miss much! I enjoyed making their acquaintance. I am so glad you sent them.

There has been an alarming visitation since, an American publisher who took the trouble to come all the way from London in search of a book that does not exist. Alexander McKay. He produces very beautifully illustrated books, there is no question about that. It would vex my old publishers very much, and I don't like breaking with old friends. Possibly I may arrange to have published something in America for the American market only. That was an odd book you sent. I couldn't thank you because I had lost the address, and I did not know whether I liked the book or not! I respect dogs to a certain extent; but I don't think they are moral characters – leastways I have been acquainted with some rascals. I know my favourite she-colly [sic] is looking out for a chance to quietly remove my favourite tabby cat. She has already killed a semi-tame fox belonging to the shepherd; but it was no loss, a snappy little beast.

With kind regards to you all (are the girls all quite grown up?)

Yrs sincerely
Beatrix Heelis

Watercolour study

To Joseph Moscrop

Jan 18. 28
Sawrey
nr Ambleside

Dear Joe Moscrop,

I am glad you are coming. The tups [rams] were turned out Nov 18th to 20th. They started rather slow, there won't be much doing till the week beginning April 20th, I think. As for the Galloways – I don't know how things will go on; but I wish Jimmy Hislop had not said they were a bad colour – you were right about them; they were lovely calves, and the red sold just as well (or just as *bad*) as the grays. Considering the dreadful slump in cattle they did better than I expected, averaging just under £8 a head. Either the new bull is not so useful, or else the heifers were too much pulled down with their calves. They will calve late this year, and I fear the crop will be smaller. I am sorry I changed the bull.

The sheep are in good condition and there has not been much snow this side of the country, we only had a little sprinkling at Christmas – it was a piece of luck! The new dog is *not* very promising at present; Martin says it will make a useful dog for hard work on the fell, but at present very noisy and barks while running, which does *not* sound like settling for a lambing dog, so please let me know if you hear of one to sell or hire. Mr Heelis & I have kept well. There is a lot of illness about, and the weather is horrible.

With our kind regards and looking forward to seeing you again.

Yrs sincerely
H. B. Heelis

My top prices were 23/– for a small early draft, but lambs got down to 10/– to 12/– later on! The clip was satisfactory. $9\frac{3}{4}$

Pen-and-ink-sketch of Nip, 19 July 1929

Beatrix had responded to the American interest in her work by rewriting some of her early stories and putting them together into a book, which she called OVER THE HILLS AND FAR AWAY *(later to be* THE FAIRY CARAVAN*).*

To Henry P. Coolidge

Sawrey
nr Ambleside
Westmorland
June 28. 28

Dear Henry P. Coolidge,

I have taken such a long time to answer your two letters that I am almost ashamed to write! I hope the bantam hen did her duty more conscientiously than Jemima Puddleduck, and hatched her eggs successfully. Things have "hatched" badly here this spring; which is in part my excuse for not writing sooner. There are seasons when things go wrong; and they just have to be lived through; like the old inscription "Good times and bad times; all times get over". It is strange where all the rain comes from, after such a wet winter of rain & sleaty snow we *did* hope for a fine summer.

All my spare time last winter I was working at the guinea pig story. I became so much interested in it – it grew longer and longer, and I kept re-writing earlier chapters. In spring, before lambing time I came in sight of a halt (or convenient pause) in the tale; but before I could finish off the series of stories up to that point – the spring work outside commenced – and various disappointments and annoyances; so that I had no time to "finish" the adventures of the caravan. Besides being out of tune and cross. The wanderings of the circus company go on and on without end or "finis"; next winter I hope to write out carefully a sufficient number of varied tales up to a point that is a convenient breaking-off-place. I could have finished it after a fashion; but I like to do my work carefully.

The yellow-and-white Mrs Tuppenny-guinea-pig is such a beauty, she looks twice the size now. The little dark one died in the cold weather, I do not think it was the cold though. It was rather badly treated by the other, and always seemed scared and thin. Nip my favourite colley [sic] has a promising puppy, a blue gray coloured dog. I have not started to break it in yet for sheep work.

I was very much pleased with the way you wrote about your visit here; it was well done in every way, no word too much nor anything one could dislike; and it made me understand so well the sort of interest that readers of the books feel when they see the real place. A very pleasant account of the old house. I wonder what you had for tea – was it pear jam? I forget! This cottage is nearly smothered with roses, the rain has weighed them down over the porch and door. There was a spell of fine weather early in the spring between Easter & Whitsuntide. Tell your mother it was pleasant to see the holiday makers sitting on the grass on the new recreation ground; the walk beside Windermere lake is much appreciated. We had a jolly camping party of girl guides at the farm. They brought 5 tents.

I will send you a copy of the first chapter of "Over the hills & far away"; but you must understand there is not so much exclusively guinea pig in the other later chapters after Tuppenny joins the caravan. I don't know what Miss Mahony is thinking of my delays – but I *can not* write if I am out of humour. I hope you have been well, as we have – With very kind regards to your mother & you, and thanks for the Horn book which I will always keep.

yrs sincerely
Beatrix Heelis

Yes, it has been a lovely spring of blossoms. The hawthorn bushes were like snow, and the bluebells like a bit of sky come down.

Tuppenny from The Fairy Caravan

Beatrix had signed a contract for her new book with David McKay Co. of Philadelphia but only after a certain amount of heart-searching, fearing that she might be revealing too much of herself. 'Sometimes I feel I don't want to print the stories at all, just keep them for the private edification of Henry P. and me.'

To Alexander McKay

Castle Cottage
Sawrey
nr Ambleside
Westmorland
Feb. 20, 1929

Dear Mr McKay,

I regret that I have been delayed by influenza – thought it would happen!

I hope to goodness the story is tolerable. The last tale of the oak fairy is rather over sentimental; but the children it was written for, New Zealanders in 1911 [the Hadfields], were always very anxious to have it printed – they liked it. I could have stopped at the pig's recovery, but it seemed more appropriate to round off with Xarifa & Tuppenny like the book began – better balanced.

I do not intend you to print the notes on the back of opposite pages; they are intended to explain the text to you and your children; and I hope that *you* can pick out from them any word that requires translation – for instance "Keld-well".

I am afraid I am longwinded about my sheep. I have two sheep stocks; rather jumbled up in the story. We keep the old pedigree flock here – on the low ground farm; and the main flock goes on the fells that you crossed when you drove from Penrith. The young sheep and rams are brought down in summer. Picturesque farming. I am conceited enough to say I am the only person who could have written about the sheep; because I know them and the fell like a shepherd; but the Herdwick men are not articulate.

I don't want you to pay *me* anything for drawing. Only to pay for help, which I could safely say under /40 [?] – Between influenza & writing the stories – I have not got on with arranging, but the coast is clear now. There is nothing in the book that anyone can take exception to. Old Mrs Scales is alive still; but she would be flattered to have a portrait of "Mary Ellen". You may notice "*her*" in 3rd line from finish – please *not* "*his*", as the real pony was Dolly. I don't want all this stuff published in England, at all events not this year; I would really prefer to print it privately first – anyway I would like to see whether it looks silly in print – and no immediate intention of printing is a strong reason for

313

not wishing to charge for illustrating. I have a few old drawings that will work in, which I will send in a few days as a sample – and I will inquire next week for some student who can draw human (or fairy) figures. I have kept rough copies and paging – 1 2 3 etc in case you want cutting down.

As regards language, I have purposely used "Yes", instead of the local "Aye" which has been exploited "ad Nauseam" by local colour writers.

Every anecdote is fact – except possibly: the fairies?

With apologies for delay.

Yours truly,
H. B. Heelis

Very pleasant about the Horn Book – but for your new printing, please note that there are a few corrections in the early chapters. [*The Horn Book* published the first chapter of *The Fairy Caravan*, 'Tuppenny', in February 1929 as 'Over the Hills and Far Away'.]

To Alexander McKay

Castle Cottage
Sawrey
nr Ambleside
Westmorland
Feb. 21, 29

Dear Mr McKay,

Forgive me troubling you! Do you have dedications in children's books in U.S.A.? I would have liked "To Henry P. Coolidge". And if there is room anywhere, the motto of the book in my mind has been

"As I walk'd by myself, and talked to myself,

Myself said unto me –"

on p. 129 [of the MSS] "*Meg* and Fly and Glen". My favourite sheep dog *Nip* has a line to herself elsewhere; but poor Meg has been left out! a meritorious, hardworking little dog.

The last p.192 gave me trouble – possibly I may see a proof?

Tune up little fiddlers; begone! – too many "always"? You may think me fidgetty [sic]; but I believe that is why children learnt by heart the rabbit books; I took trouble with the words.

I posted the mss. yesterday in a linen envelope, registered letter post.

With apologies,

Yours truly,
H. B. Heelis

I conceived that the words "Gigit" (−20) and "gingel" are pedantic – they are not used commonly, even amongst the men.

To Alexander McKay

Castle Cottage
Sawrey
nr Ambleside
March 28. 29

Dear Mr McKay

Thank you very much for your cheque for £100 and letter enclosing sample page. It is clear good type – a few errata – 'cats' should be 'rats'.

I have found no assistant yet. I wrote to an art school which did not even reply, and lost time. I think you said 8 colored [sic]; I have 3 more on hand, & another designed. Should you get 2 or 3 designed in America? *How long have I?*

F Warne & Co are very jealous of my passing over the NY branch, and wrote me rather an unpleasant letter. It was *not* personal to you, as I had not named David McKay & Co, only told them I was "intending" etc. They sort of apologized afterwards; but endeavoured to frighten me about 'pirates'. There are black sheep on both sides of the Atlantic; I might have retaliated about people in glass houses. It is evident that the English copyright must be secured by me. I told you – in our back yard – that I am shy about publishing that stuff in London. My real wish and present intention is to have 100 copies semi privately printed by the Ambleside printer – a small local publisher – just a paper-backed thing. A few would have to be sold over the counter, and there are certain formalities about depositing copies for registration purposes. I should have to know the exact date when you propose to publish in U.S.A. and I wonder whether you would do me the favour to let me have a few sets of the colour plates? Not necessarily 100, but enough to register the copyright.

I cannot imagine that it would be to the interest of a decent American publisher to do me an injury – apart from being a gentleman! – But their unpleasant letter may be correct in saying that my publisher in U.S.A. could not prevent others doing wrong.

One design I think I will get engraved in England, it is rather peculiar and may be too small in detail – especially the fairies. Would you mind cabling *me size in inches of colour illustration plates*; and approximate date for *me finishing*? I can do these – but I am slow and this inquiring for help loses time. I doubt they are too grand to work to order, these artists.

It looked rather well in the Horn Book. She should not print too much, because of this copyright bother.

I never really wanted to print at all; but the money has been useful.

I remain yrs truly
Beatrix Heelis

One hundred complete sets of unbound sheets (with the colour plates in place) were sent to England and Beatrix arranged for an Ambleside printer to reset and reprint the first section of eighteen pages with new copyright details before binding, so she could register the copyright at Stationers' Hall. No attempt was made to match up the typeface or the paper colour and the five line illustrations in that first section were hurriedly redrawn by Beatrix, as the originals were still in the US. She gave the copies away to friends and relations.

THE FAIRY CARAVAN was published in America by David McKay in October and Beatrix was delighted with the edition. 'Thank you for turning out such a handsome book, and I hope it will give satisfaction to both of us – and I may add – to my most exacting critics – my own shepherds and blacksmith. I do not care tuppence about anybody else's opinion.'

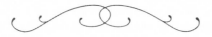

The Assistant Secretary of the National Trust, Bruce Logan Thompson, had been born and bred in the Lake District (where he regularly returned) and many of the problems relating to the Trust's affairs there were routed through him. He was preparing for publication a small but important book, NATIONAL TRUST PROPERTIES IN THE LAKE DISTRICT, in which he dealt specifically with the preservation of the area and with the threat to it of the spread of buildings, forestry plantations and electricity cables.

The National Trust meanwhile was considering the appointment of its first Land Agent, who would manage the Lake District properties locally rather than from London. Beatrix was concerned that it appoint the right sort of man, 'some educated fairly intelligent gentleman?'

To S. H. Hamer

Castle Cottage
Sawrey
nr Ambleside
Oct. 20th 29

Dear Mr Hamer,

Thank you very much for your letter. I ought to have had more confidence in your judgement and caution than to allow myself to be needlessly alarmed. G.A's [George Aitchison] swagger was such that it looked as though he already held the appointment in his pocket. He is very popular. The Windermere society that yachts, golfs and plays tennis with a strong leaven of Manchester & Liverpool – that society would not understand my misliking. I see these men from another angle altogether; the village smithy and the joiners shop. A man's attitude towards his subordinates, and their opinion of him, is an acid test of character.

Mr Heelis stands the test. He *can* be very disagreeable, as overbearing as the popular "George"; but he usually offends his equals! The two men never get on well; petty jealousies; some not unconnected with architecture. A. supports his friend Whitwell; Wm. employs Stables; I won't employ any architect at all. (By the way I have got my plans passed and begun the shepherd's cottage at the Pass). I was not aware there was any ill feeling with Porter; probably he was just siding with the other in a rather ill-bred attack in presence of many harmless sheep. I was reproved by suspecting them tipsy; I am told neither gets "drunk". There *is* a lot of hard drinking in the set.

It is so kind of you say my words of wisdom are not useless – here's a few more. I think you need a better class of man. At present you are looking for a purely Lake-district part-time agent. The Trust is growing rapidly in size; growing enormously in prestige and influence. Your first agent (whatever district he may start in) should be a superior man with more than a merely local outlook, a clear head, a good presence, presentable in London; honourably independent above local politics and squabbles. I can imagine such a man growing with the Trust, growing in influence and public usefulness, as well as growing in private usefulness to you. A poor specimen would only grow in swelled head.

I doubt Wm's "retired business man" except he might be cheaper, if he had means; better take good young material & mould it; as I hope you find successful with Bruce Thompson.

We all grow older. I grow a bit more clumpay [sic] on my lame ankle; but I can still wade the Troutbeck. When I am beat, I would like my agent to be an educated gentleman and *interested*; not merely professional.

I know the man for me. But he has not yet been "Geddes axed" [Sir Eric Campbell Geddes was chairman of the committee on national economy]; and *honestly* he had slipped from my memory when I wrote that indigent [sic] letter. He is a Scotchman (no noticeable accent), Mr Duke. He must have been very young at Jutland and he was only a commander when the war ended. It speaks for his capability and trustworthyness that the Admiralty kept him on. At present he and another officer are inspecting ordnance at Armstrong's. Six months, and more on – the Clyde; Plymouth; Portsmouth; Woolwich next. Keen, interested, alert but quiet mannered, used to command but apparently good tempered – I and my friends & servants could teach this paragon(!) to be useful for my own purposes in six months, and proficient in twelve. For wider scope and more extensive training, I would not venture to say without inquiry; but he has a good manner and modest assurance that would serve anywhere. A citizen of the world, but very fond of the country. I fancy his grandfather was a small Laird; he seemed to have lived in that atmosphere as a youngster. His wife is daughter of Sir Wm Hyde Parker of Long Melford, who married my cousin, Ethel Leech. A silent pretty young woman, not over strong; but she went up Great Gable on a very hot day without turning a hair. They spent a week's perfect holiday here in June. Mr Duke was shy and reserved at first; but proved to have a sound head and sense of humour, a good sample of the Navy – I was taken with him. He enjoyed himself and the Lake district with enthusiasm. Never shall I forget a certain night-poaching fishing by moonlight (and the difficulty of disposing of those monsters – I got sick of cooking them!!)

When he was taking leave he said if "I'm 'axed' you must have me back as your agent". It was said in joke, and it had slipped my memory till yesterday when I was sliding down the Kirkstone banks. He was a bit anxious about the future; and he said the constant rumours were hard on Stephanie and the two little girls. When I can scramble no longer and he is 'axed' – I might do worse than think of Mr Duke.

I am rather a forlorn person. Next summer if Bruce Thompson is on holiday – couldn't he spare a day in Troutbeck with me? I want neither praise nor thanks, but it would be pleasant to show him what I have done and planned – a labour of love, and much scraping, and hard work.

How easily one can make a mistake. The gable end is standing at Esthwaite Hall; half one side is down, and the whole of the timbers are exposed to the weather. The S's have not the excuse of the Parkers, who are as poor as rats. Mrs Duke gave sad accounts of Melford Hall. Her mother's money repaired it for a bit; but one wing is falling into ruin. It is a house like Hatfield; and not much smaller.

With kind regards (and renewed confidence!) yrs sincerely

Beatrix Heelis

It is not that I am suggesting Mr Duke, or aware that he is even available; but is not that the better sort of man? I think he is about 32 or 33 – his wife is a year older than he is.

News had come, through Willie Heelis, that Monk Coniston Estate was for sale, over 5,000 acres of prime Lake District country from the head of Coniston Water into Little Langdale. Determined that the Estate should not be split up, Beatrix proposed to buy it, but only on condition that the National Trust then bought half of it from her as soon as the money could be raised. An appeal was launched at once.

To Mr S. H. Hamer   Troutbeck Park
                     Oct 23rd 29

Dear Mr Hamer,

Thank you very much for your letter, which gives some hope. If the money cannot all be raised in this country – I would try hard in the United States. Roughly speaking and "without prejudice" the Trust should aim at £7,000, supposing the price to be £15,000; or in proportion if more – say another £500. With the object of buying the 3 larger farms

£7,000 { Yew Tree, Low Oxenfell, Tilberthwaite } 2,090 acres
& some small pieces that dovetail; say 60 acres

Yew Tree includes Tarn Hows and Glen Mary, and Tom Craggs
Low Oxenfell includes Holme Fell
Tilberthwaite includes the Ghyll and Waterfall and the chief part of Witherlam joining the Cockley Beck Fell at the Carrs.
The odd parrocks [small fields or paddocks] and coppices would round up Tarn Hows and join Tilberthwaite to Holme Fell, Yew Tree by a narrow strip.

The farms are well let, I mean settled tenants and a fair return. Mr Heelis will get full particulars, but it will take a few days to do, and offer a scheme.

I would be left with something under 300 acres [of this half of the Estate], I'm not denying that they are the more paying portion – at present – but as they largely depend for income on small holdings and the *quarries* I do not think anybody could say I was imposing! There are quarries on Tilberthwaite but I do not think they are working now. The Hedge Close quarries and the cottages may last, or may not, they are let on lease.

You can tell your friends that the matter *is* urgent. There is a bus service between Coniston and Ambleside passing through Yewdale; and on the Colwith side of the rise there is a building development creeping up from Skelwith Bridge. Some better houses are inoffensive; but the recent ones are bungalows, in fact the latest is a wooden house with a redtile rigging.

I am sorry to say WH Heelis & Son are selling a 26 acre plot for the Allonby's close to Colwith waterfall – it will do no harm provided it is a reasonably neat house.

With regard to the Thwaite, I have no particulars yet. If it could be bought also, I would give the Guards – the rough woodland joining the Thwaite wood. You will know that Yewdale Craggs and the main part of the Old Man is common land.

The thing must be done somehow. Mr Heelis is very strongly for it. He thinks it would be a good bargain for both of us, but too dear at £18000 so he may have to haggle.

I have been vexed again, on the same road. I am awfully sorry if the Trust is having to pay interest on account of the delay in completion of the last purchase. He *is* slow but I do not think that one has any authority from you to attack him. Please put our good will in the balance against the slow.

I remain yrs sincerely
Beatrix Heelis

High Yewdale Farm today

From The Fairy Caravan

To Henry P. Coolidge

Oct 27th 29
Castle Cottage
Sawrey
nr Ambleside

Dear Henry P.

I hope by this time you have received your copy of Our Book! I have got my English copies bound in gray paper backs; it looks well. I am already in trouble – I cannot give the correct name and ownership of the horse waiting at the smithy. It is obviously not really "Maggret", because she was a pony, belonging to Joe Taylor, and Maggret and her master have been dead for many years. If it is a white horse it would be Ambrose Martindale's. But to the best of my recollection the animal was brown, when I sketched the smithy – so it's either John Kirkbride's or William Postlethwaite's. William is quite enough in the book being owner of Fan, and Dick, Duke, Sally; but he wishes to claim that horse. Sally was white in old age; a grand wagon mare but a kicker. In fact it was always suspected 'Sally' had 'done something' in her youth; William bought her so cheap, it was suspicious. I did not intend to draw a white horse. I left it light to try and look as if its hind quarters were in the sun.

I hope you and your mother are very well. This year has been hard work, (apart from the drawings). I shall be glad of a quiet winter when the last of the fairs are over. We are selling 300 sheep at Ambleside on Tuesday; and same day my stirks [yearling bullocks or heifers] go to a Scotch sale at Newcastleton. Prices have been good up to now, and we had a grand haytime & harvest.

The weather has been wild and rough. Today is glorious, after a white hoar frost. The autumn colours are still splendid. After dinner Mr Heelis & I are going to Coniston. There is a lovely stretch of mountain and valley to sell there and the National Trust are trying to buy it. Did you drive that way when you came here I wonder – past Tilberthwaite and Yewdale. I am very interested because my great grandfather had land there and I have always longed to buy it back and give it to the Trust in remembrance. I was very much attached to my grandmother Jessy Crompton and said to be very like her, "only not so good looking!!" according to old folks. Perhaps I will be able to help out of this book – it would be like a fairy tale, would it not? I would be glad to hear from you and your mother how it is received. Mr McKay seems quite satisfied with the advance sales.

I have 52 copies bound here with the English title page and copyright notice.

I remain with kind regards to you and your mother

yrs sincerely
Beatrix Heelis

Tuppenny is flourishing – Charles [the cockerel] is having a severe moult; but I hope to nurse him through. He is very old, but still fighting. I had to hold a young cockerell [sic] this morning and let Charles give it a good kicking. He will get killed someday I am afraid.

From The Fairy Caravan

To S. H. Hamer

Castle Cottage
Sawrey
Oct 28. 29

Dear Mr Hamer,

Mr Heelis says the purchase is quite sure to go through. He is getting out a plan – but it is the most perplexing business. We were round yesterday – Sunday afternoon. It is an enormous scattered piece – we did not attempt to go to Tilberthwaite, or to the south end. We went through the Tarns roads (where we met about 15 cars and no room to pass). Without the headman, Eddington [sic], it is most difficult to identify enclosures, because some woods are cleared, and other places are new plantations. The latter bother me a little. They run into land that you will have. If they are properly looked after they will be worth thousands of pounds some day. There is much more timber than we expected. The worst devastations have been along the roads, especially on old Mrs Marshall's share, which *she* sold away.

We can make out very *little till you see it*. Could you see it – spare a week end? but if it is as wild and misty as today, it might take more than two days to go over. What about Mr Baillie? [sic; John Bailey was Chairman of the National Trust.] it is a very big thing, and worth looking at. Yesterday was a cloudless autumn day, and the panorama from Tarn Hows was bewildering – we could see the top of the Carrs opposite.

Tarn Hows is too theatrical for my own taste; like scene painting. I think the south bank of the Brathay is very pretty.

If you would like to come here as being nearer – this is a bigger house than it looks – 2 spare rooms and an upstairs sitting room and the telephone. We would gladly meet you at the station and put you up. If not next week end it would be better to aim at a visit within the next ten days, for I cannot tell how it will devide [sic]. For instance a bit of Tilberthwaite farm is a mile away. And those woods are such a mix up. The present man at Monk Coniston Hall wants a piece of Fell End wood – but I think it would be a mistake – provided the Trust could buy it. The more money you can find, and the more land you can take – the better and simpler in the long run. I think there were originally about 700 acres of woods, but without Eddington's [sic] help we cannot understand the plans, or know what has been cleared and thrown into farm land. It is a bewildering place. I do prefer a single large valley like Troutbeck. But it appeals to the public to judge by the numbers yesterday.

I remain yrs sincerely
Beatrix Heelis

To Mrs. J. Templeman Coolidge

Castle Cottage
Sawrey
nr Ambleside
Westmorland
Dec 9. 29

Dear Mrs Coolidge

It has been a great pleasure to receive such kind *understanding* letters from you and others in America. And it is appreciation that is worth having. I feel that you take me seriously! The Peter Rabbit books have had an immense success and popularity; but I have always been irritated that the Tailor of Gloucester was the least popular and successful – irritated a little because it was my own favourite, but still more so because I know that it was less generally cared for *because* it was less *comic*. I think the vogue of children's books in this country is far too much governed by the shop keepers; and mine have always been toy books – not literature. Certainly my English publishers considered the pictures first; and the words a poor second. The shop keepers like something comic and showy; I used often to buy stray copies in London, and encourage perplexed shop keepers to say how strange it was how they were asked for! There is nothing like the Horn Book or like Miss Moore's organization of storytellers to direct the choice of children's reading in this country. And it does seem such a pity that children should be encouraged to like things grotesquely ugly.

I am sure the average Londoner would care nothing about Herdwick sheep! That chapter made my old shepherd cry with pleasure; that is appreciation worth having. I don't feel at all as if I want to reprint it in this country. I had about 80 copies bound with an English title page.

Now I am very glad that you and Henry P. and Mr McKay – amongst you – extracted the book! It would have been rather a pity if I had shuffled off this mortal coil with most of those chapters inside my head. And it surprises myself that some of the late written chapters are as good as any, for instance the sheep anecdotes, and the woods by moonlight. It seems I can still write and invent. I think I had better write down some more, not necessarily for publication, but to preserve them.

It is most kind of Miss Mahony to take trouble again about selling drawings etc, in a good cause. I sent her a parcel at once in case they might arrive in time for Christmas sales, but I doubt it. There were some misprints in the Caravan; I sent a list of 'errata' to Mr. McKay for the second edition. Miss Mary Gould Davis of the NY public library seems to say the book is going to be a permanent favourite. Very funny. I could not judge it in the least. Sometimes I thought parts of it must be real fine. Other times I thought it was dreadful rubbish. I like the pig the least. He was rather an after thought; his losing himself & [his] illness was used to string the chapters together. I hope Henry P. has a good long vacation to stretch his mind and his legs at Christmas time! Here we have shocking weather; but the stock is under cover, except the sheep and they can get down to the woods. The fells are very white and the gates are open. We are having a party for the folk dancers on Monday night. Now with love and best wishes for Christmas & New Year

believe me yrs aff
Beatrix Heelis

From The Fairy Caravan

To S. H. Hamer

Castle Cottage
Sawrey
nr Ambleside
Dec 12. 29

Dear Mr Hamer,

I have been accustomed to solace myself with two mis-quotations from the Scriptures. "Blessed are they that expect very little for they shall *not* be disappointed" and "The Lord helps them that help (i.e. assist) themselves".

I am very much amused about Sidney Jones; but that *Book* [*The Fairy Caravan*] may save my financial situation.

Like you I have met with no spectacular success. But I am informed by the NYork public library, juvenile departt., that the book is likely to be a *permanent* seller. It was published rather late for this season – no time for reprints – but if it has a certain future I feel less anxious about the cost of holding the estate.

I think you had better give up Tilberthwaite & the quarries and concentrate on Tarn Hows and as much of Yew Tree as you can buy. I still feel very averse to public begging; probably you will gradually get it in tens twenties hundreds amongst friends.

I have not yet asked my Mother point blank and she has steadily taken no interest whatever! She will have to do something with her bank balance about New Year and I will try then; though it is some risk. Once when I pointed out the unwisdom of saving – she startled me by making a large unnecessary gift to a relative-in-law!

I have not got over again to Coniston, it has been wild weather, and lumbago. Eddington [sic] writes very good business-like letters – quite competent.

By the way you had better beware of disturbing cock robins; one well-to-do elderly spinster may give *something*; but she is wroth about the buzzards' nest! Such stuff.

I think I had better write another book. They say in Boston they can sell as many autographed sketches as I can send, but it takes time. I may get £100 that way.

I take it if I do get anything from my mother it had better go into the general subscription – unless it were a big amount for an example, but I'm afraid she won't.

With our kind regards yrs sincerely
Beatrix Heelis

To Alexander McKay

Castle Cottage
Sawrey
nr Ambleside
Dec 17th 29

Dear Mr McKay,

Thank you for yours of Dec 6th, we are always here, and will gladly put you up, if you can spare a longer call than the first one – about 25 minutes! At all events – get out of the train at Windermere Station – (unless you are in an express that does not stop at Oxenholme junction).

I am glad to hear that the Caravan has done so well.

I will think things over. Only you must remember that I am *not* a prolific scribbler. I wrote myself out on the rabbit series. We must talk over the future of the caravan and consider where its wheels can travel without upsetting – not "most haste worst speed". My present inclination is to appease my English public and publishers with an inferior book next season; and make a sequel to the caravan the year following, if spared; which would give time for more adequate illustrations.

If I made another caravan for autumn 1931, it would be rushed; and there would be a blank in 32.

You will let us know – approximately – lest I should be on the hill tops or stuck in a bog, when you arrive.

With all good wishes from Mr Heelis & myself for Christmas and New Year

yrs sincerely
Beatrix Heelis

To Henry P. Coolidge

Jan. 1. 1930
Castle Cottage
Sawrey
nr Ambleside
England

Dear Henry P.

I am glad to hear that the dedication has given you pleasure; and you show dis-criminating appreciation (as Louisa Pussycat might say) in your choice of favourite pictures. I was perplexed what to do with the hair brushing picture till I had a sudden inspiration about pig tails. But do you not notice it should have been Xarifa who '*brushed* behind"? And on p 183 [154] Jenny Ferret should have worn spectacles.

The coloured plate of the blue bell wood is bound into a wrong chapter; pony Billy is without the caravan; I intended it for the chapter where he goes back alone to look for Paddy Pig, and hears a faint tingle ringle of laughing from the thousands of blue bells in the wood.

Now for the old words – *sneck* is the sort of door latch that lifts/ opens by pressing a flat thumb piece.

327

All our cats from generation to generation learn the trick; Tamsine jumps up and opens the door into the kitchen. She tries the house door if she is left loose at nights; it is rather weird and troublesome, but I usually shut her in the granary. I had a dog, old Fleet, who "went one better". She used to open a similar latch in the iron garden gate, and what's more she (standing on her hind legs) holding the latch used to step backwards pulling the gate open towards herself. I could never teach her to close it; I have heard of a fox-terrier which would shut the door obediently. *Midden stead*, a 'stead' or place where farm-yard manure is heaped. *Clothes swill* Swills are flatish [sic] baskets woven out

of interlaced thin broad parings of oak wood. *Uveco* a cattle food, yellow flakey rolled indian corn, from which the oil has been extracted. It is a waste product and comparatively cheap. *Lish*, active supple energetic; an expressive adjective; an old man who has preserved his youth and worn well is said to be "as lish as a lad". *Coppy* stools, three legged stools such as are used for milking. "*Shippon*" a stable-like building containing stalls – or 'boosts' – for tying up cattle. *Ring widdie* the double ring, with a swivel between the rings which slides loosely up & down on the rett-stake to which the cow is haltered. It would be possible for a

ring widdie to "clink" on the stone floor of the bruist [rough bed or shelter]; but "clink" is *not* the right word for a very pleasing sound. When anyone opens the shippon door, there is a sort of scraping noise of the rings, usually followed by a gentle 'moo', if it is feeding time. There are new fangled ways of tying up cows; but I prefer the ring-widdies. 'Keshes', wild parsnip, tall coarse plants – does not Shakspeare [sic] speak of "rude kecksies-burrs"; burrs doubtless were burr docks = teazles. Wither [or] "widdershins", contrary way – there is an old verse "The stars shall gae wither shins Ere I will leave thee" *Demerara* sugar. A soft sugar not much refined. I suppose in old times it came from Demerara. What would you guess if I had put in the puzzling numerals of the old sheep counting,
"Yan tyan tethera methera pimp (is it 'pimp' or dick?) 'bumfit' is 15.
  1   2   3   4   5
Very interesting words they are, for they are supposed to be one of the few remains of the old Celtic language. Sheep have been kept in this district from early times. A fragment of woolen [sic] cloth was found in

a "barrow" or ancient burial mound with a funeral urn, and bronze implements. I guess the stone men who set up 'Long Meg' and the stone circles had sheep. Now I wish you and your Mother a very Happy Year. Tuppenny is still flourishing; and we are all pleased with the success of the book.

yours sincerely
Beatrix Heelis

John Bailey was Chairman of the National Trust from 1922 until his death in 1931. In a letter to THE TIMES *on 15 February 1930 he reported that the appeal for the Monk Coniston Estate had raised £5,000 to date, securing Tarn Hows, Holme Fell and Yew Tree Farm. Only the Tilberthwaite portion remained and for that a further £3,500 was required.*

Beatrix was in weekly contact with the National Trust during the first half of 1930, encouraging them in relation to the appeal and keeping them informed of her work on the Estate. 'I have been "doing" the place thoroughly in the splendid dry weather of the last fortnight [Feb. 25] – drains, fences, plantations.' The Trust had still made no decision about the appointment of a local Land Agent.

To John Bailey

Castle Cottage
Sawrey
nr Ambleside
Feb 15th 30

Dear Mr Bailey,

Thank you for your kind letter, and for your dignified appeal in today's Times.

Those of us who have felt the spirit of the fells reckon little of passing praise; but I do value the esteem of others who have understanding.

It seems that we have done a big thing; without premeditation; suddenly; inevitably – what else could one do?

It will be happy consummation if the Trust is able to turn this quixotic venture into a splendid reality.

Yrs sincerely
H. B. Heelis

On his visit the previous December, Beatrix had shown Alexander McKay a story about a pig that she had started writing as long ago as 1893 (LITTLE PIG ROBINSON) – and he had bought it on the spot. Beatrix decided that this time the new book should be offered to Frederick Warne as well, for they had been angry and disappointed at not being allowed to publish THE FAIRY CARAVAN. Now Beatrix found herself working for two masters.

To Alexander McKay   Castle Cottage
                                                         Sawrey
                                                         nr Ambleside
                                                         June 21. 30

Dear Mr McKay,

Are you going to use the same type as in the Caravan? I presume so. But I wish I could see yours, *set up*; because of ends to chapters. If FW & Co use another size of type – there may be more – or less space in the British edition. In the meantime I have no print at all; and I dislike typewritten matter. Probably it is my fault for having said I would extend the last chapter; but I am so much "at sea" on land; upon the subject of boats and desert islands, that I find it prudent to concentrate upon Robinson's Devonshire adventures; and I am sure everyone will be tired of him before the last chapter.

Minor corrections and alterations I could make on the galley – if I had it. I am putting in a sentence after passing Styford mill to bring in the big dog called Gypsy who barks, but the big dog smiled and wagged his tail at Robinson. And please put your children's names on the dedication page if it would please them. [The U.S. edition was dedicated to Margery, Jean and David McKay. The Warne edition carried no dedication.]

I have done a great many illustrations, and I think they are fairly good, but I had a disastrously slow start, getting bronchitis. I was not really bad but it left me so dull & *lazy* for a long time and ever since I have been desperately busy, indoors & out.

FW & Co have a good drawing (2 copies plain & coloured) of Robinson, for the cover. They submitted an ugly design – doubtless they will send you the pig, and you will make your own framework, for U.S.A.

It seems as though they want all my blocks before setting up any copy; I must write to them also, I have no idea how many pages.

I remain with kind regards

                                                         yrs sincerely
                                                         Beatrix Heelis

To Alexander McKay

July 15. 30
Castle Cottage
Sawrey
nr Ambleside

Dear Mr McKay

I send with this 10 full page and 16 heads and tails of chapters none of which will appear in the English edition except 4 marine subjects which I have redrawn more compactly for inside the book-covers, by suggestion of Mr Stephens. [Arthur L. Stephens had been appointed Managing Director of Warne in June 1928, after the death of his brother-in-law Fruing Warne in February that year.]

It is difficult to judge ones own work, but I think myself that some of the chapter ends are the best drawings of any. I hope you may care to include them. There is one proof that they don't want, as the subject is illustrated by another drawing. They have 22, full page pen & ink.

It is a good book to illustrate; I should quite enjoy doing a few more! If you want any to fill up – just tell me the number of the (typewritten) page as I have kept the duplicates.

I got this typed from the altered copy; FW & Co will be setting up letter press like enclosed.

About the cheque – would you please keep it back just a bit – I shall be re-investing something presently, and I will ask for it later on.

I am thinking it might then go direct to Messrs WH Heelis & Son who invests clients money for them.

I wonder how you make hay in hot weather in America! There was a run on the *barrel* last Saturday – we had a grand day, with lots of helpers; refreshments were gobbled up.

With kind regards from us both I remain

yrs sincerely
Beatrix Heelis

I am not very particular about illustrations coming exactly opposite words – you may find them rather in bunches.

Betty Harris was the niece of Marian Frazer Harris Perry from Philadelphia, who had contributed to the Windermere fund in 1927, buying three of the special Peter Rabbit pictures. In August 1930 Mrs Perry had brought Betty Harris to meet Beatrix.

To Betty Harris   Castle Cottage
                                                          Sept 4. 30

Dear Betty Harris

I am extremely amused with the snap shot – had there been a third victim – the (tea) caldron is there alright! Your long-suffering Aunty looks rather like an elderly sheep. But I am more like a good tempered witch than a cow. We had speeches at lunch, at the Hawkshead Agricultural Show, and an old jolly farmer – replying to a 'toast' – likened me – the president – to the first prize cow! He said she was a lady-like animal; and one of us had neat legs, and walked well; but I think that was the cow not me, being slightly lame.

We had our pretty little Baa's at Ennerdale Show last week, and yesterday at Keswick; on perfect autumn days – still, sunshiny mists. The Buttermere fells were in golden haze. We did not try the 'passes', we took the road to Cockermouth.

The sheep have been very successful in the female classes; 16 first prizes, and several shows yet to come. Including Loweswater.

It is raining again this afternoon, but the fine hot week has been most acceptable for finishing hay & harvest.

I don't know whether you are still in England, but will send this on the chance. Hoping to see you and Mrs Perry again some day,

                                                          I remain yrs sincerely
                                                          Beatrix Heelis

The two editions of LITTLE PIG ROBINSON *were turning out to be quite different, the American edition having chapter head and tail pieces and twelve more illustrations than Warne could find room for. The Warne edition, published with a small run of 5,000 copies in September, was already reprinting by December and again in the following March.*

To Alexander McKay

Castle Cottage
Sawrey
nr Ambleside
Westmorland
Sept 9. 30

Dear Mr. McKay,

I return these by first post. You may possibly have received suggestions for *legends* already. They do not suggest anything specially bright. I agree with all your corrections, except possibly "fatter er"! Of course there is no such word; but it is expressive! If you don't like it, say "fatter and fatter and more fat". It requires 3 repeats to make a balanced ending. [The published version was "fatter and fatter and more fatterer".]

I like the appearance of the book *extremely* – the head & tail pieces give it much more character than the English edition; and it is grand print.

It *might* make a hit. It is much more concise and understandable for children than the Fairy Caravan. If such a thing should happen, – a future edition would be improved by a few more illustrations, as some chapters are rather bare. I think P. R. looking into a shop window is the best black & white I ever did. I feel most grateful to you for turning out such a handsome letter press & general set up.

When it is convenient to you to send me another cheque would you please draw it to W.H. Heelis & Son, that is the name of the firm WH Heelis and Son, Hawkshead nr Ambleside.

Trusting you will receive this parcel promptly,

I remain yrs sincerely
Beatrix Heelis

The National Trust appeal for the Monk Coniston Estate had been successful, and the Trust was now in a position to begin the repayment to Beatrix for their share. In September they had asked her to continue managing the entire estate on their behalf, about which she was very pleased, 'interesting work, at other people's expense!'

Sir Samuel Scott had subscribed to pay for Tarn Hows, Lord Esher had given for Holme Fell and Beatrix had given – under the promise of anonymity – for her great-grandfather's former farm in Tilberthwaite, Holme Ground.

To S. H. Hamer

Castle Cottage
Sawrey
nr Ambleside
Oct 8. 30

Dear Mr Hamer,

We think it would be quite a good plan to put a list of subscribers in the Westmorland Gazette (my mamma *might* feel stirred to send a trifle! – only she has just had the car varnished).

Don't please hold me up as either pressing for money, or in pecuniary difficulties – but it is quite right to publicly thank those who have subscribed; and gracefully allude to the small remaining requirement. Considering the times, it is wonderful how the money has come in.

I am very sorry to hear about Mr Horne [Benjamin Horne was legal adviser to the Trust and to the Society for the Preservation of Ancient Buildings]; I hope it is not a serious illness. I had been thinking about him – thinking I will plant some chesnuts [sic], for colour, in the hollow way where it is sheltered – and mend his spinning galleries. But I fear the art of pegging is a lost art! I have been studying sign boards. There is a well designed real oak expensive board at Queen Adelaide's, *made with pegs*. Three of the pegs have already come out.

I read in the Times the death of your old friend and treasurer. [Harriot Yorke had died on 1 October.] My husband received the cheque & Sir Samuel's lease.

I remain yrs sincerely,
Beatrix Heelis

Beatrix's cousin, Caroline Hutton, with whom she had often been to stay in Gloucestershire, had married Francis William Clark (Frank) in 1910. As well as owning the Isle of Ulva, Frank had substantial holdings on Mull and in Argyllshire, and Beatrix and Caroline regularly exchanged farming news. The Clarks' only son, another Francis William, was born in 1912 and Beatrix had dedicated that year's book, THE TALE OF MR. TOD, *to him. He was now serving in the Argyll and Sutherland Highlanders.*

To Caroline Clark

Castle Cottage
Sawrey
nr Ambleside
Dec 13. 30

My dear Caroline,

It sounds as though you had been battering on the Daily Mail. Things are so bad I do not envy any minister who has to tackle the problem of economy, which goes (or ought to go) deeper than the public deptmts wastefulness. There is such a mania for getting 'something for nothing'; witness sweepstakes; and foreign bacon at 9d per lb. Our grocer says some of it comes from Poland. It is pretty mad to talk about smallholdings without protection? There is no demand for very small 'holdings' here; moderate sized farms are much run after. That idea of building and forcing the ground landlord to buy is a caution! To begin with a cottage ought not to cost £600 under those circumstances.

I give it up – as regards politics; it is beyond me. All I can do is to prepare for yet more evil days by getting the land & stock into tip top order while one can still afford to do it. – by the way we got the lime wagon through a small bridge the other day but the R.D.C. [Rural District Council] repaired it without remark. They don't care what they spend.

I wish I had sold my wool. I dropped from $9\frac{3}{4}$ to $4\frac{3}{4}$ and now it is not wanted even at that price and I am afraid of the rats getting into the heap, 1600 fleeces is a big stack. Except for wool it has been a good season, and the barns are full which is a comfort. It was very slow work getting the hay, but not much was wasted. The black cattle are still running out, there has not been much snow. I had 18 blue gray calves and 4 Galloways, they seem to stand the wet climate best of any breed, the halfbred calves averaged £12 at six to eight months old. I wonder how anyone makes a profit later on, but blue grays are the fashion. I think I could carry more cows, so I have been breeding some Galloway pure bred heifers – I don't feel sure that they will be as good as imported stock – but Galloway heifers from Roadend[?] fair cost up to £30 and there is the risk of buying a wrong one!

My mother is 91 and very well. I wish I were as little troubled as she is, if she gets a cold it is only a sniff – and I have been in bed twice this winter already. If I survive to be an old lady I'm afraid I shall have bronchitis. She is very lucky in having good lungs, no rheumatism and good eyesight. She amuses herself with needlework and knitting. It is annoying that she is so difficult about money – a regular miser in reluctance to spend money, which will simply be wasted in death duties when she has hoarded it up.

My garden is a case of the survival of the fitest [sic] – always very full of flowers and weeds, presently it will be a sheet of self sown snow drops, and later on daffodils. It always seems too wet or too busy at the right time for digging over – consequently I just let the plants alone until they *have* to be divided, and small things like gentians have got crowded out. I think they will stand wet if you mix pebbles or old lime with the soil, for drainage.

I have been much gratified to get back the bit of land at Tilberthwaite that belonged to my great grandfather Abraham Crompton. I should have liked to keep it for my lifetime but on the whole it seemed wiser to make a gift of it to the National Trust when they bought the surrounding property – especially as the secretary has asked me to look after the place. I wish the weather would dry up, I have got an interesting bit of planting in hand for the Trust.

I am sending you a copy of a belated book [*Little Pig Robinson*] – the story was invented 30 years ago. It is selling well. Fancy you with a grown up son in the army!!

I think one way is to keep a pure W [?Wyandotte] cock every other year – and ring the hens. What I dislike about Wydts. [Wyandottes] is the scaley leg. There seems no ideal dual purpose breed. Try a game cross instead of Leghorn for table.

With love & best wishes for 1931.

Yr aff cousin
Beatrix Heelis

I like Indian runners better than Aylsbury [sic], never had Karls [?]. An Orpington drake is a better x than Aylsbury [sic]. I have a few left but they are very old & really not worth their keep except as pets. Our sheep did well this summer at local shows. Had the best Herdwick ewe & gained the challenge cup to hold for a year.

To Joseph Moscrop

Castle Cottage
Sawrey
nr Ambleside
Jan 15. 31

Dear Joe Moscrop,

Our letters might have crossed, for I have often been thinking about the time of year for writing. Now you have paid me the compliment of reading the Caravan with careful attention – not merely skimming, but digesting the immortal work (!?). I had an enthusiastic criticism from an American admirer, who harped upon the merits of the "sleepy" *guinea pig*. Which was bad, as natural history; and *in*attentive as reading; as it is the *dormouse* which hibernates. My little old guinea pig is lively and twittering. I rather doubt if it will get through the winter; it is thin, and its peculiarly long coat has fallen away.

Now we shall be as glad as ever to see Joseph again at the Park; and this time you must please be sent for rather earlier, as over 400 ewes were marked first weekers; they seemed to come with a rush. The tups were turned out Wednesday Nov. 19th. Sheep have wintered well this year; so far there has been little snow, south of the passes. I believe we had a heavier fall here from S.E. than any that fell in Troutbeck, but we have never had snow and frost together.

If you are not fixed up with a lambing dog – will you use Lassie? I would not suggest it "on my own", as I might be thought to recommend a useless favourite. Tom Storey recommends her strongly for a lambing dog. His bitch Fly was heavy with pup, and I was indoors with a cold, so I sent Lassie over to Hill Top about six weeks ago. I miss her, as she was good company; but she was so keen I was always in difficulty to keep her back. She got to work at once; rather excitable but very obedient. He says he never saw a young dog better at holding, and very gentle with sheep. She is still a bit inclined to bunch a flock at a distance and sit down. I expect she will get out of that at Troutbeck, I will send her there as soon as she is over the time of keeping up. She has one fault; biting humans who get her by the scruff of the neck if she is laid hold of. I feel sure you would have no trouble with her, she is an in-worker, and she would quieten down with daily work, when there is lambing.

We hired old Wedgewood the celebrated Herdwick champion last autumn. Mr Cockbain warned us the ram was failing. It has gone rapidly down hill lately and died yesterday – rather to our consternation! Of course it could not be helped; it was done; but I would have preferred to see it live to go home to Threlkeld. It worked alright, we should have some good lambs next spring if lucky.

You must have had a wet job in the peat drains; the land is fairly rotten this winter.

We have been troubled with colds here – one cold after another. First I had my cold and then Mr Heelis had a cold that seemed like influenza – and I must needs catch that from him; so I was in bed twice, which I do hate – but I suppose one has to expect to take things easier as one gets older. There are not so many like my mother who seems just the same at 91 as she did at 81 – but then she has never exerted herself to work, in her life. I would rather keep going till I drop – early or late – never mind what the work is, so long as it is useful and well done. If the majority of citizens would use their one talent honestly, giving value for what they receive, instead of [?] canny and go on the dole – the country would have a better chance to pull round within reasonable time.

Wool does not mend! I see Herdwick has dropped another $\frac{1}{2}$d = 4d! Mine is still unsold. The men are all at Troutbeck the same – for a wonder! I do not think E. Parker has very much interest in farming; in fact I have always understood he would go back to one of the packs if there were an opening, but at present – we jog along.

There should be a calf, first week in Feb. by the black bull. There are disputes whether she is in calf at all; she walks very heavy. The cows have been running out, but they are laid in this week – we want the manure.

I will drop you a line to Mosspetral nearer the time. There was one ram out that they could not keep in, but the main turn out was Nov. 19th. You remember you were sent for a week late last year by some foolish mistake. It gave the new man a lesson on the difficulties of Troutbeck lambing! I'm sure there were some lost before you arrived, they were over run with lambkins.

I hope there will be fewer cockroaches, we have given *every ewe* we could get hold of fluke pills, because there was a far better crop from the pilled-and-crossed-ewes although some were old sheep, than from the large *unpilled* flock; I think a lot of the trouble is fluke. The sheep looks to be thriving, at a certain stage of fluke. Some good looking ewes produce the smallest lambs; it may be that they do all for themselves – or it may be fluke. With kind regards and best wishes for 1931 from Mr Heelis and me,

I remain yrs sincerely

H B Heelis

Its funny that story of the wee wifie spinning – it occurs in German, Norwegian, etc and always the *lazy* daughter scores! bad moral.

Wedgewood   [January 1931]

[Draft letter] To the editor, dear Sir,

A grand old champion of the fells is dead. Mr Joseph Cockbain's celebrated Herdwick ram, "Saddleback Wedgewood", has died on Jan 14th at Hill Top Farm, Sawrey. The ram was bred at High Row, Threlkeld by Mr Cockbain; his sire was Mr Jerry Richardson's 'Gable'. He was lambed in 1923 – he was not very old as Herdwicks go – but he had been failing for six months and his complaint was incurable.

Wedgewood's successes in the show ring were past counting. He won 54 firsts and championships. In 1928, he was exhibited eleven times and eleven times he came out champion. And there were giants in those days; Wedgewood; Roamer; Grayknott. Old Roamer is still living; but shrunk into little room. Wedgewood was the perfect type of a hard big boned Herdwick tup; with strong clean legs, springy fetlocks, broad scope, fine horns, a grand jacket and mane. He had strength without coarseness. A noble animal.

It is too early to tell what mark he will leave upon the Herdwick breed. Not all fine rams are as impressive as Gatesgarth Ned, whose line reappears again and again in Herdwick pedigrees. Judged by his young stock, Wedgewood will prove to be a successful sire. I am proud to have had the use of him in my flock; though I could have wished that he had survived to go home to Threlkeld.

'Ram's Head, drawn from a stuffed specimen. Beatrix Potter.'

To S. H. Hamer

Castle Cottage
Sawrey
Feb 25. 31

Dear Mr Hamer,

This letter applying for a camp has come before I am prepared to deal with it. I have put off the Scout master civilly, telling him I must refer to you; and in case of difficulty *this* season he would be welcome to use Hawkshead Field, or might try Wray Castle.

The question wants going into. If Bruce Thompson is up at Easter I would like to go to the Tarns with him. It would be a pity to refuse facilities; but promiscuous choosing of sites by campers, and permission by old John Thompson won't do at all. These Scouts would be careful, but the public in general are *not*. And possibly the Trust and Sir S. Scott might not like a camp in the foreground of the view over the Tarns? I think we should fix sites; and probably have to burn brackens ourselves.

What words do you use for notice boards?

"Visitors are requested not to light fires." or "No fires allowed" By Order

"No road for cars" By Order

"Car Parking." By Order

"Teas & Minerals. Tarn Hows Cottages"

"Camping. Apply F Edington Highwater Head Coniston"

We have the painted boards ready when weather permits; but we want a few painted small notices. We have boards for them & can letter them.

I am afraid if you saw the estate you would think there was little headway. I am sustained by remembering the struggles at Troutbeck Park – like old Sisiphus [sic] – 2 fences put up, and 3-4-5-6 rolled down! Then suddenly order came out of chaos. I have paid more than my half of the wages anyway. If I had given the Trust gratis every blessed(?) wood on the property I would be better off! Not only fencing, but double tax, 4/6, and occupation tax 2/3 for no return whatever.

Have you heard anything from the Yorkshire Insurance? I am most awfully sorry. I described Edington as a "forrester" [sic], and they jumped to the conclusion that it was wood felling, for which the premium is over 90%.

The Japanese thinning was rough work, but it was finished last autumn; and it is too absurd to call the young plantation work dangerous.

Hawkshead had a narrow escape yesterday. The parafin [sic] pump place in the Co-op Stores caught fire – groceries burnt, smoke & fire. The Miss Pussycats timbered house Thimble Hall was in great peril. Indeed if it had got upstairs, or into the 200 gals parafin [sic] cistern it would have been a mess. There is no hose or standpipe and no pressure. It was put out with extinguishers & buckets.

I remain yrs sincerely
Beatrix Heelis

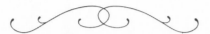

Beatrix welcomed Scouts and Guides who applied to camp on her land, or if it was very wet even in her barns. She was always ready to help them and one year lent her car and chauffeur to drive a suspected case of appendicitis home to Manchester. She continued to keep in touch with Nora Burt, who started training as a nurse in 1935.

To Nora Burt

Castle Cottage
Sawrey
nr Ambleside
June 5 31

Dear Nora Burt,

It is always a pleasure to help Guides, and it brings its own reward – for surely it is a blessing when old age is coming, to be able still to understand and share the joy of life that is being lived by the young. If *I* slept in a tent I might get sciatica; I enjoy watching Guides, smiling in the rain.

You and I, Norah [sic], are doomed to go through life *grinning*! even upon unsuitable occasions, like appendicitis, we find it difficult to keep a straight face. I hope to see Dorothy again, but without her appendix, please. It might have been extremely awkward, for I have not very much faith in local doctors; and although this attack may subside completely, she will never be quite safe from another, until it is removed.

The weather has not settled yet, yesterday was sultry and today there is a cold east wind.

I hope you will all come again and have better weather next time, though you did not seem to mind the rain.

Yrs aff.
Beatrix Heelis

Remember the tent available, with ground sheet & loan of blankets but no sleeping bags.

To Mr S. H. Hamer

Castle Cottage
Sawrey
nr Ambleside
Feb 27. 31

Dear Mr Hamer,

I am rather unhappy about the Coniston accts. The Trust has had a larger share of wages, and there is a belated mason's bill from the time when a corner of Rose Castle fell down. About £60 rents are still owing; but should come. There is nothing to hand over, just about enough for next half year.

I *hate* accts! Wm. gave me such a lecture about wages that I was awake nearly all night. I presume the Langdale farms are in better order, quite certainly there are not these miles & miles of straggling woods which "fence themselves". The place will clean up by degrees; but I cannot see myself how the estate can ever be worked without *2 men*; what with floods, roads, drains and fence renewals. The future prospect should be 2 men and enough scope (land & rents) to make 2 men worth while. When Wm. says it would be cheaper to pay no wages at all, I disagree with him. It is perfectly unlikely that such rambling work could be done by outside contract cheaper, especially when I lend Dolly; he has never walked over the south end of the estate since it was bought.

He knows what the cottages are like, and he says the rents are so low they aren't worth repair! but one *has* to!? I was asked to look at Yewdale farm house windows (mine) last week, panes falling out with rotten wood, one bedroom window had only one pane of glass in it. I understand the tenants could have asked for paint to put on themselves – careless landlords make careless tenants. It means new window frames, all through neglect of painting.

I have Dr Patterson bothering at Far End cow shippon, I think I can pacify him; but it is to be hoped he does not go all round. The sanitation is not nice at the Trust's Tilberthwaite cottages – and as for Stony [sic] End – there are 15 people using one earth closet. When one is up against such problems – I think it was rather unkind of Wm. I will see if I can get a talk with Miss Edington; her father *is not* worth his wages, & he is comfortably off. I think he might be persuaded to just do time keeping, only.

I went to Grasmere to investigate furniture and find out what Mr Horne is at! We were extremely amused with him; but surely he is a *very* talkative lawyer? Is he eccentric? I could not make out whether he was serious about buying old oak. The scheme is very attractive; but with reservations of common sense. He cannot plump quantities of goods upon the top of sitting tenants who have furniture of their own already and I should think he was indiscreetly talkative to Telford. He said how interesting it would be to have Dungeon Ghyll furnished with fine oak, and the dealer naturally encouraged the idea. The women nearly always appreciate a fine piece to rub up. I do not know Mrs Dawson; it is probable that if tactfully approached she would be willing & careful. I know nothing about the Dawsons; they seem successful, & Wm. thought Pro. Trevelyan [George Macaulay Trevelyan was Chairman of the National Trust Estates Committee] rather liked them? Mr Horne mentioned Mrs Rawnsley as a possible co-committee on antiques. I was taking notice yesterday, but Telford never mentioned anybody except Mr Horne. He is a chatterbox. I reproved Mrs Telford for gossiping.

There is a card for an Ambleside meeting, re Hostels, Dec 5. I think of going, from curiosity. If the sanitary inspector got to the Castle there might be words. Talk of overcrowding in a slum! There are 8 beds in a small chamber, formerly servants bedroom with one narrow window; much tighter packed than the Far End cows.

I am having a bit of cementing at Thwaite, whether solvent or not.

I remain yrs sincerely
Beatrix Heelis (depressed, but still arguing & spending!)

You see the unlucky Edington is blamed for every dmd thing, including painting; but how *can* the men do everything? I have a dozen jobs waiting for them. I admit it would be better to save his wages & get in the joiner or plumber more often.

Pencil study of roof tiles and skylight

To Henry P. Coolidge

Castle Cottage
Sawrey
nr Ambleside
Dec 15. 31

Dear Henry P.

How is the algebra? Still troublesome? or have you mastered it? I have got along fairly well in the world without ever having acquired the art of doing sums! Never by any chance did they come right. What is the old rhyme?

> "Multiplication is vexation,
> Division is as bad.
> The Rule of Three it puzzles me,
> And Fractions drive me mad!"

But I fear *you* will have to learn to understand Euclid – bother him!

I am struggling with another volume of the Caravan. I think of calling it "Cherry Tree Camp". There are a number of stories that were not used for the other book – though I do now think I was rather extravagant in using up all the prettiest in one volume. This collection does not wander up amongst the hills, it is in a sunny pasture, surrounded by woods. As a matter of fact the site is where the Girl Guides camp in summer, and the Scouts. We had such a number for the August holidays, over 80. And one troop arrived in such a downpour that they could not get their tents up so there were 30 sleeping in the barn and cooking in our small kitchen, for 2 hours.

The country is very lonely and deserted now, in winter. Last week one of the shepherds, searching for stray sheep, found the bones of a poor man who had been missing for many months.

The sheep sales have been bad this autumn, disastrous prices. I am fortunate in not having to pay rent, as I farm my own land. The tenant farmers are having a severe struggle; if things don't improve next year many of them will have to give up. There has been a sprinkling of snow twice on the top of the fells, but none in the valleys, and it is very mild and muggy weather. We are quite well here (amongst measles and influenza epidemics!) I hope you and your mother are well, and with all good wishes for Christmas and New Year,

I remain yrs aff
Beatrix Heelis

I hope we will meet again in more prosperous times. Very few Americans have been to the Lakes this season.

I wish someone would tell me how to address the friends in U.S.A.! Do you put Esq or Mr on the envelope? I am always puzzled if I write to Mr McKay.

To Joseph Moscrop

Castle Cottage
Sawrey
Jan 23rd 32

Dear Joe Moscrop,

I shall be very glad to see you again at lambing time. It is always something to look forward to – you manage to keep smiling! I note that you will come for £13 instead of £16; and I cannot deny that sheep farming is not at present a very profitable trade (what is?) so I am obliged to you, and it seems reasonable. The more so as I am taking on another servant here which in a way is an extravagance. He is a man who used to be groom in my parents' service, but last 10 years has been chauffeur to an old lady in this village who died lately; "Walter" [Stevens] is stranded – rather old to get a chauffeur's place again; but willing to do any odd jobs. And it seems to me it would be a kindness to *myself* as well as to the man, for I would be able to get about more, as he is competent to drive (carefully) anywhere – which is to say, I was laid up again with a nasty bronchial cold at Christmas & I have been rather afraid of driving in an open car in the wind. I got up to Troutbeck on Tuesday in the lorry, which is warmer than the open car; and I was delighted to see the first calves, 2 bulls. One beautiful blue gray; the other cow always brings a funny coloured calf, she was gold last year. G Walker thinks *all* the cows are in calf this year. Too good to be true; but a good crop I expect. The sheep have wintered well; but we are just wondering how they will stand the change to dry cold. It will likely come later; this would be perfect *April* weather – constant showers, but only once white over for a few hours. My mother is surprising. She had the cold before Christmas but she just stopped in bed 3 days and no worse. She was so very ill last spring, we thought her dying; but she got to coming downstairs again. Mr Heelis had the cold – nearly everyone had it – but it is working through.

Lassie will be the better of work, she is just as lively as ever, but no harm in her, except rabbiting. We have a young dog out of Fly, so there is no scarcity of dogs here. Tommy Christy has been doing drains too; its a grand time for tracing "boiling ups". He had a turn of influenza early on – we seem to have been rather a sick lot! Very glad you have kept so well.

With our kind regards yrs sincerely
H B Heelis

To Mrs. J. Templeman Coolidge

Ap. 29. 32
Castle Cottage
Sawrey
nr Ambleside

Dear Mrs. Coolidge,

Thank you for your interesting letter. I can read that "Henry P." is still the same eager unspoilt boy. Students in these later days have to absorb such an enormous range of knowledge, that it is pleasant to know that he has energy & time and strength for subjects outside the regular routine of school learning. I can believe he will make a good editor; he had originality and an inquiring mind.

Talking of editors – a curious thing has happened about my next book. I wrote out so many chapters and posted them. I never have much control of my subject; it ambles along, like the Caravan. By way of variety (and my own inclination) I made this sequel book more of tales told by, than of adventures happening to – the little animals. I remarked to Mr McKay that the book seemed likely to be over weighted by the tale of the Second Cousin Mouse; an absurd and grisly version of Bluebeard which grew to a big length. I suggested throwing it out. Which he has done. But he suggested printing it first and as a separate book under title of "Sister Anne"; and "eliminating the mice". Alright; it will suit me well. Only if the mice are "eliminated" the tale becomes deadly serious. I am recopying it and trying to improve the writing; but I am uncertain whether it is a romance or a joke. It certainly is not food for babes. He will get it illustrated in USA, which will relieve me from the difficulty of trying to illustrate human figure scenes. I think it had better have a blood curdling picture on the cover to warn off the babes! As it stood originally, the mice afforded comic relief; for instance after Fatima's discovery, the chapter ended – "Then the First and Third Cousin Mice with nerves and fur on end, fell upon the Second Cousin Mouse and bit him". I leave the responsibility intirely [sic] with Mr McKay. But I am not sure whether he is right. It wanted alteration, taking out of the frame work of the Caravan; but I am not sure how it will stand by itself. I wonder what Miss Mahony will think of it, it will be a queer book. I am glad to have more time for Cherry Tree Camp.

Trade is so bad there may be other reasons for delaying a larger book. I should like to do a set of fairy tales in thin volumes; Habbitrot [Chapter XI in *The Fairy Caravan*] might be reprinted, with a coloured illustration, for one of them; and I have others more or less written, for instance a version of Cinderella.

Mr McKay sent me the "Epic of America" [James Truslow Adams], a fine brave book, face the facts. Your task of regeneration is even harder, for your country has not a background of centuries of developing character. But every country is suffering from the same complaint of coming on too fast; all the world; not only America – forces and knowledge that are out of control; a curse instead of a blessing. Free education has not done much for this country. Clever children could always get educated in the past; and shallow education without character is proving to be a snare. It is a pity all these unstable young people of both sexes have votes. The National Govt. has such an immense majority, it should last this Parliament out, but I fully expect they will lose most bye elections that crop up – that is replacing vacant memberships.

We have had a mild wet winter, a dry early spring; and a heavy snow shower at the end of April. The leaves are coming out and the country is beginning to look lovely. The shepherds are very busy. In spite of tempests we have lost very few lambs.

I hope we shall meet again in better times. I have the pleasantest recollection of your visits with Henry P. My husband & I have kept well; we don't grow younger, and always almost over busy; but one must do ones bit.

With our kindest regards yrs sincerely
Beatrix Heelis

Sepia ink sketch of Newlands in Cumberland

In 1932 Bruce Thompson left London to look after the National Trust's affairs in the Lake District, with the title of Northern Area Representative. Living in High Cross Lodge in Troutbeck, he was the first full-time representative of the Trust's headquarters' staff anywhere in the country.

Meanwhile, in addition to her gift of Holme Ground in Tilberthwaite, Beatrix now donated to the National Trust the smaller estate of the Thwaite, under the strict assurance of anonymity.

To Mr S. H. Hamer

Castle Cottage
Sawrey
nr Ambleside
July. 20. 32

Dear Mr Hamer,

I have read – today – the report of the annual meeting and I am exceedingly annoyed about it. The announcement about Thwaite farm, in direct contradiction to my expressed wish, was quite gratuitous, when two other acquisitions were described as anonymous. I am very much annoyed about it.

You had better tell Prof. Trevelyan what I say; and at same time tell him what he has done. Willie and I had made up our minds to give a good deal more if my mother had died last time when she was so ill. *Now I won't.* It must take its chance.

I remain yrs sincerely
H. B. Heelis

Holme Ground farm today

To Bruce Thompson

July 23rd. 32.
Castle Cottage
Sawrey
nr Ambleside

Dear Bruce Thompson,

I am obliged for your letter. I did not think for a moment that Mr Hamer would commit a breach of confidence and put me in a false position – a position already uncomfortable at Coniston, if I were thin skinned.

As for Prof. Trevelyan, he is not a man of business.

Perhaps you do not realize that I got back ¾ of the original purchase money of Monk Coniston while I kept the more valuable half of the estate. The purchase of Thwaite was made possible by previous re-sales. As I took the initial risk I was entitled to reap any advantage. But it was not in my opinion a proper occasion for any further indulgence in what I can only describe by the vulgar word "swank".

The shocking condition of the Coniston property will prevent either the Trust or myself from getting a reasonable return in *income* for a long time; and it will always be rather an expensive estate to keep up, owing to the floods and the woods' fences. But as far as *capital* value in land is concerned I got a very large area of valuable land out of the deal. The Thwaite itself was not worth my keeping in its bad repair, since I could not sell the timber and build villas.

I do not like humbug in the newspapers on one hand, and on the other hand neighbours who have a shrewd guess at the truth. And I think Pro. Trevelyan made an error of judgement in talking; apart from offending me. But it is – raindrops on the sand. The Trust is a noble thing, and – humanly speaking – immortal.

There are some silly mortals connected with it; but they will pass.

I remain yrs sincerely
Beatrix Heelis

To S. H. Hamer

Nov 28. 32
Castle Cottage
Sawrey
nr Ambleside

Dear Mr Hamer

My husband says I ought to give you some account of the work at Yew Tree, which is now well advanced. It has been economically done and it is satisfactory; I do not think a stranger would detect the new walls. I cannot give you figures until I see Sandford's wage sheets. *I think* the cost will be round about £120; mainly wages. I have had to buy 2 tons slate, price £15. Any timber that has been used was *mine*; I propose to recoup myself by prigging larch timber from the Trust – (you can scarcely buy, or price, seasoned oak, 8 years in log?) The house is roughly this shape.

We have had off all the shaded slates, & put new latts on. We have rebuilt 2 walls.

The south gable came down like this and took the 'coign' and a bit of

front with it. It *might* have survived this winter – it might even have stood ten or twenty; but the crack in it had opened a lot in six months, and it might have gone any time in wind or snow. I can only say I was very thankful when the roof was safely propped.

And I can only say if I have spent too much – I am totally unrepentant. I consider Yew Tree is a typical north country farm-house, very well worth preserving. Besides, you cannot let a farm without a habitable house; it would have tumbled down piece meal; like Lane Head farm house.

I am in no apprehension about the Bank. If there is any shortage, it would at any time be possible to sell £40 £50 of larch; inconspicuous trees that would not be missed. I have cut down one very big one that was splitting (like the gable end) there is 200 cubic foot of timber in it = £10.

It is not possible to estimate in advance for patchy work, you never know what will happen amongst old walls. All the main timbers are sound. We have treated some parts with the preservative recommended by Mr Powys.

A lot of work has been done by our own men, all the carting & sand for mortar stone getting. It has been a big job, but I think well worth it. The inside plastering is still to do in the roof, & floors to patch with my oak planks.

If I put in a new kitchen grate, a good solid farm range costs about £12 – I will see if the old one would mend.

The only thing I regret is that I did not scrap the washhouse which is a modern-built excresence [sic]; but useful. I do not like the flue.

The mason Cookson & his labourer have been most conscientious in their work, doing it the old fashioned style.

The weather is very wild now; but things are improving – only us on the fells have sold all our lambs. Sheep that made 10/- at Ambleside fair were resold at Ulverston last Thursday at 26/-. A bit aggravating; but I trust the slump is over, and that there will never be such another.

I remain yrs sincerely

H. B. Heelis

Yew Tree Farm today

Alexander McKay commissioned the illustrations for SISTER ANNE *from the American artist, Katharine Sturges. The book was never published in England.*

To Alexander McKay

Castle Cottage
Sawrey
nr Ambleside
Dec 18. 32

Dear Mr. McKay,

I am agreeably surprised with "Sister Anne". The magenta is a crude color [sic]; but it is only a wrapper [*see Plate 17*]. The illustrations are fine; Katherine [sic] Sturges has conveyed the sense of giddy height so well in the outdoor subjects; and the black backgrounds give an effective air of mystery.

Brother John who "rode light" could not possibly have scrambled up & down a dry ditch in heavy plate armour; but that is a mere detail. The women's figures are beautiful, especially Fatima on horseback behind the Baron, and Anne coming down the cellar steps.

She cannot draw dogs – but no more can I. I should have sent a photograph of a wolf hound; they have *not* flap ears.

I should like to have the draft sent direct to me; not to Brown Bros.

I hope you and your family are having a Merry Christmas. I am *not*. My old mother is refusing to die. She was unconscious for 4 hours yesterday, and then suddenly asked for tea. She cannot possibly recover, and she suffers a lot of pain at times, so we hope it will soon be over; but she has wonderful vitality for any age – let alone 93.

With kind regards yrs sincerely
Beatrix Heelis

Beatrix's mother, Helen Potter, died on 20 December.

To Joseph Moscrop

Jan. 31. 33
Castle Cottage
Sawrey
nr Ambleside

Dear Joe Moscrop,

We shall be very pleased to see you again. The tups were loosed on Nov. 19th. Sheep have had an open winter and have thrived; except there have been some deaths amongst hoggs. Perhaps the wintering sheep have come down to over much grass – too green a winter. We have our first white snowfall here today; but the glass is down and the wind changed west, so I hope it will not lay long. I went with Tom in the lorry this morning, and we stuck on the Church hill, till he got chains on – being jeered at by a facetious farm boy with Mrs Leak's 2 carts. He turned out of the "Low Lane" got in our way; and we had a big load of coal. However, we got home, all well. Lassie is as hysterical as ever; she will be at liberty when you come, she was shut up before Christmas.

I wish I could say my Mother had not suffered. She was happy and cheerful, like a child, the last week. But she had a long struggle, and it is very sad to see an old person sick and cross. She was too strong, she lived on after her works were worn out inwardly. It was a nice notice that Mr Skelton put in the Wd. Gazette, which I suppose would be copied elsewhere. Last week's full reports of her affairs strike me as rather an impertinence; but the newspapers respect nothing private in these days. They don't mention that there is over twenty six thousand to pay in duty. In this case it is an easy matter to sell out securities – but what an upset it must be where there is a family business, or all the property in land.

You speak of Bright and Cobden, I don't remember the latter, but John Bright the Quaker was a very old family friend. A fine man – but I would not use the word "brilliant" (I believe it applied more to Cobden) J.B. was impressive by strength of character; a noble simplicity and transparent honesty – absolutely fearless & sincere; and as obstinate as a mule. I often wonder what would have been his ultimate opinion about tariffs. After his death his own business at Rockdale (hearthrugs & small carpets) was completely ruined by foreign competition. Mr Bright believed that all the world would be converted to Free Trade; that's the rub.

My grandfather was a very dull speaker, very plodding and useful on committees at awfully dull subjects. I have been looking over a bundle of his papers – notes and figures – factory acts – trades unions – education. I see one pathetic note to the effect that there were more than 45,000 children under 13 working in factories.

I think in those days trades unions were illegal. Now – alas – they are a worse tyranny than the masters used to be. And the children seem out-of-hand; in England. Education has grown and been valued in Scotland, grown from deep roots. I doubt whether free education has been altogether a blessing in the south. There ought to be a better class of teacher anyhow.

The world is a perplexing problem at present. After all these years of legislation, it is sad that there should be so much unrest and suffering.

Things are much as usual about here; seasonal unemployment, and several larger houses closed through deaths.

Mr Heelis has had colds and colds – now he has a sneezing cold, which he hopes will clear his head, he has been so deaf. We have not had flu – yet.

I remain with kind regards yrs sincerely
Beatrix Heelis

To Mr S. H. Hamer

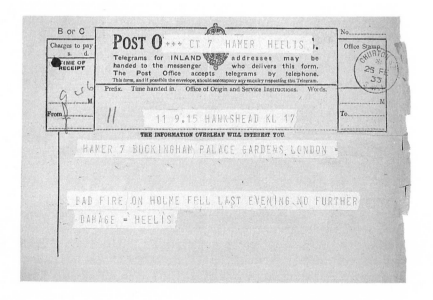

To Mr S. H. Hamer

Castle Cottage
Sawrey
Feb 23. 33

Dear Mr Hamer

This fire is a wicked thing – incendiarism. There are 3 or 4 sheep burnt and perhaps ½ square mile of heather. But what worries me is what may happen tonight. The police have it in hand; but the bracken is like tinder, any one could drop a match. It was most deliberate yesterday evening – I found one fire spot on my own this Oxenfell side of White How intake that could not be the work of a child nor a visitor. I was going up off the road to try and call Mr Slack's shepherd who was working sheep off the tops, & I came on this thawed circle and a nasty little stacked up heap of green savin [juniper] branches. I found the bush they had been hacked off with a knife; they were as thick as my walking stick. Apparently the violence of the wind had blown this fire out.

The lad said they had found 3 or 4 spots where it had been separately lighted, and I got the same news at the quarries. I think there was more than one lad in the mischief.

It was a terrific sight about 7 p.m. and we thought nothing else but it was Tarn Hows as it was straight in line. It burnt out on the craigs [sic] above the Tilberthwaite valley; about 8 it was all over. Nobody could have stopped it, had it been on low land; the flames were racing and leaping. Miss Roberts intake next Tarn Heights is burnt also. It is a blessing the fire near Oxenfell did not spread, it would have taken all the north end also. The burning does not show much from below; it is on the top. It began some distance above Hodge Close Cottages. There are some wild lads there; but I did not think they would do such a trick.

Perhaps the poor sheep may make them shamed. Wm. & our shepherd & Slack from Rydal who has the wintering were up last evening, but of course could do nothing in the dark.

Yrs sincerely
H B Heelis

To Mr S. H. Hamer   Castle Cottage
                                                    Sawrey
                                                    nr Ambleside
                                                    March 5. 33

Dear Mr Hamer

I have nothing satisfactory to report about that fire. There is suspicion against a young man, resident at the quarry cottages, but unless he gives himself away by alleging an untrue alibi or some other lad splits, there is no proof.

The police were up at the fire on Wednesday night and they made some perfunctory inquiries next day. I am provoked with the sergeant's attitude; he seems to consider the affair amusing. *Do you?*

It is beastly cruel, whatever. My men were up on Thursday (a week after the fire) helping Slack, but conditions were very bad for gathering. They only got a few sheep and they saw none of the scorched ones. It is thought at least 2 are dead under the snow. It is to be hoped so. Slack says the skin was peeling off in strips next morning; the wool burnt off back & buttocks.

The event was like this. There were 2 series of fires on Feb 22nd. Both series showed the curious trick of cutting and upending branches of savin. The first series started at Oxenfell about dusk. (I do not connect Miss Roberts intake). By 5.30 the series (of at least 5, – more likely 8) had reached a part in a line above Holme Ground cottages, the reservoirs, & the south heights of Holme Fell. As two witnesses told me "it was popping about"; probably more than one box of matches. After that the fire wandered on the top and burnt out over the south crags. At 9.45 *when Wm and the police* left High Yewdale it was dying out amongst the rocks. There was a hurricane of wind, but the thawed ground was mercifully wet. As soon as it got over the edge out of the wind – it went out. That was *9. p.m.* when the High Yewdale farmer Atkinson & a man called Wilfred Parry decided to take a walk up the Hodge Close road. Parry said he thought he saw 2 men going off amongst the bushes. Atkinson saw nobody. But a little further on they came to 2 new fires, newly lighted, 3 hours after the first series. It was a starlight night, but a fearful wind; no tramp or stranger would have hung about 3 hours on the hill side *out of doors.* Yesterday I went up to investigate these latter fires. It was almost uncanny: but you know I have long sight. First I found yet another fire place of savin branches; like the branches cut off on my intake. Next I came to the fires extinguished by Atkinson, the larger is an annoying disfigurement. I could not make out whereabouts it started being very rough. The second patch near the old road back of Holme Ground wood, I went to examine a patch of neighbouring junipers – old bushes – no need to cut with a knife. It appeared that sticks had been pulled out. And something had been pulled *off* – a neat new calico bandage for a sore finger. Not a *cut* finger – a pad . . .

I remain yrs truly
H. B. Heelis

Benjamin Dawson, the Lindeth How gardener

Castle Cottage
Sawrey
nr Ambleside
March 25. 33

I have much pleasure in recommending Benjamin Dawson. He was nine years in the service of my mother, the late Mrs Rupert Potter at Lindeth How[e], Storrs, Windermere, and he has left in consequence of the house being closed. He has been accustomed to herbaceous border, some bedding out, green house, peach house, early vegetables, and the use of the motor lawn mower.

He has also looked after the central heating of the house, and understands it.

Mrs Potter had a high opinion of Ben's usefulness, he is a thoroughly reliable man, and strong in health.

H. B. Heelis
(Mrs W. Heelis)

357

Ivy Hunt, the milliner's daughter who had emigrated to Canada in 1920, had married a Scot and fellow immigrant, Jack Steel. Now living in the United States, the couple had a daughter, June, to whom Beatrix wrote regularly.

To June Steel

Castle Cottage
Sawrey
nr Ambleside
May 8. 33

My dear June,

Thank you for your nice little letter – I am glad to hear you are getting on well at school. I will write to you while I remember a pleasant walk I took this afternoon in Mr Todd's [sic] big wood. But first I must tell you I heard a noise just now like somebody talking in the kitchen – there was Mr Drake Puddleduck and 6 Mrs Ducks *sitting* on the *mat* before the *kitchen fire*!! Our servant had gone out and left the back door open and it was raining very hard. But that is no excuse for ducks, they like rain. Had it been hens, or turkeys, I should not have been surprised. I said "Whatever are you doing here Mr Puddleduck?" And out they waddled in a hurry, Mrs Possy duck always last; she is quite blind of one eye She runs against apple trees etc, but she seems as fat as any, so I suppose she can find worms & corn to eat.

The woods are lovely now, wild cherry trees covered with blossom as white as snow, and violets and primroses and blue bells amongst the nut bushes. The deer have been making a noise at nights, they make a curious gruff barking noise like a dog that is very hoarse. I wanted to see them. It is a time of year when the stags have no horns. It is very strange their horns fall off in spring, and grow again.

First I saw lots of rabbits, big old rabbits, and tiny baby rabbits of all sizes. One was peeping out from the root of a big fir tree. I saw nothing of Tommy Brock or Mr Todd [sic]. I was looking out for Mr Todd [sic] because something carried off one of my young lambs into the wood. We were afraid others might be taken so I hung up an old jacket for a scarecrow – at least I did not hang it up, I folded it and put it down as if someone had taken their coat off while at work, and I moved it every few days to a fresh place, & Mr Todd [sic] kept away afterwards. I saw footmarks of deer. I saw Mr Todd's [sic] old house, long deserted; the walls made of sticks & bits of wood have gone; only the chimny [sic] stack is standing. A wood pigeon has a nest in a holly tree near the door way. I went on and I saw the stump and the fallen tree where Mr Todd [sic] sat and read the newspaper. I was getting tired and very warm and thought I would turn back, only I could hear a cock pheasant calling cuck! cuck! Cuck!! very excited and cross, so I knew there was something stirring. I saw two light coloured patches that moved beyond the nut bushes – light brown ends of deer. I wonder why they have a light patch at the tail end. They were reaching up, eating the young leaves on the ash and oak saplings. I stood quite still and watched them for a time then I climbed up a little hill in the wood and got a view sideways, looking down. The biggest deer were in front, five very big animals, taller than donkys [sic]. They are rather like donkies (how do you spell donkys [sic] at school?) only they are red brown and they have awfully thin legs. One of the young bucks  had knobs about an inch long on his head that was the horns growing. He looked dirty, in fact I saw him splashing about in a bog, they often roll in the mud to get away from flies and midges.

I watched them for some time keeping behind them. When the stags have horns it is not safe to go near them as they sometimes run at people like a bull. They seem to think the woods belong to them. They wander about for miles and miles. I only saw 10, but sometimes there is a drove of 40. They can do a lot of mischief if they come out onto the turnips and potato crops. It was a pretty sight to see the herd of deer moving away slowly. They never took any notice of me.

I hope you are very well. It is sad times in the big world but we must learn our lessons and hope for better days to come. There are nice showers of rain here, plenty of grass for the lambs.

With much love to you and your Mother

yrs aff
Beatrix Potter

To Caroline Clark

Dec 19. 33
Castle Cottage
Sawrey
nr Ambleside

My dear Caroline,

It is a long – very long – time since we wrote to one another. I hear news of you through Mary [?Caroline's sister]. Have you better times with the sheep trade? The autumn fairs were wonderfully better here, but my sister-in-law in Roxburghshire did not appear to be getting much benefit – our small Herdwick lambs in October made as much as her big half breds in August & September. Fat beasts are a very bad price, and while that lasts the store cattle won't make much either. There is decidedly a more hopeful feeling, on the sheep farms. As for milk marketting [sic] – we don't know where we are. I should think I am not under it, I have had no notice what to charge so went on at 5d. It is not suitable for small farms & retail custom. More & more red tape.

We had a glorious spring summer & autumn; and the glass is now standing on its head, set fair. Unless there is snow to fill up the springs it is a queer look out for next year. The Manchester supply at Thirlmere [reservoir] has never filled up since the summer drought. And Kendal is at present short of water. There has been plenty here, and the ground was never parched as there were welcome thunder showers in summer. There was the first fall of snow last Tuesday. At present there is a thick raw mist. I have been indoors a good deal, I got a chill in Nov. and it left me with lumbago & upset in my 'tummy', the mist disagrees with me. It is fine weather for those that are well.

Francis will be in a very different climate, Mary said he had gone or was going – to India? She did not mention Frank lately so I hope he is well again. Willie is alright & so far he has not had a cold, last winter he had one on top of another & went almost stone deaf. He was persuaded to go for the day to Liverpool to see a specialist who wrought a miraculous cure by blowing or injecting or clearing up the tubes between nose & ears. It really is a thing to know of; but doubtless would require careful doing.

I have been very much interested to read about the beast in Loch Ness. I can remember the controversy more than 50 years ago, when some such creature was in the Highland lochs, I have always believed in its existence, in spite of the incredulity of the Nat. History Museum.

– Post –

With love & much good wishes yr aff cousin
Beatrix Heelis

To Caroline Clark

Castle Cottage
Sawrey
nr Ambleside
Ap. 8. 34

My dear Caroline,

Your letter is welcome and very interesting. This village has been possessed by mumps all winter, I had it 50 years ago and have escaped so far! Your epidemic sounds rather similar. I agree intirely [sic] about school teachers. They do untold mischief and they have got such a hold, & such a good conceit of themselves, they are unsnubable [sic].

I am afraid I am not likely to be in London, I am feeling very much better, but I am still stiff, always over busy, & feeling old – I sometimes doubt whether if we did meet whether I could keep up with you and Mary! one cannot completely judge by letters but it seems to me that compared with me you must be more fresh and active in mind & body. I do not resent older age; if it brings slowness it brings experience & weight. I am not "on" things; but I pull strings. The regional planning is very interesting just now. Compared to the south this district has escaped wonderfully well, thanks to the landowners & the National Trust. The surveyor for North Lonsdale is a most satisfactory man, and I suppose he has enough weight as he is a govt official. As far as he has gone he is trying to work by persuasion and he will have little difficulty with the larger landowners getting lake shores declared "private open spaces".

The worst of 'zoning' is the small amount of land in the valleys; if it is zoned for houses with 20–40 acres of land it will stop bungalows; but it may also destroy farms. Our pretty old white washed farm houses in the sheltered valleys are a feature of the district.

I remember Harescombe perfectly. I don't think I should like to see it again. I remember Edith Pirton & her father perfectly; and the gallunus [?]; & the cowslips (which don't thrive here) and the blue distance looking over the Severn plain. I can imagine the horrid creeping out of building along the roads.

It has been the same sort of winter here, not really severe, but often frost, & a backward dry spring. We are getting lambs here, & should be in full swing on the sheep farms in another week. I have a third farm in hand this year, one of the Trust tenants having thrown up & left things in a mess.

Wool has slipped a little, but on the whole sheep farming is looking up. I was at the Herdwick Association meeting at Keswick yesterday. There was a resolution about subscribing to the Scottish Wool Growers Ass. Glasgow, with the object of eliminating the local small dealer; it was not carried. I am a little surprised that a large Scotch firm would care to buy Herdwick wool. If they get tired of it after our local agents had been squashed – our last state might be worse than our first present state – which has mounted to the magnificent sum of 6d per lb.

I see a neighbour has bought a mixed lot of Highland x heifers, its a pity the pure breeds get pinched down by the better paying xbreds. Our grand old local breed the Fell ponies has had a narrow escape, what with the govt grant being withdrawn and the temptation to breed Clydesdale cross foals (most useful & sort after [sic] in a hilly district) – there were plenty of mares but only 12 entires [stallions] left including colt foals & old "Jacky" "Blooming Heather" 20?th who is still ploughing at 30 odd years. I hope your West Highlanders don't shrink to such straits. This year the War Office has reappointed 3 premiums of £35, and the breed is looking up. They are said to be descended from the moss troopers horses, Dandy Dinmont's 'Dumple' would be a typical example specimen.

I have never tried Highlanders again. I go in for Galloways – I have just bought another 7 heifers. We are so plagued with bull calves, last year there were 11 pure bred calves and 8 were bulls. [For] the blue gray x we want bullocks, I do like the little black cows, they are so quiet, I have only had to get rid of one savage; it would not be possible to go amongst shorthorns with sucklers at foot.

I hope Francis will become reconciled to India. I had a cousin at Pekin[g], he liked the Chinese best of the Eastern races. The world is a perplexity; one can only strive to do ones bit. I think the milk marketing will have lost a lot of votes. It is very annoying to see the moderate party dragged at the heels of Mr Mc [Ramsay MacDonald was Prime Minister]. The old liberals had their failings; but they were at least an alternative.

I shall be very glad when warm weather comes. I get really pulled down with sleeping badly but my shoulder does not hurt now, I am afraid it will always be a bit stiff. I hope you and Frank do not catch the epidemic, we have both been very lucky here escaping flu or bad colds. The daffs. are not quite out in the garden. The wild ones are lovely.

With love yr aff cousin
Beatrix Heelis

Donald Macleod Matheson, Assistant Secretary to the National Trust,
was to succeed Samuel Hamer as Secretary on the latter's retirement at
the end of the year.

To Mr D. M. Matheson

Castle Cottage
Sawrey
nr Ambleside
June 15. 34

Litter at Tarn Hows

Dear Mr Matheson,

It was very tidy last week when I was up. If the *Crows* have been at the boxes again, I will get wire lids. It is a remarkable fact that the crows occasionally turn out the whole collection of paper bags, cartons, etc in search of sandwiches.

Bottles I regret to say I picked up 7 or 8, two were near the Tarns; some glass was almost too hot to handle.

Happily the rain has come. There was a slight fire last Friday which burnt itself out against a wall. It is not possible to patrol the whole estate. The men were working close by till 5 o'clock; and saw nothing. They think it was a cigarette.

One way traffic To restrict the whole length from Hawkshead hill to the bottom of Monk Coniston Hill would be rather cruel to nervous drivers; and rather asking for trouble also. Perhaps the R.A.C. secretary does not realize the terrific drop into Yewdale. Very many quiet harmless drivers go up to the parking place and there turn back, because they are afraid to go down the steep hill into Coniston.

The R.A.C. letter is singularly ill informed. To begin with the road *is* "in the ordinary sense a public road" under the jurisdiction of the Lanc. C.C. Moreover it was inquired about and scheduled by the L.C.C. sometime ago. *But they do not take the trouble to put up official notice boards anywhere.* I think Tilberthwaite is also scheduled. They notified all local char-a-banc companies. But there is no warning for long distance excursion drivers. A Newcastle driver got into the hill downwards & was nearly frightened to death, he could not turn back. I wish *you* could ask the Highway people to put up an official notice, (but don't let the R A C do it. Theirs would be mustard colour)

I have been speaking to the Highway Dept. Ulverston, & asked him to give you the date of scheduling and particulars. I am afraid he & I think the letter from Mr Armstrong is rather "butting in". The Trust does not want a wide tar macadam road through the Tarns – do they?

I am sceptical about the road mender. The road fireman & his men certainly do not approve of cars going up from Coniston; there was a complaint of a tradesman doing so.

Widening Our policy has been for the roadmen to nibble off corners and projections. It is greatly facilitating passing; and is less noticeable than a big alteration.

So much disfigurement has been caused by exaggerated widening in the Lake district that it makes one cautious of schemes. Our own two estatemen could do a lot of improvement at the Parking place – if only we could get through other work – cannot it wait till next winter?

Bathing We look another way, when it is at the further side.

Grass verge I suppose I must have the rails put up again. Cars went on objectionably at Whitsun. It is such a pity to have to put up barriers; but it seems it will have to be done.

If the secretary of the R.A.C. would take up the question of Motor Cycle Trials it might be more useful – but I suppose he would side with the Cyclists. The gates which the Carlisle Club broke did not belong to the Trust and I can get no satisfaction for the inconvenience caused to the Trust's tenant at Hall Garth Farm. I enclose Chief Constable's letter, also copy of letter handed to Messrs W H Heelis & Son by an indignant farmer.

Yrs sincerely
H B Heelis

Early landscape in grey and blue wash

Marian Frazer Perry first visited Beatrix in 1929, and since then they had met regularly. They exchanged books, Beatrix introducing Mrs Perry to Alison Uttley, and she in turn sending American authors.

Her niece, Betty Harris, had married Richard Stevens in April 1931 and their first child was called Nonya.

To Marian Frazer Harris Perry

Castle Cottage
Sawrey Ambleside
Oct 4. 34

Dear Mrs Perry,

I have just *re* read the Child in Old Chester with great enjoyment after getting it back safely from a borrower; it is a sweet book and you gave it to me! Little Ellen with her hair brushed back and the plain band behind her ears; mine used to be black velvet on Sundays, and either black or brown ribbon week days. I don't think my "Betsey Thomas" (who was Scotch and named Mackenzie) would ever have allowed a pink band. I remember the bands fastened with a bit of elastic, looped over a button behind the ear; it hurt.

My Scotch nurse was a stern Calvinist. I learnt nearly all the Lady of the Lake by heart when I was very young, perhaps 7; and I remember crying bitterly because Ellen Douglas was an R.C. and therefore *must* have gone to hell. Children take things seriously; at least the old fashioned ones did. I have another American book that is a favourite; "Hitty", about a doll.

It is sad that we shall not meet this time, but we will look forward to your next visit. And you are wise not to come north now, for the weather is completely broken, and sometimes bitterly cold at night after a stuffy day; probably thunder.

We are taken up with sheep fairs just now. I had a good sale at Ambleside fair, and there is another at Keswick tomorrow. I have about 700 sheep to draft out of the flocks this season. The nuisance of sheep stealing has cropped up again, at a season when so many sheep change hands lawfully it is too easy to put a wrong lot through a distant market. It is probably a motor van, and a clever dog trained to hold a sheep, without barking.

I hope the weather will be less windy when you sail; and I hope you find all well – give my love to Betty and Nonya.

yours affectionately
Beatrix Heelis

If you really really want to send me one more book at parting – please send another of Willa Cather's? I just have the Shadow on the Rock, it is a lovely book

To Eleanor Rawnsley

Castle Cottage
Sawrey
nr Ambleside
Oct. 21st. 34

Dear Mrs. Rawnsley

There was no letter to Dorothy Wordsworth amongst my father's collection. The only autograph letter of William Wordsworth's is addressed to John Gardner Esq, complaining about Messrs Longman the publisher. It is dated May 19th 1830; a long letter, a little bit sententious, but characteristic. If you think it is likely to be interesting I will gladly lend it?

Perhaps the letter to Dorothy may have been on approval. My father bought autographs from [Walter] Daniell's Mortimer St. and Tregaskis, Holborn; both reputable firms. He did not always buy. I remember a discussion and doubt about a signature – I thought it was Dr Johnson's, but very likely my memory is at fault and it might be the Wordsworth letter – the one sent to Canon Rawnsley for his opinion. I am afraid if HDR's [Hardwicke Rawnsley] reply is still existant [sic] I could not read it; and I cannot read much of RP's [Rupert Potter]!

My brother could read his writing; but my mother & I – living at home & not receiving letters – found his hieroglyphics quite illegible.

Your letter speaks of many memories of HDR. With how strong a mark his memory lingers! I don't know if it is the same with other people – I think it is. The other day there was some question about Portinscale bridge reported in the Herald and inevitably there followed the name of Canon Rawnsley.

I sometimes ponder over what he would say of recent developments – changes for good, for evil, and for doubtful good. It is to the good that there should be this new widespread interest in the overworked new word "amenity"; but personally I mistrust and definitely dislike some recent feelers towards a new policy.

The Canon's original aim for complete preservation of as much property as possible by acquisition was the right one for the Lake district.

If I hear you think the letter likely for publication I will send it, it is under glass but can get it out.

Yrs sincerely
Beatrix Heelis

To Eleanor Rawnsley

Castle Cottage
Sawrey
Oct 24. 34

Dear Mrs Rawnsley,

It is curious about that letter, I hope nothing disastrous happened to it. All the autographs were in two parcels.

You will find the Gardner letter at Allan Bank when you return. It has been in a case, hung up in the tea room at Yew Tree farm Coniston. The room will not be reopened before spring; and most unfortunately it has been closed this summer owing to Mrs Jackson's ill health. It was such a success in 1933 season, it has been disappointing this year having to close.

Besides the farm can scarcely pay without the teas & visitors.

It is a complicated subject. You see there are drawbacks to farming in a semi public situation; crowded like Tarn Hows is in summer.

And yet there are great advantages to farm upon land under the Trust. The Trust without income tax to pay, & without death duties, can afford repairs & be a fine landlord and lasting security to good tenants.

That is what I feel & mean about mere "covenanting".

I think the little white farm houses and green fields in the dales are part of the character of the Lake district, and I take such a pessimistic view of the future of our local farming – *unless under a good landlord*, that I wish there may be a sufficient representative number of the old farms in the hands of the Trust; and no doubt Baliol [sic] College [owners of much Lake District property] will also preserve them. Manchester Corporation & the Forestry Commission are protective against *building*, but they destroy rather than preserve the character of the countryside.

And small holders are hopeless. First they sell off the sheep stocks; and then they cut all scrub timber, & concentrate on hens.

Forgive this expression of views! but you are influential, and the new policy seems to be a sort of new toy to some people who ought to know better! It is good. But it is not enough.

Do not hurry about returning the Wordsworth letter.

Yrs sincerely
Beatrix Heelis

To Bruce Thompson

Castle Cottage
Sawrey
nr Ambleside
Nov. 11th 34

Dear Bruce Thompson,

Old Francis Edington died this morning at Coniston age 78, peacefully, after 3 weeks in bed.

He picked up strength in summer and was working in the joiner's shop until his last illness.

But he has been failing for the last year. It was kind of the Trust to pay his wages for so long. The two estate workmen George Wilson & William Wilson (not related) are very honest workers, trustworthy; and the former is a good scholar & joiner capable of keeping the time sheets.

I do not say that he could "take out quantities" and measure timber like Edington who was a trained forester; but there is very little commercial timber left on the estate and it would be easy to get outside help if any were ready & available to sell. He – Edington – has been little able for overlooking work, as foreman, for a long time, as his heart was not fit for bicycling.

He was a charming old man and I shall miss his friendship – though little use lately on the estate.

It will be a saving of wages, while there are still some structural repairs needed.

I remain yrs sincerely
Beatrix Heelis

Landscape in sepia ink and pencil

Helen Dean Fish, the editor of children's books for J. B. Lippincott Company in New York paid her first visit to Beatrix with her friend, Miss Street, in 1930. In answer to a recent letter Beatrix had sent her a copy of the privately printed TAILOR OF GLOUCESTER.

To Helen Dean Fish

Castle Cottage
Sawrey
nr Ambleside
Dec 8. 34

Dear Miss Fish,

I think your Children's Almanac is delightful, and it brings back so many favirites [sic] to my remembrance. Of course I have many of them still. I have been reading Miss Edgeworth's "Simple Susan" lately, again; with as much pleasure as ever, in a little old dumpy edition that belonged to my grandmother.

It is comical that I offered you a *second* copy of the pink "Tailor"; I must have felt you would appreciate it for I am not in the habit of throwing it about! So I will send a photograph instead, reprinted from an old one. It had no date, but probably I was six or seven. I know it was about that time that I was playing in the same garden when a friend of my father's, Professor Wilson from Oxford, came in and produced a book from his pocket and discussed with my Mother whether I was old enough – or whether the book was too old? which was the same thing. It had been written by another Oxford don and was attracting attention. I became immediately so absorbed with Tenniel's illustrations that I don't remember what they said about 'Lewis Carroll'. It was not the first edition – neither was the Water Babies. I had Mrs Molesworth's as they came out, with Walter Crane's pictures.

It is curious – the books that appeal to some children. I was very fond of "The Wide Wide World" – the farm life part of it [Elizabeth Wetherell, pen name of Susan Bogert Warner, the daughter of a prosperous New York State farmer, published in America in 1861]. I did not meet with "Little Women" until much later.

There has been time for reading lately; outside work is mostly finished for the season, and the country is rainswept and misty – but always beautiful. The fells are even more impressive in mist and snow than when you and Miss Street saw them in August.

With kind regards & all good wishes to you both,

yrs sincerely
Beatrix Heelis

I've had a cold and I'm feeling rather old and slow, but we both keep well.

In September 1932, at the age of fifty, Bertha Mahony, editor of THE
HORN BOOK, *married William Miller, the owner of the W. F. Whitney
Company, a business which manufactured reproductions in maple of
colonial furniture.*

To Bertha Mahony Miller

Castle Cottage
Sawrey
nr Ambleside
Dec 13. 1934

Dear Mrs. Miller

I have just been reading again your most interesting letter of Jan 3rd
– never answered by me yet. I think time slips away faster and faster as
one grows older; partly because this person when tired falls asleep;
which is not conducive to writing letters, or any thing else. I have only
done a Christmas card [for the ICAA]; the proceeds go towards
maintaining 2 beds in a children's hospital

I *do* get the Horn Book regularly. I thought it must be sent to me
from the Bookshop? I really ought to pay for it? There is the postage too.
That feeling of indebtedness was the reason I did not cash a little cheque
for a drawing; but it may have been a childish way of balancing accts. I
wish I could think of something worth while writing for it. It is a splendid
publication; the articles and critiques are so alive; and real criticism,
speaking out. Here, the review of the new crop of children's books is
either indiscriminate exaggerated praise, or silence.

I think your mind is occupied with two delightful interests – books
and old furniture. There is a periodical on this side – "Country Life"
which publishes views of old houses, indoors and exterior, and there
have been several of Georgian houses in the States. We used to feel that
rich Americans were carrying off too many treasures, but it seems as
though you have Chippendale & Sheraton furniture of your own.

I think the new style furniture & architecture is hideous; it is a craze
that will pass. But the old mahogany styles will always survive and be
beautiful. I have a few good pieces – no complete big set of chairs, but a
few very good 2's and 3's. We have got 2 chairs which were lying in a
garret over my husband's office 40 years ago, rather elaborately carved
Chippendale. There were usually good mahogany chairs in lawyer's
offices. I have a Queen Anne style fiddle back chair which had been
painted green, in a farm house in Wales. The local furniture in this
district was oak; rather out of fashion in the sale room now, but I collect
any genuine pieces I can get hold of to put back into the farmhouses.
The court cupboards with carved fronts are the most interesting as they
are usually dated. It is a great shame to take them out of the old farm

houses for they really don't look well in a modern room. There are a good many in cottages belonging to the National Trust which will be preserved safely. The oldest I know is 1639. I was in a farm house this morning looking at some good oak pannelling [sic] which the young woman had uncovered under many coats of wall paper & whitewash, the country people are learning to appreciate polished oak; they have discovered that tourists – American & British – are interested. There is a very fine old house Yew Tree Farm near Coniston belonging to the Trust. We fitted up a tea room with good furniture and pictures. Unluckily the woman has been ill; it was a great success the first summer it was open.

I am "written out" for story books, and my eyes are tired for painting; but I can still take great and useful pleasure in old oak – and drains – and old roofs – and damp walls – oh the repairs! And the difficulty of reconciling ancient relics and modern sanitation? An old dame in one of the Trusts cottages wants new window frames because only 2 little panes open. A date March 1826 is scratched on an old pane.

Such are the problems that occupy my declining years! I am 68; we have both had colds, it rains & rains & rains & is nearly dark. Things might be worse.

I only hope things may *not* be worse. I am one of the sceptics who refused to sign the L[eague] of Nations manifesto. Your government has not sent troops to the Saar. It is a nightmare. If the Saar vote goes *against* Germany and the Germans advance – it is not our handful of troops and the League's talking that can stop them; another retreat from Mons. It will be an anxious time.

If they *will* fight, let them exterminate each other; and hope that England the Colonies and the States may survive to see rule – *really* rule by power, not by preaching a better world.

I wish you and your husband a happy Christmas, and success in two good works – providing wholesome beautiful literature for children and continuing a fine tradition of furniture.

yrs sincerely
Beatrix Heelis

This photograph is pretty – is it not? it was taken by my father & is not copyright. – I don't know what to think about it? I could have written a few words about the little girl who used to be me – the books she liked or the pets? Or would it be egotistical. I do hate anything like advertisement.

The original print is not dated, I might be 6 = 1872. I was born [in] 1866.

To Caroline Clark

Castle Cottage
Sawrey
nr Ambleside
Dec 19. 34

My dear Caroline,

I hope you are well, and Frank not rheumatic. We all have to go slower as we get older. I am said to have a very strong heart; but I go slowly uphill, physically; and of course down hill in the years. It has been a wet dark dismal time lately. I do not know what you & Frank think about it, but I am alarmed. Their dd League of Nations is more likely to drag England into war than peace. It is the limit of infatuation to send British troops to the Saar. The Germans hate the English more than they hate the French. A handful can do no good; only endure another Mons if there is an outbreak. It is rather curious how extensively that foolish manifesto has been signed about here; I should have thought the distress in Barrow would have affected local opinion. If the money that has been wasted on the dole had been spent at Vickers' this country might have stood independently. It is not political; I noticed one socialist family would not sign; whereas Conservatives, & of course parson, do so, and revile those who won't sign.

We have had an awfully wet summer & autumn – November was less wet, but very dark – now December is very wet, I understand your climate is the same. The hot spring & early summer was a delight to remember. Sheep prices went up at least 6/- at the early fairs, but slipped a little before the big fair in October. Wool stationary at $4\frac{1}{2}$ during summer; also slipped since. The fat market is chaotic owing to the beef grading. Dealers are bringing in Irish heifers to grade. Young fat cows with teeth up are thrown away, we had luck to make 13.10 for a white one that had slipped her first calf; practically heifer beef. I think a great many are being killed that ought not (though some get graded & don't get killed!) which may make cattle dearer later on. We did alright with the blue gray suckler calves, bullock calves £8.10 to £9.17 but there is much more competition now. Instead of a few hundreds at Newcastleton market, the auctioneers were refusing entries after 1000 as the market was full.

I see a Windermere gentleman has some West Highland heifers in his park; they are delightful beasts. My little Galloway cows are next best; one of the heifers has just calved a funny little black baby. I keep a Galloway stirk [yearling bullock] as well as the white bull.

I see in the papers the Scotch milk sellers are in revolt. There is a little less grumbling here; farmers are getting used to the returns nuisance. We are getting a little advantage; I receive more for my milk 11/4 per month,

& pay the Board 3/11 + postage + poundage on produce + nuisance of forgetting to fill return ÷ selling a little less milk, at 6d instead of 5d.

I remain yr aff cousin
Beatrix Heelis

Detail from pen-and-ink sketches

To Mr D. M. Matheson

Jan 22. 35
Castle Cottage
Sawrey
nr Ambleside

Dear Sir,

I am forwarding for your inspection (and return) plans which I propose to deposit in duplicate with the proper authorities for the purposes of the Act – Rights of Way Act 1932.

After careful inquiry and after discussing maps with the officials at Ulverston, we have come to the conclusion that there are no public footpaths on the Trust's Coniston estate.

There are 3 on my own land. Fortunately all three are approached through stone stiles, not practicable for motor traffic. I am afraid in cases where ancient footpaths are entered through gates there may be serious trouble with motorcycles in this district. They have no right whatever to use footpaths either public or private, or occupation roads, but it is difficult to keep remote places under observation. During a reliability trial last summer 16 motorcycles went up a sledge track to the High Fell quarry on Wetherlam. The secretary of the club tried to argue that it is a public footpath. In the end he apologized and promised that his club would not offend again.

All the tracks marked on the ordnance survey on the Trust's estate are merely occupation ways. I venture to suggest that it is in the true interest of pedestrians & hikers that these pleasant walks should continue to be subject to the Trust's byelaws. Therefore it is important to lodge these plans.

I remain yrs truly
H. B. Heelis

To Joseph Moscrop

Castle Cottage
Sawrey
nr Ambleside
Jan 31. 36

Dear Joe Moscrop,

We look forward to seeing you as usual, it wouldn't be like lambing time without Joseph and *his dog*. I am expecting that the remuneration will include the four footed assistant again. The young dogs have turned out well, but G Walker's old Rap cannot do much work now. Mat seems to have a good nose for finding sheep, there were a lot to dig out, most of them above the Mires at the south end of the Tongue, the sheep had come down. I have not heard of any serious loss on this side of the fells. It has been a *horrible* winter – rain, rain, gales, and snow more than enough. The sheep look well, poor things they are never dry but they seem in good fettle. And we humans are well. G.W. got a bad cold in the wet snow but he was partly through it on Sunday afternoon when we were up at the Park.

It has been a sad time [King George V died on 20 January]. There is one reflection that is comforting – don't you think it is to the credit of human nature that a plain honest – not very clever man should have gained so much love and respect?

It is creditable both to himself and to Great Britain – still "great" in spite of a lot of nonsense talk. He has set a good and noble example and it has made an impression. There is much that us old ones don't like in modern life; but it would have been a much worse country without the good influence of King George and Queen Mary.

I believe I have you to thank for a copy of the Carlisle paper with the sale prices. You would know we did not send to Newcastleton because Messrs H & H. requested their southern clients to send sucklers to Carlisle. It was much the same – no harm. We kept a good many calves back, and sold some; as well or better, at Penrith – and kept back all black calves. I have just sold two little black bulls locally for £10.10 and £8.8 and we have a young bull and 5 heifers left. The hay is a problem, I bought some straw, there are only 3 geld running out; and they can get through some hay! Poor old twin mother, the big heavy cow was put away, she reared a splendid calf but she was so lame we did not try her again. The 6 top bullocks made 9.2.6.

With our kind regards.

yrs sincerely
H B Heelis

In January 1936 Beatrix had invited Ivy Steel and her husband, Jack, to bring their daughter, June, on holiday to Britain. The Heelises had recently acquired two Pekinese puppies, Tzusee (Suzee) and Chuleh (Chu Lee).

To Ivy Steel

Castle Cottage
Sawrey
nr Ambleside
Ap. 14. 36

My dear Ivy

I think most decidedly you would be wise to register as a naturalized American citizen. I cannot see that you gain any advantage by remaining a British subject when your husband is American, and it might be a disadvantage – more's the pity! Things looked so bad abroad that for several weeks I doubted whether it would be wise for you to come at all. It looks more hopeful now; but one never knows how soon, or when, there will be a flare up in Europe or whether this country could keep out of it. As an American citizen you would have a better chance of a passage home in a neutral ship.

I wrote to Cook's, the shipping agency, and got much the same information, "Summer season June 1st July 20th 49.7.10" other dates 46.18.0 Tourist class. "Above fare applicable to Berengaria Acquitania etc but not the Queen Mary." I think it is worthwhile inquiring further; these very grand ships with swimming pools and extremely quick passages are the last word of luxury; but surely an 8 days passage in a not-the-very-fashionablest would be alright, provided it were tourist class. What they don't ever mention is *How long does the return ticket hold good*? how long can you stop? I don't want you to be in Sawrey at August bank holiday – it's the one week in the year when Mr Heelis and I go away from home, to relations in Scotland [Bertram's widow], also we usually have visitors staying here at end of July till the last minute before we go. If the fare is a little lower after July 20th – why not the next boat after that – and go to Jack first and come on with Aunt Jessie here in August – I think her holiday is August? or was it September? It would not be half such fun without Aunt Jessie.

Cook's advise me paying fare on this side through them – they are the big travel agency, and absolutely reliable. If for any reason (such as measles etc!! or war etc) it fell through at last moment, they would refund the money to me, and we would hope for better luck next year.

The smudge is the paw of my little Peke dog who has a habit of getting on the table – tell June there are no guinea pigs now, but there is a Peke puppy very like a guinea pig or a Teddy bear with a tail. In this cold weather it sits up at the fire with its feet on the fender. It is bitterly cold again with snow on the hills, not nice weather for the little lambs, we have a lot and more to come. I will write to Cooks again and try and get more information, now that things are looking more settled – I really put it on one side for a bit. If there were a wider sea between here and Germany we would feel safer. Suzee and Chu Lee are going round and round under table and chairs like a hurricane, the puppy chasing the older one, they are sisters. Suzee has finished on the table again, I must stop & take her out. With love to you & June

yrs aff
Beatrix Heelis

In 1936 Bruce Thompson was appointed the National Trust's first Land Agent in the Lake District and it was proposed that the management of the Trust's share of the Monk Coniston Estate should be transferred to him.

To Mr D. M. Matheson

Castle Cottage
Sawrey
nr Ambleside
Ap. 22. 36

Dear Sir,

I have carefully considered your letters of Ap 16 and Ap 20th, together with our previous conversations with Pro. Trevelyan and Bruce Thompson.

I think that the proper course is for my husband and myself to retire when Bruce Thompson takes over at the end of the year.

At anytime I shall be glad to give him any information which may be useful for the management of the Trust's Coniston estate. This management will be a much simpler matter when the delapidations [sic] consequent on 30–40 years of neglect have been remedied.

The estate should show a fair income afterwards; though there will always be current chronic expenses, such as renewal of fences; repairs to buildings damaged by tempest; woodlands; drains, occupation roads and paths etc. At least I sincerely hope that the Estates Committee will not contemplate allowing the property – especially the farms – to fall back into ruin.

I should be obliged if you will read this letter to them.

I remain yrs truly
H.B. Heelis

In the year following their first visit to Beatrix together, Richard and Betty Stevens had a new baby, a brother for Nonya.

To Betty and Richard Stevens
Castle Cottage
Sawrey
nr Ambleside
Sept 10. 36

My dear Dick and Betty,

Most hearty congratulations upon the arrival of the dear pink Baby! I expect you are home again. I have been slow to write; but not through want of sympathetic pleasure. I had been thinking very hard about you and wondering from the end of July; and directly I saw the letter I thought here's news! I am so glad you had not much trouble and I hope you are well again. Nonya will be most interested and full of funny remarks.

We are having a wet dreary season. The hay is in the barn at last and some of the corn. What is still out in the field is nearly black and spoilt. There is a good deal of grass still uncut in the district and nearly all the corn is spoilt. It is not a corn growing country; but we use the oats & oat straw for the cattle so it will be a loss of fodder next winter. Some of the small farmers will be half ruined. They are all wanting a reduction on their rents. Sheep are a better price, as the fields are deep in green aftermath – what we call fog grass – so store lambs are being bought to eat it off. I think that is the reason you have so few sheep comparitively [sic] in the States; I am told your fields are bare after the hay is carried.

I have had a good many American visitors. Two delightful girls, (niece & friend of a friend known of old). They had come over 3rd class and were tramping all over England, doing it economically. Also a young woman, a Londoner, who went out as a young girl and married. I had not seen her for twenty years. She came over to see her brother bringing her own child. I was very relieved to find I liked "Ivy" [Steel] as much as when she was a young girl, and I was interested in her girl. I suppose you have no classes in America?! Anyhow Ivy's husband is in the telephones and her child goes to what would be equivalent to board school = council school here. It was the first time I had ever heard the native accent of Bronx. I am tempted to say I hope I may never hear that accent again. She was a dear child. When one got over the accent she compared favourably with the average English child of the same class; obedient, intelligent and natural manners without forwardness. But the accent was a caution; on her father's side descended from Glasgow Scotch which is even worse. I was not edified with what Ivy told me about graft in N.Y. Your politics are beyond comprehension, but there's "something rotten in the state of Denmark". I also had two charming Boston boys whom I had seen six years ago.

But Mrs Perry is a missing visitor – and I have missed her.

With much love to Betty – and all of you,

Yours sincerely
Beatrix Heelis

Detail from a pencil sketch

Esther Nicholson was Willie Heelis's niece, one of the five children of his sister Grace and her husband James, who was a barrister. (Another daughter was Nancy, for whom Beatrix wrote the unpublished story, THE OAKMEN, *in 1916.) In 1915 Beatrix took on the financial responsibility for Esther's education and over the ensuing years encouraged and supported her in her studies. Esther became a teacher and in the late 1920s was English Mistress at Amberley House in Christchurch, New Zealand, where one of her pupils still remembers her as 'a most excellent teacher'. From Christchurch she moved south to Invercargill and taught for many years at St John's Girls' School. She retired to Te Anau in the beautiful lake country of Southland and when she died there in the early 1980s she left her house to the little Anglican church next door, St Michael's and All Angels, of which it is said she was 'the practical founder'.*

To Esther Nicholson

Nov. 17. 36
Castle Cottage,
Sawrey,
nr Ambleside

My dear Esther,

I doubt if I have written to you or heard from you since last Christmas, but I heard of you and the school when your Mother was over here in summer and she said how well you had started off, which we were very glad to know.

I hope times are mending in N.Z. it is a most uneasy world. The belated catching up in armaments for defence has helped unemployment, but what after I wonder? And the miners in Cumberland and Durham are still on the dole. As far as the Maryport and district men are concerned – I doubt if they want *work* – and as for removing – they refuse to go as far as Kent; let alone N.Z. Perhaps Australia and N.Z. don't want them. It is a pity how emigration has completely stopped.

There is no news to write about. We have not been to Appleby for some time. By all accounts Aunty May [Willie's sister Marion] is wonderfully better, we never thought this time last year that she would see another spring; and she has been well enough to enjoy the garden. The present Battlebarrow gardener is a treasure, he gets through so much work, keeping the lawns well mown, and the beds full of flowers. I had a letter from Nancy yesterday saying Mr Coop is dead, from pneumonia at last, after several attacks. I wonder if it will make a difference. Nancy has good influence and control over the spirited boys.

We have kept well here – a little battered by the weather. There was just one short fortnight in October to warm us up, but we have paid for it since! The fine weather came in spring, fine, cold at nights, a regular drought in May & June. By the time there was any grass to cut – the weather was gone. I never remember a more tiresome hay time, week after week. It interfered with shows; we missed several. The sheep got many prizes, but not so many as the previous year. We had not such bad luck with the hay, but so late of finishing; about 3rd week of September.

Uncle Willie has only had one afternoon shooting, Saturdays seem always to be wet. It would do him good to get out a bit, he gets bothered with overwork, and he is getting stouter. So is Jack [Heelis, Willie's nephew and partner] – quite fat and middle aged in tortoiseshell spectacles. He and Wynne [Jack's wife] have gone in strongly for the Oxford group which is active in Hawkshead. They and the Ushers have prayer meetings on Tues. Fridays at each others houses. They say it has made them much happier. Jack does not seem to come to the office any more punctually; but it is harmless. And where people are quarrelsome probably quite beneficial. Its spread is phenominal [sic]. I think the fiasco of the League of Nations has a good deal to do with it; the earnest people who clung to Geneva are now clinging to Oxford as a plank in shipwreck. I am not conscious of hating anybody; and your Uncle cannot publicly confess his sins as a solicitor nor other peoples. But if it is to spread like Free Masonry, he thinks it may be quite useful for one partner to belong. They, J & W, have not approached the subject with either of us yet. I hope a letter will come from you at Christmas – though I expect you are kept very busy. With love from Uncle Willie and yr aff aunt

Beatrix

Beatrix was eager to pass on to the National Trust's newly-appointed Land Agent her experience of the past years, and she showered him with practical information.

To Bruce Thompson

Castle Cottage
Sawrey
nr Ambleside
Jan 4. 37

Dear Bruce Thompson,

Nanson, the Yew Tree tenant, is asking about a broken fence against the Beck. If it is a short length of wire, near Yewdale Bridge – it has always been considered an estate fence, repairable by landlord; probably a bit of scrub or coppice in old days. It is much patched and wants reerecting. It is usual to put *round* wire near flood water, because woven wire netting gets clagged with drift.

I sent 350 yards Hercules woven wire, and 1 stone staples, to Tarn Hows out of my own stock, but the Trust has no round wire – you want *1cwt No 9.*

Messrs Warhurst Ironmongers Ulverston, send their van round Coniston about once a fortnight but it is not coming this week. I wonder how you intend to get things, I have carried small articles in the car. You can get round wire, from Mr W. Middleton 21 Stricklandgate Kendal, or Hoggarths, Sandes Avenue or possible Musgrave's Windermere, (but do not be put off with anything thinner than 9, you understand 10 is thinner and 8 is thicker) If you at any time want more Hercules it is obtained *on order* from W Middleton. There is a cheaper netting called 'Wrylock' obtainable from Hoggarths or anywhere – besides the ordinary flimsy sheep netting – but so much of the cost of fencing is comprised in labour, posts, nails etc., that it is good policy to buy good wire.

The men call *all* square mesh "Yankee", whether good or bad. If a farmer asks for a roll to stop a gap, sheep netting is good enough. But for a permanent fence properly erected by our own men with a jack stretcher there is none so good as Hercules.

G. Wilson says you inquired about wood. There are 3 trees at Nibthwaite saw mill marked for rails and boards. I sent 3 on acct of horse hire, it is a day's hire of three horses whether one tree is snigged [dragged along the ground with a horse and chain] or several; also the wood is better of drying. We are clearing a place in the cart shed.

I told Wilson to use my old horse for small jobs of estate carting until Atkinson comes to Yew Tree, when it would be a help for him if you hired his cart. Should you require a lorry I would recommend Barr, Torver; not Fury.

I have been up to Tilberthwaite this morning and I was very glad *not* to hear of any more slates off, it has been wild weather.

I remain yrs sincerely
H.B. Heelis

There is one Ulverston-Coniston carrier, but I have never yet discovered where he is supposed to dump goods. They do not arrive at High Water Head.

Study in black crayon drawn when Beatrix was not quite thirteen

To Caroline Clark

Castle Cottage
Sawrey
Feb. 15. 37

My dear Caroline,

Crompton tenacity, obstinate, indomitable to the end. By all means let her go her own way – would not you and I choose so, if choice is left to us? I am glad you got her to a doctor, because I have sometimes wondered whether her "good osteopath" was allowed to give death certificates? I believe in bone setters, and think the medical profession go too far in jealousy; but osteopaths go too far also when treating complaints that do *not* come from bones or nerves. Thank you for writing; I appreciate it, and will say nothing to anybody – indeed who is there left to say to? except Carrie Halpin at intervals writes a note; with little in it.

I should think Mary will just doze away. In her last letter she said she had her Aunt Annie's nurse near at hand. I can just see her! by your description; dear Mary; obstinately obstinate. Your father, a true philosopher, gave in, and enjoyed his Greek and his nursing; but I'm sure it must have been by his own choice.

I was rather surprised when I got Mary's last; her letters had dwindled to about twice a year. I won't write again till Christmas card time – unless she asks, which is unlikely. It will be a relief to you when she finally falls asleep, in her bed, without accident. You ask how I like growing old. I have felt curiously better & younger this last 12 months! Last year I felt so peaky it was irksome. I mind it little (with one or two reservations) For one thing to quote a friend "Thank God I have the seeing eye", that is to say, as I lie in bed I cannot [sic] walk step by step on the fells and rough lands seeing every stone and flower and patch of bog and cotton grass where my old legs will never take me again. Also do you not feel it is rather pleasing to be so much *wiser* than quantities of young idiots? But perhaps you Caroline had always a good conceit of yourself!! I begin to assert myself at 70. What worries me at times is so many dependents. I have always favoured married servants; and had many good ones. It will be a slump when I come to an end.

It is a pity that the wisdom and experience of old age is largely wasted – (except in the case of Judges who sit for ever, usually without falling into dotage).

I eschew tea parties, but was inveigled into quite a highbrow tea recently, 6 persons, the hostess an old Jewess. One person started the proposition that it was unfathomable why brains should be wasted and every scholar have to start afresh with A.B.C. I thought that youth would be perfectly horribly unbearable if it started ready made without having to learn to learn. There is little enough discipline as it is. I did not venture to mention the wasted wisdom of old age; but I don't agree that it is a hardship for youth to have to commence afresh at the bottom.

I have just bought a very nice little Galloway bull at Carlisle £20 – I did not go to the auction, I know a very useful farmer-dealer if you ever wanted an agent buyer. He bought me a white scotch shorthorn elsewhere & charged 2gs commission for the two & a lot of telephoning.

I am glad you enjoyed the trip – your description was not dull at all, very amusing. I should think ocean cruises are even worse than a smart hotel, in the social line, and the only escape would be sea sick or suicide in the sea. The birds must have been very beautiful & interesting. I have met several who have been the trip but you are the first to mention humming birds.

remaining yr aff cousin
Beatrix Heelis

The white shorthorn bull is off a good breed, but not quite as much bone as I hoped for, its impossible to get *beef* bulls now; all milk recorded. I wonder how a Hereford would cross. Irish are using them.

Detail of pencil study

To Mrs M.C. Grimston

Castle Cottage
Sawrey
Ambleside
Feb.12.38

Dear Mrs Grimston,

Thank you for your pleasant letter. If Kathleen has not posted back the 'Fairy Caravan' I hope you will keep it and accept it – I don't give it away to *everybody*, but I should like to bestow a copy on such an understanding correspondent. If all the chapters had been as charming as 'Birds Place' – it would have been a fine book! As a whole I think it is too rambling; and the pig is tiresome.

It is interesting about your wild rabbits. I used to tame house mice – so tame that I could pick them up, with food in my hand. But I never had a satisfactory "wild" rabbit. Usually the little rabbits picked up, or apparently unhurt when caught by a dog, did not live. I had one called Mopsy that grew up, but she was painfully nervous, and I let her go, before firelighting time in autumn, because she always made a dash for the chimney whenever startled. 'Peter' was drawn from a very intelligent Belgian hare called Bounce. You will notice the ears are too long for the native rabbit. The Belgians are undoubtedly rabbits – not hares. But I always thought poor old Bounce resembled Cowper's tame hares in his ways – the verse about 'The Turkey Carpet was his lawn' – he used to bang his hindlegs & rump against the wire fender in the school room as "he frisked around". A noisy cheerful determined animal, inclined to attack strangers.

I remain yrs sincerely,
Beatrix Heelis

Detail of pencil study dated 14 February 1899

Josephine and Delmar Banner were two young artists in whose work Beatrix was interested. She was helping them in their search for land on which to build a house and occasionally she drove over to have tea with them when they were staying in Heathwaite, below the Old Man of Coniston.

To Josephine Banner

Castle Cottage
Sawrey
Feb 28.38

My dear Josephine,

It was disappointing but not unexpected by *me*. I am afraid your originals are too delicately beautiful for the modern publishing world which caters for shop keepers at a competitive price. Goupil could have reproduced it as an art book years ago. What is to be done in face of such a world? Children deserve the best. Rather than have the vexation of seeing your work reproduced badly I should advise you some day when you don't feel too disgusted to re copy some of your pages in darker ink (not necessarily *black*, tho' *black* reproduces more correctly in values) and adapt them to a *smaller* page – or arrange to have more white margin. Or, if the music publisher wants the full size music – compress the design so that there is a wider margin. A design spread over a page the size of your sample would require a very large plate, reckoned by the square inch, its formidable. They are too good and pretty to be left in the cold of rejection. Neither do I see – though I can understand – the feeling that there is something superior and more satisfying to the artist in a very choice very limited small edition – But there!! Peter never aspired to be high art – he was passable (except the covers which I had nothing to do with and always hated), but if not high art his moderate price has at least enabled him to reach many hundreds of thousands of children, and has given them pleasure without ugliness.

I do hope you will get your book published in some form. If you recopy I do not think you should give yourself the labour of beautifully transcribing *all* the music pages. You don't know what a dirty mess printers etc make ! Music on ordinary bought music paper is good enough for them.

We have had a pleasant dry spell, with occasional still days. Today is wild rain. I have been in Little Langdale and Coniston on days when the fells were very lovely. On Oxenfell on Tuesday I looked away – away – there was another behind Bowfell, in the gap between Bowfell and Langdale Pikes. The fells are never twice alike.

There has been an *amazing* show of Dick Yeadon's watercolours at Kendal. It is a tragedy that he died last summer of pneumonia at 40. He was 'finding himself' the last six or eight years. He was mainly self taught, and weak in perspective which he had obviously never learnt, but he did understand the How Barbon & Tebay fells. Not successful in his few attempts in the Lake District proper which one can understand as he worked much from memory and pencil notes, and would not remember the forms of unaccustomed hills. When Delmar can get as much *light* into his studies as poor Dick??! I have a sketch of Shap moor before me which reminds me of a slight sketch by David Cox which belonged to my grandfather. All done in the spare times of Saturday Sundays after driving a laundry van 12 hours a day during the week. It was a very remarkable and sad show – closed yesterday after one week. Your husband has learnt clouds. Light next please. He has the *drawing* which is the foundation.

Yrs sincerely,
Beatrix Heelis

Early pen-and-ink drawing

To Mr D. M. Matheson
Castle Cottage
Sawrey
Ambleside
May 9.38

Dear Sir,

In the course of a telephone conversation this morning with your agent Mr Bruce Thompson about fencing, I told him that I intended to write to head quarters. Mr Thompson's usual excuse for delaying farm repairs is that he "has no money".

He said this morning that there was "plenty of money" but that "he did not think the Trust is under obligation to fence land that has not been fenced before". In the first place the pasture land in question at Holme Ground *is* and has been for many years fenced, but the fence is worn out and quite unsafe for cattle in proximity to a public motor road and dangerous quarries.

And I think that the observation comes strangely from an agent who has wasted money on nearly half a mile of unnecessary and objectionable fence along the open south side of Holme Fell.

Is it the policy of the National Trust to take no interest in its farms? or is it not? I regret heartily that I ever presented Holme Ground to the Trust.

If Mr Thompson is really short of money (which would not be surprising) I am willing to lend money for the Holme Ground fence, by advancing wire and wages; in which case I should at least have the satisfaction of erecting proper woven wire netting. I have asked Mr Thompson 3 times not to buy the "wry-lock" type of netting, but he seems to have no understanding about anything; and he is not learning either.

I told him and I take this opportunity of repeating that if cattle come to harm after he has been warned – the Trust will be held responsible. I could have claimed for 2 sheep last year. If my cattle hang themselves or get lost you will have to pay for them.

I remain yrs truly
H.B. Heelis

Bruce Thompson wrote to Head Office on the same day putting the case from his side, but continuing, 'Because the National Trust are anxious to do everything to please Mrs Heelis I have given instructions for the work to be done'.

To Mr D. M. Matheson

May 11.38
Castle Cottage
Sawrey
Ambleside

Dear Sir,

I am glad to receive your assurance that the National Trust appreciates the importance of good farming. An institution which pays neither income tax nor death duties should be in a position to give a useful lead to less fortunate landowners. As regards advice – a man must have judgement to sift the value of advice and of advisors, otherwise it is like the fable of the old man and his donky [sic].

I understand that the new fence along Holme Fell was put up by request of a new in-coming tenant who had no previous acquaintance with the land. From long observation of Holme Fell – I should be afraid *now* to put on sheep of my own. The new fence cuts off the sheep from the only satisfactory water supply on that side; and it would be a death trap in case of fire. It shuts out the public from a pleasant piece of heather & rocks – a happy spot too steep for car parking! Some part of it is iron standards drilled into rock. An utter waste of money. Like the prolonged cutting of firewood last winter.

It is not my affair or wish to interfere with Bruce Thompson; and most emphatically I cannot take any responsibility for anything he may do. But when I was blamed for the Holme Fell fence last summer by a party of Oxford gentlemen, and when Mr Thompson says he cannot afford reasonable repairs – it is time to speak out.

Thanking you very much for your letter

I remain yrs truly
H.B. Heelis

P.S. What is the feeling of the Estates Committee about corrugated roofing?
P.P.S. And would there be any objection to my taking up to Tilberthwaite a wooden loose box (weathered not new boards & wooden roof) to supplement the existing buildings? The box would of course be a "tenants fixture". H.B.H

To Alexander McKay

Castle Cottage
Sawrey
Ambleside
July 13th 38

Dear Mr McKay,

I am pleased to hear you have given leave for the transcription into Braille of the Fairy Caravan – rather a bulky volume in embossed form.

I have an old interest in Braille; years & years ago when it was all to do = i.e duplication by hand, my mother transcribed many volumes for a Blind Association in London. A process of stereotyping was invented later.

We are having a very very wet summer here. I hope you are all well – I'm alright, but feeling old. My book days are done – I'm afraid Margery [Alexander McKay's daughter] will look in vain for mss. from me.

But you are well off for excellent writers of children's books in USA.

What an amusing picture book that [*And to Think I Saw It on*] Mulberry Street by Dr Seuss – someone sent it to me at Christmas.

With kind regards yrs sincerely
Beatrix Heelis

P.S. I *hope* I acknowledged safe receipt of the package of originals – beautifully mounted – they came safely.

I'm dreadful for not writing receipts and thanks.

From The Fairy Caravan

391

To Marian Frazer Harris Perry

Castle Cottage
Sawrey
Ambleside
Oct. 4. 38

Dear Mrs Perry,

I have been very neglectful about writing letters this unpleasant summer – and now one has a feeling of stupifaction [sic]. Anything – "nearly" anything – may be better than war. It is not an honourable peace – and doubtful whether it has any permanency.

Can you hear Hitler over the wireless as far as America? Did you ever hear such a brutal raving lunatic. I could not understand a word of his clipped rapid German; but the ranting note and the smiling face in the telegraphed photographs are not sane. If Mr Chamberlain believes in his promises he must be an incurable optimist.

We did not take gas masks very seriously in this remote district; which was just as well for our peace of mind as they were supplied wrong size – so few small & medium compared with the large size that the police sensibly decided it would be best to withdraw them. It is the Air that has let us down – the Navy was ready. I wonder whether a new and more solid frame of mind will emerge from this slap-in-the-face; there ought to be conscription. Czechoslovakia would have been wiped out in any case; but it is a set back for England.

The season has been wet & dismal, not to be called "summer". The hay was a wearying long task; it was finished on the same day as our small harvest, Sept 19th. The corn was got well. There is still a good deal out in the north; but taking one place with another there are heavy crops. We burnt some of the last of the hay, the barns were full and it seemed little worth, after repeated wettings. This last weekend there has been a wild gale.

The sheep sales are coming on, up to date they are bad, prices 5/per sheep down from last year. Everything is in an upset way.

That is a most curious book you have sent me, so "alive" [The Yearling by Marjorie Kinnan Rawlings] – I find myself trying to make out how the illusion of reality is done? I liked it extremely until I came to the rattlesnake which gave me creeps and horrors! The end chapters are too horrid.

My brother years ago had a very bad accident with a viper; he sucked the bite and the poison got into his throat & inside him. I wonder if it is a superstition, or true, that newly killed flesh will draw the poison! I have heard or read it before, but it scarcely seems explainable. One of our little peke dogs got bitten on the nose this spring, and was very ill; we dosed her with whisky & carbonate of soda. The actual bite did not swell; but the swelling & pain went down the glands of the neck & paralised the hind legs. She got quite well again within a week. They are good company, but sad pickles, always hunting. Tzuzee [sic] had killed 2 large rats successfully, so she must needs tackle a snake.

I have not been at all well lately. I got a chill, and the weather has not been helpful. My husband has been over worked; old friends and neighbours dying, and their affairs to wind up. There are these black depressing seasons! I hope we are properly thankful that there is no war. For which we may thank the unhappy Czecks [sic].

Perhaps a better, more wise, world may emerge. I have not much faith in Mr Chamberlain, and if we are ever in the "same mess" as the Czecks [sic] it would be little use to wait for U.S.A.!!? Everyone for themselves – and underground in tunnels! Thanking you for the book.

yrs very sincerely
Beatrix Heelis

My old American friend [Rebecca Owen] went back to Rome; she feels safe with her dear Duce. We all think the mobilisation of our Navy stirred Mussolini to intervene.

P.S. I have been reading your letter again – of *June*! The book did not come quite so long ago as *that*, your cousins had sensibly read it first. It is a curiously graphic picture of the Florida swamp life.

I never heard of "trench mouth" – Shingles does go in epidemics in this way – that it so often coincides with chicken pox – too often to be a coincidence. Thus, I had chicken pox being nearly 60 when William had shingles; but which of us started the infection or where caught from cannot say – I hope Dick [Harris] got clear of it. Shingles leaves ticklings which can be mildly troublesome for years.

It was well that your kind thought for your friend kept you out of Europe this summer. Surely things must settle one way or another.

The best chance would be realization by the German people. I do not believe they could have won a war. But I am afraid they will be strengthened by the acquisition of Bohemia. And this country is kept in the dark too. We are completely perplexed about Russia. Not an agreeable idea to have to line up with Russia. But its silence seems strange; unless it is completely rotten.

Was it you who sent me The Country of the Pointed Firs [Sara Orne Jewett]? I have been re-reading it with great pleasure. I shall never go over the sea; but I think I would like the New England states.

To Joseph Moscrop

Castle Cottage
Sawrey
Jan 23rd 39

Dear Joe Moscrop,

You must be an incurable optimist if you think this a suitable time to make jokes – I do *not*. We may be under 'exemption' orders like the last war and sent where the board pleases before lambing time comes round; or it may be past over like last September. I shall be very glad to see you again at the Park, all being well. But you will please come down a pound Joseph – take it or leave it! not even King Canute could control the tide – or the slump. Not the most cheerful person could say anything favourable about the sheep trade last year. In 1937 I sold 876 sheep for £727.14.9 and in 1938 I sold 843 sheep for £533.16.8. Wool about halved. It has been a disastrous year; so bad that I think things must have touched rock bottom.

Tell your brother the heifers seems [sic] to be all in calf and done well. Perhaps the 2 best are no longer quite the best in condition – (had they been on better land I wonder). They certainly were expensive. But what I can buy locally are not so good – and its hopeless breeding Galloways at Troutbeck, another 2 have just been knackered with Johne's disease [a chronic intestinal infection] – one was as fine a heifer as I ever saw, last spring, scoured to bits, and infecting the pastures. So long as we only bred cross [?] which go for baby beef – the evil was not apparent, but it is the old trouble, in the soil and pasture. The new heifers are at Coniston. I do not think adult cattle catch the disease.

I wonder if you have got over this influenza epidemic in Scotland. It has been mainly throat & heavy colds – very prevalent. I have been out in the sun for the first time since New Year. It pulled me down a good deal – and very awkward our maid is still away in bed with it. Mr Heelis is better.

Have you a dog? They have been unlucky at Park – a young one died of distemper (early December) and Walker's good dog Matt has been so ill with pneumonia I don't know whether it is still alive or dead poor thing. He was a good dog, he is jiggered for work this winter. We have had little snow to lay long.

These wretched stamps have been looking at me since last spring!!

Yrs sincerely
H.B. Heelis

Bertram Potter's widow, Mary, had continued to farm in Hawick after his death in 1918, and Beatrix and Willie had visited there every August Bank Holiday weekend. Now Mary had died.

To Daisy Hammond   Tower Hotel
Hawick
[Feb 1939]

My dear Daisy,

We are here – or hereabouts – till after the funeral on Tuesday – we may get part way homewards that afternoon. Poor Hetty [Douglas, Mary's niece] is so upset, and nervous about undertaking any business that we cannot shirk stopping. After being in close attendance for a fortnight, the doctor told her to take an evening off. Her married sister from Hawick took her place, and was present when Mary collapsed, with another attack of anguina [sic], from which she died in an hour. It is a sad business. She was a nice Scotch body; homely quiet and sensible. They are regretting that the house was enlarged – which sounds as though they think of keeping it on at present? I hope they do so. The disposal of pictures & furniture would be distressing.

It is said to be cold here, W. says so, but I according to my perverse habit feel *warmer*, so I hope the change of air has stopped my sneezings, it is the best cure for a hanging on cold. There was a lot of snow on the fells beyond Dunmail Rayse [Raise] and today the Cheviot looks most lovely, with a white cap, beyond the blue expanse of the Merse. There is a wonderful view from Ancrum village towards Berwick and the east coast.

I hope the little dogs are well behaved and not too disconsolate. Chuleh was dribbling tears during the packing; Tsuzee [sic] aloof, grave in disapproval. Our clothes are sniffed by terriers at hotels. We slept at a very nice hotel where there is salmon fishing, the Cross Keys Canonby [sic], but it was too far off. Provided the weather does not turn to snow.

We came through 2 big hail showers yesterday. I will try to ring up Mrs R. [Rogerson, the housekeeper] tomorrow Monday morning.

Love to you & Cecily and the 3 pekes [Daisy Hammond had a peke, too, called Yummi.]

yrs aff.
Beatrix Heelis

Since her marriage Beatrix had made the acquaintance of Rebecca Owen, an American who made infrequent visits to her large house just north of Hawkshead, Belmount Hall, which she had bought through Willie Heelis in 1899. Miss Owen was an admirer and friend of Thomas Hardy and had a considerable Hardy collection.

In the summer of 1938 Beatrix and Willie agreed to buy Belmount Hall, for Rebecca Owen had decided to live in Italy, and when she died in February 1939 at the age of eighty-one Beatrix was faced with clearing the garden and sorting through everything in the house. She discovered that a number of books were signed by Thomas Hardy, and that there were autograph letters from him, as well as scrapbooks, magazines and press cuttings all relating to him.

To Caroline Clark

Castle Cottage
Sawrey
March 18.39

My dear Caroline,

What next? Has France also made a fool of Mr Chamberlain?

We are enjoying rather better weather, it is a treat to see the sun again. Perhaps it may be like last spring, when March ending and April were the finest months of the year – too dry in fact. The cattle are trying to eat the hay from a late wet haytrimming – lots of it – mostly overgrown & mouldy. It has been a bad winter, so gloomy, in every way. We all had influenza. The farm people had it one at a time; and I got up the day our maid went to bed; which was some blessing. But I wasted 5 weeks indoors. At present it is nice weather for gardening. Some plants have perished, through damp and through a sharp frost upon rain.

My eccentric old friend Miss Owen has died in Rome (U.S.A. citizen, and executor a N York bank) so I have a free hand in an old walled garden of over an acre [at Belmount Hall]. The old fan-trained fruit trees in the last stage of old age. I have planted some clematis against them, and some shrubs, such as ceanothus, between, to gradually grow into their place. Is chimonanthus fragrans a bush that would grow? I have witch hazel, and shrubby spiraeas, and syringas. I remember you said you were going in for shrubs – and for the same reason. I should like to plant some bushes that might grow on at Belmount Hall without much attention? The garden is not seriously weedy. It is carpetted [sic] with jonquils & spring flowers. The house is scarcely habitable, though it seems a pity to let it fall in – fall *down* it will not. Georgian building stone. Perhaps some time it might be repaired for a hostel. The police have it down on their list; and the NY executors would not be asked leave for the mouldy furniture. One room is locked up, and she took away the key. I have had over a ton of good leaf mould removed from the roof & gutters and the rain no longer runs downstairs; but it is in a mess. She went away suddenly because her Italian chauffeur knew what was coming; he was in a fever to get back to Italy last August. She admitted that he belonged to a fascist organization – she was a horrid old fascist herself, in spite of being R.C. The floors were strewn with her belongings, valuable and rubbish. I wonder who will finally deal with them. I had expected it would be Father Taylor; but apparently not. There is her shroud in a cardboard box; presumably blessed by the Pope. I did not post it after her as I thought it seemed like "carrying coals to Newcastle." Father Taylor has obligingly buried some unpleasant remains of the early Christians in consecrated ground. He is in hope that *I* may not meet the monk and be converted. [It was said there was a ghost at Belmount Hall.] I was too surprised and amused to tell the worthy man that I saw 'it' months ago. It is a laurel bush, which in certain rare conditions of wind, wet leaves and slanting sun rays is startlingly white in a dark angle of wall – but it is the greenish bluish white of fleeing Daphne – not the Cistercian flannel. Miss Owen saw it only once, although she hung a rosary upon a tree, to tice the monk to come back! She was so very shortsighted that I told Father Taylor that she was unlikely to be able to see a real ghost. He seemed puzzled.

I wonder what is going to happen. How can we get at Rumania to help? It is not Chamberlain's failure to save C. Slovacia that is wrong; it is his density & smug satisfaction that is so hopeless. He does not seem ashamed of having been blind & wrong.

I remain yr aff cousin
Beatrix Heelis

Any names of shrubs suitable, on P.C.?

Soon after Rebecca Owen's death Beatrix had received a letter from Professor Carl Weber of Colby College, Waterville, Maine, USA. Carl Weber was a keen and aggressive Hardy collector and his letter was a request for any Hardy material found in Belmount Hall. Beatrix was under the impression that Rebecca Owen had bequeathed all her Hardy material to the Bodleian Library, but it soon became clear that she had sold some of her books to Carl Weber through Sotheby's the previous year. Beatrix now agreed to sell him what material was left, and to pass the money on to the Red Cross.

Beatrix had been in the Women's Hospital, Catherine Street, Liverpool, for a few days in November 1938 with what was then diagnosed as 'an insignificant carbuncle'. Now she was back there again, this time for what Beatrix knew was to be a serious operation, a hysterectomy.

To Daisy Hammond and Cecily Mills   Liverpool
                                                     March 30th 39

My dear Daisy and Cecily,

What a mess! but not intirely [sic] without premonition. I have failed in strength more than people know this last 2 years. Most times it has been an effort to walk to Hill Top. I am so glad I was feeling particularly well last week; and I have seen the snowdrops again. If it was not for poor WH I would be indifferent to the result. It is such a wonderfully easy going under; and in some ways preferable to a long invalidism, with only old age to follow. Moreover the whole world seems to be rushing to Armageddon. But not even Hitler can damage the fells.

Now Margaret [Daisy], the tongue is an unruly member! If I return in charge of the inconveniently-fond-of-me Nurse E [Edwards] – remember that she is an extra good nurse, though her dense self complacency can be annoying. Wherefore put forward the more concise Cecily to assist Mr Heelis to check interference. I think a big bed should be chucked. Consult Nurse Heaton & Mrs R. What about big room? If I do not return Wm will have a list of things I want eventually to go to Hill Top after his death. A few could go now, he would not miss the china in the big room. I want the dogs china!! of course etc in the bureau to go into an empty corner cupboard at Hill Top. The bureau itself from Castle big room to go near the door in big room at Hill Top, with china put in, which china is now in the mahogany glass cupboard at C. Cottage. Oh dear I wish I had done it and arranged it. I am conceited about arranging china. Let Cecily sketch how they stand at present. I like her little dogs! I am not sure about Chuleh; they are sometimes almost fighting, which might end in spoiling Suzee. You need never hesitate to have a dog "injected" to sleep. In some respects a younger pup-sister might be better.

I hope that Cecily and Wm will walk out little dogs on Sundays; they are old enough to face comment! *Could* she learn picquet or could you play 3 handed whist? It would be far best for the poor man to follow Willy Gaddum's [Beatrix's cousin] example and remarry, provided he did not make a fool of himself by marrying, or not marrying, a servant. The misfortune is that I have acquiesced in such slovenly untidyness and unpunctuality that I am afraid no old maidly lady would put up with it; and he is old to remodel. So I hope & feel sure you will do your best for him in the winter evenings. I have very great confidence in the good sense and kindness of both of you. If I did a kindness in providing a nice house – a lovely house – you provided me with my delightful neighbours.

I will never make him understand about my clothes. Ask Nurse Heaton if Matty Coward & Gladys Chapman would like some under clothing – some to the Friends of the Poor 40 Ebury Street – and some I think the Manchester Museum Curator seemed to fancy; there is an Indian shawl that belonged to my grt gr.mother Mrs Ashton of Flowery Field, some muslins and green-silk-high-waist and purple cloak & bonnet of Grandma Leech and a lot of Brussells lace. If not wanted in Manchester they might be put in a drawer at Hill Top, some Brussells given to Stephanie [Duke]. There are a lot of things there want clearing out & burning. At Hill Top books of no interest; some might sell. Tell Wm to be careful burning at C.C. I very nearly burnt some autographs the other day. Now I shall have nurse spanking me for burning the electric at night. I slept too early. Much love to you both and to Yummi.

Yrs aff

Beatrix Heelis

Sketch drawn in pencil on card

Beatrix also wrote to her American friends from hospital, among them Mrs Perry.

To Marian Frazer Harris Perry

The Women's Hospital
Liverpool
March 30 39

Dear Mrs Perry,

You may be surprised to see this address. I was in last Nov. for what seemed a trivial matter. There was [sic] some disquieting symptoms of bleeding a fortnight ago, so I came again and the surgeon is somewhat serious. I don't suppose it will be worse anything than "curetting", but anything in the womb is apt to be the beginning of the end. I am in no pain or discomfort, but awfully worried about my husband. You might have noticed I am the stronger minded of the pair, also the money is mine; death duties would make it awkward for him and the servants. He belongs to a family who have the privilege of dying suddenly – in their sleep. I have always hoped to survive! At all costs I hope he will remarry happily and sensibly. I have felt very tired and aged the last two years. Maybe the surgeon will put me right – but he cannot put me young again.

I think you stop on the safe side of the Atlantic. You see the feeling of confidence was only a ruse. Now the Italians are doing "says the spider to the fly; to France this time, and perhaps France also has made a fool of our Chamberlain and his umbrella (which he lost in Rome). It is a weary world. I have done my bit – here's fame!! The surgeon says he backed a horse called "Benjamin Bunny" and it only got half way round the race course.

What do you think I am reading? "Uncle Tom's Cabin". I had not read it to myself. I remember my nurse reading it to me when I was a small child – Eliza springing across the ice on the Ohio River. Hospital is very comfortable; ward sister is such a nice sensible woman. Give my love to Betty and Dick and 3 of a family, and with love to you dear Mrs Perry

I remain yrs aff
Beatrix Heelis

The surgeon has just been in again. He does not anticipate a severe operation, but it is not a pleasant prospect to envisage anything wrong at all. What a pretty country it is at the Lakes is it not? Hitler cannot spoil the fells; the rocks and fern and lakes and waterfalls will outlast us all. I can see the tower of [the] unfinished cathedral from the hospital windows, it seems a waste of money, apart from air raids. And councils still pass plans for great institution buildings and block[s] of lofty flats – it all seems so inconsequent and unreal. Why don't they have conscription if in earnest to defend?

I hope to see you again in better times, but I trust not as an invalid! I would rather go to rest. I am a very good patient & cheerful, in spite of this rather morbid letter. I want to say how much pleasure I have had knowing you and other delightful New Englanders.

HBH

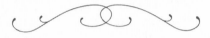

To Mr D. M. Matheson

In hospital Liverpool
March 31.39

Dear Sir,

In case my husband Wm Heelis is too upset to remember to write, I beg to give formal notice to give up my tenancy of Tilberthwaite Farm Coniston in the spring of 1940 but I make the request that you will not announce this publicly or advtz the farm for a time till we see whether I survive a somewhat serious operation. If I don't you will of course hear & I think my husband would recommend one of my men as tenant.

Please keep this quiet in the meantime. I give the notice as a precaution as my executors might otherwise be embarrassed, sheep farming is so bad. If & when I retire the Trust should purchase a sufficient landlord's stock of sheep – it would be wicked to let them be dispersed a second time after the labour and profitless expense incurred by the shepherd and me, in founding a new heafed flock.

Yrs truly
Beatrix Heelis

Beatrix also wrote to the niece of Mary, Bertram's widow. Hettie Douglas had lived with Mary Potter in Ashyburn on the Borders.

To Hettie Douglas

Liverpool
March 31.39

My dear Hetty [sic]

Thank you for your letter, I am so glad you came and glad to hear that Ina [Hettie's sister] was not ill, and both enjoyed your visit. I did not tell you I was going to hospital because I feared that you might think yourselves in the way whereas it was a nice distraction and pleasure to have you. And you went the right day – Mr Heelis & I had a nice Sunday, and we went after dinner to "Tom Kitten's" house & hung pictures. I liked your interest in the dolls, Lucy, Carrie and the china American – they really ought to be labelled. Carrie's skirt is [blue?] silk. I had intended to put away some of the downstairs things in the doll's house and have one room all for the "Two bad mice". I can't think what has become of "Lucinda and Jane", perhaps you and I may find them some day. They may never have been unpacked since leaving London, perhaps in some cardboard box in the cellar or the shippon or the barn. Jane is a cheap wooden doll who was bought in "Petticoat Lane" Shoreditch. Their little wooden furniture was made by the Disabled Soldiers shop – Lord Roberts soldiers of the S. Af war. I am a bad person to lose things; there should be copies of the "Times" with the battles of Waterloo and Trafalgar. It is to be hoped that "spring cleaning" has not devoured them. I cannot say how long I shall be here, perhaps Mr Heelis will send you a post card.

With love to you and Ina,

Yrs aff
Beatrix Heelis

From The Tale of Two Bad Mice

To Daisy Hammond   Liverpool Hospital
                                    Sunday [early April 1939]

My dear Daisy,

No one can be more surprised to be writing to you again. I do not think it is merciful to put an old woman through such an experience. I was sick again on Saturday, and burst the stitches, so had a third journey "downstairs" to be sewn up again, and have had pain which is considered of no consequence. I hope WH well got home on Tuesday, he has a heavy cough & remains of a cold and it is a small room. I have no idea when I will be fit – the stitches was an unfortunate breakage. I have been so pleased to hear news of little dogs, little dears. I have had a fine bunch of carnations, I wonder whether they come from Mrs T.Ed? It has been a lovely day – I feel a craving to go to Troutbeck Pk again, & lie out in the sun on a cane chair. Most things I am tired of, & would not care if I never saw again. I wonder what it will leave me like. The trains [?trams] are awfully noisy, but I manage to sleep. I suggested nurse had better order a bed of the small hospital pattern from Wright & Wright. If it were not very cold weather I have a fancy to sleep in the "big room" – but I don't want the geraniums destroyed, I nearly lost the scarlet one. There is a cutting of it on the landing windowsill opp. bathroom.

Love to you & Cecily. I have got nightgowns washed

Yrs aff
Beatrix Heelis

Pen-and-ink study for The Tale of Samuel Whiskers or The Roly-Poly Pudding

THE TALE OF LITTLE PIG ROBINSON, *which had appeared in 1930, was the last of Beatrix's books to be published by Frederick Warne during her lifetime. Although there are no letters from Beatrix in the company files between 1929 and 1940, it is certain that she continued to be involved in all matters concerning her books and the merchandise from them. She also kept in touch with various members of the Warne family.*

To Miss Louie Warne

Castle Cottage
Sawrey
Ambleside
May 19.39

My dear Louie,

I heard of your father's death – at a time when I was uncertain myself. Mr Stephens wrote from the office. He said how ill your father had been, and suffering a long time. It was well you were able to have him. You were in China once – or was it Nellie [her sister].

How well I remember you both and your parents – on hot Sunday afternoons in the garden behind the house on Primrose Hill. And your Father & Mother, & Nurse – it seems a lifetime ago.

I am glad the little books are giving pleasure to another generation – they go on and on.

I have been in hospital and I am said to be completely cured. It seemed a good deal of bother over an old woman! I walk with a stick yet.

Thank you for your letter. Remember me to Nellie also,

and believe me yrs aff
Beatrix Heelis

Two months later Beatrix was rushed back to hospital by ambulance with appendicitis.

To Daisy Hammond

Liv Hospital
Catherine Street
Liverpool
July 12.39

My dear Daisy

I have been getting on extremely well. I thought I should have been up tomorrow but Mr Gemmell is going to London for the day and he says he would prefer to put off till Friday when he can observe the result. The delay makes my return on Sunday less certain. If it has to be Monday or Tuesday perhaps I might come home by train, if Nurse Heaton were not too busy to fetch me – she has been known to fetch patients. Young Irving is driving a bus during the season.

I have been wondering whether anyone has picked black currants? There ought to be a picking ready (unless a bird has been shut into the net!) I should like to have some jelly made; the jam is less liked. Please take some for yourself too, there should be plenty.

It is very hot this evening with sun streaming through 2 large windows, I did not realize it was so late; I have missed the Glyndbourne [sic] Mozart which I intended to listen to. There is no clock but my ears were saluted by advice to farmers about white scour in calves. The professor recommended increasing Vitamen A [sic] in the cow's calostrum [sic] (= first milk) by feeding her on a special diet for 6 weeks before calving; whereby the constitution & resisting power of the calf would be fortified. The diet seems a costly one. Calves are worth from 7/ upwards; average 15/!!

I feel remarkably well. No callers today except bevies of pretty nurses – advanced to other posts since April, one of the Welsh girls looks particularly charming, and improved.

Love to you Cecily and Yum

yrs aff
Beatrix Heelis

John Stone, a young journalist born in Christchurch, New Zealand, was visiting England from Fiji where his father was editor of the FIJI TIMES. *Brought up on the Potter books, he was anxious to see the places where the stories were set and wrote to Beatrix, care of her publishers, asking for a guide.*

To John Stone

Castle Cottage
Sawrey
nr Ambleside
Westmorland
Aug 19th 39

Dear Mr Stone,

Your letter has amused me so much that I am answering it, (with my address, in spite of the alarming "journalist"). I hate publicity; and I have contrived to survive to be an old woman without it, except in the homely atmosphere of Agricultural Shows.

Peter Rabbit's garden – various. The most panoramic view with Peter in a wheelbarrow was done in a garden at Keswick which was completely altered afterwards. Mr MacGregor [sic], gardened near Berwick – the only gardener I ever saw who weeded a gravel walk lying flat on his stomach! Mrs MacG. [sic] imaginary – (sorry for the lazy Mc's real wife!) "Tom Kitten's house and Jemima's home = Hill Top Farm Sawrey. The old part of the farm house is very charming.

The views in Jemima & Jeremy Fisher are Sawrey & Esthwaite Water nearby. Pigling Bland other side of Windermere Lake, looking towards the Lakes hills. Squirrel Nutkin, Derwentwater and Lord's Island, near Keswick. Tiggy Winkle, Newlands near Keswick.

The pictures which show little flowers & such details were all drawn at the Lakes. Benjamin Bunny at Keswick, the later books all at Sawrey. Pig Robinson the earliest inventing was made up of old sketches done in South Devon – some Sidmouth, some Teignmouth, and the market streets at Lyme Regis – lovely backgrounds to which I should have liked to do better justice. I have not done any for a long time. I always liked the story of Pig Robinson and tried to do the pictures before finishing.

You are evidently one of the individuals who never grow up, and belonging to the age of Alice and the Water Babies. I don't remember Alice coming out, but my copy of [the] edition is an old one.

If you come north during your visit to England – ring up Hawkshead 16 – and I will show you Tom Kitten's house. I cannot ask you to stay here unfortunately, for I am occupying the spare room since a severe illness in April, but I'm well enough to be interested to meet you, if you happen to visit the Lakes. We live between Windermere Ferry and Hawkshead, though Ambleside 7 miles off is the post town. There are buses from Ambleside &, with one change, from W'mere via the Ferry. Many visitors stay at Grasmere as a centre.

With thanks for your letter

yrs sincerely
Beatrix Potter (Mrs William Heelis)

Lyme Regis main street drawn in sepia and pen-and-ink

Britain declared war on Germany on 5 September.

To June Steel

Castle Cottage
Sawrey
nr Ambleside
Oct 11th 39

My dear June

I have been a long time in answering your letter. I am feeling very much better than I have felt for two years past. Provided I get through this winter without any serious illness I hope I shall get along comfortably for a while longer. I am 73 but I have no wish to give in and live as an invalide [sic]. We all want to see the end of Hitler! He has upset the world badly. I think he must be in a shaky way or he would not have given up so much to Russia. There is no want of food here, we put by a fortnight's supply; but we have never needed it. The continual filling up of forms & gradings and papers is a nuisance; everything that farmers produce has to be arranged for marketing so that the Govt knows what there will be to draw upon for supplies. This is always a busy time, the sheep fairs are in Sept and October. Shows were starting, but of course came to an end when war began. The sheep went to Penrith and Ennerdale and took some prizes. I was waiting for shows nearer home – so I never went at all – but I enjoyed Keswick Fair last Saturday – such a lovely autumn day, and meeting all my farmer friends. It was a lovely drive past Thirlmere. So far we have plenty of petrol. There are not many gone to the war from this district as there are few young men on the farms, mainly older men & young boys. Some of the Coniston quarry men have been called up. The young people seem to look upon the war as a huge pic-nic. They have got a new song instead of "Tipperary" – they sing 'We'll hang [out] our washing on the Siegfried line!' There were two local boys on the 'Courageous'; one of them from Kendal was drowned, the other was saved. Mr Heelis & I are both busy with useful work, but not hard work this time. I am too old to take charge of the pigs & calves this time. The little dogs are well and very good company. I bought 3 bags of "puppy biscuits" in case of famine, at present they turn up their snub noses and won't eat them, they prefer rabbit – Susie [Tzusee] caught a very large rat one day, she pounced on it successfully like a cat, but Judy [Chuleh] unfortunately dragged it out of her grasp; where upon the rat turned round & bit both of them. Which had the effect of making them more eager. The bites soon healed.

Now I must stop – Walter Stevens is waiting for letters. Everybody is quite well – hoping you & your mother are the same.

Yrs aff
HB Heelis

To Mr D. M. Matheson

Castle Cottage
Sawrey
Ambleside
Oct 17.39

Dear Sir

Although it is probably useless I am writing about your agent Mr Bruce Thompson. There is a keen demand for all sorts of wood, and he may do irreparable damage. It is useless for me to talk to him. A man cannot help having been born dull. Thompson is supercilious as well.

He destroyed the finest group of oaks on Thwaite, dealing with a man he had been warned against. Recently he was negociating [sic] the sale of Tilberthwaite coppice with another unsuitable man, a rough dealer in firewood. Parts of the coppice are overgrown and require cutting. An experienced agent with any taste for the picturesque would have decided to thin it in patches, deliberately and cautiously; employing the estate woodmen (the Trust's servants) and selling the cut wood. This first negociation [sic] fell through because W Fury only wanted part of the coppice and Thompson wanted to sell the whole 24 acres.

The whole was bought afterwards by R. Wren, a wood man, who has that taste for Preservation of Natural Beauty which the Trusts agent lacks. Wren told Mr Thompson that it would be a "shame" to cut the scrub wood amongst the rocks – that "it would spoil the picture of the valley". To me the idea of indiscriminate cutting appears *wicked*. There are coppices in plenty – acres of coppice – of no interest – but the coppices in Tilberthwaite and in Yewdale which clothe the lower slopes of Holme Fell are specially beautiful; glorious in autumn colours, and in winter & spring. Wren told him that the dwarf scrub is of small money value. There is an old saying that some folks would sell their soul for 6d.

Wren bought the whole coppice for £20. I have now bought it from Wren. I could have trusted Wren to exercise good taste and discretion; but I am in a stronger position if there is argument.

There were 2 conditions attached. (1) "All standards and any trees marked with white paint to be excluded." (2) All the coppice to be cut by March 25th 1941 at the latest."

As regards (1) I agree. (remarking incidentally that the standards if they ever grew into large trees might be out of scale, like 3 tall trees which I felled below Yewdale Crag. The extra trees are birch which will blow down. But I agree of course. (2) I repudiate. Possibly Mr Thompson intended merely to say that no cutting or removal must continue after March 1941. If he or *you* propose that the whole coppice must be razed by that date – I refuse to do it. It is disgraceful.

With regard to heavy timber, bearing in mind the mistakes which

Thompson had already committed, I endeavoured to give him a hint about a dealer from Bolton, who has been going round endeavouring to buy large oaks. I could see that the hint was not well received. The dealer is substantial and respectable – only he was talking more than needful about "commandeering"; since he is buying for his own sawmills; not buying directly for Government.

It is a matter of opinion. I consider Mr Thompson has *no* capacity for dealing with tradesmen. Shortly after he became agent he "sold" another fine group of trees, near Tilberthwaite. In that case Mr Heelis interfered just in time. Not only were the trees outstanding fine ones, but also they are the only protection against the river bursting a new course north eastward.

He seems to have no sense at all. And not capable of learning. Indeed, excusably; because it is impossible to inculcate a pictorial sense of trees arranged in landscape, when imagination is a blank.

He wastes time & wages in the woods; yet there are no new plantings – no judicious thinning of hardwoods. The men in the woods seem to be employed picking up dead sticks – or cutting down the wrong thing.

My husband & I never drive through Coniston without vexation.

There is a great quantity of possible hardwood that might be cleared with advantage, but Mr Thompson is too deficient in experience and taste to be trusted to choose it.

You would be well advised not to allow him to sell anything extensive without reference to the committee. I shall be obliged if you will show the Estates Committee this letter.

Yrs truly
H B Heelis

I do not intend to suggest that Mr Thompson intends to sell to Mr Kay of Bolton – but he has had no discretion in the past; and no experience (except disastrous) in timber & wood selling.

The National Trust's internal comment on Beatrix's letter was that it was 'a rather exaggerated outpouring of an injured lady's mind'. But they were most anxious not to upset the Heelises and advised Bruce Thompson to consult them in future so that any criticism would be directed at the Trust rather than personally at him. The Secretary, Donald Matheson, also arranged to visit Beatrix 'as soon as possible'.

To [?]

Castle Cottage
Sawrey
nr Ambleside
Dec 7th. 39

Dear Sir,

The first coloured edition of Peter Rabbit, published by F Warne & Co in 1902 had greenish-gray endpapers with a small leaf pattern all over.

I think I remember a few copies bound *experimentally with a clouded* or marbled stiffish paper, more brightly coloured and without definite pattern. Its a long time ago. I do not remember that they were copies of Peter Rabbit; but it is likely enough; as the present type of end paper, depicting the little animals of the series, came into use in 1903. You can 'place' editions of other books, approximately, by looking at there [sic] animals. (Where there was a *reprint* within the first twelve months I cannot distinguish between *reprints* – except that the first imprint might be brightest)

After Peter the books mainly came out in pairs. Thus 1903 – Tailor of Gloucester & Squirrel Nutkin 1st edition end papers show Nutkin & a Tailor Mouse as well as Peter. Next year these 3 were joined by the next pair of books + Two Bad Mice and Benjamin Bunny. Mrs Tiggy joined them early on, but she was concealing the title of her book, until it was published. The brightness or otherwise of the impression of plates is no guide, because the copper blocks wear so badly, and they have all been re-engraved. I kept all originals for that purpose, and sometimes I worked on the drawings – for instance I had had a bad sample of white and had to redraw some that were badly discoloured; and some B. Bunnys were temporarily mislaid and I supplied new ones, duplicates very little different to the originals for fresh blocks.

I forget the number of the 1st edition of Peter, possibly 1200 [8,000 copies were printed] – children did me the compliment to read their copies to pieces, so the number still in existence must be much reduced, I have 3 myself.

There were a few early copies of the Tailor of G. bound in a flowered lavender chintz, very pretty. I think the 1/6 binding was rather better than the 1/- but I have always thought the bindings ugly; only when it was known & a success it was best to stick to the same pattern. The attempt to vary colour & shape of inlay, for convenience of sorting & handling stocks led to some ugly shapes & crude colours.

I hope this information may be of some interest to you.

Yrs truly
H.B. Heelis "Beatrix Potter"

411

Watercolour of Kep, Beatrix's collie

To Joseph Moscrop

Castle Cottage
Sawrey
Ambleside
Jan 9th. 40

Dear Joe Moscrop,

How very nice of you to have the thought of sending New Year's Boxes! There are still some kindly folk left in this unkindly world. I have a toffee in my mouth and I think of Joseph. And I have read the Lord's Day Magazine – with sympathy – but I confess still with one doubt. When I see a parcel of lads loafing at a corner on a Sabbath afternoon – I wonder whether they would not be better on the recreation ground instead of idling and shouting bawdy talk to get rid of their superfluous energy? It is a very difficult question, very difficult where to draw the line. The Lord's Day editor gets rid of the difficulty completely, as regards his own point, by going in completely and consistently for the Jewish Sabbath. The boys remain a problem.

We look forward to seeing you – and dog – again! I was going to say "all being well". If things are *badly* we will be all the more glad to see your cheerful smile. You are over the age for calling up. I think only one of my shepherds comes within the present age limit – at Tilberthwaite. There seems to be no tribunal to hear appeals this war-time, but surely the authorities will not take key men off the farms, while so much is said about production of food. We are doing some extra ploughing, but not more than 3 acres at Troutbeck. It might improve the quality of the herb, but there is the risk of losing the corn crop in a wet season. This back-end has been favourable both for sheep and black cattle. George says there are 30 "blackies" content at the top of Hallilands.

There has been scarcely any covering of snow on the fells yet. We will get it later! They are well at the Park but Wm & I have not had a pleasant New Year (apart from apples and good wishes!). He has been in bed with a chill, and I have sciatica. I felt the cold in my bones, it will go when a thaw comes. I wish Mr. Heelis would get right, he has not been so grand this winter. I think there is a sort of flu that gets hold. But one should be very thankful to have fires indoors and food, when one reads of the awful suffering. And no end in sight, the war seems to spread.

The frost has been bright and sunny here, today is rather thick fog. With kind regards and all good wishes from us both.

yrs sincerely
H.B. Heelis

To [?]

Castle Cottage
Sawrey
Ambleside
March 17. 40

Dear Sir,

I am sorry for unavoidable delay in answering your letters and returning your quaint book. As regards the folding copies of "Miss Moppet" etc, I have not kept any. To be candid, this minute study of first editions seems very silly when applied to recent picture books. Its a pity you have not some more useful pursuit or hobby to employ your time.

I am sorry I cannot give any further attention to the matter.

Yrs truly
HB Heelis

To Betty and Richard Stevens

Castle Cottage
Sawrey
Ambleside
May 25. 40

Dear Dick and Betty,

I have your pleasant message before me as I write, and a little snap of Nonya and her brother, taken in August 38. She looks a little pickle! Quite respectably clothed. I remember a lovely Aphodrite [sic] – or was it Milton's "Sleek Panope" – dripping from the wave and water lilies of Grasmere Lake. The pleasant peaceful days – do you remember wriggling a large car past a large bus on a very narrow twisty lane near Buttermere? Your aunt had a confiding faith in your skill as a chauffeuse which emboldened me to keep my seat. The bluebells are lovely in the woods, and the hawthorn hedges sprinkled white like snow; the beauty of the countryside that will survive. I am glad your little folks are across the Atlantic. I see in the paper that one of your ships appropriately named Roosevelt is coming to take off Americans. Times are extremely anxious; there are such swarms of foreigners in this country. We have been too easy; like the Dutch.

I suppose your immigration laws permit "foreigners" i.e. English to land in U.S.A. provided they are self supporting? I am far too old to dream of bolting whatever happens. I am thinking of two young girls, children of a favourite cousin (I have scarcely any young relatives) The elder is training for an agricultural diploma with intentions to go to S. Africa at present off the map, the younger is a school girl. I was telling their mother if the worst came to the worst she should get them over to Canada or U.S.A. Of course their first duty is to their country; there will be work for women in English Agriculture if we survive.

Their names are Rosemary and Jean Duke, their father Leut. [sic] Commander Duke is a naval officer. Rosemary is a self possessed level headed girl; got away from Brussels in Sept 38 in a troop train – and doubtless any "evacuating" would be done through consuls & officially – but if they ever have to go – I would give them the names of some of my good friends in U.S.A. in case they required advice. Their mother has money & expectations. At present we are solvent in spite of taxes! I have been selling pitwood – what you call "hemlock"; and wool is a better trade.

It has been a very severe winter, unusual snow and protracted frost. We both had flu – my husband picked up quickly but I stopped in bed through the cold weather – of course getting up, but mostly like Mr John Dormouse – 'very snug'. I got over a severe operation, but I am rather crippled, though still smiling and very busy. Tell Nonya how

414

many baa lambs I have on the sheep farm, 999, and the shepherd thinks there are a dozen more not counted and marked. It is surprising how well the flock got through the severe winter. Thank you Dick for the letter & pamphlet which was very interesting & instructive. Love to you all– there are 2 + 3 now are there not – or is it 4? Good luck!

yrs sincerely
Beatrix Heelis

Beatrix wrote to a number of her American friends at the same time, including Mrs Perry and Anne Carroll Moore, and asked for their help in looking after the Duke children if they came to America.

Sepia ink and pencil sketch

War was declared only two weeks after John Stone's first letter to Beatrix. Immediate travel restrictions were imposed, with the result that it had been March before he had finally reached the Lake District. His telephone call to Hawkshead 16 brought an invitation to lunch at Castle Cottage. Nearly thirty years later he wrote a graphic description of the magic day he spent with Beatrix in Sawrey for the Christchurch STAR, the paper on which he was then working.

To John Stone

Castle Cottage
Sawrey
Ambleside
Westmorland
June 5. 1940

Dear John Stone,

You say you will return? *Not* in the guise of McCaulay's N.Zealander??! We have been through anxious days since you saw the English primroses & daffodils, now droughted with the fierce heat – under a cloudless blue sky. We are longing for thunder & rain. April was lovely; showers & green grass; and May was full of flowers, sheets of bluebells in our northern woods (I'm glad you saw bluebells in Oxfordshire) and the hawthorn hedges and big thorn bushes in the valleys have been like snow drifts.

I enjoyed reading your account of your rushed tour; you found *some* of England that is still unspoilt. I can imagine Oxford. My father had an old friend, an Oxford don, & I remember 40-years ago how they lamented a street of new houses that were being built beyond the 'Parks' – (N.B. the Parks were Oliver Cromwell's gunparks & had not altered much, until the day when "Fellows" were permitted to marry & require family residences); and the green Cumnor country was unsullied by Morris cars "en masse". What a world; mechanized to destruction. Us old ones had not long any how; so it's comforting to think that the N. Zealander & the Canadian will someday shake hands on one of the Thames bridges. The best bridge – Waterloo is already pulled down. I remember when Putney bridge was timber – I seem still to hear the clump clop of our carriage horses' feet.

It is most unfortunate how much has been wilfully destroyed in the English country side. I have tried to do my humble bit of preservation in this district; and I can assure you that the pleasure of your visit was mutual; it was a real treat to meet an intelligent listener, a clever well-bred fine young man – tell your mother from me – that your visit gave me *great* pleasure. I only regret I was so crippled, & you so hurried, that I could not go about with you and show you more antiques – but you have seen lots elsewhere. There is practically no domestic antiquity in this Border country, prior to the Union, because it was continually harried & burnt by the Scots. A few of the old castle towers (peels, or fortified farmhouses and church towers) are older; but most of our old oak and old buildings date from the rise of the wool trade in the early 17th century. Hill Top farm house is of about that date, though we found portions of older walls and previously-used oak timber when I made additions. It's a pretty old place, and I have taken much pleasure in collecting some oddments, hoping that some day the National Trust might care to preserve it along with my land; it would be easy to maintain it – separately yet under one roof – with the modern farm house. I cannot help reflecting ruefully, if the N.T.'s present secretarial representative were like you!

At present – I pack things away – in case refugees arrive. Miss Mills next door has the true enthusiasm & I hope she will remember where to put things back, if I cannot. At present I am able to get about again and superintending works in the woods and on the farms. No one can foretell the end. A number of our local men have got back from Flanders. I should have no fear if it were not for the swarms of aliens, you remarked upon them. We must do our bit, and the colonies will carry on the cause of freedom if we go under. And the mountains & fells and green land of pleasant England will survive her smoky towns & ugly suburbs.

Give my kind regards to your Mother, and also if you look her up remember me to Miss Elsie Shrewsbury, Brighton Road, Parnell, Auckland, C.4. She and I have corresponded for very many years and told each other about our gardens – and politics. I do think one very good thing has arisen from this war, it has opened the eyes and minds of the British working man to the value of the British empire, and all it stands for.

There is still no shortage of anything, except paper, no doubt some temporary adjustments were necessary owing to the influx. Its a long way to send children to Australia. I think it would be a very good thing – quite apart from the war – to send more to the colonies – Canada is the nearest. My husband and I are too old and too tied up in the land to contemplate moving, whatever happens. If things get worse I think I'll bury some tins of biscuits in the woods!

Yrs sincerely
Beatrix Heelis

To Marian Frazer Harris Perry

July 24. 40
Castle Cottage
Sawrey
Ambleside

Dear Mrs Perry,

I received your letter of July 5 on the 22nd. Its kindness and understanding overwhelmed me. I am disturbed about the date – July 5th – surely by that date you would– in normal times – have heard that *none* of the children are coming? I am wondering whether the congestion of cablegrams does not cause them to be slower in transit than the air mail letters? The little boys were first 'crossed off'. Then Jean Duke was refused a permit, after passport and passage difficulties appeared to have been surmounted. Her father looked in here while on his round of inspection last week; he said it seemed a last moment disappointment after putting everyone (including you) to much trouble. He said he felt one relief – he had begun to wonder whether there might be the same difficulty in getting her back, to England, if "duration" proved to be a lengthy exile; he had not contemplated more than a year – or two at most – but we all think it will be a long time before the war is over. There is a great change of feeling – a complete recovery of confidence compared to that black ten days. And the delay has been invaluable. I may not tell you how martial we feel even here! The other day turning a corner I suddenly met a company of soldiers practising route marching in gas masks. They did not look human – more like antediluvian tapirs or short nosed elephants! We are quite cheerful, and the country is full of troops – and more & more of the Kendal boys are heard of; the local regiment was in the rear guard at Dunkirk. Some were killed, some taken prisoner, one has been heard of alive & unhurt in Morocco. The troops got mixed up and landed at random, north & south. It was just like what General Smuts said in his fine speech, a triumph of strategy & endurance; an army that could fight its way back safely is not beaten. Very few appear to have been killed. The guns and other stores were the worst loss.

There have been no air raids within hearing distance yet. Occasionally stray planes go over at night which are thought to sound like Germans; and it is very likely we may get raids yet on this coast perhaps from Ireland; but they do very little harm; the death rate is less than the toll of the roads. People *will not* take cover. I was in a cottage yesterday when a plane flew very low and every child ran out to watch it; it was obviously a Spitfire, but it would have been all the same had it been a Heinkel. A farm house was hit further north, but no one hurt. The Germans got the nearest doing serious damage in their first attempts; they have flown higher & higher ever since, except when they dive bomb. People who come from towns complain of being kept awake by our own sirens. So long as they are not hit – its a case of "familiarity breeding contempt". An old gentleman from this part who went away to live in the south has met with a strange fate – he was playing golf at a s. coast watering place and stumbled upon a live bomb which blew him into bits. He was a great invalid, and he did not suffer; it must have been a shock for his fellow golfers.

We have very unsettled weather. We make hay (& drill) between showers; not both at same time. The authorities are reasonable in apportioning the men's time between soldiering & farming.

I hope Ken & Stephanie [Duke] have thanked you properly. We never can thank you enough for your willingness to do so much. Steph is not very much of a letter writer, but I know how grateful she is – it was a *very* black time while it lasted. Thank goodness we are on our own now, with our backs to a strong wall and the sea in front. It may be hard & cruel, but we can and must hold out. I am still keeping in better health, and able to get through a fair amount of work. W. goes on the patrol one night a week, they let him off at 11, which he can do comfortably without knocking up; he is the oldest on the job. He has a "tin hat", which he refuses to wear – until Hitler comes! He's a long time about it. Now I don't know how to thank you. I do appreciate your letter. Mr Duke cabled to you directly he knew that the permit could not be granted. I suppose it must have been after July 5. Time seems to fly away.

yrs sincerely

Beatrix Heelis

In the summer of 1939, Bertha Mahony Miller read THE FAIRY CARAVAN *aloud to her granddaughter, Nancy Dean, who was then aged seven. Some time after the reading, Nancy expressed her pleasure by patting the book and saying 'Oh, lovely* FAIRY CARAVAN, *if only there were ten of you.' Mrs Miller described the incident in a letter to Beatrix and later included an account of it in her article, 'Beatrix Potter and Her Nursery Classics',* THE HORN BOOK, *May 1941.*

From June 1940 Beatrix's letters to America had been examined by censors and often had words or phrases cut out. She, in turn, sometimes addressed a remark to the censor.

To Nancy Dean

Castle Cottage
Sawrey
Ambleside
July 30. 40

My dear Nancy

So you would like news of the Fairy Caravan? Where is it camping? or whither is it wandering? I wonder if I can tell you! When we grow old and wear spectacles, our eyes are not bright like children's eyes, nor our ears so quick, to see and hear the fairies. Just a glimpse I catch sometimes through the trees, and I hear a tinkling tinkle tinkling of little pots and pans & cans. I seemed to know last week that they were in Clogger Meadow. I saw something white through the trees; I looked hard – and alas it was a cow! Two wood cutters were working in the wood. Until the underwood of nut bushes grows up again – Sandy and Pony William will not stay more than a night or two in the lovely green meadow that lies hidden amongst woods. And they did not go to Cherry tree camp where I *know* they have always camped in May, when the cherry blossom & hawthorns are in flower. And now in August the Girl Guides cannot camp there either because there is a footpath leading to another sort of camp.

So the Guides are camping in a little larch wood near our cottage, and their tents are dyed green. Where can the circus have wandered to? I believe I know!

Right away amongst the fells – the green & blue hills above my sheep farm in Troutbeck. Such a lonely place, miles along a lovely green road. That was where I first saw the mark of little horse shoes. There is an old barn there that we call High Buildings – it is never used except sometimes by the shepherds; and when I was younger and used to take long walks I used to eat my bread & cheese at High Buildings, or shelter from the rain. That was where the Caravan sheltered in a very wild rainstorm, and

Xarifa made acquaintance with the melancholy Mouse. There was a story about that place and that very wet night – but it was so silly I really could not print it. Besides it might have offended my friend Joseph, who is not really a mouse. He is a shepherd. Every spring Joseph Moscrop has come to help with the lambs; for 14 springs he has come from Scotland with his dogs and fed the weak lambs and the twins with his milk bottle. And in very cold springs Joseph has a little gin in a little bottle and last March Joseph told me "the corrk had coom oot" in his pocket!! There was a smell of gin; but Joseph is a total abstainer – what Americans call "dry". He does not like being laughed at, especially on Sundays. He is wonderful with lambs and dogs; we all love Joseph. I do not think he would approve of me calling a mouse "Joseph Mouse-trap", perhaps the censor would not tell him? If I copied out that very silly story? There was one about Cherry tree camp – but it was long and tiresome.

Good night Nancy, I am going to bed.

Yours aff
Beatrix Potter

Preparatory sketch for The Fairy Caravan

To Bertha Mahony Miller

Castle Cottage
Sawrey
Ambleside
Nov. 25th 40

Dear Mrs Miller

I hope this is in time for the Horn Book – it is my own fault if you have not waited. I found the old copy – and somehow in these times it read a little petty and egoistical [sic]. We are still unbombed here and there are fewer planes at nights.

Perhaps I will post a duplicate in a week. Some letters go lost. And having got-a-going I had better write out Nancy's Christmas story before the scribbling fit passes.

I remain yours sincerely
Beatrix Heelis

I have been asked to tell again how Peter Rabbit came to be written. It seems a long time ago; and in another world. Though after all the world does not change much in the country, where the seasons follow their accustomed course – the green leaf and the sere – and where nature, though never consciously wicked, has always been ruthless.

In towns there is change. People begin to burrow underground like rabbits. The lame boy for whom Peter was invented more than forty years ago [Noel Moore] is now an air warden in a bombed London parish.

I have never quite understood the secret of Peter's perennial charm. Perhaps it is because he and his little friends keep on their way, busily absorbed with their own doings. They were always independant [sic]. Like Topsy – they just "grow'd". Their names especially seemed to be inevitable. I never knew a gardiner [sic] named "McGregor". Several bearded horticulturalists have resented the nick-name; but I do not know how it came about; nor why "Peter" was called "Peter". It is regrettable that a small boy once inquired audibly whether the Apostle was Peter Rabbit? There is great difficulty in finding, or inventing, names void of all possible embarassment [sic]. A few of the characters were harmless skits or cariacatures [sic]; but "Mr McGregor" was not one of them, and the backgrounds of Peter Rabbit are a mixture of locality.

"Squirrel Nutkin" lived on the shore of Derwentwater Lake near Keswick, and "Mrs Tiggy Winkle" in the nearby valley of Newlands. "Jemima Puddleduck", "Jeremy Fisher" and others lived at Sawrey in the southern part of the English Lake District.

The earlier books, including the later printed 'Pig Robinson', were written for real children in picture letters of scribbled pen and ink. I confess that afterwards I painted most of the little pictures to please myself. The more spontaneous the pleasure – the more happy the result.

I do not remember a time when I did not try to invent pictures and make for myself a fairyland amongst the wild flowers, the animals, fungi, mosses, woods and streams, all the thousand objects of the countryside; that pleasant, unchanging world of realism and romance, which in our northern clime is stiffened by hard weather, a tough ancestry, and the strength that comes from the hills.

'Beatrix Potter'

Early pencil sketch for The Tale of Peter Rabbit

To Arthur Stephens

Castle Cottage
Sawrey
Ambleside
Feb. 23rd 41

Dear Mr Stephens,

I am very glad you are considering the question of a cheap edition [of *Peter Rabbit*]. I cannot see any reason why it should interfere with the coloured edition – and *if* it did so I am afraid *I* would not be inconsolable. I do so dislike that idiotic prancing rabbit on the cover! If it were properly spaced (which my rough sketch is not) the running rabbit figure is more effective. Perhaps you could have a simple colour cover; but not the frontispiece so you could avoid clay faced [paper] altogether. Try all black & white and a cheap simple form of get up.

The price 2/6 is really too much for a little gift book for "infants", or school baby-classes.

The history of the first edition was that the story had been refused by several publishers, so I got it printed myself. As far as I remember it cost me about £17 – I sold enough at 1/- to pay expenses & have enough for my own use at Christmas. There was a first printing of 250 in Nov. 1901 which was soon used up. I remember I went to Messrs Strangeways and inquired anxiously if they had broken up the type and the old gentleman said with a twinkle that he had kept it for a while, set up, and "he thought some more might be wanted" – so I had another 200 which are dated Feb 1902 and bound in rather stouter boards. I think your firm subsequently had the coppers of the frontispieces.

In the same way – you took over most of the colourblocks of the 1st edition of The Tailor of Gloucester which was printed for me by Messrs Strangeways in Nov. 1902. It cost me £40 I had 400 copies done, at one printing.

The cost of blocks was much less in those days. I think I heard the name & address of the printers through a friend at the N History Museum with whom I was working. Her father Dr Woodward edited the Geological Magazine; and she knew something about engraving & printing; you are obliged to have clay faced paper for the coloured books but [it] is inartistic. I rather remember there were 2 many pages for folding economically therefore some were not used for the coloured book; they might be scrapped in a reprint.

Yrs sincerely
HB Heelis

Certainly you may send it to N.Y.

424

Two illustrations from the privately printed The Tale of Peter Rabbit

To Professor Carl Weber

Castle Cottage
Sawrey
Ambleside
March 31. 41

Dear Pro. Weber,

So many letters go missing that I am writing again to tell you I have not posted any more Hardy books since the parcel March 7th. I am so much afraid of inserted memoranda being lost or destroyed if the parcel is opened by the Censorship authorities as well as risk of sinking at sea. I shall be glad to hear that the "Greenwood Tree" which contained some notes on the first Mrs Hardy's funeral reached you complete?

Belmount Hall is being taken over for a hostel. The old rambling house has been pretty well ransacked, but it yielded yet another literary curiosity last week; inside a volume of Kipling's "[*The*] Seven Seas". Miss Owen did not know Kipling; the book is not autographed (for a wonder it is a first edition). In later years Rebecca[h] being soured, and rather spiteful against the world in general, and the lands of her birth and adopted residence in particular – did not whole-heartedly admire

425

Rudyard Kipling's robust patriotism. Very possibly she thought him coarse. I was pleasantly surprised to find that she had any of his works at all at Belmount. Inserted amongst the pages of "The Seven Seas" are numerous cuttings, and some old letters from Miss Georgina Craik (later Mrs Walter May). She and Miss Owen corresponded in the 90s; and Georgina told Miss Owen about the wonderful success of – and her own pride & interest in – the the [sic] young man "Rudd Kipling" – "who came from India six months ago, where he had been sub editor of a newspaper since he was 17" etc "We have a special interest in him because during three years of his boyish life – his parents being in India – our house in his holidays was his only English home (and a pretty weight upon our minds the budding genius was during those times!" etc "He is a busy little fellow with a hard voice & an eager powerful face, etc. Miss Rebecca[h] does not seem to have been appreciative – a further letter from Georgina to RO in NY says, "Rudyard Kipling was in America this month but I suppose you didn't see him? – nor desire to do so! etc." ... "Tennyson did him the honour of writing – etc etc. Rudd was enraptured, he told Auntie it was the greatest thing that had ever happened to him" etc Along with these letters of Mrs May's is an envelope endorsed by Miss Owen – "Two autograph Poems (unpublished) by Rudyard Kipling sent by him from India to Mrs A.W. May (Georgina M. Craik) & given to me about 1894–5 when Kipling had become famous. RO 1903" The enclosed sheet of notepaper has a poem on either side. The m.s.s. is undoubtedly authentic. Whether the poems *are* by "RK" (signature) or copied in his handwriting from a contribution by another to his newspaper – I cannot guarantee. They are bad enough to be the work of a "budding genius". The longer one is sentimental. The short one is characteristic. It does not scan, but in subject and lurid forcefulness – it reads like original early "Rudd". I have deciphered another of Georgina's letters in which she remarks that Kipling sent her "quantities" of verse after he first went out to India. She adds that she is afraid she destroyed most of his letters!! So the Belmount fragment is probably authentic and original.

Would that he were alive to write the epic of the air! Your student contributor to the review does not understand about the RAF. No youth is conscripted to go up. The boys volunteer for the air; and glory in it. The same voluntary coming forward applies to service in submarines.

Yrs sincerely
H.B. Heelis

To Arthur Stephens

Castle Cottage
Sawrey
Ambleside
Ap.19.41

Dear Mr Stephens,

I received the parcel containing the Peter Rabbit original drawings today – safe and unbroken. I suppose you have sent them for safe keeping. No place is safe, but the chances of any individual house being hit is small in the country. An isolated farmhouse has been destroyed, with 11 killed, in consequence of army lorries with lights on a main road. The lorries were not hit. There were bombers over head all night long, we are on a "route" here, they fly over and come back; and to judge by the noise some go lost and wander round.

There were over a hundred killed in a town. It must have been terrible in London. But there seems to be no rush of evacs. [evacuees] like last summer – poor things some begin to call them "Jonahs". There were 5 in that farmhouse who got no safety in the country. The first killed last summer was a little evac. girl, in bed.

I think – with you – this is the climax – every country spreads him out & must weaken the communications. I think if we have to leave Greece we had better concentrate on thrashing France & Southern Ireland – whatever they call themselves – a bad lot. I hope Bedford Street is still standing. With thanks for yr letter & parcel

yrs sincerely
Beatrix Heelis

Mr Heelis is much obliged for letter with figures

From the Warne edition of
The Tale of Peter Rabbit

*Beatrix had asked Joseph Moscrop if he could find her 'a careful clipper',
not knowing that he himself was practised in the art.*

To Joseph Moscrop   Sawrey
                                                     Friday Jun 27 [1941]
Dear Joe Moscrop,

I thought it was very strange if you had never clipped – they had got
the idea at the Park – you have been too modest. I trust you have got my
letter of apology about writing 60/- instead of 70/-, I thought I had
done so directly the letter was in the box. As regards hay time it would
not have surprised me if you had asked more, it is a little under the
current rate, but you will not of course be working on Sunday which has
become a local bad habit. We never did so in past times – then the
powers that control affecting the weather sent us a series of wet summers
when the only fine days were Sundays (missed!) so next season we
succumbed to temptation, which came from the D; and made hay on
Sundays when we could get it; I hope this season the weather will be
heavenly. Anyway please understand I would never wish anyone to go
against his conscience. Without discussing the question of Sabbath
labour generally speaking – the conscience of each individual is a guide
in addition to the law of Holy writ.

About clipping, as you are *not* a mere roller up – you should have
60/- per week. The other man is getting £6.10 for the fortnight – a
fortnight won't see us through with it. I am very thankful you are
coming. I do not think G.W. is worse or seriously ill – probably he is
healthier than for years past, but he is in a state where he might crock
up, with heat or exertion, and then he tries to look [at] the cattle when
he ought to be resting.

I wonder if there would be a chance of getting a puppy of Lassie's
breed – poor old thing I would have liked another litter but Tom Storey
says she is too old now for pups.

                                                     Yrs sincerely
                                                     H B Heelis

To [Mr Fildes] the Surveyor, U.D.C. Castle Cottage
[Lakes Urban District Council, Ambleside] Sawrey
Ambleside
Oct 26.41

Dear Sir,

I understand that Mr Schofield has forwarded a copy of my remonstrance about the foot bridge over the Brathay – at Fitz Steps, Little Langdale.

It is to be hoped something will be done *soon* – if only patching.

Today, I am told the younger child John Stoddart – being unable to stride across the hole – the elder child has been jumping him over it.

Also a woman taking fright on a dark night, stumbled & dropped her parcels through into the river.

Do get something done before there is a bad accident.

Yrs truly
H.B. Heelis

What is the difficulty about mending it? – Apart from the fact of being between *2 councils?*

Are you short of timber? Can I help you any way? I am felling Tongue intake & could arrange for 2 or 3 larch from Mr Crossdale.

It has been unsafe for months past.

Sepia ink with pencil sketch inscribed 'Sept 19th '04 The Greta, Near Portinscale, Keswick. H.B.P.'

At the top of this letter a bit of silvered material was attached and marked 'Blitz'.

To Anne Carroll Moore

Nov. 12.41
Castle Cottage
Sawrey
Ambleside

Dear Anne Carroll Moore,

We have not been feeling very cheerful; but it seems as though wind and snow and winter frosts may save Russia. America is going through the stage that we did at first – talking a little too big, but not ready or able to save other countries from going under. *You* who visited devastated France after the last war will know what a fate it is. We have had noisy nights even in this remote district, as the German planes go over on passage elsewhere, and sometimes unload their bombs when running for home; but there has been very little damage, they usually fall in fields or water. There was one bad tragedy, a lonely farm house, where the farmer his mother his wife & 2 children, maid servant, and 5 evacuees were all killed. There have been none near this village. If it were not for pity one might say it is a fine sight! The red glare of Liverpool & Manchester burning last spring. The searchlights and flares when towns on the coast are attacked. People take it calmly; with temper, not fear. Also animals; I had 2 horses in a field next to a pasture where 11 bombs dropped and my man found them grazing quietly when daylight came. We thought those bombs were dropped because the German suddenly realized that he was heading straight into the fell side in the darkness. They were only small bombs; it is interesting to look at the holes amongst the turf & rushes. Next morning there were little bits like tinsel on the grass; there did not seem to be any heavy metal – a thin bag of explosives? We have had a pleasant summer apart from the war, and good crops. It has been very hard work for farmers. This is really no suitable district for much ploughing and corn. We have plenty of food, and plenty of fodder for the cattle. I do hope it may not be such a severe winter as the two last – which were terrible for the hill sheep. I did not lose so many in the snow, but they lost their lambs in spring, they were so weak. As regards ourselves we are both very well – of course feeling older.

I don't know if you will get this by Christmas, I ought to have written earlier. This paper has done some travelling – it was sent to me by a friend in Australia! You will have heard Mr Churchill say in Parliament that there is plenty to eat! We here personally feel cheerful about a Christmas dinner. We are going to kill a fat pig!! We are allowed 2 pigs a year amongst us; but may not kill any other sort of animal, except hutch rabbits. The rationing is very just; a bit inconvenient for country people far removed from shops. I have received a wail from Bedford Street – orders without cease, and enough paper, but they cannot get books bound. The Warne business has not been bombed. A large edition was lost last Spring at the printers. Other things have gone that matter more! It is sad to think of the City. And the same in Europe; senseless waste and destruction. The blitz has done one useful purpose, it has opened the eyes of the British trades unions; well if the Americans realize in time.

With our kind regards yrs sincerely
Beatrix Heelis

Detail of a pencil sketch

To Bertha Mahony Miller

Castle Cottage
Sawrey
Ambleside
Nov. 24.41

Dear Mrs Bertha Miller,

The winter's cold and bad weather is here again, I hope it has not brought any more bronchitis to you? I have only got a cold in my nose; and let us both make good resolutions that "a stitch in time saves nine" with colds that are obstinate: stay in bed.

I happened to look through a packet of old letters from USA and I have reread some questions which you asked about the books. "Stymouth" [in *Little Pig Robinson*] was Sidmouth on the south coast of Devonshire. Other pictures were sketched at Lyme Regis; the steep street looking down hill into the sea, and some of the thatched cottages were near Lyme. The steep village near Lynton is called 'Clovelly'; I have never seen it, though I know parts of the north Devon coast. Ilfracombe gave me the idea of the long flight of steps down to the harbour. Sidmouth harbour and Teignmouth harbour are not much below the level of the towns. The shipping – including a pig aboard ship, was sketched at Teignmouth, S. Devon. The tall wooden shed for drying nets is (or was?) a feature of Hastings, Sussex. So the illustrations are a comprehensive sample of our much battered coasts.

Old John Taylor was the Sawrey joiner and wheelwright; his wife, and later his stout elderly daughter 'Agnes Anne' kept the little general shop for years and years. After their deaths a daughter-in-law took it on. In turn she became old & invalidish and made it over to a niece-in-law – who has closed the long chapter; Ginger & Pickles is no more. Multiple stores had almost killed village shops before the war. We were very vexed; indeed I would have put in a friend who was anxious to take it on. But the Taylor niece-in-law sat tight! She kept on the cottage, made the "shop" a parlour to let, and threw away the goodwill and connections because, being a young person, she would not be tied keeping shop. Agnes Anne was a big fat woman with a loud voice, very genuine in her likes & dislikes; a good sort. Old John was a sweet gentle old man, failed in his legs, so he kept [to] his bed; but was head of the family and owned several cottages. He professed to be jealous because I had put his son John in a book as John Joiner [*Roly-Poly Pudding*, later *Samuel Whiskers*] [censored] When I saw old John who was very humourous [sic] and joky, I asked him how could I put him – old John – in a book if he insisted on living in bed? So a week afterwards, enclosed with an acct, there came a scrap of paper "John Taylor's compliments and thinks he might pass for a dormouse".

It really is too bad to have closed "Ginger and Pickles". And the village blacksmith's is gone; turned into a bungalow for a Taylor daughter-in-law. And the village post office is gone [censored] 2 miles from Hawkshead P.O. And nearly all the older generation – all that were "old" when I was younger, are dead. To be dead is in the course of nature – and war – but [censored] we are alive seems to me to be generally for the worse, & disagreeable.

I have heard lately of the death of an old cousin. She had been living in a country hotel since her London house was destroyed; she was 80 so it doesn't matter; but can you wonder the Germans are hated? Her daughter writes me that a [censored] frightened her into a stroke, followed by pneumonia – "She was ill only 4 days, but the night she died there was another raid & guns & bombs going all the time. There is nothing I would not do to those murderers. She could not even die in peace."

Another cousin of mine was killed in London last spring. The raids have been only small affairs for many months though more serious than might appear from the news reports & evacs have gone back to towns. Indeed there is as much in the country; but of course less chance of being hit. One night there were 4 planes, on the way home unloaded their sticks over [censored] some sheep were killed. I had 2 farm horses in the next pasture to a bog where there is a line of small craters. The German would have flown into the fell side in the dark, if he had not tipped out his load; [censored] but only small ones. The horses were grazing quietly when daylight came. There were the saucer shaped holes, about 4 foot deep, and quantities of shining flecks like tinsel on the grass & rushes. The bombs probably weighed only about 50 lbs each. Thin light bags of explosives.

A friend (evacuee) from a south Lancashire town tells us frightful tales – a shelter containing 300 people got a direct hit. Some bodies were got out and the rest sealed down with quick lime. Only 10 days ago she looked down into a chasm large enough to hold a lofty building. It had fallen on vacant ground; she found her friends in a nearby house undamaged, though a whole row had collapsed. The effects of blast are most peculiar; windows may be unbroken on one side of a street and *everything* gone on the opposite side. Everything literally. A young woman from the village went to Barrow to look for her sister last spring and there was not a shred. Its a pity the U.S.A. strikers cannot realize, by seeing and feeling, what it is. Destruction & *beastly* cruelty.

We have had a fine summer; enjoyable but for the overwork and anxiety.

I am too late posting for Christmas. I wonder whether "Nancy" will care for the stories? [*The Solitary Mouse* and *Wag-by-Wall*] Of course I wrote the introduction for my own pleasure – and it might appeal to Anne Carroll Moore because she knows the Lake district. I cannot judge my own work. Is not "Wag by the Wa'" rather a pretty story; if divested of the "Jenny Ferret" rubbish? I thought of it years ago as a pendant to *The Tailor of Gloucester* – the old lonely man and the lonely old woman: but I never could finish it all; and after 9 months occasional nibblings – it seems likely to go into the post – unfinished yet!

What a *pity* you did not come to Sawrey! A.C.M. [Anne Carroll Moore] came & Miss Gould & Miss Davis & Mary Haigh & Mrs Coolidge all delightful – why not Bertha Mahony?

I do not know of any treatise upon credit; ask Mr Micawber of David Copperfield! I think both Ginger & P.[*ickles*] and the Pie & Patty are feeble in plot: the ovens are absurd, quite wrong.

My books are off the market – wails and lamentations from F.W. & Co. They have enough paper but they cannot get book binders, so they have to refuse the whole Christmas market. It would hit me also, but farming has looked up; hard work but fair pay at last.

With kind regards yrs sincerely
Beatrix Heelis

From The Pie and the Patty-Pan

To Hettie Douglas

Castle Cottage
Sawrey
Ambleside
Jan 14.42

My dear Hetty [sic],

How very awkward about Dave [the gardener and handyman at Ashyburn] having to go. I should have thought you had almost enough garden under vegetables to "reserve" him, he grew such fine crops – but likely it is a clean sweep of younger men, except ploughmen. Geoff. Storey registered, but nothing further so far. And there is more ploughing, I think it is perfect nonsense in this poor soil. I am to plough a field in Troutbeck that has always been used for twin lambs. I would not object if they would allow me to sow down at once; but if the rotation is carried through there will be so very little lowland grass for lambing time while 3 fields are under crops. And the potatoes were a disgrace last year – all they would say was "try another variety" next time!

I hope you and Ina keep well; its nasty weather here, wet snow, and fog. Up to Christmas it was fine and open; then we had white frosts. We did not have an agreeable Xmas. Mr Heelis took the pekes a walk on the intake in the afternoon – after a chicken for dinner – as usual lost them rabbitting and Chuleh returned to him covered with blood and an eye like a disgusting marble. He blames a stray dog but I feel *sure* it was a cat, perhaps a village cat also after rabbits. She had a scratch an inch long on the top of her head, no depth but bled a lot which was not at all like a dog bite. He heard her scream. She was taken to the vet right away, but the eye by that time was too swollen to put back, and Miss Lawton (the vet) said to bath[e] it over the weekend – the dog seemed to have no pain & could see with it. However, it took bad ways & burst on the following Tuesday; & now there is scarcely a shred left in a clean socket, healed and clean empty.

They are tough little dogs. We were more upset than Chuleh. It does not show a great deal; and she is rabbitting again. Tzu-zee [sic] was very shocked and rather unkind. If her poor sister went near her – she got up and turned away. I don't know if she will ever wash its face again; it would be useful now.

They have played again last few days. There is one advantage of a Border terrier, their eyes don't stick out! They are very active independent little dogs and better able to look after themselves. I think you have made a good choice of breed. One can never tell how a Border puppy will turn out; a nice thick little dog is very pleasing. Sometimes they grow bigger than expected. We are well here, I had a few days in bed with a cold at New Year (with peke as a footwarmer) I got off with a small cold. The Russian news is very heartening, and its a grand move to have Chinese troops. If they are like our 2 ruffians they have courage & not much feeling for pain. Miss Mills is very anxious about no news of her brother in Hong Kong, she has gone back after 3 weeks leave, she had a bad cough but she got over it and is not quite so thin. Poor Miss Hammond looks woe begone. It would be better if she could pull herself together and undertake something to do – surely she might do something at home. With love to you and Ina

Yrs aff.
Beatrix Heelis

Pencil sketch of a dog

To Anne Carroll Moore   Jan 31.42
                                                         Castle Cottage
                                                         Sawrey
                                                         Ambleside

Dear Anne Carroll Moore,

Your letter and the snowy trees reached me two days ago, in a world equally white. I am so very glad to hear you are lecturing. I was half afraid your retiring from the Library might mean ill health. The Library Journal was not explicit on that point. Your country is truly in the war at last! How glad we are to know that American troops are in Ulster! I have never thought that invasion of Britain could be successful; but while any landing was being beaten off it would be horrible for people living as near the coast as we do here. The orders have always been to "stay put", we would not have stampeded like the French; but the choice of sitting indoors – or taking to the woods is not attractive to the aged! There is about a foot of snow at present – no doubt it has come from Russia, the wind has been in the east. It is the third severe winter in succession. I feel the cold a bit; but I have had the luxury of breakfast in bed some very cold mornings, as we have an evacuated friend here, for the winter months, who is helpful. This paper is a bit off an old proof sheet. I have been sorting papers & books this afternoon – a perplexing task as regards books. "Salvage drives" are a craze, at the present moment being overdone. Things are being destroyed that ought not to be. There is a drive for old iron and the local council has made such a muddle of listing railings. Pretty old fashioned light iron work on walls is listed to go, while a next door heavy gate is not on the list. It is causing much annoyance, they are taking so many garden railings which are not of sufficient weight to balance the wreck. There is any amount of modern ugly bar fencing, but the Council unfortunately selects "*old* iron". I am sure mine is Georgian. I am trying to ransom it by offering a pump, a stove, a field gate and some hurdles. Nearly all the little old railings in Hawkshead are scheduled, the square will look bare. I have been telling the sanitary inspector (!) who is the author of the list that he should have taken many hundred tons of horizontal bars from the black modern fencing which disfigures our widened roads, for miles & miles. The middle & lower bars could be drawn out, and replaced by sheep netting.

Books also are perplexing. Books of reference that one cannot scrap. Books that one is fond of, though one does not constantly re-read them. What about the Horn books for many years? which I dip into with pleasure. What about little old books for children which I have collected? I have shelved the question with regard to a quantity of general literature by sending it to the Sailors Home at Barrow; the port missionary is anxious for books for the ships, and he can "salvage" what is unsuitable, though he does say they "will read anything".

How quaint and pretty to drop into a backwater of old France in 'Arcadia'. I think some parts of the States must be as charming as other parts must be as unpleasingly modern. In this small island we have not room for back waters, and the few that still linger are to be listed and swept away by sanitary inspectors!

Someone sent me Rachel Field's "All this . . . [*and Heaven Too*]" the "second volume" – the New England sequel is delightful, and the American historical personages are alive and natural. The French part has no atmosphere, rather flat.

My husband keeps well – touch wood! There is a good deal of influenza about. It is going the round of the farms. Not severe; but if William gets it he – does get it – with depression. I am fairly cheerful about things. This snow – 4 falls since New Year – is becoming serious for the sheep, but it has done a good turn in Russia.

With kindest regards from both of us,

yrs sincerely

Beatrix Heelis

Watercolour of Sawrey under snow, 7 March 1909

To Joseph Moscrop

Castle Cottage
Sawrey
Ambleside
March 11th 42

Dear Joe Moscrop,

I agree with hearty approval to pay you £22.10.0 for the 4 weeks lambing. I do hope the poor dogs stand up to it, I have felt sorry for them – their food is such trash. I am getting some more oatmeal ground at the mill. It may not be lawful to feed it to animals, but we cannot do without sheep dogs (or without Joseph?). It is always a pleasure to see the swallows again and Joseph's smile.

Things are very black at present; but it was so last time; the Germans cannot be very cheerful in view of the retreat in Russia.

We had another fall of snow at the weekend, it has melted in the sun, but the Troutbeck fells look white. I wonder if the lane is still ice over. I went to Windermere to shop – which is a tedious job with "points" and ration cards, I had not time to try the lane this morning.

One of the mares – the big one – nearly died after it was laid in. I don't know how it will be for spring ploughing. I have heard of a 4 yr old. The Committee order the ploughing of "little Dawson", I told them it has always been used for twin lambs. If only the snow would go! I want to get on some sulphate of Amon. to help pasture grass; we will be short of 2 fields, so want all the "early bite" possible. With kindest regards

Yrs sincerely
H.B. Heelis

To Bruce Thompson
Castle Cottage
Sawrey
Ambleside
March 30th 42

Dear Bruce Thompson,

I regretted – too late – that we had not taken old Mr Newton from Ambleside. It was not wise to have the inspector propound a scheme. Apart from *sheep*, the farm is scarcely more than a small holding. At present there is *one* milk cow standing in the shippon. There is not sufficient in-land, or hay, for a shippon full of cows.

There was a nice little trade of selling glasses of milk (now unlawful); but its unprofitable to make butter, and remote for sending milk away in kits [small wooden tubs]. Any future tenant should be a sheep farmer, with a small local milk selling; it might be worked up to 2 cows, at a time, milking in winter; and say 4 or 5 in summer.

The buildings are uniformly & depressingly *all bad*. Apart from Milk Marketting [sic] fads *I* think the dark damp hulls are much worse than the shippon?

It does want some money spending on it, after the war. What is pressing in this next summer season is to do the drains and to put a new floor in the shippon – the existing shippon. I did not say anything when he made a silly joke about carrying the milk through; what is more serious is that the wet "muck" sipes [sic] north through the site of his proposed new shippon. And I am not competent to say whether that north wall would support the weight of a slate roof leaning against it?

Before you meet the inspector again I think it would be wise to be prepared with a practical man's opinion on the buildings as a whole. The official is an affable little fellow – (a dnd. sight too pleasant if you'll excuse the expression!) When he brought that book into the kitchen he asked Stoddart about the water supply; when he heard it came from above he suggested a bath. Tommy did not tell him the beck runs dry. Doubtless he would suggest a reservoir. Some people do not realize that there is a war on.

It is human nature for a servant to want all he can get of labour saving. I detest bowls. In a town the wretched cows cannot take exercise; but in the country they should walk out daily and drink clean water in a beck. Ball-cocks in troughs are not like flushing a W.C. Unless the bowls are washed daily (by attendants in white overalls) they are not sanitary.

I remain yrs sincerely
HB Heelis

Jacqueline Overton was a protégée of Anne Carroll Moore and children's librarian at the Bacon Memorial Library, Westbury, Long Island, U.S.A.

To Jacqueline Overton

Castle Cottage
Sawrey
Ambleside
April 7th 42

Dear Jacqueline Overton,

I received your letter of March 2nd. It renews an old regret. I never met Caldecott. My father bought some of his work, through a dealer, and he could easily have made Caldecott's acquaintance; but he did not do so.

We bought his picture books eagerly, as they came out. I have the greatest admiration for his work – a jealous appreciation; for I think that others, whose names are commonly bracketted with his, are not on the same plane at all as artist-illustrators. For instance Kate Greenaway's pictures are very charming, but compared with Caldecott – she could not draw. Others who have followed him were careful & correct draughtsmen, but lifeless and wooden. Besides; Walter Crane and Caldecott were the pioneers; their successors were imitators only.

Caldecott, & Crane's Baby's Opera were engraved by Edmund Evans; wherein they were fortunate. The Racquet Court Press turned out fine work. The last pair but one of the picture books were not so well engraved, an unpleasant mealy stipple spoils "Come lasses & lads" and in "Ride a Cock Horse". I seem to remember that Evans tried an experiment with the engraving – the last pair of all "Mrs [Mary] Blaize" & the "Great Panjandrum [Himself]" were strong & clear again. No doubt Caldecott's health affected his work – he was consumptive. How sorry we were to hear of his break downs. He went to Florida I believe one winter; and to Switzerland or Northern Italy? I have a little Swiss picture of cows in a mountain landscape. He painted a small number of oils, tentatively. This "Swiss Cattle" is about the size of the paper I am writing on [approx 240 × 210 mm]; it is painted on a bit of pasteboard, with a small brush. The cows are very good, but the general effect is wanting in light – as though it had been painted on brown paper & sunk in. On the back of the cow's picture is an unfinished view of Caldecott's house, in Surrey (or Sussex). A red brick house with a foreground of untidy garden flowers. It was bought at the sale after his death. Another larger oil painting was bought by one of my Manchester cousins. I doubt if she was acquainted with him; & anyway she is dead. We were all interested when he achieved success, because he had been a clerk in a

Manchester bank. He must certainly have had some art training, for instance in perspective, but I gathered that he was an original genius. No doubt Blackburn's Life will give you particulars of his training & career, with dates. What one remembers is the tragedy of his lungs. But he had reached the summit. He would never have done finer work than John Gilpin. The later picture books declined a little; though there is one of my first favourites in the last – the Great Panjandrum – the maid and the cabbage leaf. I *know* – because *I* tried to draw cabbages when I drew Peter Rabbit [*see opposite*].

I remember Sir John Millais [who was a friend of Beatrix's father] saying it takes an artist to appreciate an artist's work – (he was speaking not of Caldecott but of Charles Keene who drew in Punch.) Keene used a peculiar scratchy style of ink work, but a splendid draughtsman. Caldecott had 2 drawings in Punch. One of haymakers sheltering under umbrellas, I forget the other.

There used to be a small gallery in Bond Street called the 'Fine Art Society'. It was a good class dealer's, not "society" like the "Water Colour Society" etc – The Fine Arts used to have a one man show; several of the Punch artists; Miss Greenaway; other water colourists & etchers; and Caldecott, at the height of his picture book fame. My father bought at different times – perhaps there were 2 shows? as well as the sale after his death at Christie's I think. His work very seldom comes up for sale now. There was never a large output. And at the sale after his death the greater part of his pen & inks were bought for the British Museum print room.

Anyway we had the color [sic] pictures of the [Three] Jovial Huntsmen (8 in one frame, but not the cover that is used for the Horn Book) and a frame of coloured designs for the "Curmudgeon's Christmas" which appeared in the Graphic, and 4 Brittany Folk, and most of the pen & inks of the Mad Dog, and 4 little pen & inks of the frog a wooing. They came into my possession after my Mother's death. I gave them with other water colours to the Manchester Art Gallery – except about a dozen. The ink has faded sadly – though I kept them out of strong light. He did a lot of correcting with white paint, which has stood alright, but its a pity he used Indian ink. Its much easier to work with, for free flowing work, than the stodgy process black. His water colour has stood well. He was fortunate in having his work reproduced by Edmund Evans before the advent of process colour-photography & horrible clay faced paper.

I do not know if Wilfred Evans is still alive, he must be an old man if he is. All the three sons of Frederick Warne (& Co) are dead. Warne succeeded G. Routledge. When I gave the Caldecotts to the Manchester

Art Gallery – the curator Mr Lawrance Hayward [Laurence Haward], Curator, spoke of him with affectionate regard, but I scarcely think Mr Hayward is old enough to have known him; I am afraid it is too late. I distrust my own memory. I seem to remember my father saw him at a private view & he was like the poor sick gentleman in the Babes in the wood; tall with a reddish beard? or am I thinking of someone else? The pretty maid hanging out the clothes was the Caldecott's maid at the house in Surrey. ? which was the maid's picture? Which was his wife's? My memory is not clear. I think the Queen of Hearts was a portrait of his wife. The other oil painting is a hunting piece; good, but rather flat & finicky as a painting. It is sad that I cannot give more help. He was one of the greatest illustrators of all. I hope you will succeed – try Mr Hayward – and write to A. L. Stephens, F Warne & Co, Bedford Court Bedford St Strand WC2 to ask if they can put you in touch with any elderly person who knew Caldecott.

yrs sincerely
Beatrix Heelis

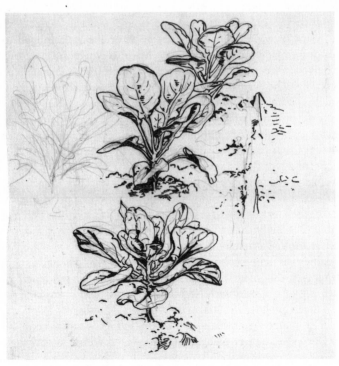

Pen-and-ink sketches for The Tale of Peter Rabbit

In an article in THE LADY *of 7 May 1942, Meriel Martin claimed to have visited the real Mr McGregor's garden when she went to Gwaynynog in Denbigh, North Wales.*

To Arthur Stephens   Sawrey
                                                          May 12.42

Dear Mr Stephens,

I must explain my neglect in not thanking you immediately for 2 letters, being in bed a few days with flu, which is rather an epidemic but only mild. We were amazed with the report of the probable royalties; "Buy British" in spite of no paper! I suppose the shortage of toys for presents explains it. I had been thinking dismal shrinkage. The assessor of taxes seems to have known what he was talking about, when he said it had *not* been a book year of poor sales.

The article in The Lady is interesting – it brings back mixed memories. It is nicely written; curiously inexact. It would not be surprising if it led to argument or inquiry by better informed rabbit fans who claim for the Lakes. The well meaning Miss Meriel makes any mistake she can! The photograph shows a south front [of Gwaynynog] unhappily refaced with sham gothic; the unspoilt side of the house was the original Welsh border 'black & white', beams & plaster. It originally belonged to the Myddeltons (of New River water fame). My uncle (in law's) elder brother Oliver Burton, a wealthy cotton spinner bought it from a decayed branch of the family. The Burton brothers were self made self educated men, but had the taste to appreciate the place. There was a good deal of original oak furniture and Uncle Fred added to the collection a truly wonderful collection of mahogany. I wonder what became of his magnificent Chippendale. It was a true pleasure & treat to me to go and stay there for a week's change every spring. But as to a happy place – ? It was exchanging one unhappy home circle for another. I disliked 'my cousins' heartily. How angry they were at the purchase of another water colour, or another complete set of chairs. The old man had earned his own money. Latterly they let him alone, & he lived alone in a corner of the house, looked after by 3 pretty Welsh maids and the old Welsh joiner estate odd man – John Evans was a character – I am afraid I don't remember a gardiner [sic] at all! I suppose there *was* a gardener. There were cauliflowers mixed with paeonies & roses. The lawns were never mown. They were hayed in summer.

Two years since a granddaughter of Uncle Fred's called here. 'Eileen Bowen Davies', daughter of his daughter – half Welsh, whole musical, frouzy looking, garrulous, rather coarse – I didn't like her at all either! When families have no background of true affection and real love to remember – what's the good of raking up an unkind past?

Jean Duke who should have gone to U.S.A. and her mother got away from Bath, leaving a flat on fire, unhurt. Her father got leave & hurried from his present station to find they had left 2 hours in their own car which would start. The girl is waiting to join the Wrens, & her mother hopes to rejoin.

We heard the York raid – nothing near here. I believe it is true that York Cathedral escaped. The choir of Exeter Cathedral was destroyed and the centre of the town.

It is still an east wind here but there has been a welcome shower of rain.

With kind regards yrs sincerely
Beatrix Heelis

To Arthur Stephens

Castle Cottage
Sawrey
Ambleside
May 14.42

Dear Mr Stephens,

Prodigious! When one thinks of the paper and the string and the wrapping up that must have been expended on the distribution of nearly two hundred thousand copies – what about war work?

The world goes mad on astronomical figures. You must have had a worritting year. Such a result could not be achieved at any time without a [?] much work; this last year it is a triumph.

I have also by same post a cheque £5.17.0 for a few cwts of potatoes, grown, under protest, on unsuitable land. They made me plant an acre, and actually gave a bounty of £10 per acre without inspecting the crop. Oats get £2.

I remain with thanks & kind regards yrs truly,
HB Heelis

I have a bronchial cough, so I write in bed, but its nothing – no rain here

To Professor Carl Weber

May 20 42
Castle Cottage
Sawrey
Ambleside
Westmorland

Dear Professor Weber,

I received your letter of April 20th punctually and expeditiously this morning, enclosing your $1.25 cheque for Red Cross – how kind of you! I do assure you American sympathy is appreciated; we never doubted the better Americans sympathized, but for a long time it was sympathy which did not include serious understanding.

I had your earlier letter about the Dynasts three weeks ago, and would have copied Thomas Hardy's earlier, but have been in bed with flu & bronchitis (not bad). I forget exactly where I found the packet at Belmount Hall – probably in Pandora's (hat) box. It is an envelope addressed by T.H. to Miss B. Owen [Rebecca had changed her name to Betty] Belmount Hall, endorsed by her "Auto letter of much interest to go with vol 3 The Dynasts as also inserted cuttings." The letter is on 3 sides of a sheet of note paper with printed heading Max Gate Dorchester, 6. Dec 1907["] Dear Miss Owen, My best thanks for what you have sent (which I return herewith as you request) Anything about the Brussels ball on the Eve of Zuctre Bras is interesting.

In respect of "the Dynasts" it does not matter that you write too late. (the proofs of the ball room scene were returned to the printers sometime ago) the question of where the ball took place being of no importance to the drama. But, as I told you, I had been struck with the curious historical uncertainty about the spot, when one would have supposed it would not have been forgotten. My opinion is still that, though well-guessed at, it has never been *proved* to be at any guessed place – despite Sir W. Fraser whose book (containing the plan reproduced in the newspaper cutting you send) I read when it came out, but was not convinced by it, having visited the same hospital, coach house etc. in 1876 – years before he investigated the buildings. It is, of course, *possible* that he may be right. But I prefer that the site of the room should remain unknown, as it helps the romance of the event – unless, indeed, it could be where Byron puts it – at the Hotel de Ville, the only place worthy of the occasion.

I am glad you have got back safely. Your hills must try the motor car a little. With renewed thanks I am sincerely yours T Hardy."

The writing is firm and without erasure. It is not for me who never could spell to doubt the spelling of the battle? Zuctre? Enclosures are 2 newspaper cuttings – a review of Sir W Fraser's book reproducing plan, and an article in the "Sketch" about Byron's reference to the ball. And a letter written to Miss Owen by old Mrs Whitaker, wife of Rev. Edmund Wemys Whitaker vicar of Bath. "Fanty" was a charming old lady, her husband was a son of the Whitakers of Belmount Hall, Miss Owen was very fond of them & she had apparently set on Mrs 'Fanty' to make inquiries about the ball amongst descendants of those who were present at it.

"14 Widcombe Crescent Bath, Dec 1907

My dearest Bet. I enclose Lady Mary FitzWilliam's answer to my letter. She *ought* to know for her cousin Lord Anglesey's daughter (the Waterloo man who left his leg on the field of Battle!!) married in 1817 a Duke of Richmond. So surely such an event as the giving of a Ball on the eve of the great Battle and *where* cd never be forgotten in the family – but people are so contradictory! they remember things much better to be forgotten – and forget what it wd have been as well to retain. So dear Bet make any use of the letter you like – it is very likely Lady Blanche will have been making some enquiries. In great haste and with much love to you both my dears ever yr aff "F"."

That is all except a p.c. addressed to Mrs Whittaker [sic], redirected to Miss Owen & endorsed "Forgot to enclose this so send it on F." In old fashioned copper plate hand "I have written to ask for the information you require to a member of the family of R. & will let you know the result the moment I get an answer y.v.c BE Nov 25".

If Mrs Fanty got any information from any member of the Richmond family (Gordon Lennox) and sent it to Betty it is to be presumed that she passed it on to T.H. and that he did not return it. He does not seem to have been impressed, probably he lost it. I am sure Betty would have preserved any such aristocratic fragment if she had got it back. Hardy's own expression of a preference that the site should continue unknown is very fine. There is something petty in trying to pin down the exact locality. How fine the description in Vanity Fair; though of a different quality of excellence to the Dynasts. If it comes to trivialities I have a little much creased copy of the 'Times' with the acct of Waterloo; and the death roll commencing with the Duke of Brunswick, ending with Ensign Brown. The guns of Waterloo. How they frightened poor Amelia! How trivial they would sound today. Mrs Wemys Whitaker was right about people forgetting & remembering. When I asked my grandmother about Waterloo she remembered very clearly that she had been at school in Liverpool and they had been walking 2 and 2 in the street when the news was called out 'and I was wearing black for Sister Laura', which the family bible confirms, nothing more!

You spoke of rewriting or adding to? the account of Miss Owen's friendship with Thomas Hardy. I wish you had seen those letters. I wish you would hold back printing till I have *extracted some of Florence Hardy's* anyway? I have never known what you got from Sotheby's? Were you founding on purchased diaries? or partly on information derived from *me*, or someone else? Until I read Florence's letters carefully, *I* had no idea the intimacy between the Miss Owens & Max Gate [Hardy's house] persevered after Mr Hardy's second marriage. To copy *all* Florence's letter would be scarcely worth while; a lot of them are mere notes of invitation, none dated, but apparently very frequent. She Betty was more intimate with the second Mrs Hardy than with the first. I should think most of the people must be dead now? Florence was not a discreet letter writer; there were one or two so spiteful I burnt them. She was not an attractive woman; but I end by being sorry for her.

Belmount Hall is unoccupied. The third last proposition was the Society of Friends proposed to make it a rest home for aged evacuees; they had started many homes; but, alas, they had to drop the project because they were largely dependent on help from America for running them, and there would have been preliminary expense on plumbing etc. The house is perfectly dry since I repaired the roof. Taking no harm now, and the daffodils & azalias [sic] are a dream in the deserted gardens.

Thanking you again for the cheque

Yrs sincerely
HB Heelis

Early sepia ink drawing inscribed 'H. B. Potter'

In the May issue of THE HORN BOOK *Bertha Mahony Miller was publishing an essay by Beatrix called 'The Lonely Hills' in which she reminisced about the colour and excitement of local folk-dance festivals, and about her solitary walks on Troutbeck Tongue.*

To Bertha Mahony Miller

June 18.42
Castle Cottage
Sawrey
Ambleside

Dear Mrs. Miller,

Your charming present arrived unexpectedly this morning – *Lemon Juice*! Also Butter, Dextrose, Onion flakes, Chocolate, Bacon & Cheese. I was very thankful for a tin of lemon juice in a Christmas parcel – I think from Mrs Coolidge – it helped my cough when I had bronchitis, all through the month of May (which is too good a month to waste when one is nearly 76). I am not coughing now, so I shall save your lemon juice till next winter; and sprinkle the dextrose on my breakfast porridge, to promote energy as promised on the label. I have nobly given the tin of bacon to a friend who was lamenting the smallness of the ration. We have half a pig hanging up here, and I am not altogether glad, as it proves hard. And it will be very hard indeed if we are nibbling at it for twelve months. I do not think the pig itself had been so well fed as poor Pig Robinson. We usually pride ourselves on home cured hams. The onion flakes are welcome, this season's onions are just beginning to grow as seedlings.

The May number of the Horn Book has not come, perhaps it might have traveled [sic] with the gift parcel, and it may arrive yet. I am curious to see how the essay looks in print.

I thought I might have written out some others, while I was a prisoner, but my energy only went so far as sorting books – rereading one – before consigning to the pulp collection. I dislike the task, even if one does not read them often, they are friends. As regards old letters, they are usually best burnt – no that's a fine! – best torn up. I have been surprised at the number and the friendliness – of the packets of dozens of letters from [the] U.S.A. and they are only a few tied up in bundles from amongst the numbers received through many years. I don't receive English letters like that; a good many from children, some wanting autographs, some enthusiastic grateful parents (also in U.S.A.) but never does anyone outside your perfidiously complimentary nation write to tell me that I write good prose! Its a wonder the censor does not cut it out. I think he must have suppressed the Horn Book; if it does not come by next post.

I eat your chocolate at the moment. We are getting a fair amount of chocolate here, but it does not taste very nice. I had 2 oranges when I was ill, I had nearly forgotten the taste. The crops are looking well, it is not much like summer, such cold nights.

With renewed thanks.

yrs sincerely
Beatrix Heelis

The chocolate is *good*!

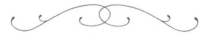

Mrs M.E. Wight was the wife of the forester for the Graythwaite Estate. Her only daughter, Mollie, a great fan of the little books, had died in 1928, aged thirteen. Beatrix had given Mrs Wight a copy of the limited edition of THE FAIRY CARAVAN.

To Mrs Wight

Sawrey
June 26.42

Dear Mrs Wight,

. . . This warm weather is a treat. We are starting hay tomorrow – the crops look good – and what a crop of apples! I am thinning ours with a pair of scissors, so high as I can reach.

I am so glad to hear that you are well and occupied – there's nothing like open air for soothing present anxiety and memories of past sadness. I think of you in your garden with "Primrose".

Yes – Kenneth Grahame ought to have been an artist – at least all writers for children ought to have a sufficient recognition of what things look like – did he not describe 'Toad' as combing his *hair*? A mistake to fly in the face of nature. A frog may wear galoshes; but I don't hold with toads having beards or wigs! So I prefer Badger.

With very kind regards yrs sincerely
Beatrix Heelis

450

To Mrs Hall

Castle Cottage
Sawrey
Ambleside
Aug 11.42

Dear Mrs Hall

I was disturbed to read your letter. I am sorry to say I detest goat keeping in the Lake district, from experience in the last war, and afterwards. The original Nannies in the hands of a careful owner *may* be tethered – though I take leave to doubt its lasting. But they have *kids*. People have sentimental objection to drowning the kids, like kittens new born; they are sold, or given away, to neighbours, and presently the neighbourhood is infested with them. There was a flock of half wild goats above Coniston after the last war that became such a nuisance they had to be shot. And I had a wood devastated in Troutbeck by a goat which had been given to a small holder by a well meaning lady – so I decided to put my foot down – no goats again!

The fact is our district is so stony it is impossible to drive pegs firmly. I had a tenant who kept a Nanny goat for many years in a district of deep red earth; there were hedges & appletrees, but it never got loose or did any damage. But I know by experience what would happen in Little Langdale. You could not fasten them by tethering. I am sorry to refuse so far as my land is concerned.

Yrs sincerely
H.B. Heelis

Detail of pen-and-ink sketch for
The Tale of Little Pig Robinson

Reginald Hart had first visited Sawrey with his wife, Betty, and young daughter, Alison, in the autumn of 1940. As a keen collector of children's books he was tracing the backgrounds of Beatrix's little books and he sought permission to photograph Hill Top. Beatrix welcomed the Harts into Castle Cottage where she showed them her collection of original Caldecotts and her extensive china collection, which was another of Reginald Hart's interests. He was an architect by profession, working at that time in the Ministry of Works in Blackpool, where he issued permits for building and for the allocation of materials. He returned to Sawrey a number of times and was able to help Beatrix through the complexities of applications for building plans.

For Christmas 1942 Beatrix sent Alison Hart a slightly different version of her story THE CHINESE UMBRELLA, *also given to Louie Choyce.*

To Reginald Hart

Castle Cottage
Sawrey, Ambleside
Oct 24.42

Dear Mr Hart

I am quite delighted with the photographs of the little dogs – and *Alison* is even more delightful! The square shaped picture where she is looking down, just commencing to smile, and I am holding Chu-leh's [sic] paw is lovely. If I could ask for 3 more copies? I should like to send two – to friends in the States. Its very good of my lace edged cap (which seems to have hitched forward over my nose) and not too bad of the old woman!

Alison is rather serious in the other holding up picture, as though the dog were a great weight. Samuel Whiskers' doorway is an interesting study in light and shadows. You have a good lens – it does not distort.

I ought to have written sooner to thank you. I have been been [sic] over busy about sales – mud – rain – transport difficulties – and now the corn threshing machine has arrived unexpectedly – and it has been working in heavy showers – as though the corn were not spoilt enough already! I am afraid there is a good deal rotting in the fields all over the north. We have a few carts still out, but it is too rotten to bother about. The weather is very wild, with hail showers. Some trees are bare of leaves but the autumn tints are fine. I went to Coniston this morning – (on the subject of Broughton sheep fair) and the colours of gold birch coppice, red bracken and dark blue hail storm clouds were wonderful. But it will be a long winter.

I shall wait till the 12 months is up, in November; and apply about that unfinished house; apply in the formal way – but there is surely no harm in telling you when I do so. I do not think I have enough plaster boards; nobody seems to use the old lath & plaster method now.

I am glad you had a pleasant holiday at Sawrey.

The little dogs should send their love to Alison – and with my kind regards to Mrs Hart and yourself

I remain yrs sincerely
Beatrix Heelis

THE LISTENER *of 21 January 1943 carried an article by Janet Adam Smith called 'The World of Beatrix Potter' in which she compared Beatrix's work to earlier English artists including Blake, Palmer, Constable, Bewick and Caldecott.*

To Janet Adam Smith (Mrs Roberts)   Feb 2.43
                                                     Castle Cottage
                                                     Sawrey,
                                                     nr Ambleside

Dear Madam,

I am obliged for the 'Listener' – some one had already sent me a copy which I read with mingled gratitude and stupefaction – the writer seems to know a deal more about the inception of the Peter Rabbit books than I do! When first published another outraged authoress (and her publisher) said they were a crib of a horrid little book called "Little Black Sambo". Now you say they are founded on the work of the Immortals – all names which I revere, but the only one of them I really tried to copy was Randolph Caldecott, and you say there is no resemblance.

I am very glad the books have given so much pleasure and continue to be useful. I can no longer see to overwork my eyes; and I think I have "done my bit"; – unconsciously – trying to copy nature – without affectation or swelled head.

Its well I do not depend on the BBC – they "conveyed" one of my books without asking, and paid – was it £2.2.0 or £1.10.0? I wonder what they paid you.

Again thanking you I remain

Yrs sincerely
H. B. Heelis (Mrs W. Heelis)

PS When a person has been nearly thirty years married it's not ingratiating to get an envelope addressed to 'Miss'.

To Arthur Stephens

Feb 7 43
Castle Cottage
Sawrey
Ambleside

Dear Mr Stephens

Thank you for sending me the 'Listener' – a while ago; I did write to thank you and tore up my letter (*not* burnt!) The article is nicely written and well meant – but surely great rubbish? Absolute bosh. I revere the names of the Immortals, and I have this much in common with them, that, like them I have tried to do my best from love of painting, and taken satisfaction in so doing – whether printed or not – and without swelled head – but to compare the manner of my work with theirs is silliness – especially the great, and *broad*-painting-Constable. I did try to copy Caldecott; but I agree with Mrs Roberts that I did *not* achieve much resemblance.

When I was young it was still the fashion to admire Pre Raphaelites. Their meticulous copying of flowers & plants etc influenced me.

I have had 3 of the wretched things sent; one from the author, an evacuated mother at Penrith. You may not remember – as regards "Peter Rabbit" – a Mrs [Helen] Bannerman & her publishers Grant Richards said Peter was imitated from their Dumpy book series and they were rather nasty about it. As a matter of fact, Peter was spontaneously written before "Little Black Sambo" was published.

I hope you are keeping in better health? We have kept well here, although there has been flu about the village, and rather trying times. Too much rain – endless rain – and too much work. This morning it is snowing which will stop the ploughs again. I have not been inconvenienced by calling up, my men are mostly older, except the plough boy who is reserved, but every body is tired and "edgy". I am running a tractor outfit, but its most unsuitable country for a tractor plough. The neighbours ask for it without regard for the steepness of their fields. And Mr Hudson [Robert Hudson, Minister of Agriculture] asks for more and more potatoes where potatoes won't grow a decent crop! And its wicked to grumble when one thinks of the suffering in other lands.

Are the little books out of print? They have been on sale locally. I like the light coloured jackets – I like them much better than the sunk binding. I did not write for any at Christmas because I had some in reserve which you advised, some months ago.

I hope you are not finding business too difficult – it must be aggravating to be short of paper & labour when books are much sought after.

With kind regards yrs sincerely
Beatrix Heelis

P.S. I think "Sister Dorothea to whom we used to send a parcel must be dead or gone into a nunnery, she faded out of sight and knowledge some years ago. Her relations that I knew are dead.

To Janet Adam Smith (Mrs Roberts)   Castle Cottage
                                                     Sawrey
                                                     Ambleside
                                                     Feb. 8.43

Dear Mrs Roberts,
    "There is nothing new under the sun". We seem so much 'at cross purposes' that its not much use pursuing the subject. I have too *much* common sense to resent a suggestion that my painting-manner is not original & founded upon another painter's manner, but I think it is silly to suggest it is founded on Constable – a great artist with a broad style. When I was young it was still permissable [sic] to admire the PreRaphaelites; their somewhat niggling but absolutely genuine admiration for copying natural details did certainly influence me; also F. Walker & his school and Hunt.
    You write nicely, but in this case you have been trying to write an article without quite enough knowledge. Try and write some articles about country wayside objects – if you are a beginner – and write them for your own children – that is the secret of good writing – have something to say – and write with an end in view. I must not say write "with a purpose" because that is next door to a moral – and Miss Edgeworth (who did influence me!) is out of fashion.
    And for goodness sake don't write any more rubbish about me.

I remain yrs sincerely
Beatrix Heelis

To Arthur Stephens

Castle Cottage
Sawrey
Ambleside
Ap. 13. 43

Dear Mr Stephens

I have just received your letter and accounts this morning. It is an extraordinary record, in face of difficulties and restrictions – I dont know how you have managed it – I assure you I realize and appreciate.

I notice one curiosity – that Peter is not at head of the sales, no doubt this reflects the difficulty of buying him in shops, he was out of stock. The war seems to have encouraged book buying, which must be provoking to firms who are short of paper – but certainly neither you nor I have reason to complain about the Rabbit books.

I am afraid you must be very tired. We have kept well in this house. A good deal of illness round about; and it increases short handed over work, 2 men laid up when corn wanted sowing, but its coming up quickly. There is more & more to plough. I don't think the M[inistry] of Ag.[riculture] is so bad, its Lord Woolton's endless forms and muddles. Retail milk selling – only undertaken to oblige neighbours – is absolutely beyond undestanding.

Thank you very much indeed for the cheque. Its a coincidence I wrote one for £1025 just before post came in. *Not* "Wings" – a piece of land near Hawkshead village very important to keep under control from jerry building; and let at fair rent. Wings Week [when money was collected for the RAF] here is in June.

With very kind regards and thanks

yrs sincerely
Beatrix Heelis

Elizabeth Booth was a school friend of Isabella Halsted, a daughter of
Charles Hopkinson.

To Elizabeth Booth

Castle Cottage
Sawrey
Ambleside
Westmorland
June 12th 43

Dear Elizabeth Booth,

Thank you for a very pleasant letter. Yes! the Peter Rabbit books seem to have filled a gap! In spite of of [sic] paper shortage they are circulating after 40 years; indeed they are more useful than in normal times because there are fewer toys to give to children.

"Toys" makes me think – and try to say – what real pleasure I have had in return from American unknown correspondents' letters. You really appreciate my little books; whereas in this country it is the popularity of a "best seller" toy book – enormous sales, but mainly *toy* book; a convenient present. For instance in this country the Tailor of Gloucester my own favourite has never sold so well as in America.

I am interested to know that your father recognized the archway – into the precincts of the Cathedral. I remember I sat on a door step on a blazing *hot* day to sketch it. The Tailor's shop was copied from a print of houses in old London city – probably destroyed. I do not know what happened in Gloucester. I used to stay with cousins who lived on the Cotswold hills between Gloucester & Stroud; dead long ago.

How funny about the nurse and the rat! She would not have liked "Sammy". I have memory of him waddling along the floor, wanting to be picked up by my Aunt – a stout elderly lady who did not altogether appreciate his friendly advances. Poor Sammy. White rats are not very long lived; and he was always wanting to be petted in his declining months. But not everybody liked him. One of his scrapes was to cut a neat round piece size of our ½ crowns out of the middle of a sheet. He carried a curious collection of stolen articles to his box.

I remember the Aunt providing a hard boiled egg, and watching the rolling of the egg along a passage; but she requested that his nest box might be kept firmly fastened. Like your nurse she was not fond of rats!

I reciprocate your good wishes – and agree with you, you and Timmy Willie, in preferring the country – there is more room for bombs! We have not had any for a long time near here, and in the worst times they always fell on rough land.

Sincerely yours,
'Beatrix Potter' = Beatrix Heelis – Mrs W. Heelis

Bertha Mahony Miller was planning to publish 'old Sally's story' by Beatrix, called WAG-BY-WALL, *in the Christmas issue of* THE HORN BOOK.

To Bertha Mahony Miller

Castle Cottage
Sawrey
Ambleside
Aug. 23rd. 43

Dear Mrs Miller,

I posted an airmail letter to you two days since to say I had no objection to the use of the photograph and I am trying to get at Mr Reginald Hart who took it. I should think he would make no objection or charge. His little daughter Alison Hart is holding my Pekinese dog Chuleh in the picture. I wish it had been the other, Tzu zee [sic], but she is very proud and objects to being photographed.

I hope you will think old Sally's story is improved by being shorn of some trimmings? It seems better balanced without the longer verses – one too good, and the last – too doggrel [sic].

About the name. Have you any reason in U.S.A. for always referring to the clock as Wag *on* the wall? I have looked in the history of Colonial Furniture and it is not mentioned therein. I think I have once heard that form of clock mentioned as "*at* the wall" – but never *on*? I went to see Mrs Cookson, Gallowbarrow, Hawkshead yesterday who has a fine specimen, and I asked her what she called it. She replied without hesitation "Wag b' t' Wa". The nearest phonetic pronunciation would be "Wag by twa" = Wag-by-the wall. Mrs Cookson said "never *on*". They are uncommon; older than the long case.

The sequence was first the brass "lantern" clock – I have one, imperfect, date 17th century – then "wag-by-wall", then wag acquired a hood, a wooden head cover to slip on; and 18th century invented the long case. No doubt some over-lapping of dates. The wag is of course the pendulum. The weights on Mrs Cookson's are this ▲ shape, instead of the normal cylindrical in a grandfather.

Unless you have strong reason for contrary I would like the old clock to be Wag-by-the-Wall – or "Wag-by-Wall."

We have a big crop of corn, we are waiting for settled weather to cut it, it is scarcely ripe yet in the north.

My lantern clock had a curious history. A man in Ulverston who buys secondhand furniture at sales bought a long case at an auction. When he got it home and looked inside, he found this much older brass clock was fixed in, in such a way as to use the face and fingers of the grandfather. I bought the old one which he pulled out; unfortunately its own face is missing. It has the brass dome which was the bell and the pretty pierced brass fret, with dolphins, which is usually considered about 1650–70.

The wag-by-wa's were plain; a plain face in a plain wooden border frame, or merely a face unframed.

With kind regards yrs sincerely
Beatrix Heelis

To George Wilson

Castle Cottage
Sawrey
Oct 13.43

Dear George Wilson,

Mr Heelis has been at Hughes the builder, and at Dewhurst. They both make promises. W. Brockbank says he wants the floors so that he can stand on them to work at the window sills. If only a bit could be done, to fasten up the house before winter.

I want them to do the cement in the larder if Dewhurst would fix where the staircase reaches, which controls size of larder.

There has been a message about wet coming in near the chimney at Mary Brockbank's cottage. She is at the Central Cafee [sic] Ambleside, and her tenant is not always there. I should think Saturday is the likeliest day to find them in. They talk about a "stain" – there are plenty in this house!

I have not been out in the car yet. I am getting sick of the doctor coming. My heart has been too quick since I had rheumatic fever at 20 – so if I stay at home till it mends to "normal" you will not see me for a bit! I am not short of breath now.

It has not been a very grand fair – Troutbeck hoggs did not average so well as last year – 23/6 top, down to 5/6. I could not see them, the ½ breds were good; but Herdwicks on the high fell have been backward this season.

Yrs truly
H B Heelis

To Reginald Hart

Castle Cottage
Sawrey
Ambleside
Nov.2.43

Dear Mr Hart,

I am much interested in the catalogue. The slip ware is almost incredible; how can such a collection of elaborate and *perfect* monstrosities survive unbroken? I recognize several as the originals of illustrations of early pottery in sundry text books. A few years ago a Kendal dealer had a Toft dish, brown & yellow, unbroken and very ugly. I sometimes dig up chips in the garden that seem older than modern glazed jugs.

I wonder why one digs up so many pipes? bowls & stems, broken, some of them very pretty.

There are a good many old sites of tumbledown ruined cottages. I used to look for kitchen middens, without one success. The absence of pottery fragments is so complete that I have come to the belief that old inhabitants of this district used exclusively turned *wooden* ware: its not unlikely as it was a country of woodworkers; and turning – witness the old turned legs of tables & chairs. I am vexed to have missed a table that has been through a sale in Bowness lately; it was genuine untouched from a Troutbeck house – a long table. The gatelegged tables are not rare, but there are few of the so-called "refectory" left. You may have noticed a fine gateleg at Hill Top, it belonged to the Dixons at Low Greengate, Sawrey.

I see some kind person – Mrs Tittlemouse or Hunca Munca had been round [at Hill Top] with a mop and a duster? And my bed vallance straightened up, for which many thanks. I have been across there once. I got on very slowly till last week, when I got outdoors again and was much refreshed. I have not quite got rid of the doctor, but I hope if the weather improves I may get back to my usual health – or nearly so – one must expect to lose a little ground as one gets older. I took over some early mss of the books and put them in the chest in the oak bedroom; I found an incomplete portion of Pig Robinson dated 1893. I still have not found the data which you ask for; but I will hunt it out by degrees. I have got up to various – farming – complexities – sales – fairs – Martinmas term – 2 servants leaving – which has rather absorbed my energies; I am beginning to see daylight however. Did Alison send the little black book which tumbled out of the parcel? Chuleh & Suzie [Tzuzee] think it belonged to a black cat? They send most kind regards to the new Siamese kitten, but they would bark at it unless properly introduced. It may be rather the same colour as Chuleh.

The weather is no better, there was one day of perfect sunshine last week, followed by rain and fogs.

I shall hope to post you the early Peters someday soon. With kind regards to all including  no tail?

Yrs sincerely
Beatrix Heelis

Mrs Miller had asked if WAG-BY-WALL *could be delayed until May 1944 and be printed in* THE HORN BOOK's *Twentieth Anniversary issue.*

To Bertha Mahony Miller

Castle Cottage
Sawrey
Ambleside
Nov 5.43

Dear Mrs Miller,

I cordially agree with the delay until May for printing the story in the Horn Book. It leaves time to see proofs, and I would like to make it as nearly word-perfect as I know how, for the credit of your 20th anniversary.

The winter's snows will be over by then. Would you desire to drop "Christmas Eve"? I am inclined to *leave it in*, with perhaps an added sentiment about the return of spring. (How the sad world longs for it!) I liked your suggestion of Christmas Eve because I like to think some of your storytellers may read the story turn about with the old Tailor of Gloucester, at Christmas gatherings in the children's libraries. Twenty years is soon vanished. I was turning out a drawer, sorting waste paper, setting aside, and I found an old draft of Pig Robinson's first chapters dated 1893 – ! I remember that story stuck on board the Pound of Candles; and Sally's story stuck because the kettle was obstinately dumb.

Mr Hart's name is Reginald. Reg. S. Hart he signs himself. He is an immensely tall thin man, with lengthy limbs .. a gibbon monkey. He hung up some plates – old blue delph – opposite my bed last time he and his family were on holiday, it was comical to see him reach up to the picture rail without the stepladder. Mrs Hart is short & shy, Alison is a little dear. He is an architect, on civil service job at present; interested in books & china.

I have spent more than enough time upstairs; I had bronchitis and the doctor forbid me coming up & down. I am out and about now – when the rain stops – which is seldom. My heart has never been normal since I had rheumatic fever as a young woman, so my prolonged bronchitis cough upsets it; but I hope to do a bit more active work yet – and anyhow I have survived to see Hitler beaten past hope of recovery!

No letter has come except dated Sept. 18th. I am interested to read about your woman minister. The *right women* are exercising an increased & hopeful influence in all spheres here. The majority of the young ones are going through a horrid phase; but I think it is a phase, and that there will be a reaction of common sense and decency; though it may take another generation to achieve it.

Amongst old papers I found a nice letter from Maresa [Marcia] Dolphin Rye N.Y. [Librarian of the Rye Free Reading Room in Rye, New York] I wonder if she is still at that library! I will write to her on the chance. I am afraid I never answered her letter.

With kind regards.
yrs sincerely
Beatrix Heelis

To Stephanie Duke

Castle Cottage
Sawrey
Ambleside
Dec 10.43

My dear Stephanie,

I don't know whether you will have been moved? perhaps your Wren number may find you. When last heard of you were hoping for leave together in Devon – last spring. Please don't think I'm grumbling! time slips away and everyone is over driven and over busy. I wrote to Ken six weeks ago and tore up letter as I have *mislaid his address?*

I have not had a good "summer", one cold on top of another, bronchitis in Sept which strains my heart. I got fairly alright beginning of Nov – but the least damp brings it back, so I shall just stop indoors. At present I am in bed recovering from a cold; *not* flue [sic] or any temperature, just a creaking & thumping. As my heart has never been normal since I had rheumatic fever as a girl – I don't think much about it, and I was often worse in London. But if an old person of 77 continues to play these games – well it can be done once too often. I have plenty to do indoors and the little dogs are great company – most efficient foot warmers.

We had such a wet summer – no floods, but no sunshine. The crops were very lucky on this farm – a very big crop of hay. The oats were some shook out, but got in good order. There was a good deal of waste on hill farms. Wm is fairly well, very overworked – the office is getting too much for him, deaf & edgy – but what can be done; he has to take a court case at Kendal tomorrow for another solicitor with flue [sic]. I think most people have had it now. Mrs Rogerson is on a week's holiday, should be back tomorrow. Nurse Edwards is here over the New Year, so I am looked after. We have had some nice bright sun, since frosty weather – but seemingly I had better wait till spring.

The war news is taking a turn at last. It is sad to think of the occupied countries, waiting through another winter – and its exasperating to think of 'neutrals' – Turkey – Eire – Sweden – 'he that is not for us is against us?'

Have you any news of Rosemary? And where is Jean? And where is Ken now? I have lost his address.

With love yr aff cousin
Beatrix Heelis

To Joseph Moscrop   [?]
                                          December 13 1943

Dear Joe Moscrop
   Very far through, but still some kick in me. Am not going right way
at present. I write a line to shake you by the hand, our friendship has
been entirely pleasant. I am very ill with bronchitis.
                               Best wishes for New Year.
                                          Beatrix Heelis

Beatrix Potter died on the night of 22 December 1943 at Castle Cottage.

LETTER ACKNOWLEDGEMENTS

The author and publishers are grateful to the following for their kind permission to reproduce the letters in this book, which appear on the pages listed below.

John E. Benson, 255 (*bottom*)
Winifred Boultbee, 135, 166 (*bottom*)
Special Collections, Colby College Library, Maine, 425, 446
Henry P. Coolidge, 306, 311, 321, 324, 327 (*bottom*), 344, 346
Country Life, 193
Cumbria Record Office, 302, 303, 310, 337, 345, 353, 374, 394, 412, 428, 439, 466
Rare Book Department, Free Library of Philadelphia, 63, 181 (*top*), 244, 264, 266 (*top*), 279, 313, 314, 315, 327 (*top*), 330, 331, 333, 352, 365, 386, 391, 392, 411, 413, 414, 418
The Field, 58
Doris Frohnsdorff, 265
Betty S. Hart, 127, 452, 461
John Heelis, 272, 277
Jean Holland, 464
The Horn Book, 304, 370, 420, 422, 432, 449, 459, 462
Richard Hough, 260
Department of Printing and Graphic Arts, The Houghton Library, Harvard University, 42, 46, 68
Mrs Hilary Hutchinson, 450
Urling Sibley Iselin collection, 99
Trustees of the National Library of Scotland, 18, 19, 37, 39, 40, 41
The National Trust, 190, 295, 296, 316, 319, 323, 326, 329, 334, 335, 339, 340, 341, 342, 348, 349, 350, 354, 355, 356, 360, 361, 363, 368, 372, 373, 377, 382, 384, 389, 390, 396, 401, 409, 429, 440
Rare Books and Manuscripts Division, The New York Public Library (Anne Carroll Moore Papers, Astor, Lenox and Tilden Foundations), 270, 369, 430, 437, 441
The Pierpont Morgan Library, 14, 29, 33, 51
Private Collections, 11 (*bottom*), 20, 152, 228 (*top*), 281, 302, 303, 310, 337, 345, 353, 357, 374, 394, 402, 404, 406, 412, 416, 428, 435, 439, 466
Rosalind Rawnsley, 230, 251, 366, 367
Robin Rogerson, 184
The Board of Trustees, Royal Botanic Gardens, 38
The Simmons College Archives (The Horn Book magazine records), 459

Janet Adam Smith, 454, 456

Toronto Public Library (the Osborne Collection of Early Children's Books), 358, 375, 408

The Times, 223 (*top*)

Alexander Turnbull Library, National Library of New Zealand (Beatrix Potter Ms. Papers 461), 173, 186

Victoria and Albert Museum, 11 (*top*), 12, 28, 131, 175 (*bottom*), 178, 208 (*bottom*), 212, 214, 241, 252, 275, 300, 387, 395, 398, 403, 405, 451, 458, 460

Frederick Warne Archive, 55, 56, 57, 59, 60 (*top and bottom*), 61 (*top and bottom*), 62, 64, 65, 66, 67, 69, 70 (*top and bottom*), 71, 72 (*top and bottom*), 73, 74 (*top and bottom*), 75 (*top and bottom*), 76 (*top and bottom*), 77 (*top and bottom*), 78 (*top and bottom*), 79, 80 (*top and bottom*), 81, 82 (*top and bottom*), 83, 84 (*top and bottom*), 85, 86, 87, 88 (*top and bottom*), 89, 90 (*top and bottom*), 91, 92, 93 (*top and bottom*), 94, 95 (*top and bottom*), 96, 97, 98, 103 (*top and bottom*), 104, 105 (*top and bottom*), 106, 107, 108 (*top and bottom*), 109, 110 (*top and bottom*), 111, 112 (*top and bottom*), 113, 114, 115, 116 (*top and bottom*), 117 (*top and bottom*), 118 (*top and bottom*), 119 (*top and bottom*), 120, 121 (*top and bottom*), 122 (*top and bottom*), 123, 124, 125, 133, 134, 139, 140, 141, 142, 143, 145, 146, 147, 148, 150, 151, 153, 154 (*top and bottom*), 155, 157 (*top and bottom*), 159 (*top and bottom*), 160, 161, 162 (*top and bottom*), 164 (*top and bottom*), 165, 166 (*top*), 168 (*top and bottom*), 169 (*top and bottom*), 170 (*top and bottom*), 171, 172, 174, 175 (*top*), 177, 179 (*top and bottom*), 180, 181 (*bottom*), 182, 183, 185, 187, 188, 189 (*top and bottom*), 190, 192, 195, 196 (*top and bottom*), 197, 198, 199, 200, 201, 202, 203 (*top and bottom*), 204 (*top and bottom*), 205 (*top and bottom*), 207, 208 (*top*), 209, 210, 211, 216, 217 (*top and bottom*), 218, 219, 220, 221 (*top and bottom*), 225 (*top and bottom*), 226, 227, 228 (*bottom*), 229, 231 (*top and bottom*), 233, 234, 235, 236, 237, 238, 239, 240, 242, 243 (*top and bottom*), 245, 246 (*top and bottom*), 247, 248, 249 (*top and bottom*), 250, 253, 254, 256, 257, 258, 259, 261 (*top and bottom*), 262, 263, 266 (*bottom*), 268, 269 (*top and bottom*), 271, 274, 276, 280, 283, 284, 285, 286, 287, 288, 289 (*top and bottom*), 291, 292, 293, 299, 300 (*top and bottom*), 301, 305 (*top and bottom*), 307, 380, 424, 427, 444, 445, 455, 457

Every effort has been made to trace the owners of the material included in the book, but the originals of the letters on the following pages have changed hands and the present owners are unknown: 213, 215, 223, 255 (*top*), 309, 332, 378, 400.

ILLUSTRATION ACKNOWLEDGEMENTS

Where an illustration is part of a letter it has no separate acknowledgement. The illustrations on the pages listed below were chosen by the editor and publishers to complement the letters and they are grateful to the following for permission to reproduce them.

Book Trust (National Book League), 87, 132, 191, 197, 232, 303, 339, 373, 407

Winifred Boultbee, 131, 156

Betty S. Hart, 453

Jean Holland, 12, 62

David W. Jones, 320

Museum of Fine Arts, Boston, 376

The National Trust, 348, 351, 431; Plate 9 (*left*)

Perth Museum and Art Gallery, Plate 1

Private Collections, 298, 357

Robin Rogerson, 144

Victoria and Albert Museum, 28, 82, 92, 97, 113, 114, 115, 125, 145, 151, 158, 163, 209 (*top*), 235, 238, 248, 250, 256, 260, 262, 273, 282, 308, 309, 343, 347, 364, 368, 379, 383, 384, 386, 388, 399, 403, 412, 415, 423, 429, 436, 438, 443, 448; Plates 3, 6, 12

Frederick Warne Archive, 13, 50, 57, 67, 69, 83, 86, 107, 111, 119, 153, 155, 160, 177, 182, 184, 185, 188, 202, 209 (*bottom*), 214, 215, 226, 245, 252, 276, 279, 280, 286, 287, 301, 310, 312, 321, 322, 325, 391, 402, 421, 425, 427, 434, 451; Plates 2, 4, 5, 7, 8, 9 (*right*), 10, 11, 13, 14, 15, 16, 17

The present owner of the photograph on page 332 is unknown.

SOME FURTHER READING

The Tale of Beatrix Potter Margaret Lane, Frederick Warne 1946, revised editions 1968, 1985

The Journal of Beatrix Potter transcribed by Leslie Linder, Frederick Warne 1966, revised edition 1989

A History of the Writings of Beatrix Potter Leslie Linder, Frederick Warne 1971, revised edition 1987

Beatrix Potter's Americans: Selected Letters edited by Jane Crowell Morse, The Horn Book, Boston 1982

Beatrix Potter: Artist, Storyteller and Countrywoman Judy Taylor, Frederick Warne 1986

That Naughty Rabbit: Beatrix Potter and Peter Rabbit Judy Taylor, Frederick Warne 1987

Beatrix Potter 1866–1943: The Artist and Her World Judy Taylor, Joyce Irene Whalley, Anne Stevenson Hobbs, Elizabeth M. Battrick, Frederick Warne/The National Trust 1987

Beatrix Potter's Art paintings and drawings selected and introduced by Anne Stevenson Hobbs, Frederick Warne 1989

BOOKS BY BEATRIX POTTER
Published by Frederick Warne, unless otherwise stated

1901   *The Tale of Peter Rabbit* (privately printed)

1902   *The Tale of Peter Rabbit*

1902   *The Tailor of Gloucester* (privately printed)

1903   *The Tale of Squirrel Nutkin*

1903   *The Tailor of Gloucester*

1904   *The Tale of Benjamin Bunny*

1904   *The Tale of Two Bad Mice*

1905   *The Tale of Mrs. Tiggy-Winkle*

1905   *The Tale of The Pie and The Patty-Pan*

1906   *The Tale of Mr. Jeremy Fisher*

1906   *The Story of A Fierce Bad Rabbit*

1906   *The Story of Miss Moppet*

1907   *The Tale of Tom Kitten*

1908   *The Tale of Jemima Puddle-Duck*

1908   *The Roly-Poly Pudding;* later renamed *The Tale of Samuel Whiskers*

1909   *The Tale of the Flopsy Bunnies*

1909   *The Tale of Ginger and Pickles*

1910   *The Tale of Mrs. Tittlemouse*

1911   *Peter Rabbit's Painting Book*

1911   *The Tale of Timmy Tiptoes*

1912   *The Tale of Mr. Tod*

1913   *The Tale of Pigling Bland*

1917   *Tom Kitten's Painting Book*

1917   *Appley Dapply's Nursery Rhymes*

1918   *The Tale of Johnny Town-Mouse*

1922   *Cecily Parsley's Nursery Rhymes*

1925   *Jemima Puddle-Duck's Painting Book*

1928   *Peter Rabbit's Almanac for 1929*

1929   *The Fairy Caravan* (David McKay, Philadelphia)

1929   *The Fairy Caravan* (privately printed)

1930   *The Tale of Little Pig Robinson* (David McKay, Philadelphia and Frederick Warne)

1932   *Sister Anne*, with illustrations by Katharine Sturges (David McKay, Philadelphia)

1944   *Wag-by-Wall* (The Horn Book, Boston)

1944   *Wag-by-Wall* (limited edition, 100 copies)

1952   *The Fairy Caravan*

1970   *The Tale of the Faithful Dove*, with illustrations by Marie Angel

1971   *The Sly Old Cat*

1973   *The Tale of Tuppenny*, with illustrations by Marie Angel

1987   *Wag-by-Wall*, with illustrations by Pauline Baynes

1987   *Country Tales:* 'Little Mouse', 'Daisy and Double', 'Habbitrot', with illustrations by Pauline Baynes